BOOK ONE
BETRAYALS
OF THE
BROKEN

JAIME L. TLAX

Edited by Joyce Fernandez, ReJoyce Literary Editing Co. www.rejoyce literaryediting.com and Alex Moyer, Alchemy Edit www.alchemyedit.com
Editorial Assessment by Sarah Beaudette, SB Editorial Services www.sarahbeaudette.com *"Unflinching honesty, unapologetic passion, and audacious authenticity are your gifts. Give them freely, so others may follow your map to their own hidden treasure."*—Sarah Beaudette
Proofread by Larissa Wright of FictionAlly LLC www.fictionallylarissa.com and Adele Lindfors
Cover Design by Miblart www.miblart.com
Interior Layout by www.formatting4U.com
Blurb by Book Blurb Magic www.bookblurbmagic.com
Map Design by Hannah Truelove of Centaur Maps www.instagram.com/centaur.maps

Author's Sanity Maintained by
Jessica Harris, www.instagram.com/jesssssreads
Self-appointed PA; alpha, beta, ARC and mood reader; therapist; writing coach; head of concussion prevention team; Kelter enthusiast (not); first fan; book buddy; "co-author" and forever friend *"Press G!"*—Jessica Harris

First Edition Published 2025 by Jaime L. Tlax

ISBN Ebook: 979-8-9985713-1-2
ISBN Hardcover: 979-8-9985713-0-5
ISBN Paperback: 979-8-9985713-2-9

Website: www.jaimetlax.com
Social: @jaimetlaxauthor

To anyone who questions the stability of their own mind—
Sanity is optional.

To anyone who seeks escape—
Find yourself a broody, possessive guard… and reconsider.

AUTHOR'S NOTE

This is a dark fantasy dark romance for readers 18+ years of age. It is a work of fiction, and I do not condone any situations or character behavior in this book.

If you do not like the dark and twisted side of the mind, and possessive, morally gray men, kindly pass it on to your quietest, most uncorrupted-appearing friend. They will probably secretly love it.

For those still here, however many times you've been broken and put back together, I swear the glue and scars and cracks and sharp edges only make you stronger.

CONTENT ADVISORY

Contains indirect spoilers. Includes but is not limited to:

Crude language and frequent swearing
Descriptive pain and violence
Blood—dripping, gushing, oozing, etc.
Death by fire, knife, falling, beating, tongue, brain hemorrhage, neck-breaking, rock, spikes, needle, tree, darkness and boot
Stabbing and slicing
Physical abuse
Emotional abuse
Verbal abuse
Parental abuse
On-page intimate relations
Bodily fluids
Outdoor nudity
Biting
Animal caging
Torture
Vomit
Mild, non-graphic infant harm
Food withholding
Dehydration
Mouth covering
Abduction
Imprisonment
Suicidal thoughts
Blood tasting
Handcuffs

Restraint by clamps and chains
Confinement in small spaces
Confinement in dark spaces
Forced intoxication
Choking
References to self-gratification
Substance use
Bare feet
Light knife play
Attempted drowning
Clothing theft
Testicle abuse

PRONUNCIATION GUIDE

Ametrine	AM - uh - treen
Blitzer	BLIT - sur
Caldera	kaal - DEHR - uh
Coen	COE - ehn
Eli	EE - lie
Elivander	el - ih - VAN - dur
Ever	EV - ur
Everielle	ev - AIR - ee - el
Jace	jais
Kaleida	kuh - LIE - duh
Kelter	KEHL - tur
Lirica	LEER - ih - kuh
Malachite	MAL - uh - kite
Mallace	MAL - ihs
Milo	MAI - low
Oreyla	oh - RAY - luh
Peridot	PERR - ih - doh
Poett	POH - eht
Rayde	rayd
Sola	SOH - lah
Sonnet	SAWN - eht
Sypher	SAI - fur
Teva	TEE - vuh
Vaile	VAY - ull

PART 1

BROKEN

CHAPTER 1

Consciousness should be optional.

It's not so much to ask, to be sent into oblivion when the world is unpleasant, to slip away into the kind of darkness where even nightmares can't get me, but that's not how it works. Consciousness is forced upon me.

It's a flaw, a fatal flaw.

But whose? I don't believe in the gods. No creator could be so cruel as to forgo a back door to the mind. Or maybe it's only mine that holds me captive and solidifies every horror into memory. *Such brilliance.*

I'd let all the memories go if I could.

If the gods were real, if an immaterial force capable of creating life and writing the laws of nature lurked among us, the decent thing to do when their creations are abducted would be to grant them unconsciousness, or at least drug them.

Decency is hard to come by, so I'm still conscious, stuffed in a full-body sack, trailing along the root-laced forest floor in a pull cart that jostles my insides.

It's not good.

I wait for the panic to set in, to take over. The tightness in my chest, the emotional itch. I should be terrified, even hysterical.

But I'm not.

I'm too busy puzzling over that little boy. I've never seen anyone this deep in my forest. I bring his dirt-smudged face, almost lost under the shaggy mess of golden hair, back to mind. My ears rang when I saw him with his toothy grin. The air got so heavy I thought it might fold me in half, then the sack slipped over my head, and he disappeared with everything else, leaving only a memory for me to stow away.

But I'm no fool.
The panic will come. It always does.

"Kelt?" I whisper into his stubble.

My sight is narrowed to the daylit space within the confines of the sack and the view through its tiny square windows, but that's enough to confirm we're heading away from all we know. Even though I can see right into Kelter's pores, and the heat of his breath clouds around us, I need to know he's really inside this sack with me, that I'm not imagining his warmth. That I'm not alone.

No answer.

His silence is too loud, thundering through my head. I turn my face toward the sky and drift back to nature, something I can trust. The late afternoon air is warm and sticky, enough to taste the pine, and through the thick weave of the sack, the tops of trees skip through the cloudless sky to the rhythm of our captor's footsteps.

"Answer me."

Nothing.

Maybe he's dead. Maybe the up and down of his chest is really mine. Maybe I'm pressed up against my friend's corpse, and the warmth and softness will fade to cold death and rigid limbs that trap me in their grasp. Maybe those gods I don't believe in let him off easy with a torture-free death, a swift blow to the head that I missed in the chaos of the moment.

Is it wrong to be jealous of someone else's death? And pissed? I'd lose what's left of my mind if he took the easy way out and left me alone in the hands of a madman.

Past our tangled legs and beyond the tight tie of the sack at our feet, two black-gloved hands belonging to two black-sleeved arms clutch the handle. The cart weaves around boulders, the mountain peaks on either side rising up and up and up, farther than I've ever ventured. I lose track of the turns, direction becoming a concept of the past, home so far, far away.

When my body is numb from the vibrations of the cart, dusk falls into place in shades of ripe orange. The bumping and swerving ends, and we're motionless except for the breath I draw, barely there. Running water trickles in the distance.

Something about the encroaching darkness and the ominous thud of footsteps in the still night strips away my cloak of denial. The panic I was waiting for sets in, choking the air right out of me.

Then finally, *finally* Kelter's corpse speaks to me, oh so alive and well that I could kill him for making me think otherwise. Or hug him, because I can't even fathom taking a life.

He sighs, a warm caress on my cheek. "Ever? Are you hurt?"

I will away the throbbing pain in my arm and the back of my head and gather up my nerves. "I'd never forgive you for dying on me. Don't you fucking dare."

"I'm not going anywhere." He turns his head, and his hot breath meets mine.

"You should be." I squirm in the sack, the rough fabric chafing my skin. "We have to get out of this thing. This is our chance."

"There's no point. It's tied shut." His calm voice scrapes over me, and I reconsider how capable I am of taking a life.

Water sloshes in the direction of the footsteps, and my fear liquifies. No shape, no walls to hold it back.

"*Please* Kelt."

"I don't have anything to cut the sack." His tall body shifts against mine. "Don't worry, I have a plan for when he takes us out."

"*If* he ever does."

"He will."

"I'm not waiting here for *him* to decide what's next. He could drown us... or beat us. Kelter—" I swallow the terror rising in me. "He could rape us. Anything he wants." I plant my feet and thrust backward, only managing to smack my head i...nto the edge of the cart.

"He's not going to—" Kelter goes quiet.

The lower half of our captor comes back into view through the small holes in the sack. He carries a bucket of water, spilling onto his leg as he walks.

I hide my face in Kelter's neck and press myself against him, his heartbeat grounding me, but the tightness works its way around my chest, and I fall into a vision.

Black gloves grab my ankles. My lungs won't let me scream. I grab on to Kelt, my nails ripping through the velvety skin of his arms in red lines as I'm pulled away. His thighs smash together around me, an attempt to keep me for himself. Fists strike the sack, hundreds at once, beating the blood and life right out of us, beating us into one. Bones crack and snap back together, crooked and jagged, marrow mixing with blood. Red tears paint his face so beautifully, his hazel eyes gleaming until the light flickers out, and I'm not sure which of us is gone.

I shake away the illusion, returning to reality, but it creeps back with such ease, blood and bones, fists and fear. It always comes back. I escape behind my eyelids, only finding winding pathways leading deeper into darkness.

I squeeze Kelt's hand, the sweat on our palms blending.

"I got you." He delivers the warm whisper to my ear and returns a squeeze.

"No you don't, Kelt, unless you mean you plan to hold me through our gruesome death," I hiss.

"I would."

"That's not helpful." All I can do is focus on the tightness of his hand until the boulder lifts from my chest. The panic stays.

Our captor's back is to us, so untroubled on the mountaintop, no fear of death. I long for ease like his—the looseness of his stance, the surety of his hands that lift away his shirt. He squats down, barely more than a shadow, only his back illuminated in the moonlight.

I can't see clearly through the holes in the sack, forced to rely on the noises of the warm night and my violent imagination. A splash of his shirt in water. A flash of a knife in his hand. The scraping of steel on stone. Over and over, sharper and sharper, a skin-piercing, muscle-slicing, bone-chipping blade. He rolls his back, wrings out the shirt and slips it over his head, smothering a large tattoo—two dark towers.

This is it. He's going to slice us to pieces. He'll cut through this sack, and the last face I'll see will be his before the knife goes straight through my middle, then splits my heart in two.

But death doesn't come.

He slides his fingers back into the gloves, picks up the handle and drags the cart onward over *my* mountain, through *my* forest. They hold my secrets, my footsteps, my tears, and he can't take those from me.

A sensation crawls over my body, thick and constricting. I'm flattened. No room for air. Only strangled notions. Fragments of thoughts. Broken feelings.

As soon as the tightness surrounds me, it's gone, as though I imagined it.

"Kelter." I rummage between our bodies for the security of his hand. He may not have answers, but he's my certainty when all else falls away, like now…

The forest I know by heart is left behind, the red-barked trees and moss-covered boulders replaced with the obstructed view of jagged branches and a craggy path that promises deception and disaster. And somehow, it calls to me. The sudden assault of wind summons me, and the trails beg to be trodden.

Kelt's fingers lace with mine, but it does nothing to stop my spiraling mind. *Don't just hold my hand, do something. Anything.*

The cart comes to a halt again. Hands drag us to the ground with a painful drop. Face down, pine needles poke through the fabric into my mouth. A slice of knife at the drawstring near our feet lets in a rush of icy air.

Death. Next comes death.

"See you tomorrow," our captor says, then pushes us headfirst into a tunnel.

We careen down and down and around, too shocked to scream. Cool, pitch darkness consumes us. My stomach leaps to my throat, and I dig my fingers into any bit of Kelter I can reach, not releasing my nails from his skin until we shoot out of the tunnel and tumble across a rough floor, crashing into a stone wall and racking up uncountable scrapes and bruises.

Kelt doesn't say a word—typical of him. He works his feet into the loosened opening of the sack, pedaling them up and down, forcing our exit into existence, then wriggles out, leaving me behind in the dark.

He grabs my ankles and pulls, the sack dragging along with me. Laughing softly, as if *he's* the one walking the fine line between sanity and madness, he lifts me upright, grabs the bottom edge of the sack and works it up my body. He hesitates, holding it suspended over my head, as though reconsidering my freedom.

CHAPTER 2

The room is a perfect cube, six sides of rough gray stone. The kind of room you never get a chance to describe as the last place you ever saw. Because you die there.

Moonlight beams through the opening in the ceiling, but despite the glow, the room embraces darkness, seeking it out and spreading it. Shadows with no apparent source skitter along the walls, and frigid air surrounds me. It smells like damp wood and the end of time, but tastes like the past—stagnant and stale and stuck.

Lovely. *Where the fuck are we?*

The crumpled sack on the floor haunts me. We went from one prison to another. But I'm not staying here. I'm not waiting for the man to return, to beat or rape or torture and kill us in this death trap of a room.

I reach for my backpack and realize it's still in my forest, leaning against a tree near where Kelter and I stopped for a drink. That was right before the sack. We'd been hiking for hours, like any other afternoon with me mapping the expanse of the forest and Kelter scanning for predators at my side. But not abductors. No one else goes into my forest. Or didn't. Until the madman. And the boy.

I begin to search, as limited as it'll be in a ten-by-ten-foot room. There has to be a way out. I scan the walls. Baskets, woven from untrimmed twigs, moist and rotting, discarded on the stone-carved shelves. A toilet and a sink, both strangely made of stone instead of porcelain, chipped and bathed in a grayish grime. Three wooden wheels, their broken spokes jutting out like splintery threats, softened by blankets of gray spider webs, heavy with what must be hundreds of years of dust.

That's it. That's the decor of my death.

Unless I can escape.

"Aren't you going to help?" I ask Kelter, my numb fingers groping the underside of the shelf.

"No."

I sweep away dust and crunchy insect carcasses from the corner, finding no way out, no crack to hint at a door, and turn to him. "You're just going to stand there while I get us out of here?"

He knocks a single knuckle against the wall, a resigned look on his face. "There's no way out."

"So damn optimistic of you."

"Realistic," he says with a gentle nod of acceptance.

"Fine. You wait for death, and I'll escape."

I explore crevices and chase shadows. I climb shelves, roll wheels and press my ear against every inch of the cold wall. No trapdoor. No hidden knob or handle. A tunnel too steep to climb and a metal grate out of reach. The room is as much a prison as my mind, plagued with visions of death. Every day. Over and over.

I'll never make it out of either.

I lean against a bare wall, icy stone and defeat rippling through me. I'm stiff and hurt all over. My favorite jade green pants are ruined, the corduroy dirty and ripped from crawling on stone. I shiver, my bloodied white T-shirt not cutting it. It had been warm in my forest, even as night crept in. I've never felt the air this cold.

"Are we even still in Caldera?" I ask, poking at the fleshy edges of a cut on my arm and cleaning out the dirt with an even dirtier nail. Caldera—my home, my realm, one huge city where my rented room above the coffee shop is waiting for me. It's only a little bigger than this room, but it's all I need.

Kelter doesn't move from his resting place on the opposite wall, arms crossed and knee bent, the sole of one shoe flat to the stone behind him. His loose blue jeans fared as well as my pants, and the deep blue of his fitted V-neck shirt only hides some of the dirt and blood, making him look rugged and rough and tough—which he's not. He takes in my appearance with discerning eyes, as I do his.

Even now, trapped with no way out, he has that same air about him as always—arrogant and sweet at once. Twenty-three years old, like me, a man of few words and little spine, often unseen and forgotten, but loyal and loving and not at all bad to look at. He's confident in his tall body, owning his tan skin, his movements as slick as a lion's prowl. It all comes together like a masterpiece, even his ears that stick out far enough that I get the urge to press them down and see what happens when I let go.

"You look cold," he says, pulling me from my musings and not bothering to weigh in on our whereabouts.

How helpful. "I'm freezing. Where do you think we are?"

He gestures toward the sack, his brows rising in challenge. "You could get back in."

I can't tell if he's serious. We've known each other for a year, and I still find myself questioning his humor.

"I'd rather freeze." I hug myself because he's too much of a fool to think of wrapping me up in his arms. But he's my fool, my friend. My voice softens in response to the invasion of fear. "You think he'll kill us?"

He strokes his chin in thought, a little too dramatically. "Are you hungry?"

I slide down the wall. "So you think we're doomed then?" Why else would he avoid answering?

"I think you're hungry."

"Stop trying to take care of me, Kelt."

"Stop not letting me."

"Fine. I'm hungry. What does it matter?" I pull my arms tighter around me as the cold ventures deeper into my veins.

"It doesn't, I guess. It's just…" He seals his lips in thought.

"What?"

He tilts his head, pondering. "What would you have wanted for a last meal?"

"You can't be fucking serious."

He shrugs. Such indifference for a man waiting for death.

"You want to talk about an imaginary meal instead of figuring out where we are and how to get home?" That's it. I'm going to lose it. All the years of faking sanity will be for nothing when I'm found slumped against the wall with a melted brain. Thanks to Kelter.

He crosses his arms and looks thoughtfully at nothing. "I would have wanted chicken."

"This is serious, Kelt." I try to hide my shivers.

"I *am* serious. What else are we going to do while waiting to die?"

I stand up, rising with my rage. "We keep looking. We scream. We dig a hole and crawl out—anything but talk about chicken."

"We can't dig through a stone floor."

"I know!"

He asks question after question, none mattering, none saving us, none comforting. All pointless words, teasing my temper and getting me nowhere except wrapped up in resentment. I pace back and forth, spinning the rings on my fingers and pivoting every five steps in the small space, my heart beating violently. He gave up. On escape. On living. On *me*.

And when I think he couldn't be more maddening, that I've reached my limits of lividness, and I wish again for the quiet corpse in the sack, he taps his chin and says, "I think you'd want a baked potato."

I stomp past him. "You're so morbid imagining my last meal."

"Somebody should."

I stop in front of him, such a fire in me that I could singe his long lashes with a scream. "Why won't you help me?"

"I am!"

Finally some emotion out of him. "How so?"

He lets out a breath, his chest flattening, and looks away. "I'm keeping you from freezing."

My mouth hangs open. I'm warm, flushed with anger, pacing, stomping and flailing about, heat pulsing through me. No shivers. No cold bones. No achy muscles or goosebumps.

I march back to the opposite wall and drop to the floor, hugging my knees so tight that my chin rests on them. The cold ices over me.

I look up at his set jaw and mismatched hazel eyes—one with a little extra green, and one that glitters with gold—and because I'm a liar, and I really do want him to take care of me, I say, "It might be our last night alive. I'm scared shitless, and I'm bleeding and bruised, and all I have in the whole fucked-up world is you, and you're way over there, pissing me off. On purpose. And you're still the only one I want here with me."

Kelter pushes himself off the wall, aiming his gaze anywhere but mine as he approaches, a tower that crumples at my side. He wraps his arms around me and nestles his head against my shoulder, radiating warmth. His thumb brushes over the open cuts on my arm, and the smattering of freckles on his nose wrinkles into a yawn. I can't make sense of the last few hours, but this fleeting moment asks for nothing—no logic, no explanation, no words.

My anger melts away, and the throbbing in my arm returns with all the other pains, inside and out. I cradle my arm to my chest and rest my cheek on Kelter's head, his soft, golden hair tickling me.

I fight to keep my eyes open, scanning the shadows and expecting them to peel from the walls and rise over me with a knife. My mind churns. The thoughts clash together, accelerating into spirals, but as the minutes pass, as time becomes as indiscernible as the threats in the night, I lose the battle. My eyes drift shut, taking the whirling thoughts of death and doom into my dreams, creating nightmares.

Daylight intrudes on my sleep, slipping through the ceiling grate.

Not a dream then. And not the awful, sunny kind of daylight in Caldera. It's beautiful—dark and gray with only enough clarity to know the night has ended.

I pull away from Kelter, shivering, my breath fogging.

Baskets, tunnel, wheels… It's all the same as last night. A madman really did put a sack over our heads, take us from my forest and dump us in a stone prison. I try to deny reality and slip back into sleep, but something nags at me—something I thought I saw but couldn't have. I force my eyes open, and across the room, where Kelter plastered himself against the wall and stoked my hot temper, is a tiny door.

"Kelter." I shake him and point.

He sits up straight and pries his eyes open, lids fighting the weak light. "That wasn't there last night."

"Doors don't appear out of nowhere," I remind him. And myself.

"Well… it was dark." He relaxes back against the wall, letting darkness take the blame.

I don't know which part of finding a door to escape death makes him settle in for a morning snooze, but I scurry across the room on my grubby hands and black-and-blue knees. "Get over here."

Kelt lets loose a spiteful sigh and follows. We kneel in front of the square door, just wide enough to crawl through. Made of wood, with a golden handle in the center, it looks entirely out of place in this stone room.

"Wait." Kelter thrusts his arm out in front of me as I reach for the handle. "It could be a trap." He inspects the door, feeling along the edges and flattening his stuck-out ear against the wood.

Waiting is a noxious concept. He knows how I feel about it. I'd avoid it if I could.

"Or… it's our only way out of here." I grab the handle.

He presses his hand against the door, eyes flaring with fear. "We can't trust this."

"Are you insane? Are we supposed to sit around and wait for that man to come back to…" My voice fails at the possibilities.

Kelter shakes his head softly, his forehead wrinkling. "I'm not worried about him."

"We have a way out of this nightmare, Kelt. I don't know why or how, but I'm taking it. You can stay here and think about your last fucking meal until he guts you, spilling it on the floor with your intestines."

"You know I don't like when you get like this."

"Then let me out of here."

His hand stays steady on the wood. "We need answers first. We can't go through a suspicious door. What if something dangerous is waiting for us on the other side?" His eyes are pleading, but they're locked on the door, not me, as if he were asking it to disappear once more.

"Answers?" I slam my knees into the ground, inviting bruises on top of bruises. "How do you expect to get answers inside this room?" I wrap my fingers under my knees, my anger tempered by the pain as it gives way to fear. Even though I face death every day, I still want to run from it. My voice is small. "He said he would see us tomorrow… and that's today."

Kelt's hands engulf my shoulders, heavy and firm. "I know you're scared, but I need you to trust me."

"I am so damn beyond scared. I can't trust anyone." *Not even you.*

"I need some time to figure things out," he says with the softest squeeze.

My eyes pivot to the door, to his mistake.

I'm going home.

CHAPTER 3

My fingers feel the way in the dark tunnel, more stone floor and walls, only as wide as the door itself. Kelt grabs my ankles from behind and pulls as I crawl away, bringing me to my stomach.

"Let me go!"

"Quiet. You'll get us killed."

"Now you're worried about dying?"

He tugs me toward him. "Get back in here."

"I'm getting the fuck out of here and going home, with or without you, Kelt. I have to finish my map." An absurd priority, but it's the closest thing to an escape for me. He has to understand. I need the lead between my fingers, the sketches forming one stroke at a time, the landscape in my head pouring onto the paper. My latest map unfolds in my mind, evoking the smell of pine and unbeaten paths. The lure of unturned corners. Rivers that seek to be followed...

"Ever!"

"Huh?" I turn onto one elbow, looking behind me at Kelt's weary face staring back at mine.

"I'm asking you to come back and talk this through with me, and you're not even answering, as usual." He mumbles the last bit.

I maintain a delicate line between friend and person he tolerates, and my temper doesn't help. Some days, I think he'll walk away, that when I say goodnight, it might be the last time, like everyone else in my past—too put off by my *quirks* to stick around for the good stuff. If there is any.

It's my visions of death that drive everyone away. They don't have to know I have them to see my reaction, the way I freeze or fall to my knees, the look that must take over my face. Maybe that's why I don't know who my parents are, why I've spent my life trying to find them—I scared them off. Or maybe I'm lost, and they're looking for me. Or not. But every incomplete file and dead end only makes me crave answers more. Whoever and wherever they are, they're mine, dead or alive, and I'm going to find them. Because the pain of the unknown—the questioning and searching—has to be worse than knowing.

Only Cam was aware of my visions. I've known her since before I knew better than to tell anyone. I asked her why I had them, what they were for, how to stop them, but she always shut me down. And I still can't explain them. Cam was always there when each family I lived with inevitably sent me away, claiming I had strange behavior and wandered off far too often, as if curiosity were a defect. She would hand me a tiny package with a ring inside—a gift, an attempt to keep my heart in place, I suppose. Then she'd take my hand and lead me away, from one family to the next. Soon, I had more rings than I could fit on my fingers.

I didn't go through all that to die at the hands of a madman. "Say what you're going to say. I'm not going back."

Kelter adjusts his grip and slides me along the tunnel floor, closer to him. "We're safe in this room. We can keep watch."

I dig deep into the depths of my self-restraint for some patience, but my tone doesn't reflect it. "How long?"

"A few hours." His eyes crinkle, desperate.

"That's long enough for us to be brutally murdered six times over. Are you trying to make it easy for him? I'm going to fall apart here, Kelt. We both are. We couldn't even see a door right in front of us."

"I'm not sure it'll be any better outside this room."

"Anything is better than this room." *Better than certain death.*

"You don't know what we're up against." He's not pleading anymore. It's a warning.

"You don't either." I tug my ankles free, and he drops his forehead to the tunnel floor, flattened by defeat. That's the thing about him. He gives in. Not only on trivial things, but also when I want him to fight… with me, for me, for himself, for anything. Like when the cashier at the pastry shop refused to ring me up because part of her roof caught fire when I burned down the house next door. He hauled me away, kicking and cursing.

I continue my slow upward crawl. Kelter follows, no doubt

revolting in silence. With the wooden door far behind us, the last of the light dissolves. It's funny how everything sharpens in its absence, how the darkness becomes so alluring. The stone grates my hands and jabs at my knees. I try to match Kelt's steady breaths, but I have no rhythm in me, only a mess of erratic vital functions.

"There's nothing here," he whispers. "Let's go back."

No. I'm silent—as quiet as the pitch black—undetected and on my way to freedom, away from the stifling death that awaited me in that room. Up and up. Faint voices hum in the distance. I check the walls for openings, a fork in the tunnel, a say in my damn fate, but the tunnel offers only a single path forward—or back. And I'm not returning to that room, that much I choose.

The darkness hugs me, the walls of the passage creeping closer. I lower my head to keep it from scraping against the ceiling. Water drips on my neck and back. My hands splash in shallow puddles on the uneven floor, then my trust in all things solid falls away along with the stone below me, and daylight attacks, forcing my eyes closed.

Kelter screams, my name sounding behind me in the chaos of the fall through the trapdoor. My mind panics, and I'm thrown into a vision.

A bed of silver spikes waits below, adorned with a skeletal collection from previous victims. Skulls and toe bones, teeth clinging to jaws and still chattering. It's almost beautiful for that split second before my body smashes down, skewered in a dozen places. My blood splashes up, the warm liquid swallowing me.

My head breaks free. Water—not blood—frigid and sharp as glass against my skin.

"Look at those clothes. She's—it's one of them," a voice says, then five fingers dig into my scalp, forcing my head back underwater before I can suck in a full breath. I'm overcome with stabbing pain, the cold penetrating my skin. I try to free myself, but my stubborn limbs won't do as I say. Slow, defiant, stiff… until I can't feel them anymore. My lungs ache for air. They plead for me to inhale, to drown myself and become friends with the death that haunts me.

The spikes… they would have been a better way to go.

I fight instinct, waiting for the dreaded moment when my body becomes my traitor, raking lethal water into my starved lungs. I'm near bursting when the hand gathers my hair into its fist and yanks my head above the surface. I draw in gulps of air.

Then I'm pulled from the water and dumped onto a slick floor, pain slinging through me, my clothes and boots heavy, cold air slicing over my skin. So cold. Shivering, my brain thawing, I slide my hands over my throat. My pulse thumps—slowly, but it's there. I'm alive. I force my eyes open to a squint.

There's a crowd.

I don't like crowds. Crowds mean people. People mean judging and staring and laughing and not caring.

People are much worse than drowning.

Dozens fill the courtyard around me, still and quiet, hatred poisoning their gazes. They're incredibly tall, taller even than Kelter. They must all be related—some creepy, tall-gened family that's been living outside the city for generations. Save for one woman in a plain violet dress that cinches at her waist and flows down in sheer layers, they all wear gray jumpsuits with collars and long sleeves, like mechanics. Though their clothes are drab and fashionless, their hair is unusually glossy and their skin flawless. No blue jeans and shirts and skirts. No wrinkles and frizzy hair. Only boring perfection.

Below the overhangs of the surrounding buildings, eyes watch over the scene—guards probably, with rigid bodies and black or cobalt blue jumpsuits.

I can't find the energy to scream… or even cry. I manage a sidelong look at the owner of the hand that nearly killed me. Her olive face is young, and almost black hair sits above her shoulders. She's not tall like the others, and instead of a gray jumpsuit, she wears a black one with excessive pockets. Her pointy nose twists with disgust when she catches me staring. She snags the back collar of my shirt and drags me a few feet over the slippery marble floor, closer to the woman in the dress.

"Can I kill her now?" she says to the woman and tugs at my collar.

I almost vomit. Stomach acid burns my throat. This isn't quite the grand escape I had in mind. I look up at the stunning gray sky, crisscrossed with the tunnels above—where Kelter may still be hidden, either cowering or gloating to himself about being right.

At least I'll die outside… encircled by majestic marble buildings with green on every surface, making up for the monotonous clothes and muted colors. My eyes follow the sprawling vines. They climb the curved walls and latch onto the arched tunnels, spilling down around the giant pillars supporting the overhangs.

A square-jawed man in a gray jumpsuit steps forward, a knife in one hand. "*I* get to kill her." He pulls me from the guard's grasp, gathering me in one arm with the knife to my throat and stroking my wet hair with the other hand. "I've waited my whole life for this."

"We all have," the young guard argues.

I can no longer tell if I'm shaking from the cold or from fear. Trying to distance myself from the blade, I push my head back into his chest and scan the panorama, looking for the perfect last view before he takes my life.

Unsmiling faces. Black clubs occupy some hands, knives in others. And hate. So much hate. My eyes catch with one of the guards'—and lock. He's off by himself, the other guards keeping their distance. His jumpsuit is blue, collar flipped up, and black curls fall around his light brown face. The nape of my neck prickles, and a chill kisses each bone of my spine. He looks at me as though he can see right into my broken mind—and the damage he could do would be much worse. Somehow, I've revealed too much already.

"Not yet." Our eyes unlock, and I crank my head to the side, following the source of the voice—the woman in the violet dress. A cloak of dark hair flows past her waist. She slinks closer as the knife scrapes my skin, then pounces. I twist in the man's grasp in time to see her arm crooked around his neck and her hand splayed over the side of his face—and feel the slice across my throat.

He drops me, then the knife, casting loose a wail as though he'd been lit on fire. My kneecaps nearly crack on impact. I grab my neck, assessing the damage, my touch triggering the burn, the pain. And the blood. It's not deep, but with the flow of red comes a sweet release, my inner pain diverted, trickling down my neck.

"Tell me, how did a Hollow manage to get into Sonnet?" The woman in the dress hisses into the man's ear. "And what possessed one of your guards to put her in the old prison cell?" She looks up at the tunnel over the courtyard to the trapdoor dangling by its hinges. "Haven't you told them it's compromised? Anyone can escape if they're in there long enough."

He gurgles in response.

I inspect the blood on my hands as I take in her unusual words. Our abductor is one of them, but what's a Hollow? And Sonnet? Caldera is the only realm, an expansive city spanning most of the land, surrounded by nothing but uninhabited nature on all sides. Or so they say, but no one has bothered to look. No one cares about knowing what's beyond Caldera. Only me. I'm going to map the whole land—if I live.

I inch my fingers toward the knife a foot away, attempting to hide it from view. They slip along the wet marble, the handle almost within reach. Then a boot stomps on my hand, crushing my fingers and smashing my knuckles. I cry out and try to pull away, but the guard in black twists her ankle and sinks her weight down.

"Send guards to check the tunnels and old prison for others," the tall woman in violet adds, before letting the man fall to the floor by my side.

Others? *Kelter.*

"They already are," he croaks, then retrieves his knife.

The guard grinds my hand once more before stepping away, leaving it heavy and throbbing. I crawl backward as the man rises and snarls at me. Forget the guards—he could be the madman. And I'm a dead woman.

"Stand up," the woman says, sending her boot into my middle. Air whips out of me. Cramps strike my belly. I groan, curling into a ball, nausea sweeping over me.

I search for strength, but all I find is terror and cold air whisking over my soaked body. I can't stop shivering. A screech of marble on marble drives everyone's attention to the massive door swinging open.

"Found this one in the arch tunnels, Centress Oreyla," another guard in black says as he walks up to the woman who kicked me. He shoves Kelter to his knees, pressing a boot into his back and the end of a metal club against his neck until he folds. Kelter's cheek mashes into the marble floor, his familiar silence now striking hard enough to bruise my heart.

And I find my strength.

"Kelt!" I lurch toward him, only inches from embracing, when the hand-stomping guard pulls me away and stands me up. Kelter's head swivels to me, to my wet clothes, my bleeding neck, the dewy sorrow in his eyes reaching me in waves.

I'm sorry. I'm sorry. I should have listened, waited with you in that room... for death.

I tilt my head back to take in the woman in the violet dress. Her face is set and unfeeling and has the look of someone whose mother never loved her. I don't doubt I wear the same look, but I know every emotion is smeared across my face. She meets my gaze with her black eyes, and the faintest sharp inhale is given away by a movement in her chest. An almost imperceptible stiffening from head to toe follows— the reaction I always get when someone first sees my eyes. It's the indigo. It throws them off.

She composes herself, hands smoothing the fine fabric of her dress. "Lock them up. No one kills them until we get back what they've taken."

We didn't take anything.

The shivers overwhelm me, rattling my body and chattering my teeth. Dizziness sends the courtyard spinning. I stumble. Time stands still, my brain fogged and failing.

I want to reach for Kelt and throw myself over his tall body balled up on the floor. His green-and-gold eyes peer up at me, each wordless moment so heavy, so loud in my head. I need his warmth, the safety of his arms, but black creeps into my vision. I'm too cold. I swing and sway. My knees give out, and darkness floods in.

CHAPTER 4

I wake up with a start, raw fear crushing my lungs. I'm flat on a floor that's not mine, staring up at a ceiling I've never seen before, pain in too many places to count. I sit up, my body stiff with cold, and a headache parts me down the middle. Rain drips and drops outside.

I glance at the shiny obsidian walls and ceiling, loose shards scattered where the floor meets the wall, at the discolored stone toilet in the corner and the pointless barred window behind me—too high to see anything but the sky, and arched, as if that somehow makes the room more inviting.

The guard in the blue jumpsuit leans against the door of the cramped room—barely a room at all—arms and ankles crossed, eyes on me. Like in the courtyard, he oozes an invisible darkness simply standing there.

With only dust and shadows for entertainment, the room offers little else for him to do.

Unless I'm his entertainment.

I strike first. "Who in the ass fuck are you?"

His bored demeanor vanishes. "Your mouth is as filthy as the rest of you." The deep growl of his voice makes the prickle return to the back of my neck, like cold fingers tracing down it.

I want to run, but there's nowhere to go.

"You have no idea," I counter, because apparently my mouth does terrible things—like speak.

He switches his crossed ankles and tilts his head, his eyes so intent on me that my own travel down my body, finding no more than a camisole and underwear. My cheeks heat, and I scramble back, pulling

21

my knees to my chest. The cold wall bites into my back, and shards dig into my bottom. I clap a hand to my chest in search of my necklace. Still there—purple stone, chain and all. I breathe.

It's fine. I'm fine. He's over there, and I'm over here. A whole eight feet away.

"Where am I?"

He stares, watching me shiver.

"Where's my friend?"

Nothing.

"And my clothes?"

That interests him. A smirk plays across his stubbled face. "They were soaked, and you were unconscious, so… I helped." He shrugs, as if whatever he did was innocent, but everything about him tells me otherwise. The unmistakable taste of blood fills my mouth, and I try to disappear into the wall.

This is how it starts. This is how he'll play with my head. A dark room. Cold, dirty floor. Take my clothes. Laugh at me. Then he'll watch my slow decline into insanity. It takes weeks or months for most people, but it won't for me. I don't have much further to go before I'm already there.

"I passed out?"

"You were cold." Fascination pushes through his dark gaze. "I've never seen someone so blue. It brought out your bruises… and your eyes."

"Good to know my lack of oxygen amuses you," I spit out, hugging my knees tighter.

He arches two black brows. "It does."

My fingers coil. "This isn't even my underwear."

"Right. *I* have that." He pats his pocket. "Still wet."

"You stole my underwear?" I knock my fists on my knees and take a settling breath. "You haven't even told me who you are yet, and you're collecting my underclothes?"

He taps his thumb over his lips and ticks his jaw to the side. "It might come in handy for stuffing in that pretty little mouth of yours if you keep talking this much."

"Fuck." I try to mask the profoundly wrong sensations that rip through me at his words. I should be appalled, terrified after an attempt to kill me and the confinement of yet another prison, but with the inescapable dark walls of my mind, I'm not. Instead, I escape reality with false desire and pad my nerves with the satisfaction of stubbornness. I serve him my most menacing look, which has no effect on him whatsoever.

He stares right back at me—deep brown eyes half hidden behind a collection of loose ringlets—corrupting me from across the room.

"Get up," he says.

I lean my head against the wall. I don't particularly *like* being told what to do. His hand moves to his ear, tugging the lobe, his gaze stuck on me.

I don't budge.

Intrigue flashes across his face, the corner of his mouth lifting. "Up."

A challenge. I shake my head. *No.* Not wearing this. Not without a bra. And freezing. Not with his eyes on me. He's clearly spewing empty words to rile me, but letting him look is like letting him win.

He huffs and stomps across the small room, stopping at my bare toes, which are turning blue—just like he likes. I curl them under.

He takes me by my ear, rough fingers somehow colder than me, pulling me up and up until my legs rise, and I'm looking at his chest, the top of my head not even reaching his shoulders. The cold stone floor slices into the soles of my feet. I cry out and pull away from his grasp, only making it worse. He holds my ear tight and rakes in all the cuts and bruises as if he feeds off them. "I said up."

"I said no." *Maybe I have a death wish.*

He twists my ear. "You *said* nothing."

Oh, so true, and for some reason that fires up my insides more than the burn in my ear. I rise up on my tippy toes as though that might intimidate him.

It doesn't.

Obsidian shards embedded in my skin plink to the ground, competing with the splatter of rain, and he looks down between us. Two frozen nipples and naked legs betray me.

"Fine. *No.*"

He releases my ear and chuckles, deep and throaty… and sexy. "Too late."

I can't have thought that. About *him.*

My mind is a traitor.

I fold my arms over myself, seeking privacy. That feeling of darkness whispers around us like cold kisses on my skin as he lowers himself before me, giving off the edgy scent of an endless black cave. His knees bend, his head dipping past my chest and belly, so close his hot breath sears an invisible line down my upper half. My muscles pull taut from head to toe. Squatting in front of me, his head at my hips, he reaches a hand between my ankles.

I snap my legs shut and trap his wrist. "Nobody goes between my legs without an invitation."

His curls fall back as he looks up at me, utterly unable to contain that damn smirk. "Too late for that too." He yanks his hand free and rises again, following that line back up, the closeness of his body and the ripple of cold air around him raising goosebumps on my flesh. "You had your ass all over my lucky stone."

I tilt my head up to see the oblong black stone in his hand, iridescent blues and silvers in the grooves. "Maybe I would have noticed if my ass weren't frozen solid."

His cheeks flutter, maybe suppressing a laugh. At me. At my expense, at my bruised and chilled body.

"Come." He pulls me along with his backward steps.

"I need clothes." I wrench my arm away.

"Are you sure?"

My face scrunches in disbelief. "Yes, I'm sure."

He steps back, the harsh fingers that gripped my ear so tight now fiddling with the top button of his jumpsuit.

"I'll share," he says, sealing his lips to smother a smile.

The button pops open, exposing a triangle of light brown skin with an amber glow, pointing downward, hinting at what lies below. He moves to the next one and the next, the triangle growing, extending lower and lower.

I panic. He was serious. He's not all talk. This is why I don't have clothes. He wants easy access. To me.

Another button.

I flatten myself against the cold wall. Shit. Maybe he'd like it against a wall. Even worse—maybe I would too. But not with him. Not in this room. *Focus, dammit.* I need to stay alive.

"I have to warn you though"—he pushes a fifth button through its hole—"rumor has it I don't wear anything under my jumpsuit." Six buttons, and he slips the fabric off one shoulder.

I slide down the stone at my back and drop to my knees. *No, he'd like that even more.*

"You're an eager little one. I haven't even gotten an arm free yet," he says.

I stand, chin up. "I don't want your foul man clothes. Bring me my own."

"You give orders now?" His eyes laugh at me.

Screw him. "I do."

"Not in here, not to me." He backs clear across the room. "Either you stay like that and come get your dinner"—he pulls something from his pocket and throws it to the floor—"or you're finding out if the rumor is true."

My "dinner" looks up at me from the floor, a brown bar split in two, crumbs all about. I cross my arms. "I'm not eating your nasty pocket food."

He pops another button and works his arm out of the sleeve.

"Stop!" My heart slams into the walls of my chest. "I want out of this room."

Lightning flashes, followed by the roar of thunder, and I slap a hand over the nape of my neck to stop the sensation of fingers rippling over my skin. *What is that?*

He grins and points at the bar. "Eat. You're not going anywhere."

"So I'm a prisoner?" My voice wobbles despite the steel I thread through the words.

"Did you not notice the crowd of people who wanted to kill you?" He stalks back to me, smashing my dinner flat under his boot as he closes the space between us.

I press my back to the stone. "Better company than you."

"Before you decide, get this through your lovely little head—I'm the only one in the entire realm who wants you alive." This asshole of a man plants his hands on the wall above me and leans down—*in*—a breath away. "Outside this room, you're everyone's prisoner. In here, you're only mine."

I swallow, left with no choice but to gulp down his intensity, his scent. "*Your* prisoner? What does that mean?"

His lips stretch into a closed smile, from one sculpted cheek to the other. "That I give the orders… and you follow them." He pulls one hand off the wall and traces a finger across the slice in my neck, sucking in a breath. Then he tugs on the shoulder strap of my camisole, lifting it an inch before releasing it and flattening my shoulder against the wall. "Or I make you."

"You can't make me do shit. Who do you think you are?"

He runs that hand on my shoulder up the back of my neck and grips a fistful of my hair, pulling me closer. "Your guard, Elivander."

CHAPTER 5

Boots shuffle on stone, and a light rain raps outside. Consciousness greets me with the same hammering headache I left it with, my body punishing me for the lack of coffee.

Elivander heads toward the door, solid obsidian like the walls and ceiling and floor, the only way out of this black box. I notice it's missing right away—that dark aura around him, the taste in my mouth, the crawling sensation on my neck. It's gone. As if it faded away with the dark of night.

Maybe I imagined it, conjured it up like a vision. But in its place, a sense of light emanates from him. It pulls me in as if he weren't the man I wanted to strangle last night. My body warms despite the cold and lack of clothes, and I'm hit with the crisp scent of gentle wind before a storm. *Just my mind messing with me.*

"You're leaving?" I ask, tapping my rings on the floor. A pit forms in my stomach over who might come in his place. I survived the night, but that might not be the case with someone else.

He turns, his gaze dropping to my curled up body on the floor. His lips twirl. "Don't worry about missing me. I'll be back after my other shift." He cuffs his sleeves as he talks, revealing inch after inch of toned arms. "You'll have a day shift guard, so don't bother trying anything."

I push myself up, my muscles locking. "I'm *not* going to miss you. And why do I need a guard if I'm locked in this damn room?"

"Because in over two centuries, we haven't had a single intruder enter Sonnet. You think the Centress will risk you escaping?"

"I didn't *intrude*. I was abducted by a madman."

He laughs and runs a hand through his curls. "A guard. And his report says you were found on Sonnet's side of the border."

"Well, he's a liar."

He shoves his hands in his pockets. "No one would want to bring Hollows into Sonnet. He has no reason to lie… but you do."

"I don't even know what Sonnet is, or Hollows. Or a Centress."

"Sonnet is the realm that borders Caldera to the north, and the Centress rules it." He pulls his hands free. "I don't have time for this."

Another realm. I was right. "But what about Hollows? What are those?"

He points a finger at me as he opens the heavy door, stone scraping over stone. "Stay," he commands, then slips out, taking the warmth and suspicious impression of light with him.

"Where the fuck would I go?" I yell as the door falls shut.

Cold rubs against my nerves and cuts into my skin. Clothes would help. Food would help. And Kelter's heat. But I only have my own icy limbs to hug me, to attempt to soothe the ache, the one that settles deep inside me, as though all the shivering shook the cold into my core.

Nights at my sixtieth-something foster home were always cold. It was partly because it was winter when I lived there, and partly because all the beds, couches and blankets were already taken by the other seven parentless raging adolescents. So I slept on the floor. I got used to the rigid wood against my back or side, but I never got used to the cold. It seeped into my very being, a painful, muscle-tensing cold, and I'm not sure it ever fully left. It froze my trust—in others… and in myself.

I tried to burn it away, or maybe there was more to it than the cold.

Reggie Junior, the only biological child in the house, took to sleeping on the floor with me. He started on the other side of the room and maneuvered his way across over the course of a week, his sticky teenage skin and hungry green eyes closer every night.

He smelled like man-sweat and feet, and the first time he touched me I gagged and tried to escape, but that didn't keep him away. He whispered his nasty little thoughts in my ear and dug his hand down my underwear. By the end of the month, I was spreading my legs for him every night, letting him ram my back into the cold wood while the others slept, or pretended to. I loved it. And hated it.

Two weeks later, conveniently timed by him when I stood four feet away, he announced to his friends that he'd won the bet—that I wasn't contagious, that fucking me wouldn't cause them to have "attacks" like me. He offered me up to them in lieu of payment, but fortunately for them, they all chose to pay up. That same night I buried my trust so deep it turned to ice. I packed my bag, snagged a few things I'd had my eye on and set Reggie Junior's house on fire.

Hiding behind a parked car and watching him run outside in his saggy white underwear in the middle of the night may have been the best moment of my life.

Until I watched the house burn down.

The flames licked that house like he licked me, and that cold, hard wooden floor crackled and popped like fireworks. Smoke swirled above, laughing into the starry night.

That was the last family I stayed with. Cam, the only person I could trust as a child, hugged and scolded me for a week straight. After that I was on my own, free at the ripe age of sixteen. I quit school, left the area and never saw Reggie or Cam again.

That raw coldness, that burning, they complement and destroy each other, like light and dark, trust and betrayal.

I've spent plenty of time alone, avoiding critical eyes and hiding in narrow alleys and closets from bullies and deprived men in the houses I stayed in, but I usually had a book. And clothes. And a way out. Here, there's nothing but solid black stone—no electrical outlets, no heating ducts, no lights. Either they don't use them here, or they want to keep me in the dark and cold.

My mind stays on Kelter as the hours pass, visions taking me every so often. The gray of daylight peaks and dims again as the rain showers come and go, and twilight finds the late afternoon.

Is Kelt in a room like this? Cold and clothesless? Thinking of me? This is the first day in nearly a year that I haven't spent time with him, haven't seen his awkward smile or heard his warm voice coaxing me with its confidence. As much as he gives in to what I want, I often do the same. I have to. I can't lose him—he's all I have.

I spent years alone before he showed up, either hiding in my room above the coffee shop or hiking through my forest with a map in hand. It was only me and my visions every night, me and my tears. But Kelter forced his way into my little world. And between the deaths in my head, I found myself smiling, even laughing.

He brought me food from all over the city, getting me hooked, then persuaded me to leave home just to eat it again. I'd return, shaking from the crowds and cursing as I crawled into bed, and he'd hand me a book, a silent request to read to him. And he listened, sitting on the edge of the floor mattress until my breathing slowed and the pages no longer fluttered in my trembling hands, as if he had nothing better to do.

Though pain still lingers with every movement, at least the caffeine withdrawal is letting up, my headache finally waning. I stopped feeling hungry some time this morning even though I last ate two days ago. Maybe Kelt was right to be thinking of our last meals. But the thirst—it's consuming now, scratching at my sanity as though I were fighting the instinct to blink.

The door grinds open. I flee to a corner, crouching in the graying underclothes. Elivander enters, waves of unseen darkness sweeping in with him, cold fingers wisping down my spine. I didn't imagine the feelings last night—I'm just losing it, going mad like they want. He closes the door and waves a small stone over the handle. Metal clunks and clicks into place. Locked. It must be magnetic.

I'm going to need that.

He turns, stowing the stone in one of the many pockets down the legs of his blue jumpsuit, then sets his eyes on me, all glinty and shifty.

"Miss me?"

I tuck my feet closer, trying to make myself smaller, invisible. "What are you doing here?"

"My job. We went over this. Maybe you were underwater a little too long yesterday." He slowly closes in on me.

"I'm fine. The other guard never showed up, and look—I'm still here, still a prisoner."

He stands in front of me, locking me in the corner and looking down. The taste of metal hugs my tongue. "The day shift guard was outside the door since this morning."

Seriously? "What the fuck? Then how come *you're* inside?"

He huffs, a lopsided grin forming as he backs away. "Why would I sit outside in the hallway where there's nothing to entertain me all night?"

Dread fills my lungs with lead. I clamp my knees together and hide my perpetually frozen nipples poking through the camisole. "There won't be any entertainment inside here either."

He smirks and leans against the door. "So you don't want your dinner?"

Food. Maybe he has water. I roll my cracked lips together. I'd do anything for a sip.

"I do," I sneer, but even as the words come out, my face screws up, the cold and thirst and black walls closing in on me, *reality* closing in.

I'm struck with every emotion I've staved off since the sack went over my head, and maybe years before that. I'm locked in a room, trapped in a realm I didn't know existed and stuck with people who want to kill me. I only want to find my parents, but I'm further from answers than ever before, taken from the shelter of my forest and separated from the one person who would notice if I disappeared.

I cry dry tears, my lips trembling and my chest crushing the last of my composure. I focus on the intensifying rain outside and hug my naked legs.

Elivander fidgets at my display of misery, then lifts the flap of a side pocket and pulls out a canteen, then a food bar from the other side. He takes two steps forward and sets them on the stone floor, not far from the smushed bar that was to be my dinner last night. "Eat. Drink." He arches a single brow at me. "It'd be inconvenient for me if you died."

I ignore his cold words, the inconvenience I threaten him with if I deny the drink he offers and let myself dry out and rot. My despair vanishes, adamance taking its place.

"That better be coffee."

His rugged demeanor slips, surprise stealing his smirk. "The medicine?"

What? No coffee?

Holding the camisole flat against my chest, I crawl across the floor one-handed to the canteen. It's soft-bodied and green, as if made from leaves. I twist open the top and pour the liquid down my throat, the very same substance that nearly drowned me yesterday now giving me life and thrumming through me as I gulp down the final drop and toss the canteen aside.

I steal a glance at Elivander, at his features framed in darkness, his chiseled jaw and the curve of his broad shoulders. He watches me, masking the tiniest hint of a smile framed by a shadow of stubble as I kneel on the floor and scarf down the bar, not bothering to pick off the bits of blue pocket lint. It's bland, the texture disturbing, but worse is the flavor of blood that the nutty morsels take on as I swallow bite after bite. I curl up on my side as the last chunk goes down, groaning and clutching my middle, my gut like a rock.

"You ass," is all I find the grit to say.

He slides down the door and drapes his arms around his bent legs, the golden brown of his skin a perfect pairing with the cobalt blue of his jumpsuit, which I shouldn't be noticing at all.

I relocate to the wall when my stomach finally settles, then we're quiet, him against the door and me on the opposite wall, waiting, watching, staring so intently as the last of twilight gives way to shades of night.

When only the blue light of the moons ventures through the tiny window above me, I lie on my side on the cold, hard floor and tuck my hands under my head like a pillow, trying to ignore the earthy scent hanging in the air around me.

I wait in the dark of the black room, my back to the man at the door, my eyes forced open and my heart beating to the volatile rhythm of the unknown. Once I hear the shuffling sound of him laying his body flat on the floor, the slow breaths, and I'm the only one watching the shadows on the walls, I know it's time.

As though I'm sneaky and stealthy and swift—and not at all loud— I roll my body over the raw obsidian. One roll and I wait, sensing the air for a change in his breathing, a twitch of muscle.

Nothing.

I roll again and again, my hip bones kissing stone with each turn. He's right next to me on his back, quiet as death, save for the little drum inside his chest. My spine to the floor, I wait again, letting it beat, so steady and sure, unlike the riot inside my own chest.

I scoot, one tiny movement closer at a time until the hairs on my arm graze his. I take shaky breaths in and out, then stop breathing altogether as I roll onto my side to face him. He smells faintly of cloves.

His arms trace down his sides toward his outstretched legs, and with black curls blending into the floor, his head balances on the stone, nose pointed straight up at the ceiling.

Who sleeps like this?

I lift my head and inspect the space between us, then inch my way downward until I can reach his legs. I creep my hands closer and work my fingers into the first pocket I find, slowly lifting and shifting the folds of coarse fabric all the way down to the bottom. Empty.

So carefully, I pull my hand back out, watching his chest lift and settle, his face motionless. I feel around for another pocket, my fingers feathering over his thigh. I run into a raised flap and slip my hand inside to explore. Fabric presses against my knuckles. My palm slides against his leg.

I hit something hard.

The stone for the door. *My way out.* My fingers curl around the cold form and retrace the movements of my hand, backing out of his pocket with the treasure. As it comes into view—silver and slick and smooth— his hand clamps down on my wrist and smashes it against the floor.

I gasp and try to roll away, but he has me pinned, his hand keeping me at his side. My other arm is useless under me. He sits up, so wide awake with gleaming eyes and muscles hard like the stone between my fingers that I doubt he was ever asleep.

"That's mine." His voice grates the night air, and crisp, cool darkness wreaths around us, between us, above and below us, binding and looping around limbs, cold licking my neck and back.

I drop the stone, not able to hold it with my hand in his crushing clutch, bending my fingers in all the wrong ways. My tendons click and snick over my bones as he grinds down.

It's hard to find my voice, but when I do, I force my ire into it to mask the defeat. "Is that all you got?" I wince, giving myself away.

His eyes go wide, and he eases his grip a notch, as though he wasn't aware of his own strength. "I thought you said there wouldn't be any entertainment."

"You're such a fucking creep."

"I expect you to behave, little prisoner." He squints down at me, blue moonlight blush on his cheeks. "And I suggest you keep your hands out of my pants unless you want me to return the favor."

"You took my pants."

"And offered you *my* clothes like a fine fucking gentleman. Seems to me you like being half-dressed."

"Fuck gentlemen," I hiss. "You're deranged. You stole my underwear and started stripping. Who does that?"

That smirk returns with a vengeance. "You've obviously never had a worthwhile guard before."

He releases me, and I scurry back to the wall to nurse my numb hand. I was so damn close. I turn my rings in endless circles around my tingling fingers and take one last look at the mean man now perched in front of the door—guarding, keeping me in and others out—exactly how I guard my mind.

Despite all efforts, my eyes fall shut to the lullaby of thunder and rain. I sink further into the inky black of the wall, wishing it would slurp me into its shiny depths and spit me back into Caldera with Kelter at my side.

But it doesn't.

It leaves me afflicted with images of what the man across the room might be capable of… and the horrors of a realm without coffee.

CHAPTER 6

T hief."

I startle, taking in a gulp of frosty morning air. The rain carries on outside.

"Wake up, thief." Elivander stands over me in his blue jumpsuit. My skin flushes, fresh as though covered in morning dew, but still warm, and it has nothing to do with the slice of dawn peering through the barred window.

Lying on the floor on my side, I groan and tuck my bare knees closer to my chest. "Go away."

He scoffs. "I will, but first I have to take you to the Centress. She's ready for the Hollows."

"Where? What does she want?"

"To the school in the village. She wants to take back what you stole."

"What village? I didn't steal anything."

"The only village left in Sonnet. There's not enough of us to need another village. And she disagrees with the stealing." He pokes the toe of his boot into my ribs and wiggles it around. "Move."

I grab his boot. "What's a Hollow?"

He shakes his foot loose and crouches over my curled up body. "*You* are a Hollow." The warmth surrounding me slips into the icy air, and metal fills my mouth again. I flinch when his hand grazes my cheek, at the softness as he pushes the matted hair off my face. Then his fingers clutch my ear, twisting skin and cartilage. "And a thief. Let's go."

I pry his hand away.

He stands and smiles down at me as I sit up, glaring. I don't want to know what awaits me in the village, but being trapped in this room won't give me a chance to escape.

"Do I get my clothes back? And my boots?"

"I burned them." He looks me over, eyeing the dirty camisole. A grin wins over his scowl. "You don't want to go like that?"

I stare at him, convincing myself he can feel the hatred leaking from my eyes.

He moves to the door, waves the silver stone over the lock and pulls it open. "Hurry up. You don't want to keep the Centress waiting. She'll get in your head—and it's painful."

With no other choice but another battle of wills, likely ending with Elivander undressing himself, I stand and adjust the barely there fabric of the camisole, now a blotchy gray instead of cream colored. I tug it down past my hips, trying to look dignified as I make my way toward the door.

Elivander grips my arm, his fingers easily circling it and squeezing tight as he leads me into the dim hallway. He walks me all of three steps to the door on the other side of the hall and pulls me inside. The lock clicks with a hover of the stone in his hand.

The windowless walls are gray and white marble, the same as the smooth texture of the floor, so foreign on my feet after the rough stone of the black room. Spigots jut from the marble on the far wall, some at foot level, the rest above my head. Wooden buckets with crude metal bases and handles are littered about the puddled floor, rags draped over the sides. Shelves on the opposite wall are stocked with neatly folded clothes and linens—even blankets. Boots, dozens of pairs of varying sizes, are stowed below the bottom shelf, their twisty laces strewn about like roots. A pile of clothes sits atop a tiny stool in the middle of the room.

"There were clean clothes one room away, and you left me in this?" My face tightens, my eyes bulging as I gesture to the now stretched and saggy underwear hanging from my hips. "And you let me shiver all fucking day and night instead of giving me a damn blanket?"

His brows furrow, deep lines creasing under his curls. "You're my prisoner." He shrugs.

"I'm a person!" I yank out of his grasp, and he lets me… because where am I going to go in yet another locked room?

"You're a Hollow, and the Centress would like you less filthy."

I roll my neck, trying to push away the imaginary fingers fluttering over it. I shoot him a glance, then the spigots and the buckets and the drains. My heart knots, shoving blood through kinks and loops. "No."

"It's not optional." His boots splash through the standing water as he takes hold of me again and drags me toward the wall of spigots.

The water is cold on my bare feet, but I hardly feel it—or anything at all—as he positions me in front of the wall. I'm stuck in place, my chest hollowing out, my head trying to block the memories. The water. The tears. The voices.

"On or off?" he asks, his eyes traveling down to the camisole before his arm reaches past me to the handle.

All I manage is to shake my head, silently pleading for him not to turn on the water.

But he does.

A heavy stream of coldness hammers the top of my head, and I'm taken back.

Far back. Inside the pebbled walls of the bathroom, home number thirty-two—I counted.

What's wrong with you? His voice etched itself into my mind that day.

The vision hit in the kitchen as I helped my foster mother prepare dinner, my tiny ten-year-old fingers slicing and dicing vegetables with a knife. It took me from the paisley wallpaper and colorful foods to somewhere dark, to suffering and death. But it was the slip of the blade while I was stuck in the nightmare inside my head that caused the problem, the piece of my finger that came right off, the blood on the counter. On the floor. In the food.

My foster mother screamed, the pain and her piercing cry bringing me back to the moment. Then my foster father came stomping toward the sound and looked at me. And the blood. His veins popped. *I told you to get out of your damn head!*

He took my arm and hauled me across the tiled floor, through the bedroom and into the bathroom, leaving a trail of blood behind us. He tore the curtains down and shoved me under the showerhead. I couldn't escape when he turned the knob, when he put a violent hand on my chest and kept me pinned to the wall as the cold water pounded down on me, my clothes growing heavy, cold rippling through me.

Stop, I tried to say. *It was an accident.* But my words never found a voice. They went down the drain with the blood and the water.

I was left only with silence. And the sting in my finger.

Even as he shook me, as he scolded me—*this is my house, and I decide who stays and who goes*—I focused on the hair on his arms, the roll of fat around his neck, the bulging belly. Anything but his face and those raging, hateful eyes. *No one will ever care about you.* He lashed out at me when I closed my eyes at his words, taking in the truth of them. *Look at me!*

Hot tears streamed down my face, lost in the spray of the shower, but I couldn't open my eyes. I couldn't move at all, not an arm, a leg, a foot, not even a damn toe to get away from him. My legs couldn't hold me. The bones had gone soft.

You're a waste of space.

I claw my way out of the memory, wishing for my visions instead— of blood and gore, of final breaths and hard-earned deaths, much less painful than rejection and no one caring. I pry my eyes open, the gush of cold water massaging my skull and cascading over my forehead. Elivander stands in front of me, studying my face as the water soaks my shirt.

Through the darkness he carries, I swear I see a flash of concern way deep within, behind the black and brown of his eyes. I doubt it though when I feel those fingers on my neck again, reminding me of my precarious state of mind. They walk down my wet back, sliding with the falling water. He hands me a slippery, bubbling green bar like the soap back home, but squishy and slimy and clearly a plant.

"Wake up and wash, little thief." He moves away and sits on a low stool, not half a foot from the floor. His knees reach his chest, clothes bunched in his lap. "We don't have all day."

I work past the lump in my throat, swallowing down the memories over and over until they burn in my stomach acid, and I can move again. My body is stiff with cold as my mind constructs wall after wall, but I betray myself, tearing them down one after another and letting memories slip back in.

I scrub every bruise and cut—real scars, soul scars—and every bit of tired, exposed skin, then I face the wall and clean beneath the fabric shielding me. I turn back to catch Elivander shifting on the stool, adjusting the crotch of his jumpsuit. He gets up and holds the pile of clothes to his stomach as he approaches. I try not to look down at what he thinks of me… or let on to what I think of him.

My heart is louder than the water slamming into the back of my neck. I cover my nipples with a hand on each and pinch my thighs together. He leans past me, his chest brushing mine. Drops splatter onto the front of his jumpsuit, wetting the triangle of skin below his collarbones, and he shuts off the water… and the memories. I can't quite ignore the hardness against my side, can't dismiss it as another sensation that isn't real.

"Could you keep your cock to yourself?"

He snaps his gaze to mine, eyes predatory. "It's not my fault you're all wet and fuckable."

My nipples harden to a new painful degree beneath my hands. "It *is* your fault I'm wet."

He grins. "Then I'm doing something right."

I empty my lungs. "How are you so damn insufferable?"

"Get dressed," he says, his voice a little higher than usual. He hands me the clothes and pulls away. "Or do I need to do it for you again?"

I bite down on my lip at the thought of what he did while I was passed out, at those man hands and the lump of my wadded up underwear still in his pocket, and I'm wetter than before. Fuck. "Turn around."

"Don't worry." He smiles then turns toward the shelves. "I've seen enough of you to keep me entertained every night for the rest of the year."

"I hope it lasts through every lonely hand fuck, because you're never seeing me again."

"So far it has."

I make faces at the back of his head, shoving down the rage-lust as I pull off the camisole and replace it with a curious bra. An embroidered mountain path and rushing waterfall scene travels from one cup to the other. The bra loops behind my neck and ties in the back instead of fastening with metal clasps like the one he took off my unconscious body.

I go to put on the shirt… but it's a dress.

I don't do dresses. It's not that no one wears them in Caldera. They do—but I don't. I hike. And make maps. And run when I'm supposed to walk.

"I can't wear this. I need pants."

He folds his arms, his back still to me, and stares at the shelf full of clothes. Including pants. "It's that or nothing."

My body heats at his heartlessness. I slide the cold, dripping underwear down my legs. "I'm not wearing it."

His shoulders push back, and he flips around, eyes flaring.

"I thought you'd seen enough," I say, having just pulled dry underwear into place.

He marches up to me, deep breaths commanding his chest. "You're misbehaving again." But even as his jaw clenches and wrenches to the side, lightness tugs at me, the gentlest wind coiling around my body. His brown eyes follow the mountain path and waterfall across my chest, then trace down my belly.

That shift in him, the one that's not real, the missing feel of darkness—it whips my emotions back and forth. "What's wrong with you?" I say those words I've heard my whole life. "Do you not give a fuck about anyone but yourself? You haven't even asked for my name."

He looks away. "I already know it."

What? I give in and pull the hideous ruby red dress over my head, my necklace tucked safely inside. "You talked to Kelter? Where the fuck is he? Is he okay?"

"Kelter?" He backs up. "Shut that fiery little mouth before I wash it out. And hurry up."

I grumble and try not to imagine what might happen in the village. Sitting on the marble floor, I finish lacing a pair of black boots, not made with rubber and fake leather like the ones he took from me, but from a thick, flexible plant material. "Is everything here made from plants?"

Pulling something from his pocket, he drops to one knee before me, smirking ever so slightly. "No. These are made from steel." He slips a cuff over each of my wrists and tightens them, pinching my bones hard enough to elicit a groan, then slaps another pair on my ankles and admires the metal pressing into my skin.

CHAPTER 7

Elivander drags me down the hallway and out into the courtyard with my hands cuffed at my front. I schlep myself along under the dark clouds, the ankle cuffs only offering six inches of slack chain for each step. That lightness I felt in the shower room traces around him, walking with us.

The morning air is sharp across my face, but the ankle-length dress is oddly warm, the long sleeves like shields despite the thinness. I should feel the wind hurrying over my skin right through it, but I don't—and I still hate it. My shape is revealed. Seamless fabric as soft and delicate as new skin clings to my breasts and belly and hips and sprawls out around my legs in silky folds. I get the feeling nature has me in its grasp, that I'm wrapped up in a giant satiny petal that will wilt and shrivel before the day is done.

The loathing eyes of guards in blue and black jumpsuits rove over me as we make our way to the center of the courtyard, rather *Elivander's* way—I go whichever way he pulls me, which is right back to the helplessness and pain of my first day in Sonnet. The water. The knife. The boot in my gut. I lift the heavy cuffs, my fingers finding the soggy scab on my neck.

Then I see Kelter approaching, hands cuffed, ankles bound, shuffling along next to a guard in a blue jumpsuit. I dive for him, forgetting about the cuffs.

"Kelt!"

But two hands snap around my waist. "No touching." The gravelly voice comes straight from Elivander's chest.

Kelter's scowl at him could slice through steel. He looks at me next, inspecting the cuffs and foreign dress before landing his gaze on mine. Warmth seeps into his features, a soft smile pressing across his tan face.

"Ever," he chokes out.

He looks clean too, unharmed and like himself except for the overgrown stubble and black pants and T-shirt. I've never seen him in anything but jeans and plaid pajamas.

"Look, Eli. The Hollows are reuniting." Kelter's guard squeals and claps her hands, jiggling the curly pile of brown hair atop her head. She throws a dark brown hand onto Kelter's shoulder, and though the tightness around her eyes tells me she's fierce and hardened by life, she wears a wide grin on her freckle-covered face.

"Don't get attached, Kaleida. They're Hollows," Elivander says from behind me, still keeping me from Kelter. "Would you at least contain him?"

The guard—Kaleida, as he called her—rolls her eyes and takes hold of Kelter's cuffs.

"I thought your name was Elivander." I twist to look at him.

Fingers graze the back of my neck. His grip tightens on my hips. "Only my mother called me that."

"You gave her your full name?" Kaleida gawks at him, a smile eventually putting her jaw back in place.

"I was distracted by her incessant questioning." He turns me to grab my cuffs instead and grumbles down at me. "It's Eli."

"Sounds about right," Kelter mumbles, half-suppressing a smile.

Elivander's eyes snap to Kelter then back to me. "Walk." He pulls me along with one hand behind him, and Kaleida falls in at his side with Kelter in tow.

"You're making fun of me at a time like this?" I say to Kelter as we take stunted, chained steps across the courtyard. "Don't you care?"

Kelter deflates. "Of course I care." His eyelids grow heavy as he takes in my pain. "Did he hurt you?"

"No talking either." Elivander yanks me away.

I look back at Kelt, wordless. My eyes burn, salty wells forming.

We pass between the marble walls of the buildings surrounding the courtyard and into an area with sparse trees and golden hills in the distance. Only nature for as far as I can see—no streets dividing the land into rectangles and forcing order like in Caldera. No cars to keep people from using their bodies. No block-shaped buildings with automatic doors pulling you inside. I make sure not to show how much I love it, even though it's not home.

We walk west beneath the ever-darkening morning sky. I map the area in my head, sketching the contours of the land as I think about the strangeness of Sonnet. These people have kept themselves so hidden and secluded from Caldera that they use different materials, have their own leader and possibly don't use electricity. But of course, no one would find them if no one was looking.

Other Calderans don't venture beyond the city edge. They don't question or wonder. And they tear me apart when I do. I suppose it's big enough to keep them satisfied. They could drive for hours and not be halfway to the southern boundary, but they don't even bother to see the rest of Caldera. They get up, do their job and go home. Every day. No passion or reason. Kelter's the only one who puts up with me exploring the forest and searching for my parents. I look over at him, waiting for him to catch my gaze.

Elivander has me scurrying, the chain between my ankles tugging and snapping and the metal cuffs rubbing my skin raw. I try to keep up while still looking at Kelter, but I stumble, my foot catching on a hole. I sail forward, out of his grasp and into a vision.

My head smashes into a rock. I wait for the blood to trickle down my forehead, but it doesn't—because it's pooling in my brain. I turn over, and Kelter is at my side, his face crumpling. My emptiness inside must be showing, the approach of death painted across my blank expression. I blink, and when my lids rise one last time, the little boy from the forest stands next to him.

I rake my fingers through the dirt, grasping for reality.

What the fuck is wrong with my brain?

Trembling on my hands and knees in the red dress, cuffs clanking, I try to recover as though I'd simply fallen, like Cam taught me. *Better clumsy than crazy*, she'd say. It's the hardest thing about the visions—returning from death to find out who witnessed my fractured sanity, what kind of fool I've made of myself.

I scan the scene around me. Every leaf is greener than before. Every root pushing up through the dirt tells me its story. Every rock has an edge tucked out of sight.

I'm so alive after dying.

I catch a glimpse of green. A shift of my pointer finger reveals the tiniest seedling. It's smooth and glossy and new to the world, a crescent the size of my fingernail, bending under the weight of existence. So small it could be obliterated with the stomp of a boot, yet also so tiny it could escape between the ridges of the tread—and survive.

With delicate flits of my finger, I build a mound of dirt around it, circling it with pebbles, a small protection from a big world. We're both new here. I tap the tip of the seedling. My hand quivers inside, and a tingle darts up my arm as though the plant had reached through my skin and sent a spark of its delicate life into me. I swear it glows for a second, as if to say thank you—another reminder of how close to the edge of madness I am.

Kaleida and Kelter are a short ways ahead, still walking. Elivander puts his broad hands on my waist, lifts me from the ground and plops me down on my feet with no effort whatsoever before gripping my cuffs. I wait for the snide remark, a shove to get on my way. Anything. Instead, his eyes peel away my layers. Against all instinct I let my gaze collide with his, and meddling, rapt curiosity looks back at me. Into me. And I'm *seen*. And violated.

No one in Caldera has ever looked at me with such fascination, not even Kelter.

"I'm starting to wonder how you got along without a guard before," he says.

There's the snide remark.

"I got along fine."

His head ticks to the side. "Did you?"

It's a genuine question, and it's clear he's not referring to something so trivial as my physical safety, but rather crossing the line into an untouchable topic: the questionable condition of my mind.

No, you don't get to ask. But I answer anyway. I fill my chest with the air of false confidence, pretending I know what I'm up against. I put everything into my silent response. The whole tangled mess of mixed up feelings, every gnawing memory stinging with rejection, every unhinged thought no one wants to hear—and the rage. All the rage. Toward him, my past, myself. I pile it into my stare.

He soaks it all up, never blinking, and it's as if his hands are all over me. That's how deep he goes, penetrating my soul. My knees weaken.

"Stop staring, creep." *Because I can't stop, and someone has to.*

A black curl falls, a casualty of the wind, and even that doesn't break the spell. His lips are loose despite the tightness of his face. Fingers feather down my back, and I shudder.

"Then don't play in the damn dirt." He narrows those disastrous eyes. "I'm supposed to deliver a clean prisoner."

"Maybe you're not so good at your job, *Elivander*." I tug at my cuffs to get away.

He clenches his teeth, a low growl slipping through them as he pulls me into him, my fists against his abdomen. "It's Eli."

I look up at the loaded sky and back to him as the clouds finally give in. "Not to me." *Not out loud, and not as long as it keeps pissing you off.* Rain scatters over our cheeks.

"Doesn't your little boyfriend care when you trip and fall?"

I shove against his stomach, instantly regretting it at the feel of solid muscle, the way it affects me. "He's my friend."

"That's it? Why? He doesn't think you're as fuckable as I do?"

I expect to see that smirk find his face, but his brows draw together instead, his jaw straining.

Why? Because... he's Kelt. I could say that, but something about this man brings out the side of me that I let shrivel up, the side that doesn't fear rejection or judgment, that fights back and crosses lines... the side of me that will burn down a house.

I give him a placating smile, braving the return of my hands to his belly and the warmth between my legs that comes with it. "He knows how fuckable I am, but his cock has some self-control, unlike yours."

"That only makes him a pussy. And so does leaving you face down in the dirt."

I'm still scrabbling for a response when Kelter glances over his shoulder at us and gives me a knowing look, but he doesn't get it.

He can't see me.

He doesn't know I have visions, doesn't know how many times I've watched him die and mourned the loss of my only friend. I've never told him. He's only seen me on the outside, frozen or fallen on my ass with no explanation. He could tell I had another episode, as he calls them, because of all the times he's been there with me—holding my hand, standing me up, cupping my cheek... and looking at me as though I'm broken, like all the rest. Even though it's true. He doesn't know that look, that pitying, sundering look, hurts worse than dying.

CHAPTER 8

With every step deeper into the village, my nerves heat, the unknown strumming them until they catch fire. It's not only the open landscape that's different. There are no rows of houses and businesses along the streets, no flashing traffic lights, no print shop to buy map paper, and worst of all, no aroma of roasting beans wafting out the propped-open door of a coffee shop like where I work. Or *worked*. I could always smell it from my room upstairs.

A few people in gray jumpsuits are out walking, and it seems that's the only way to get around here.

"Welcome to the village," Kaleida says, even though we've been in it for a while. She rises onto her toes in excitement and pride, gesturing to the scattered buildings, all facing different directions. "It's nothing like it was before the Separation, but it's still home."

"Separation?" I ask and unstick my boot from the muddy path that winds between the dreary buildings, each one distractingly unique. Most are made from various types of raw stone, others with unfinished wood, crooked and leaning, as if built on an afternoon whim. Each one is only big enough to house a person or two with no space for a kitchen or living room, and definitely not a garage. None of the roofs match the supporting walls, as if tacked on as an afterthought. I try to see inside, but opaque glass covered with a constellation of scratches is fitted into every oddly shaped window.

Kelter walks with his head down, not bothering to look around. He must be as scared as I am to face the Centress.

Kaleida lets go of Kelt's cuffs to fix her tied up bunch of curls. "Oh, you don't know. The Separation—"

Eli groans and roughly pulls me along by my cuffs. "What are you running your mouth for again? Now we have to listen to one of her stories."

"You love my stories, Eli." Kaleida elbows him in the arm. Her round cheeks rise with her smile. "You remember them better than anyone, sometimes better than me."

He huffs and pushes wet hair from his face. "Your prisoner, Kaleida."

Kelt cocks his head toward Eli, flaring his nostrils before shoving his arms at Kaleida. Flipping one hand about as she talks, she takes hold of his cuffs with two fingers, as though that might restrain him.

"Why would you be willing to tell me?" I ask. She's too nice, suspiciously so.

Her face scrunches. "Why wouldn't I?"

"Because everyone else wants us dead," Kelter answers for me.

"I didn't grow up here with these *savages*." She looks at Eli, grinning, then reaches up to tousle Kelter's golden hair. "I'm a storyteller—the last one from the destroyed village of Lirica up north."

A storyteller? That's a thing?

"Everyone and everything I know went up in flames when I was ten years old. I was the only survivor," she adds in response to my silence.

"Oh." How much death has *she* seen?

A smile spreads clear across her face despite her revelation. "And if I don't share the stories I was told, they'll be gone, so I'll tell you about the Separation, and Eli will put up with it."

Eli snickers and pulls me along.

"The Separation was when a border was put up around Sonnet hundreds of years ago," Kaleida says. "Ever since then, the two realms have been advancing separately, and now they're completely different from each other and from how they once were. Before they were overthrown by a group led by the first Centress, a king and queen ruled Sonnet. Everything held beauty back then, and people weren't driven by hatred. They traveled and celebrated, families stayed together, more babies survived birth and everyone lived longer. Oh, and art was appreciated *and* encouraged, and the food—I can't even imagine. And so many more animals could be found, and clothes were—"

"We're here," Eli interrupts.

Why did everything go so wrong after the Separation? And why separate at all?

47

My chest pulls tight as I look up at the massive granite walls and blood-red roof of the school. Eli's steps slow, and he veers toward the arched entrance. Kelter and I are forced into the entry room, our boots squeaking and ankle chains scraping along the copper-flecked granite floor.

Kaleida sweeps one arm out wide. "This is where all the children in Sonnet live, from one year old to sixteen, never leaving the school grounds. They share rooms, attend classes every day and participate in combat training in the evenings. Then at sixteen they can move into any available house in the village or choose to pick or build something more remote in the woods. By the time they finish school, most parents have already died—or will soon after—so they're on their own. Their only option is to follow the rules and join the Service Sphere, like us." She signals to Eli and herself when we stop in the middle of the room.

The main foyer is crowded with people caught in discussion, pushing papers about and standing around tables with gray stones situated in the middle. Bookshelves line the walls, each spine gray and the same size as the one next to it. Tragic. Only a handful of children are among the adults, and almost everyone stops to stare at us.

A little girl at the nearest table takes one look at Eli and ducks beneath it, dragging a boy down with her. "Hide! It's him."

Some adults around us back away from Eli, knocking into each other's tall bodies in their attempt to retreat, while others pat him on the back and greet him as we pass. He keeps his face forward, not a single sign of notice.

I retreat when I see the Centress at the opposite end of the room, but Eli yanks me back to his side. The metal scrapes my wrist, and I hold in a whimper. He hasn't let go since I tripped and fell.

The Centress' dress is red today, standing out like a blood stain amid the gray jumpsuits of the others. It's almost like mine, made with that same seamless fabric that finds every curve offered. The idea of being like her in any way makes my soul itch. Kaleida and Eli are the only two in blue jumpsuits. Protected by three smug guards in black, the Centress beckons us her way with a hooked finger.

My heart searches for a way out of my chest as we near the guard that held me underwater, the supple lips and pointy nose of her hateful face unforgettable.

"It had to be you," she snarls at Eli, low enough for the Centress not to hear. "Of all the useless border guards that could have been assigned to take on a Hollow, we're stuck being around your weird ass."

The guard at her side pushes his long tail of hair over his shoulder, fair cheeks caving in despite his chilling grin. "Maybe the Centress will do us a favor and put him out of his misery after this assignment. He's bound to screw something up."

The third guard inches back as he looks the four of us over with his slashing blue-green eyes.

So much hatred.

Eli ignores their comments and pulls me as far away as he can from them without straying from the Centress. Somehow, he's a pocket of safety in this awful realm despite his constant hold on me—or because of it.

"The children live here? When do they see their parents?" I ask Kaleida in a whisper.

"They don't," Eli cuts in, his voice shady and distant.

No parents for all those years? A life without knowing my parents has left me detached and wandering the forest, mapping every path that could have been mine. Plenty of other kids grew up parentless too, but they didn't seem to mind. Maybe because they didn't have the hollow kiss of death tucking them in at night. *Hollow.* I guess the name fits.

"Bring the Hollows and follow me." The Centress and her guards turn toward a hallway branching off from the main entry room. "Better not to keep them waiting. They're impatient little things."

CHAPTER 9

N ight shift is over. We're leaving them here and heading to the border," Eli says, tugging me closer with the cuffs, despite his words indicating a desire to be far from me.

The Centress whirls around. "You stay until I say. I've arranged for a special lesson before we begin. I don't need you after that. Get out of line again and you'll find yourself with double shifts like this for the next year."

Eli's body tenses next to me. He folds his lips in, likely holding back a retort as the Centress takes off again.

Kaleida whispers in my ear, "She's been a little grumpy since her mysterious lover left her in her early days as the Centress. She thinks she's scary because she can cause pain and meddle with minds, but she's like us… only in charge."

Pain? "Who could love her?"

"Someone did. It doesn't have to make sense. Love is feral. It's not within our control."

Eli forces his feet to move and drags me down the granite hallway—toward the trill of children.

The classroom is bare, shades of gray all around except the red planks angled toward the high center of the ceiling—no colorful letters on the walls, no chalkboards, no desks and no wide window with a playground outside like the schools in Caldera. Each child wears a charcoal jumpsuit and sits on the floor with a back as straight as a wall, evenly spaced, every right leg folded under the left. Some scramble backward at the sight of Eli, then resume their stiff position.

The Centress stands in front of the classroom, towering above her three hovering guards and the four of us behind her. I move toward Kelter, his warmth and safety, but Eli grabs my wrists and pulls me to his other side. "I said no touching your little boyfriend."

"Silence." The Centress' polished voice spills over the room. The children shut their mouths as it reaches them, as does their teacher, blending into the wall in a gray jumpsuit. "To complement your lesson on Hollows, I've brought two living specimens."

Specimens.

Each pair of eager eyes finds us, flaring with loathing and fear. They look about eight years old, devoid of joy and personality.

"You've heard about Hollows in Caldera, the danger beyond Sonnet. You face them in your nightmares, the harm they cause when they steal what's ours. But now, despite the elixir, two have crossed into Sonnet. Today, you get to see them up close for the first—and hopefully only—time, then they'll visit other classrooms before we reclaim what they've stolen."

She's mad. "We haven't stolen a fucking thing," I snap.

The Centress whips around, all three guards mirroring her movement. "Silence her."

Eli moves behind me and clamps his hand over my mouth, his other hand holding tight to the cuffs at my front.

Oh, no you don't.

I twist my head back and forth under his grasp, trying to escape his fingers. His grip harshens. He smashes the back of my head to his hard chest. Our rain-dampened clothes press together. I can't escape his hand, the constraint, the pressure—I shove my tongue between his cold fingers.

He startles and removes his hand, just long enough for me to blurt out. "What elixir?"

Kelter groans, and Eli slaps his hand back over my mouth, leaving it tingling and burning under his touch.

Even fiercer this time, the Centress' voice brims with threat. "Control your prisoner, guard." She turns to face him and reaches a hand above my head, her lips spread thin. "Or I'll control you."

His body flinches at her touch, his head jerking away. Her hand trails down his arm, all the way to the hand holding my cuffs. I gather the belly of my dress into my trembling fingers. Eli's muscles flex against my head and back, his teeth grinding above me.

"Such a high tolerance for pain," she lilts.

The Centress faces the children again. "Over two centuries ago, Vaile lived in harmony with the Hollows across the land, sharing our gifts with them and living and working side by side."

Eli tucks his lips close to my ear, his voice barely more than hot breath. "I told you to behave. You're going to get us both in trouble." He squeezes my jaw. "If you wanted to taste me, you could have waited until tonight, little prisoner."

Phantom blood pools under my tongue, and I swallow away the tang. "You wish you were good enough for my mouth."

My words are a muffled mess behind his hand, but he grunts in my ear and whispers again. "I wouldn't fit."

I jerk against him at the thought, pushing into the body part in question—hard as fuck against my back—then force my attention back to the Centress to stop the vivid images in my head.

"But the Hollows grew envious of our gifts of magic from the gods when they had none. They wanted magic for themselves and their children—so they took it. They went straight to where it's stored and drained the plants with their siphoning hands, filling themselves with magic and hollowing their souls, an atrocity not even Vaile are capable of. And they'll do it again if we let them. They'll take the magic from our plants. We must be willing to destroy them when they threaten us, when they come to Sonnet and steal from us. They're more dangerous than you could ever imagine." The Centress goes quiet for a moment, letting her words sink in.

Magic? These people are insane. I thought I was the one barely holding it together. I turn my head toward Kelter as much as Eli's grip on my mouth allows. Twitchy hazel eyes look back at me... at my covered mouth, my trapped body. Kaleida stands next to him, one hand resting on his cuffs.

I got the wrong guard.

I angle my wrists until I can spin my pinky rings, around and around like my endless thoughts. The children clutch their knees and scowl.

"And so began the Separation," the Centress continues. "Hollows would stop at nothing to have the magic they craved, but the Vaile's protection was unfaltering. We put up a border, containing all the magic within Sonnet—Hollows on one side, and magic and Vaile on the other, safe from their greedy hands. We lost most of Sonnet's land and sacrificed even more magic to protect it, but it was the only way."

A boy raises his hand, holding it as straight as his back, all the way to his fingertips. The Centress tips her chin at him. "Centress Oreyla, did we get back the magic that the Hollows took?"

"No, but the border prevented them from using it, and the elixir helped them forget."

She's delusional. My breaths come faster, the air thick and lacking oxygen despite all I pull in through my nose. This is wrong. I should be home… in my room in Caldera, laughing with Kelt, drinking coffee and adding to my maps. Not here, with crazy people who think they have magic. Eli's fingers tighten on me, digging into my cheeks as if he feels my desire to escape.

"But are we safe now? Can't they cross the border?" a girl asks, fingers interlocked in her lap.

"That's what the elixir is for," a boy in front turns to tell her.

The Centress steps forward, her toes almost touching the boy's crossed legs. "Are we safe? You tell me. Two Hollows stand in your classroom. The elixir didn't keep them away. What's to say it will work for the others? The effect may not be enough anymore. This is why we must continue to guard our borders. They'll take away our magic, squander it and let it die with them. We can't get it back once it's gone."

The room is smogged with hostility. "So what do Vaile do?" she prompts.

"*Preserve the magic of our land!*" the class chants back in unison.

"At what cost?"

"*At any cost at your command!*"

"And how do we do it?"

"*Maintain the Separation!*"

"What will you give?"

"*A friend, a life, a generation!*"

"Remember those words. It might be up to you one day to turn in a traitor, give your life or take thousands more for Vaile." The Centress clasps her hands, a glint in her black eyes. "Now who wants to touch the Hollows?"

She's teaching these children to fear and hate Calderans—or

Hollows, I suppose—to be willing to die to keep us away. For what? Because she thinks magic is real and we want it? And that justifies training children to hate and kill and die for nothing? I glance at Kelter again, needing my person. But I'm stuck in the arms of one of *them*.

The Centress steps aside, and the dozens of children lose their perfect posture and crowd forward. They reach for us—some with intrigue or fear, running fingers over the damp dress covering my legs, and others with the hard hand of hatred, squeezing and pinching, pulling on the chains between my ankle cuffs and shoving me hard enough to make me lose my balance. Eli holds me up through it, still covering my mouth. My tears trickle over his hand. I can't help it… I'm a crier. It must annoy him because he shifts one finger up and strokes my cheek, the faintest motion, wiping away the wetness.

Their hands pat and poke and prod my body, tiny child hands that will grow into weapons. The crowd, the hands, the contempt—my body shudders against Eli, my chest heaving. They're meant to be happy. They're meant to laugh and play. The walls press in, crushing. They shouldn't grow up like me, with death on their minds.

The red planks of the ceiling creak and crack. A sound like thunder booms above us. Eli squeezes me tight and backs us into the wall as the ceiling opens and boulders of ice fall through. They crash to the floor, sending children scattering and running out the door, small boots bounding and leaving piles of split and splintered wood and balls of glinting ice behind. Cold air sweeps through the room. The foundation shakes as more ice falls through the open ceiling and other parts of the building. Screams clip my eardrums. The screams of children, of pain. And beyond the gray walls—of death.

I would know.

The three guards pile on top of the Centress, limbs protecting every inch of her. Four children are left behind with body parts stuck under the frozen boulders. This can't be real. A little girl struggles to free her leg from a three-foot ball of ice, pushing with her hands and pulling her body back while she cries. Kaleida leaves Kelter and runs to help.

Eli hurls me to the floor, balling me up and surrounding me—his torso above, his knees behind, his arms shielding my head and neck… and his cock pushing against my ass.

"Are you fucking hard right now? *Again?*"

"How could I not be with you under me?" he asks, squeezing tighter from every direction.

I try to get away to help, but he has me trapped, enveloped in coldness. I'm left with a pocket of air, dense and damp like a cave.

"Kelter!" I yell, unable to see him past Eli's hold on me.

"Ever, are you okay?" I can barely hear him over the crying children. My whole body reacts to the sound of his voice buried in the noise and chaos, urgency slamming through me.

"I'm okay." I push against Eli, arching my back into his stomach. "Get off me."

He starts to rise then throws himself over me again as more boulders fall. I shove my head through an opening between his arms.

The guards release the Centress, and she smacks the long-haired one in the face once she stands and gains her footing. "Fools. I don't need three of you on top of me." She scans the room. "Chain the prisoners up here, take the rest of the children outside and gather the injured in the entry room. The Environmental Sphere will be here any minute to melt the ice."

Eli peels his body off mine, grabs my ankle cuffs and drags me to the corner of the room, my bottom sliding along the granite floor.

"What are you doing," I ask. He takes another set of cuffs from his jumpsuit pocket and latches one side to my ankle cuff and the other to a metal grate on the floor. "You have more fucking cuffs?"

Squatting before me, a smirk teases his lips. "I'm a guard." That invisible darkness crowds in and sits on my skin like a layer of cold sweat. He pinches my chin, holding me in place and coercing my eyes to stay on his. "I can cuff you wherever and whenever I want—in *any* position—so don't misbehave."

"How am I going to misbehave while chained to the floor?" I yank the cuffs. Steel clangs and clatters, but that doesn't keep my freak mind from wondering *which* positions.

"You always seem to find a way." He releases my chin with a twist, then spreads two fingers apart over the crease of my brow, forcing away my scowl before backing up to the door to wait.

Kaleida leads Kelter to the corner to sit next to me. "It didn't used to be like this. It's been getting worse over the years," she says, crouching next to the grate and cuffing Kelter's ankle to it like mine.

"The weather, the disasters. It's been raining and storming since the day you showed up, and now this. I don't know what we're going to do if this keeps up."

"Those really came from the sky?" I ask, though I know it's impossible.

"Where else?" Kaleida says, compelling her face into one of indifference. She pats Kelter on the head, then me, and stands up. "We'll be back for you."

I lean back against the granite wall. The weather in Caldera is *mild*. The only disasters are in the books I read—and my head. But here, only miles from Caldera, the tormented sky of Sonnet is always shifting, stalking, menacing through that arched window in the black room. It has a life of its own. And the power to kill.

Arm to arm and hip to hip with Kelter, he rests his head on my shoulder and his cuffed hands over my raised knees.

Eli glares at us. "What did I say about touching?" he scolds, then follows Kaleida out the door. Everyone else has already left, even the children that were trapped, leaving me and Kelter in the corner, finally together, surrounded by ice and destruction.

CHAPTER 10

W e have to get out of here, Kelter," I gasp out as I rattle the cuffs and chains.

He shifts, tucking his knees into his chest and facing me, our cuffed ankles lined up. "You had another episode on the way here." He drops his chin to look me in the eyes, yet avoids what I said. "A bad one."

"I did." I look toward the gray wall. What else can I say? *Thank you for always being so damn devastated when I die?*

"Remember when you fell down the stairs to your room?"

"Yes." *Because I was busy dying in my head.*

"And I was there to catch you." He pushes my cheek until I'm looking at him again.

"You were." He carried me back inside, then spent the day adding padding to the staircase and landing while I begged him not to.

His cuffed hands hold mine. "I'll always be here, Ever. Tell me what's going on with these episodes."

Death and blood and pain and loss. No. "It's nothing. I get distracted sometimes."

Kelter holds his stare, gold sparking in one eye. He sighs at my lie, the one I always tell him, and moves on. "You shouldn't talk to your guard any more than you have to."

"Why not?" *Not that I want to.* "Because I shouldn't talk to anyone but you?"

Kelter made sure I had only his company day and night, taking up every minute of my spare time. It didn't matter. I wasn't inclined to talk to anyone else beyond the necessary back-and-forth at the coffee shop—

which I was told was never enough, nor pleasant—but I'm not sure how it would have gone if I'd tried to make another friend.

"Not when they end up hurting you," he says quietly, knowing exactly what I meant. "Watching movies with me every night was a better option."

"You don't have to keep anyone away from me. I accomplish that by being myself." I try to pull my hands away to warm them in the folds of my dress, but Kelter holds them tight.

"I *do* have to."

"You're my friend, Kelt. All you have to do is be you."

"And I'm telling you, *as a friend*, don't talk to your guard. He can't be trusted, and you don't know anything about him or what he's capable of."

"And you do?"

Despite my tone, Kelter's voice is soothing. His shoulders rise and fall with the same ease and mystery of the sun. "I know *you*."

"How come you're still my friend then?" It's what I've wanted to ask this whole last year. It's the question that makes me a rotten friend, pulled right from my mouth and into this moment to join the rest of the pain and unknown. How could he really know me and still want to be at my side?

His eyes saturate with hurt. "You're quick to shut people out."

"I'm not shutting you out, Kelt." But I am.

"And you put up all these walls. You push everyone away from the start because that's what they end up doing to you." His fingers thread through mine, an awkward, noisy move with the cuffs. "But it backfires."

My mouth parts. I search for words and come up short.

"You don't even know how you end up pulling them in. You're oblivious. You do it with those creepy-beautiful eyes. You make them want to know more, keeping them up at night, trying to figure you out."

Creepy-beautiful?

He's all riled up now, his lips trembling beneath three days' worth of forgone shaves, and I'm too stunned to stop him.

"You show how strong you are, up against yourself, dealing with whatever lurks inside your head. You make them wonder if they could be as strong as you if they had to be. You make them doubt, make them vulnerable."

Please be done.

He's not.

"And then—" His chest heaves. "You let them see a weakness, a true flaw, and you become so real, so… so *magnetic*"—his eyes flutter shut and reopen, all those colors swirling at me—"that you make it impossible to walk away."

I'm speechless.

This man rarely passes ten words at a time most days. My brain muddles through what he just said. This can't be right. If it were, I wouldn't be scarred right down to the center of my soul from years of abandonment and rejection. I wouldn't only have one friend. One friend who stuck around, one friend who didn't walk away…

And I get it. He answered my wretched question. He's not talking about anyone but himself, and why he's still at my side a whole year later. And it's too much. I don't want to be magnetic or creepy-beautiful. Or figured out.

"So please don't let that happen." A grimace distorts the face I know so well. He drops my hands. "With him. Or anyone else."

"I won't." I'll agree to anything to take the pain from him.

Footsteps thud in the hallway, and two tall men in gray jumpsuits enter. I stare up at the overcast sky through the collapsed roof, trying not to breathe. The men move through the room with ease despite the jutting planks and debris-littered floor, their black boots crushing chunks of ice with satisfying *crunches* and *cracks*. They circle the boulders, some reaching higher than their knees, then crouch and flatten their hands onto the glistening surfaces. And they melt them.

Instantly.

With their bare hands.

The ice turns to puddles.

Dammit. I thought my sanity would last a bit longer.

My mind wavers, unable to make sense of it. I reach for Kelt again, my restrained hands extending without planning or thought, instinctively searching for something right in a realm of wrong. He can fix this. He can tell me I'm hallucinating. Maybe dreaming. I turn, setting my eyes on him, but he's looking back at me, calm as ever, waiting to see what I'm going to do.

I'm going to fall the fuck apart. That's what I'm going to do.

One of the men approaches the final boulder, only feet away from us. He doesn't look more than a few years older than me, but he's tall like the Centress, his brown hair disheveled, and the angles of his face make me want to keep looking. With the touch of his hand to the ice, water gushes over the floor.

Even with his ankles restrained, Kelt manages to hop to a crouch, avoiding the rush of water flooding into the corner and down the grate. But I'm stuck in my head, observing, analyzing, panicking, my body a step behind. The ice-cold liquid soaks my bottom. I try to jump up, forgetting about my tethered ankles and end up flipped around and wetter than before. My body reacts—goosebumps prickling, hands wringing water from the dress—but it's no longer controlled by any rational part of me. I'm too far gone.

This close up, there's no denying it. I saw it melt. I feel the water, but it can't be. I know I'm on edge, even unstable, but this is approaching the insanity I feared, if not fully embracing it.

"Ever." Kelter's voice reaches my frozen figure, and I wait for everything to fall back into place—but it doesn't.

I stare blankly, my head crushing inward. "Something's not right."

"I know." He gives me a shaky smile, as unfamiliar as his borrowed black clothes. "Everything's going to be okay."

"It's not."

"We're done, let's go," the other man says, his crooked jaw clocked to the side.

"Just a minute." The brown-haired one rubs his wet hands over the chest of his jumpsuit. A perfect smile breaks across his face. "It's the Hollows. I won't have another chance."

Gray eyes glazed, tongue sliding over his bottom lip, he closes in on us. "You think you can come into our realm and steal from us?"

Kelter shields me with his arm.

The man laughs, and I hate that it sounds good coming from his threatening face. "You can't protect her. Or yourself." He kicks Kelter in the ribs, then drives his boot into my thigh. The rough tread, icy and wet, tears through the delicate fabric of my dress.

"Holy fuck." I grasp my leg and fold myself into the corner, kneeling with one side pressed to the wall and huddled next to Kelter's trembling body.

The initial shock fades, and pain crawls over me, taking me into a vision.

I'm thrown flat to the ground. The man jams his boot into my throat. I try to lift it to breathe, but it's wet. My hands slip. Everything spins, head exploding, ears ringing, black spots floating. I only want it to end. My last thought is of cursing at the stars with Kelt back home. He crushes down harder, and my last sensation is warm blood seeping from my ears.

"Just wait, Hollows. You'll get what's coming for you." The man's voice is a distant whisper, pulling me from the vision.

They leave, their cackles hanging behind, stuck in the pain-soaked air.

I can't quite make my limbs move despite the life pumping back into me. Can't find the connection between mind and body, as though it's been severed to protect myself from the hurt. But Kelter finds me. His quaking hands land in my lap. I flinch, expecting more pain. His touch is soft, surreal... apologetic. Only the burn of tears falling from my eyes lets me open them.

"Kelt," I force out past the torrent of emotion.

He looks back at me, eyes red and searching, cheeks flushed.

"I want to go home," I whisper.

"Home," he repeats, as though the concept were foreign. His gaze wanders the room. Distant cries filter in through the open door, competing with the whistle of wind over the remaining roof planks.

Why isn't he saying he wants to go home too? Has he given up? I lift my cuffed hands and lay one on each of his unshaven cheeks. "Don't you want to escape?"

His brows lift like a lazy sunrise. The fall of his eyes from mine to the puddled floor tortures me. He traps the corner of his lip between his teeth and lets it slip out so slowly that it could drive even the most patient soul to madness. "Of course."

"Then what—it doesn't look like you do." My palms slide from his face.

"I do. It's that..." He raises his hands, and with the slowest motion and the clink of metal, pulls my curtain of hair to the side with a single finger, tracing to my temple. "I have nothing to go home to." He runs his finger down my cheek and under my chin, giving it the lightest lift and forcing our eyes to meet. "And neither do you."

My insides wind up tight, tourniquets constricting every dying organ. Too tight to gasp, to scream, to draw a simple breath.

"What?!" I yell, finally unraveling. He shushes me, so I yell louder. "I don't care if you live in a damn box in Caldera, it's better than this."

Anything is better than this.

"And you're wrong. I have plenty to go home to. So do you. Things were finally okay. *You* made them okay. We can go back and pretend this never happened." Go back to coffee and sunrises on the roof. To the safety and the known. I can go back to mapping my way through the forest and find a path to my parents. I could.

But not without him.

He swallows, meeting my yell with a whisper. "You don't know what it was like for me."

Tighter and tighter. His words rip me in two. Or three. Or four. *Worse than being a waste of space? Worse than over sixty homes? And Reggie Junior?* But he can't know about that. "Then tell me, Kelt."

He tugs at an ornery strand of hair in my face and pulls away from me. "Not today, Ever. Not like this."

My heart lunges after him, trying to prevent the distance he puts between us. My pain, my fury, my fears, they coalesce into one, rioting inside me. I open my mouth to argue, beg, whine—I don't know which, definitely nothing respectable—but the splash of boots in a melted puddle of ice stops me.

"You're all wet." Kaleida runs to me and pulls on my arms to lift me up, setting sight on the ripped dress. "What happened?"

Kelter and I struggle up. "The guys that came to melt the ice," he says.

The image comes back, reminding me of my slipping sanity.

"I can't believe those guys." She sets to work on releasing the cuffs from the grate with the wave of a stone—another magnetic lock. "You know, we lost so much with the Separation, even with all we gained. Almost no one believes it anymore. They think my stories are made up."

I note her misting eyes as she rises with the spare cuffs and pockets them. She leads us back toward the main foyer, our ankle chains dragging. Kelter reaches over, his cuffed hand finding mine, fingers locking. It should be a comfort, but I'm not sure I know who he is anymore.

"We have to take you back to your rooms," Kaleida says. "The Centress won't be able to see you until a temporary school location is set up."

I could faint with relief… though it's only a delay of the inevitable.

Once inside the grand entry room, I don't see the speckled granite walls or the droves of sobbing children with sodden shoes. I don't see the gray jumpsuit wearers melting boulder after boulder of ice, or the ones in black, wading through debris. Or Kaleida biting her lip and shaking her head. I don't hear the perpetual drip, or my own breath catch.

My senses don't waste time on those things.

The quietest song commands the sweeping room. Eli kneels on the floor, axis of anguish. He holds a little girl's hand in his. She's a flower. Her skin is milky white against the light brown cradle of his hand, and her yellow hair drapes his lap, wilting petals radiating around her head.

As though she's turning toward the sun, she strains her neck to find the source of the song, then slumps back down into the surrounding puddle, letting out a final huff of air that mixes with his hushed notes. I pretend she's taken by the gods I don't believe in, and I mark my mental map. With a flower.

I try not to think about how beautiful a death it was, or how great an ice boulder it must have been to take a life and leave a puddle that size.

A polished blue stone embedded with swirls of metal calls to me from the growing pond at my feet. I let go of Kelt to pick it up. Though it's a bit of a struggle with the cuffs and my bruised body, I tuck it into my bra. That's where all my acquired treasures go—tiny things I make mine, pressed against my skin and held in place by the fabric. I don't even feel them anymore, only the calm they bring.

Kelt eyes me but says nothing as he takes my hand back. My heart beats behind the blue stone, centering me, but not enough to stop the pain, the doubt, the panic… and the confusion. How can the man holding that girl be the same one who curdles my blood? Where I expect coldness, there's sorrow. Where I expect darkness, there's pain.

It's an act. It has to be.

A woman in a gray jumpsuit enters the room and lifts the girl from his lap, and Eli splashes over to us. He looks up and down my soaked and torn dress, a flash of fury in his eyes, then smacks his hand between mine and Kelter's, tearing our fingers apart—as though he simply can't stand another man's hands on me.

CHAPTER 11

I t's been a week since the trip to the village, a week back inside the black walls day and night. The chafed skin on my wrists and ankles finally stopped stinging, and my boot-sized bruise has turned a sickly, mottled green and still hurts with every motion. But much worse is the pain that slides down and lodges in my throat every time I think of Kelter… which leads me to hands melting boulders of ice.

Magic.

That's what the Centress said they have, what she thinks we stole. Magic.

A hallucination, a profound disruption of the senses, a dream—anything is a more comforting explanation than actual magic… even insanity. So I keep denying. I convince myself I didn't see what I saw. I hide it from myself like I hide the visions from others and slip away into the hallways of my past, searching for an escape.

I held hands with Cam, walking up to my fourth new home in my third-grade year, the one with the yellow door and broken mailbox. The other social worker stood on the porch, talking to my new foster parents. Maybe he was warning them about me. I squeezed Cam's hand tight.

Now don't you fret, Everielle, you'll be great. She let go of my hand and crouched down to my level, tucking waves of black hair behind her ear and smiling sweetly.

What if they don't want to keep me? Like all the rest.

You make them want to, hun.

How do I do that? I gripped the hanging straps of my backpack.

Another smile, a brush of my cheek. *Well, you start with keeping all those special thoughts up in your head. Don't go telling people those things, you see. That ends with me. Then you control it. You stop it.*

Cam? I glanced warily at the worker coming for me.

Mm-hmm?

What if... what if I can't stop it? I whispered.

There ain't no "if" hun. You stop it, and that's that. She wiped my tears just before I was pulled away.

When will I see you again? I asked, craning my neck to keep her in sight, though I knew it wouldn't be long until I was sent away again.

You know I'm always here.

Then I was shoved through the frame of the yellow door, and I tried so hard to stop the violence and death that came for me so many times a day. I tried.

And I failed.

I lie on the obsidian floor in the dark of night, still wearing the damn red dress, now looking more black than anything. I only have my mind and the steady splatter of rain to keep me company during the day. Eli wakes me up each morning before he leaves, often a grumpy grunt of hot breath in my ear, and shows up in the evening, all broody as he tosses me a crumbly bar and a canteen of water, my one meal each day.

Once again, Eli is slumped against the stone door, staring. I didn't ask about the little girl or the grief on his face, and he didn't ask about the bruise. He glanced at the purple welt taking over my thigh when we got back that day. It peeked through the tear in the skirt of my dress as he knelt before me, removing the cuffs from my ankles, cold fingers brushing against my shin. His breath caught, and he dropped the stone for the cuffs and cursed. *Fuckers.* My mouth filled with the taste of blood, and his scent slammed into me, musky and earthy, as though I were buried underground—and losing my mind.

Despite the tattered dress and boots, I curl into myself, missing Kelt's warmth and seeking comfort in my own arms. My body shivers. My mind runs. I fight off flashes of death, tossing and turning until cold delirium reaches my bones, and sleep takes me.

It's not until morning that I have to work to suppress the

nightmare—Kelter, shoulders back, his hands at ease in the pockets of a crisp jumpsuit. Like one of *them*.

Lying on my stomach in the last of the early morning moonlight, I press my cheek into the raw stone floor. Eli is still in front of the door, but a nervous energy has him wringing his hands and tapping his toes.

"Why do you do it?" I ask. A gentle breeze rolls off him and caresses me, eroding my defenses against him. "Why choose to be a guard and sleep on the floor? Aren't there better jobs?"

"It's a good thing your little face is so damn pretty because you never shut that mouth."

I was right that it was only an act when I saw him holding that girl, for whatever reason. But I'm pulled in anyway, unbothered, needing to know more. "Don't you get tired of being a jerk?"

"No, and I didn't choose this."

I lift my head off the floor. "I'm that miserable to be with?"

One eyebrow arches, his lips awry. "Yes. Are we done talking?" His tall figure rises. "Get up. I have to take you to the temporary school. The equipment is set up now."

Equipment?

I sit up and plow my knees into my chest, panic streaking through my veins. "What happens if you don't do what the Centress wants?"

"The punishment is worse than guarding you." The contents of his pockets jangle as he nears me. "And she enjoys it. Move."

I sit up and fiddle with the laces in my boots, stalling. The last thing I want is to be handed off to the Centress.

He stands over me, a wall of cobalt blue. "How come you don't listen?"

"How come you keep telling me what to do?"

His towering figure drops before me, knees on either side of my feet. His eyes shift to the bruise on my thigh. Lightness blinks to darkness, and just as fast he grabs my upper arms and pushes me flush against the wall, his palms kneading my muscles. "Because…" He lowers his head, putting us face to face, curls falling, eyes glinting. "You're my prisoner."

I have the urge to run, but I lift my chin and ignore his aroma barging into me, musky and ancient in the best and most irritating way.

"And you're *her* prisoner." I saw the way the Centress treated him, how he goes from one shift to another, living under her threats.

As the skin on my neck crawls, I see him chewing on my words, his angled jaw jutting to the side. I hit a nerve.

"Let's go," he says, but doesn't release me.

"In this?" I gesture toward my dress, now more rag than clothes and coated with dirt and grime. It reeks of a week's worth of cold sweat from every nightmare that had me gasping for life, only to wake up and find myself sucking in the dark, timeless air surrounding this man.

I can see everything this close up. Almost hidden in the deep brown of his irises, golden specks try to find their way to the surface. An inch-long scar interrupts the perpetual stubble on his jaw, and his mouth quirks in contemplation.

"Were you hoping for my company in the shower room again?"

The cold water pelting my head comes back to me, from last week... and years ago. I stuff it down, way down along with the thoughts of him so close to me.

"Your cock pressing into my side is not company." I try to shove him away, but pure muscle holds me back.

"Yet you can't forget about it... because my cock is excellent company." He releases my arms and cuffs me, first wrists, then ankles, soft touches of his fingertips and the tight pinch of metal. A hint of reluctance slows his step toward the door. "Come, little thief. It's going to be a long day for you."

It's not raining, for once, but as if they sensed my impending doom, dark gray clouds threaten a downpour. I don't bother reaching for Kelter when we meet in the courtyard, not only because Eli would stop me, but because seeing him brings me back to that day in the classroom and his words that gnaw at my intestines. A chasm forms between us, even as we hold each other's gaze, infused with fear.

We travel north instead of west to the village. I spend the endless walk thinking of the Kelt I thought I knew—of how much I love him, how I hate when he argues with me, and even more when he doesn't. How I couldn't keep my eyes off him when we met, that I thought he was the perfect mix of tall and hazel eyes and barely there freckles, and still do.

I couldn't get him out of my head that first week, even as I refused to talk to him when he showed up at the coffee shop each day. I laid in bed thinking how those ears of his would make good handles, and—like I do with any halfway decent man I come across—I wondered if he would be the one to sweep me off my lonely feet, if he would rescue me from the mental prison I built myself into, like a sappy fairytale with an unrealistic ending that I hate, but still wish could be mine. But none of that matters anymore… because he kept coming back, and I never looked at him that way again.

Even after I fell to the ground from a vision in the middle of the street with dozens of judging eyes on me, he stayed. He helped me up, took my hand and walked me out of there. That night was the first time we stayed up cursing at the stars from the rooftop, wishing them the most awful fates. Some broken part of me took the fact that he never tried so much as to kiss me in those early days as its own kind of rejection, but I'd take that any day over no friend at all.

We reach the temporary school, an ancient stone and brick building with lush plants springing up around it and vines snaking along the steep walls. Trees and boulders surround it, and with the roar of a river rushing over rocks in the distance and wind rustling and flirting with the treetops, it would be a calming place… if I didn't have death looming over me.

Eli and Kaleida are dismissed at the entrance, and three guards follow the Centress, dragging Kelter and me by our cuffs down the stone hallway. I only get a long-faced look from Kelt as the Centress sends him through a stone door. She takes me into the next room, separating us—as if we weren't far enough apart already.

A man waits inside. He's even taller than the Centress and wears a gray jumpsuit that pulls taut over his round belly, and a hunch rolls over his back and shoulders, making his neck look squished. Each step slower and heavier than the last, I try to delay whatever's coming.

"Is it ready?" the Centress asks, surveying the room.

"Yes, Centress Oreyla. We'll get back the magic she took."

"I didn't take anything."

"Hush, save your energy," she says to me, her voice thick with false concern. "Go on, Mallace, and don't forget the serum. I'm not in the mood to hear the screams."

CHAPTER 12

The man the Centress called Mallace seizes me with callous hands and throws me onto a low wooden table. My head knocks into the wood, stunning me while he folds cold metal clamps from one side of the table to the other and locks them over my chest, waist and legs. I struggle, taken by pure instinct and terror. His greedy green eyes glare at me as he tightens every clamp, grinding them into my bones. I curse at him. And all the people of Sonnet. And the stars, which remind me of Kelter. Tears surface, then I curse at him too.

Mallace stands over me, his locks of red hair swishing as he pulls a metal crank that lifts the table, jerk after jerk, until I'm almost up to his protruding stomach. My feet hang off the end, as if the contraption was meant to restrain children.

I observe as much of the room as I can—more gray walls without windows. Dim light emanates from the tops of wooden tables pushed against the walls, but instead of lamps, a golden flame winks through gray stones slightly larger than my fist. I search for the blades he'll use to cut me open, the needles and instruments, but apart from the strange glowing stones, the tables only bear glass vials with colored liquids, cloth rags and a stack of wide, flat rocks.

"Are you ready, Hollow?" His stale breath warms my face.

Fear climbs my spine.

He cackles, the movement raising his shoulders and worsening his humped back. "You shouldn't have come to Sonnet." He rubs his thumb over my cheek, full of desire—the desire to bring life to the hate inside him. "Vaile have been through enough from your kind. You think you can take whatever you want."

"I don't." *I want to go home.*

"You don't know how good it will feel to push you to the brink. I'll take back the magic you stole, no matter how many sessions it takes."

The Centress leans into the wall, letting out a simpering laugh.

"And then we'll dispose of you." Mallace's voice pitches with glee, and he moves to one of the tables along the wall.

Glass clinks. When he turns around, he's uncorking a vial filled with liquid like melted metal. Taking my chin, he pries my jaw open and sticks his knuckles inside. Salt tingles on my tongue, and the hairs on his fingers tickle the roof of my mouth. He forces the silver liquid down my throat. It's bitter and spicy, burning all the way down and searing my insides. Heat grows and flares inside my stomach. I try to scream, but—

My mouth won't obey. The serum took my voice. The burn expands to the rest of my body, fire entering my veins and muscles, my tendons and bones.

My lips tremble, sweat beading on my face.

The corners of his eyes turn down, and I wait for him to take pity on me, to change his mind and end it here. But no. His green eyes go wide and glassy with hunger, and all I can see are Reggie Junior's starved green eyes, the way they sparked to life when he climbed on top of me on that cold floor.

I try to think of other things—home, the wriggly lines on my maps, Kelt—but my mind is scattered, spreading and connecting the fear and the worry, the past, the pain seizing my breath.

He takes one backward step after another, sliding into the corner next to the stack of flat rocks, then picks one up, requiring two hands for the task. He pulses it up and down, weighing its potential for pain, for breaking. Smiling to himself, he returns to my side and plops the huge gray rock down on my chest.

I don't feel the impact—not at first. It takes a moment to catch up to reality, for the pain to travel to my head, but when it gets there, the feeling of the stone smashing into my ribs… it's nauseating. He piles more rocks on top of me, covering my body and strapping them down with stretchy vines. Each one is unnaturally heavy, each as painful and cold as the last.

When I'm buried under gray rocks and near breathless from the inexplicable crushing weight, he taps a finger over every rock, and the real pain starts. It drives into me with intention—digging, searching, shredding everything in its path. Though the rocks are motionless and smooth, my skin splits under the assault, as though they were opening me up to find the magic they seek. My dress sticks to my skin in bloody patches, and my necklace burns against my chest.

My mouth dries out, every taste bud rough and raw. I thrash beneath the clamps, the pain reaching the folds of my brain, flames licking my thoughts. A vision saves me—and tortures me.

Kelt is clamped onto a table like mine, his face a comfort until Mallace drops a rock onto it. The crunch of bone vibrates through me. His body jolts, then droops. Blood drips from the jagged pieces of his cracked skull. Children in charcoal jumpsuits watch, unflinching, hands folded in their laps and not even a shadow of emotion on their faces.

Only the heave of my stomach brings me back, the bitter burn and rise of acid and bile and mucus, up and up and up until I turn my head and feel the warmth sliding down my cheek, followed by skimming tears. Shaking and shivering and sending air reeking of blood and vomit in and out with shallow breaths, I go somewhere far, far away. Past the Centress' midnight-calm face in the corner, past the granite walls, out into the woods, to nature. And deeper. The pain becomes a distant problem. My thoughts disintegrate, leaving only bliss.

"Did you see that?" the Centress asks in one of my lucid moments. "Keep going."

"That's—I can't extract that," Mallace says.

I don't know how long it goes on for. Every time the serum wears off and my scream starts to surface, Mallace shoves his knuckles back into my mouth and forces more down my throat. I bite down on the meat of his fingers, eventually tasting blood, but it doesn't stop him. When it's all too much, when instinct is lost and every breath is a conscious effort, I slink into the recesses of my mind. I cycle through the phases of pain and escape until rage is all I have left. Useless, squandered rage.

It poured while I was inside the temporary school getting intimate with pain until my mind shattered. The ground is muddy and slippery with wet leaves, and drops still scatter from the trees with every gust of wind.

Eli and Kaleida should be back soon. Mallace is steps away, watching me as I wait for Kelt. He doesn't restrain me, surely knowing I can't get far with cuffed ankles and a battered body, but the threat of his presence knits through me, the pain enduring.

The Centress tows Kelter out the door and sets him on a path in my direction before sliding in next to Mallace.

Kelt and I are pulled together by defeat. Fresh blood drips from the side of his mouth, but no cuts are in sight, no bruises. What did they do to him? His sandy waves lick up around his neck in half curls, and I see the Kelter I've always known. I'm blinded by the day's pain and the seduction of familiarity.

In lieu of a greeting, I lift my cuffed hands to his face and wipe the blood away with my thumb. The hazel of his eyes is subdued, the life in him all sucked out. His blood trickles around, past my rings and down my thumb like a red-carpeted spiral staircase.

"Your eyes are red," he says, reaching for my cheek.

Probably from all the tears I used up succumbing to the pain. Or the blood vessels that burst with the upheaval of my stomach. But that's too… truthful. I shy away from his hand, afraid of his touch, the return of affection.

"They're indigo," I joke, reaching into the depths of denial and trying to take us past the tension.

I want everything to go back to how it was. I want to kneel in the dirt of my forest and add to my maps with Kelter by my side, building mazes for bugs. I want to spend Saturday nights at the laundromat, spinning coins while he tugs at the threads in the knee-hole of his jeans and spoils the ends of scary movies I refuse to watch. I want to trudge upstairs after work, only to find him leaning against my door, dinner in one hand and two cups of coffee balanced on the railing. I want real food. I want books and blankets and a bathtub.

I want *home*.

"Ever…" He sighs, too heavily for the lightness I'm seeking. "I didn't mean that your life in Caldera wasn't good enough. I only—I want you here too."

I stiffen from the surge of scalding blood, my hands balling into painful fists. Each word is a whispered hiss. "What kind of life do you think you can have here, Kelt? Because it doesn't make sense. These people want us dead."

My eyelids are dams about to burst. I can't imagine a part of his past so painful that he'd rather find a way to live here. Or die here. Maybe he wasn't as happy as I thought…

"What the fuck was so bad about spending the last year with me? About hiking in the rain? Cursing at the stars?" I cut open my own scars, willingly bleeding. The wind whips my hair across my face, a temporary shelter to bleed in private.

A wealth of answers must run through his head as his eyes hunt through mine for the right one, but none of them are good enough, it seems, because silence is all he has to offer.

I stare back, a thousand words in none.

He leans down and rests his forehead on mine, and I don't push him away. I don't pull him close. I do nothing, like he does nothing to get us out of here.

The walk back is solemn, saturated with raw, lingering pain. Back inside the black room, Eli's deep brown eyes don't leave my body, soaking up the bloody cuts through the new slits in my dress. I stand in front of him, waiting for my cuffs to be removed, no defiance left in me. His face is rigid except for the twitch under his eye, his neck pulled so tight that every swallow looks painful.

He runs his hands down my blood-smeared arms, his fingers trembling over the soft start of scabs. His gaze falls to my chest, to my heart, as if he could hear its crestfallen beat. I close my eyes, waiting for the moment his touch will turn rough and awaken those slumbering parts of me he brings out, sharing pain and rage right through his fingertips. Maybe I even want it, that jolt of life. Maybe I crave his darkness to help me forget.

But that moment doesn't come.

He uncuffs me, and I collapse to the floor. Blood pumps into my head in tired, spent spurts, all thoughts dismantled. Eli tosses me a linty bar from his pocket to choke down while the obsidian floor ices my wounds—even the strange fabrics they use aren't immune to lint.

He settles on the floor, his back to the door, arms wrapped around his legs, and that lucky stone of his in hand, black with shimmery blue and silver. He rests his chin on his knees, and jet-black curls fall over his face, framing the darkness of his gaze. That's all his hair ever does, but I notice it every fucking time. Screw him for looking like a damn sculpture with ringlets and muscles and a smirk that makes my blood cells bicker, unable to agree on which body part to occupy.

He flips the stone in his fingers while I cling to the floor, too drained to pick up the bar, and wishing for death over another day with Mallace tomorrow. Then warmth blankets my body, a lightness tugging at me and bringing comfort I can't explain or justify. My mouth is sore and stretched from Mallace's fist inside it, leaving me quiet, which I'm sure delights the fuck out of Eli.

Visions strike out of nowhere as the hours pass, cruel and harrowing. I don't know if meaning is woven into them, but those visions, that suffering, may be the only reason I haven't shut down completely. All the death, all the loss, time and time again, takes the edge off the shock. Maybe I can convince myself it's all another vision, that I'll return to reality soon, and that's the comfort—and the lie—that I'll embrace through the pain.

Only the blue light of the moon defies the dark of night, morning still far off. I blink, letting the haziness of sleep fade away enough to notice the footsteps behind me.

Then a hand slams over my mouth.

PART 2
BOUND

CHAPTER 13

An arm slides around my waist, all but crushing me as I'm lifted up.

"Are you going to come willingly?"

That scent of a dark cave, of empty space and time unending shoves its way up my nose. A frantic tap of fingertips rushes down my neck and back. Eli's size is even more apparent when I'm pressed into him and can't think of anything but the hardness of his body. Dammit. He gathers me closer, his heart beating into my back, his hand on my mouth.

"Never," I spit out through his fingers.

He gains a tighter hold across my middle, trapping my arms and squeezing the air out of me. "Then we'll do it the hard way."

"I doubt you're capable of making me come," I wheeze into his hand.

"You think I don't know how to take care of what's mine?" His lips brush my ear, the shudder reaching my toes.

A rush of heat hits between my thighs. *Why does my body hate me?* "You don't own—" His hand crushes down harder, and I give up on my garbled words.

"Shh. It's okay. I know that scent of yours by now. You want to be mine, little prisoner." His hand is too tight on my mouth for any chance of him deciphering the excessive curses that follow.

He carries me out of the black room, my feet dangling above the ground, my body squirming viciously as we leave behind the obsidian walls and the crooked bars of the arched window. He closes the heavy door and schleps me through pitch blackness, then through another door, and another, a maze of connected windowless hallways. I only hear the click of a lock and the scrape of stone each time he puts me down to pull open a door.

But he must know exactly where he's going, never stopping to feel along the wall, never slowing. I writhe in his arms as he powers on, trying not to think of all the ways he could take my life—how easily he holds me in place, how little force it would take in the right spots for my breath to dwindle to rasps of nothingness until I'm limp in his grasp. Or how those same hands could do so much more.

He walks on, grunting and adjusting his clutch on me until a final door sends us out into the moonlit night air. We enter the shadowy woods. It's the first time I've breathed in the fresh pine air since I saw that little boy and the sack went over my head, though I'm not sure I ever actually saw him. The trees of Sonnet that called to me upon my forced arrival, luring me closer like the land beyond the edges of a map, now haunt me with the promise of pain. I want home more than ever.

Eli slides me down until my feet brush the ground, holding my back to him, his grip unrelenting. My cheeks cave inward with the pinch of his fingers. He has me walk in front of him, our bodies pressed together despite the bump of his knees on the back of my legs, each step cumbersome and out of sync. I struggle against his locked arm until my energy whittles down to feeble jerks of my body, leaving me slack, my head resting against the curve of his chest.

"Done rubbing yourself all over me like a feral animal?" he whispers in the dark. "Too bad."

I growl into his hand.

Deeper and denser, the air grows colder and crisper as he guides our four graceless legs through the musty dampness of the woods, the rustling of leaves below our boots turning into the snapping of twigs.

A thick fog descends and settles above our heads, blocking the view of the treetops. I try to orient myself and add to my map, but with my head pulled back to his chest, all I see is the hazy mist. It grows heavier, threatening to surround me in yet another inescapable embrace.

We venture on until we reach an old house—a ridged bark exterior, warped wooden planks for the porch and a scattering of scrap-wood shingles on the pointed cones of the roof reaching into the sky, appearing and disappearing behind the fog. No one and nothing else is around. Not a single window is visible from this angle, and I swear it's on the verge of collapse. The moonlight falls everywhere but on the ancient structure.

He drags me right past the front door and the side of the house, around to the back, then removes his hand from my mouth and stomps his boot on the double doors of a hatchway entrance on the ground.

I try to slip away. "You are *not* taking me into a basement. I've read books. Nothing but ropes and chains and blindfolds and shit."

He chuckles into my ear. "What kind of books have you been reading?"

"The dark and twisty kind." I toss myself side to side in his arms, only ire in my voice. "Now let go of me."

As if I awoke a beast, his hand clamps onto my throat, holding the back of my head tight to his chest and stilling my movements. "You aren't afraid of me."

"Fuck no," I rasp.

I should be, but apart from Kaleida, he's the only one who doesn't terrify me. And the way he riles me up, spurs a fight in me, the way his fingers press so hard into my neck… the way he decides if I take another breath—it has me panting in his grasp, my core aching.

I hate him.

He squeezes tight, cutting off all air as I sift through my final thoughts, unfortunately—or fortunately—of his hard cock at the bottom of my spine and less fatal things he could have done with my throat. He lets go and flips me around to face him, a puzzled look softening his glare. "How could that be?"

Good question. I guzzle down air as the blackness fades.

I'm about to deliver a full rant when footsteps near with loud clunks. Metal scrapes and a door swings upward. Beady eyes look up at us from under a furrowed brow. The man has choppy brown hair with a short beard to match.

"You're really doing this?" He tucks himself into the edge of the stairs, sucking in his belly to let us by, loosening the blue fabric of the jumpsuit stretched across his middle.

"Not now, Sypher," Eli says, a hint of annoyance in his voice, and drags me down the stairs and across the room.

In those few precious seconds, I try to assess every wall and door and corner to find a way out, but it's a basement. There's one way out, and it just slammed shut.

The stairs lead down into a spacious rectangular area, even colder than the black room. Two barred windows, each barely half a foot tall, sit above ground level along the edge of the ceiling, letting in the muted moonlight that seems to shy away from the house. Doors line the left wall—one, two, three, and at least one more down a narrow hallway that extends beyond the rest of the room. The doors, like the walls, ceiling, floor and stairs, are made of rough stone—not the shiny obsidian of the black room, but a dark leaden gray. Instead of blocks cemented together like I'd expect of a stone structure, it's like a slice out of a solid mountain of rock, hollowed out and cut into the shape of a room. Once again, the space offers no light fixtures or outlets, and I don't think it's because it's a basement.

The wall next to the stairs is bare, while the right wall has a corkboard—or something like cork—halfway down. Knives are stuck in it, pure metal from hilt to blade. They sit mostly near the middle, as if the thrower had a disturbingly consistent aim. A single wooden chair is pushed against the wall below the corkboard, and beyond that is a sink with a doorless cabinet beneath and a cluttered wooden counter to the side. And in the corner—

Eli gives me a shove, closing me inside a tiny cell in the far right corner of the main basement room—barely four by four feet, a quarter the size of the black room we left behind. Two walls of floor-to-ceiling bars form the cell, and while the stone of the basement is dulled with time and crumbling around the doors, the black bars look freshly installed—free of nicks and imperfections and just far enough apart to get an arm through. He locks the cell door with a jagged stone.

No no no.

The small space crushes inward, and I panic. And curse. A lot. I bang my fists against the bars, each impact shooting up to my shoulders.

Eli leans against the cabinet, arms crossed and feigning fascination with the toes of his boots while the man he called Sypher sits on the stairs, scowling. When my hands go numb and I've gone through every curse word dozens of times, I stop my racket and fall to the floor, defeated, trembling from my core and surrounded by the dirty ruby red of my torn dress.

"Good thing no one can hear you." Eli scratches along his jaw, as though I've bored him, and strolls the two steps up to the door of the cell, peering in at me. "Is your little mouth done?"

I force myself to stand and slip two hands around the black bars while I glare at him. "What is this place?"

"The castle."

Castle? "It's a basement."

He rolls his head around, perusing the room. "Strong walls, built to protect, important person inside… It's a castle, just underground."

"More like strong walls, built to imprison, *crazy asshole* inside."

He smiles. "Whatever shuts you up."

"Now what?" Sypher asks, rising from the step.

"Now, I need a break." Eli digs two hands into his hair, ringlets popping up between his fingers. "I've been away from home, working double twelve-hour shifts for a week and a half." He turns to leave.

"What do you want from me?" I ask, causing him to swivel back.

He takes hold of a bar and leans in to whisper. "Some quiet would be nice."

I groan and kick the door. Pain vibrates up my leg. "Why did you bring me here?"

"Can't this wait?"

Like waiting for my death with Kelter? A fist clenches my heart. "No, it fucking can't. I don't like waiting."

He tilts his head and flashes his bottomless brown eyes at me. "Maybe I like to make you do things you don't like."

"What?" I smack my forehead into the bars. "Tell me why I'm here."

"Is it not enough to want my little prisoner all to myself?" He taps his finger on my nose, gives me his back and strides off.

"Get the fuck back here and let me out!" Dread plummets to my gut. "Elivander," I plead. Being trapped behind these bars—with myself—is more than I can handle right now.

"I don't take orders," he says with a quick glower over his shoulder at the sound of his full name, disappearing through the first door on the left with Sypher behind him.

I stumble backward into the wall and slide down it. The cell is empty except for a broken stool, some rags and two buckets like the ones in the shower room—one empty, one with soapy water.

What about Kelt? He'll be taken back to the temporary school.

He'll be alone. He hates being alone. He had his own place, but I can't count the number of nights we climbed the ladder to my roof with a pillow under one arm and spent the night under the stars, traffic humming below.

He never questioned me about my past—about the streets I refused to walk down to avoid seeing my old homes and schools, or about my lack of family—so I did him the same favor.

I only had the guts to reveal I wanted to find my parents once I hauled him beyond the city's edge into my forest, and he let me, without judgment. I showed him my collection of folders that night, every incomplete and mismatched document, like holes in a map that kept me from finding my way.

Eli and Sypher are away for a long time, leaving me alone with my thoughts and the visions that force their way in. I breathe in the strengthening scent of peppery cloves, over and over until my eyelids grow heavy enough to let me escape.

I'm still sitting against the wall when I wake up, shivering in the cool dawn air. I pull my dress over my toes and tuck it between my legs to keep the cold out, but it's useless with all the rips in it. The door closest to the stairs swings open. Eli comes out, still in his blue jumpsuit, walking through the main room toward the hallway with loose limbs and a relaxed face. A light wind hits me despite being underground, and I stop shivering, warm from head to toe. Sypher enters the main room, leaning against the wall next to the stairs.

I return to the metal bars and call out to Eli. "Why am I here?"

He stops mid-step, as if he'd forgotten he had a woman stowed away in a cage in his basement. He takes one look at me, and I almost regret reminding him. Almost. I want answers.

He makes his way to the cell door, his brows rising, a teasing smirk piercing the side of his cheek. "Why do you think you're here?"

I consider the possibilities. "So you can kill me yourself. Maybe you changed your mind about wanting me alive."

Though… he would have killed me already if he was going to, right? Why not smother me with that hand on my mouth and leave me in the woods for the animals to feast on? Maybe he wants to do it slowly, torture me first.

I squint at him. "Maybe you hate me for all those nights you had to sleep on the floor."

"Maybe I do," he says slowly, "but not nearly as much as you think you hate me. And I don't want you dead."

My whole body lightens. "You don't?"

"I could change my mind if you ask too many questions. Guess again."

"Jerk." The gears in the back of my mind turn, connecting pieces and grinding out thoughts. "You plan to say I escaped and get rewarded for turning me in?"

"I'll be punished for your disappearance on my watch." He rubs his chin and waits for me to continue.

"How? Do I get to watch?"

"I'm not surprised you'd enjoy that," he says. "Try again."

"You brought me here to…" No—but he's warped enough for it. "To what?"

I take a step backward. "To fuck me whenever you want." I might as well find out now if they're all baseless threats or not.

Sypher flinches and moves from the wall to his spot on the bottom step.

Eli seals his lips, failing to hold back a sly smile. "I suppose that's an option."

Great, now I'm giving him ideas. "It's not. I don't want an unfulfilling life of letdown."

He pulls down on his ear, a flicker in the corner of his shifty eyes. "I guarantee you'd be fulfilled… and filled. Repeatedly."

Fuck. My face flushes. "What do you want with me?"

He looks behind him then snaps his fingers, hard and sharp, the same edginess in his voice. "Out, Sypher."

Shit, now I've done it.

"See you in the courtyard," Sypher grumbles, heading out the hatchway.

Eli sets his glossy gaze on me, suddenly heavy with emotion, but I can't tell which. He takes an eternity to speak. "I need you."

Dammit. Sex it is. "I bite. You'll regret it."

He leans against the junk-covered counter a few feet from the cell with his arms crossed. "I don't doubt that. You're a feisty little thing in the dark."

I give him my most vicious glare. Searching his pocket so I could escape was perfectly acceptable behavior. And I'll do anything I can to find a way out of here… but the metal and stone are so damn solid.

"That's not what I need you for though," he says.

Something keeps me talking—that warmth and lightness I can't explain. It makes me feel like I should trust him, even though I can't. "What then? You carried me through the woods with your hand on my mouth and—"

"I didn't want to be followed. You're loud."

"Loud?" I yell, stung by the insult, then clamp my mouth shut. So I'm loud. I need some way to dampen my thoughts. "That's what you get when you lock me up in a cage."

"It's not a cage." He gives me a wounded look. "It's a containment nook."

I stick a knuckle in my mouth to keep from laughing in his face despite the red hot blood careening through my veins. He's dead serious. And completely fucking mad. And so gorgeous. It's a terribly intoxicating combination. "Tell me what you want."

"If I told you now, it wouldn't be any fun for me."

"You have to tell me *something*."

His shoulders fall with his deep sigh. "Okay." He steps up to the cell, hooking one finger to beckon me closer. I take the tiniest steps until only the bars separate us, his whisper warming my ear. "I bite too."

Then he balls up a fist and rams it into the side of his jaw and lands another two punches to one eye, finishing with a bash of his forehead into the metal with a sick *clang*. The bars vibrate.

"What the bloody fuck?" I want to look away, but I can't. He's in worse shape than I thought.

He staggers sideways, catches himself and runs a hand through his hair, his light brown skin already turning red.

"Now sit your tempting ass down and be a good little prisoner for your guard while I go fake unconsciousness outside that empty room of yours, then scour the realm for the traitor who took you from it." He gives me a swollen smirk before climbing the stone steps and disappearing through the hatchway.

The cold returns with the slam of the door.

CHAPTER 14

Afetr being gone all day for his shift, Eli emerges from the third door off the main room of the basement, showered, curls dripping. He's in all black, his shirt tight against every mound and depression down his torso, pants loose with more pockets than his jumpsuit. I'm stuck staring, never having seen him in anything else. The outline of a knife shows through a narrow pocket on the side of his thigh. He musses up his curls, sending drops flying, and vanishes behind the first door. Ten minutes later he reappears and approaches the cell, his eyes glazed.

A clove-scented breeze whisks over my face as I breathe in the lightness around him. My defenses slip—my hatred too. I'm pulled toward him, but I push back against the sensation, reminding my brain of every dark detail about this man.

He wrinkles his nose and looks down at my week-old dress. His face is colored with more bruises than the self-inflicted ones he left with early this morning. Both eyes and cheeks are now purple and blue and swollen, and finger marks mar his neck—his punishment for me "disappearing" on his watch.

I stand up. "Let me out."

"Never," he whispers with a slight hiss, stepping so close that his face nearly touches the bars.

"What do you mean, *never?*"

"It's your word. You didn't want to come willingly, so why should I trust you?" He pulls back a smidge. "You'll run and get yourself killed, and that's not going to work for me."

"You're actually leaving me in this tiny shit hole of a cage?"

"Nook. And yes. I take good care of my things, especially the pretty ones, which means keeping you alive."

"Possessive prick." I grab the bars, pulling myself closer to him. "You only want me alive because you need something from me, but what happens after that?"

He hesitates. "I keep you."

Keep me? No one ever wants me to stay. "I'm not for keeping."

His forehead rests on the bars, and he rakes in a deep breath through his nose, his eyes fluttering shut and reopening.

"Did you just fucking smell me?" *And why does that turn me on?*

He lifts his head. "Yes."

"You're not even going to deny it?" I ask.

"Are you going to deny you liked it? I can smell that too."

Dammit. "You're an animal. Tell me what you want from me."

Eli drags the lone chair in front of the cell door, flips it around backward and straddles it, his chin resting on top. He gives me a long look, as if so much depends on his next words. Maybe he decides to keep them to himself because he lifts his chin from the chair, reaches into his pocket and hands me a bar—almond flavor today. I pick off bits of black-and-blue lint with my overgrown nails. He must have moved it from a jumpsuit pocket to the black pants, evidence of his effort not to let me starve.

Watching me swallow down the last hunk of a sad excuse for food with an audible gulp, he says, "You're a Hollow."

"So you've said." Crumbs launch from my mouth.

Eli dips out of the way, frowning at me. "Which means you can take magic, and that's what I want you to do. I'll get what I need from you when it's time."

I throw my hands into my tangled hair. "You actually believe in that magic nonsense?" *And want me to do exactly what everyone else wants me dead for?*

"You don't?"

"As little as I believe in the gods."

"You don't believe in them either?" He latches tighter onto the back of the chair. "What *do* you believe in?"

I don't know how to respond to that. Or the way he looks right into me. It's too… intimate. I thought I might believe in something after meeting Kelt, something I had squashed deep down in years past, something dangerous, yet fragile.

Hope.

But I was wrong.

"Nothing," I say.

He drums a little beat with his fingers. "Everything has to be hard with you, doesn't it?"

"Yes." *If you only knew.* "But not as hard as *you* get over nothing."

The breeze stills, and a shiver starts at my shoulder blades and rolls down my back with the return of his dark aura. He rises and smacks the chair out of his way, sending it crashing to the floor. I step back as his hand dives through the bars and takes hold of my dress, right over my belly. He pulls me forward until my body is pressed against the cell door, my dress bunched in his hand on the other side.

"One. You are not nothing." Cloves. Earth. Musk—his aroma whisks and whirls between us. His voice deepens to the crunch of gravel. "And two. I'll make you fucking believe."

For a fleeting moment, I think he means hope, but that's exactly the danger of such a thing—believing in what can't be real. I reinflate my lungs, slowly pulling in the scented air shared with his shallow breaths.

He reaches into yet another pocket with his free hand and pulls out a tragic sprout. It flaunts a spindly stem with a kink halfway up—pocket damage, likely—and four sad leaves still wet from the rain and freckled with lint. Its scraggly roots cling to a ball of dirt which shrinks with every clump that falls to his black boots below. It's comical really, but I don't dare laugh.

"Do it," he commands, holding the plant in front of me.

"Do what?"

"Whatever you did. Do it again."

"I don't know what you're talking about." I pull back against his clutch, but short of slipping out of the dress, I'm stuck.

"Godsdammit, I saw you." He yanks again and twists his fist, tightening the fabric around my middle and flattening my breasts against the bars.

"Saw me what?" I have to look up to see his face.

"You—" A tug closer. "You touched that seedling on the way to the village. I saw it glow." He releases my dress, reaches through the bars to my wrist and flips my hand over.

"It didn't glow. That was…" *In my head.* With all the other things I can't trust that I've seen.

He plops the sprout into my palm. "Do it again."

The dirt is cool on my skin, and the roots tickle. It's small and innocent, ripped away from everything it knew, its home. I lose my balance at the rush of irrational feelings for a plant, and grab a bar.

"What? Do you feel something?" His frantic eyes pour over me in search of answers.

"I have no fucking idea how to steal fake magic!"

"Touch it, for starters," he growls.

He really believes I can do this, whatever *this* is, and wants me to try.

"No." I want things too.

He passes his hand through the bars again, aimed right at me. I hurtle myself back, beyond reach, and his hand retreats, inch by inch, his voice like steel. "You *will* obey me."

I hold my chin high. "I will…" He straightens, the start of a smile at my submission. "If you rescue Kelter."

Those brown eyes. They find mine. And they scald me. "Not a godsdamn chance."

I crush the sprout in the creases of my hand, destroying a little piece of me along with it, a little piece of hope for Kelt that tried to climb its way to the surface. It's effortless. It falls apart like nothing. The dirt sprinkles down with the mangled stem and limp leaves. I position the toe of my boot over the bits, drop it to the stone and twist.

Eli slams his hands flat against the bars. "Malachite!"

"Yelling at a fake god won't help." I simper.

That cold demeanor, that control over every limb and muscle—he lets it slip. His body shakes, and he shoves a hand into his hair. "Why do you have to be so… so *you?*"

I'd really love to know too. Because it's fucking torture.

"Maybe you should have picked a different prisoner, Elivander."

His nostrils flare, eyes lush with hate, but there, tugging at the corner of his mouth, I swear a smile tries to surface before we both look at the hatchway. Sypher and another man blunder down the stairs out of sync, carrying an unattractive brown couch that they plop down five feet from my cell, as if they were setting up a sitting area to observe me.

It smells like rotting leaves. Riddled with rips and tears, the cushions look as rough as the jumpsuit fabric, and fist-sized lumps bulge from it. Sypher beams proudly at the new addition and looks to Eli who throws himself onto the couch and leans back, knees spread and arms outstretched. Sypher's light brown eyes tack on to him, a longing in them as he lets out a sigh.

The new man looks on with a laughing smile that could end a war with its sweetness. Blonde and pale, his face is thin with a natural blush over his cheekbones. The grin falls right off his face when he registers my presence. "What the fuck is she doing in there?"

I like him already.

Eli's forehead creases. "What do you mean?"

"Damn, Eli. It's four feet across."

Eli sits forward, resting his elbows on his knees. "You really think she would still be here if I left her wandering around?"

"You could have locked her in your bedroom. Or even the bathroom." He shoves the chair aside, walks up to the cell and peers at me. His eyes are the same cerulean blue as the jumpsuit that hangs loose on his lanky frame, the first I've seen of that color.

"I'm Milo, the asshole's friend." He shuffles his feet and rubs his hands together. "You look so normal. It's wild."

I stare. What does that mean? We're the same.

His bright eyes move to the buckets, then the broken stool. He bites his lower lip, disappears down the hallway and returns carrying a puffy blanket. He shoves it through the cell bars, tucking the black bunches through bit by bit.

"What are you doing?" Eli snaps. "That's mine. She's going to get her smell all over it."

Milo pushes the final corner of the blanket through. "You'll get over it. It's cold here for a Hollow."

"She's fine, Milo. She likes it."

Milo lightly kicks Eli's boot. "Be nice. She's a woman."

"It's only fair that I have something of yours," I say. "You stole my underwear."

"He what?" Milo asks, smacking his forehead. Sypher looks on in mild shock, rubbing his cropped beard.

Eli puts a hand to the outside of a lumpy pocket. "I do as I fucking please. If I want your panties, they're mine."

"And how many times have you gotten yourself off with them?" I taunt.

"Sixteen."

Oh, the untethered confidence of this man. I can't help but admire it, even under the circumstances.

Silence hangs heavy around us. Milo throws his hands up. "She wasn't actually asking, Eli. No one wants to know that."

My mouth catches up with my thoughts. "In that room with me too? While I slept?" Why am I imagining it?

He lifts one shoulder, indifferent. "You could have helped."

"Stop traumatizing her." Milo directs his smile at me. "I have sisters."

Don't these people hate Hollows?

"You don't want me dead?" I ask Milo, eyeing the blanket to avoid Eli's stare, but I'm not quite able to get the image of him out of my mind… sitting against the door, hand pumping furiously, fabric sliding up and down his length, the stifled moans and groans, the spill onto *my* underwear—all only feet away in the dark, cold room while he watches me sleep.

My mind is a fucking problem.

"Not every Vaile who survives the misery and torture of growing up in Sonnet turns into a brute. Just *almost* everyone. Locking you up is enough." Milo tosses himself down onto the couch next to Eli. "Plus, I'd do anything to annoy this guy."

Eli leans back again and deepens his slouch. Sypher sits down next to him, scooting side to side, as though he can't decide how close to get. The three men look at me, so I pick up the blanket and retreat to the corner. It smells like Eli, like cloves and wood and rain.

"You've taken your Hollow obsession a little far, don't you think?" Milo says to Eli, one foot tapping the stone floor. "You can't take the Centress' prisoner as your own."

Eli cracks his knuckles, staring at me as he answers Milo. "She is *not* the Centress' prisoner."

"Alright, she's yours, but you see the problem, right? You're lucky you didn't come home bleeding after today, or worse."

"I'm not *his*," I argue, only my head visible outside the blanket. None of them bother to acknowledge me.

Eli scoffs. "It's not easy to make me bleed, and no one can find this place or come anywhere near it unless I allow it. It's like it doesn't exist."

"We all bleed." Milo nudges Eli with his knee. "And are you really going to trust your life with your ancestors' gifts? Because the Centress *will* kill you if she finds out about the Hollow."

"I'm not worried."

"What do you want her for?" Sypher asks, rubbing his hands nervously on the thighs of his snug jumpsuit. He's thicker all around and shorter than Eli and Milo, but still muscular.

Eli is quiet, his jaw teasing out an answer. "I want to see how this magic-stealing Hollow shit works."

No... He said he *needed* me and made Sypher leave before that. Whatever he needs, he's hiding it from them. And they're okay with the ridiculous reason he gave? They have no problem with him keeping me prisoner and deceiving their leader?

"That's what the plant was for?" Sypher gestures to the smashed sprout and dirt on the cell floor. "I thought it was easy for Hollows to take magic."

"It is. She's stubborn," Eli says.

Milo runs a hand through his messy golden hair, shaking his head at Eli as though he's crazy—which he is. "You can't pull shit out of the ground and expect the magic to work the same."

"That's—" Eli starts, a fist forming, then relaxing. "That's probably true. Dammit. Let's go."

In seconds, he has me outside the cell and through the hatchway. A clearing inside a ring of pine trees sits in the shadow of the enormous house above the "castle." Hands on my shoulders, he coerces my legs to bend, shoving me down to my knees in the mud.

"Hey!"

"Go on." He presses on my upper back until I'm on all fours, my hair hanging in my face. I look over my shoulder when his hand peels away, just in time to see a muddy boot descending toward my back. Milo swipes Eli's foot in midair and guides it back to the ground without a word, saving me from the boot. Eli grumbles and replaces his hand on my back. "Do it."

"Rescue Kelter," I demand through gritted teeth.

He groans, his hand pushing down harder. "Fine. Deal. *After* you pull magic."

My heart picks up. He's actually going to rescue him.

"You can't do that. It's too risky," Sypher says, not getting an answer from Eli.

"Kelter first," I say. "Then I'll do what you want. He can't wait."

Eli huffs loudly. "I'm sure he's fine."

"They'll kill him."

"Then you'd better figure it out. I have time to spare—unlike your boyfriend."

I have nothing to barter with, so I picture Kelt in my head and pinch my muddy fingers around the stem of a plant, velvety leaves between my rings. I'll play along with anything if he'll bring me Kelt.

Nothing happens, as expected.

"Maybe she's doing it wrong." Milo crouches at my side for a closer look.

"Maybe it's because there's no such fucking thing as magic," I say. Eli's fingers dig into my back.

"Maybe she needs motivation, like us," Sypher says.

It's quiet for a moment, then Eli shifts his weight above me. "You're right. We'll start tomorrow night. Sypher, you know what to bring."

"What are you going to do?" Milo asks with a high-pitched note of worry—though nowhere near the amount that's building up in me.

Eli removes his hand from my back and circles around to squat in front of me. I lift my head, trying to read his expression beneath the bruises, but my focus is on the crawling sensation down my neck. He pushes the hair from my face, his fingers trailing down my cheek, cold determination in his eyes. "Nothing she can't handle."

CHAPTER 15

My last day in Caldera, Kelter woke me up while it was still dark, rapping on my door and whisper-yelling through it. I tried to send him away, chucking pillows at his head when he used his key to get in. But once he hauled me out of bed and threw a change of clothes at my face, we went downstairs to the coffee shop, lingering long enough to inhale the scent of a fresh brew, then balanced our sloshing cups as we climbed the ladder to the flat roof above my room to savor my day off. Kelter lived off his savings and was always around, stopping by before work, hovering throughout the day and waiting for me after my shift.

We sat on the edge of the two-story building and sipped through sunrise, watching people pack the sidewalks while remaining a safe distance from the crowds I hate. Then Kelter dragged me to all his favorite spots in the city, and even after that, he refused to let the day be done. He packed our bags for a hike in the forest, which I almost never turn down, but when I did—out of pure exhaustion—he picked me up, laughing and screaming, and carried me out the door, insisting fresh air was all I needed. It was one of the few times he didn't back down. We'd still be together if I'd fought harder, safe at home.

Daylight breaks through the two barred windows of the now quiet basement. I curse at myself for waking up. I'm still sore all over from the penetrating stones Mallace strapped to me, and no closer to escape. I slept deeper than I have any other night in the last two weeks—maybe from having Eli's blanket cocooned around me, softening the stone and curbing the cold. I don't even care that it smells like him.

I sit up, stretch my dress across my folded legs and pull closer a pile of things that weren't here before I fell asleep last night. A fresh canteen. I gulp the entire thing down, giving myself an instant stomach ache. A bar. I press it to my nose. Lentils?

And a note.

I drop the bar into my lap and unfold the paper, trembling slightly, maybe at the unknown, or because I've never been left a note before. Or maybe because the handwriting is so elegant that it looks like an artifact plucked straight out of the past.

Never,
Do I get my blanket back for this?
Eli

It's Ever, *jerk,* I lash out at the empty basement. Castle. Whatever the fuck it is.

Get his blanket back for what? I fold the note and pick up the last and largest item in the pile. Fresh clothes—black pants and a shirt, identical to what he had on last night.

He gave me his clothes.

I smile even though I don't want to and pull them into a hug against my chest. I'm so sick of this thing. Pulling the ripped and blood-stained dress over my head, I feel for the stone in my bra—a bit of security—and inspect the cuts and bruises on my front where the rocks forced my skin open, then slip on the soft shirt. It reaches more than halfway down my thighs.

But it's not a dress.

I work the gathered ankles of the too long, baggy pants up over my boots. And the pockets—side pockets, back pockets, thigh pockets, knee pockets. Endless pockets. Who knows what for. Oh right… for knives and stones to lock me up, for linty bars and dying sprouts, for underwear… and amber brown hands tucked out of sight.

No, you may not have your blanket back.

I eat the bar and curl up on the stone floor. Pants don't fix anything. I'm locked in a cell in the basement of a morally questionable man in a foreign realm where people believe in magic and want to kill me, and my friend is somewhere out there, without me. My eyes close. I stroke the fabric covering my legs, and the thoughts pour in.

I'm wound up tight, strangled by my thoughts and worn out from visions by the time Eli returns with Milo and Sypher. Each wears a jumpsuit, two cobalt blue and Milo in cerulean.

They close themselves behind the first door, and the scent of cloves makes its way to the cell, convincing me it's coming from something in that room. A half hour later the door opens, and Eli clomps down the hall and out of sight again. Sypher and Milo sit on the couch, one glaring, arms folded over broad shoulders, and one smiling, feet tapping and fingers rapping.

I avoid Sypher's perpetual pout and address Milo and his ever-moving body. He agrees with locking me up, but at least he doesn't want me dead. That's my new standard, I guess, and enough to get me to talk to him. "How come your jumpsuit is a different color?"

Milo's smile grows brighter. "Only guards wear the dark blue or black. Blue for border guards and black for regular guards. Everyone else in the Service Sphere gets this." He pinches the fabric and tugs it away from his chest.

"What's the Service Sphere?"

"It's our job after finishing school at sixteen. We're assigned to an area, and that's what we have to do. If we resist, we're dead." He pauses to take in his own words. "I was assigned to make medicines and elixirs all day."

And serums that burn and take my voice?

"Evenings at home are the only chance we have to do what we want, as long as it's not forbidden," he adds.

"What about the tall people in the gray jumpsuits?"

"They already have gifts. We get one sometime while we're twenty-three, then leave the Service Sphere and get assigned to one of the other spheres based on our gift. We're forced to use it for the good of Sonnet until death. The other spheres mostly work in the northside of the village and—"

Eli returns with a knife to his jaw and clears his throat loudly. "Consorting with the enemy, Milo?" Short angled strokes of the blade send stubble trimmings raining to the floor. His face looks worse today, the bruises darker.

"She's a harmless Hollow. What's she going to do while locked up?"

Eli scrapes the metal against his neck, studying Milo. "I would *not* call her harmless." He sheathes the knife and slips it away into a jumpsuit pocket.

A light wind ripples over me, and I'm pulled toward the scents of mint and rain. Glancing first at my uncombed hair, he rakes his gaze down to the baggy clothes and the cuts on my bare arms, not bothering to keep the smirk off his freshly shaven, black-and-blue face. "And my blanket..."

Asshole. How could he take it back? I'll freeze at night.

"You can keep it," he says as he unlocks the door. My jaw drops, and he lifts it back into place and whispers in my ear, "I'm keeping your panties."

I have to calm my sprinting heart as he hauls me across the room. We go no farther than the clearing next to the house again. After spending the day in a cell, it's a relief to feel the evening air whipping at my too big clothes, even though it's cold and almost dark and I'm stuck with Eli's hand latched around my upper arm.

Sypher pulls fist-sized stones out of a beige sack, the same size as the ones used for lighting in that room... with Mallace. I clutch my stomach.

Sypher bangs two of the stones together—and they light up, gray turning to soft white.

"How do they work?" I reach for one.

Sypher moves beyond my grasp with a swift step back. "They're imbued."

"With what?"

"Light," Milo says, walking in a circle and rubbing his palms together. "Imbuing stones is one of the most common gifts someone can get. Light stones are all over the place."

My eyes follow Milo's circles as I try to process his words. I can't. "What are these gifts you keep mentioning?"

Milo wheels to a sudden stop in front of Eli. "You spent all that time guarding her and told her *nothing*?"

"Why the fuck would I?" Eli throws back.

Milo closes his eyes, centering himself before responding. "Because it's scary not to know what's going on around you."

He paces in figure eights as he speaks to me. "We receive gifts from the gods, usually something common like imbuing stones. Each stone is assigned a purpose—light stone, fire stone, lock stone—lots of things. Or someone might get a different common gift, like heat in their hands for glass shaping, or stone manipulation for building. And some people get a rare gift, like the Centress' painful memory stealing or imbuing something with protection. Or movement, like the carriages that take the elixir to—"

Eli groans. "She doesn't need to know anything. She only has to obey me."

I can't keep up.

Milo side-eyes him. "You could at least tell her what's about to happen and why."

Another groan from Eli, and he tightens his grasp on me. "It's simple. Magic and emotions are connected. We're—"

"There is no—"

"There *is* magic." Eli releases my arm and snags my chin between his fingers, forcing me to face him. He talks fast, his voice as harsh as the wind trying to knock me down. "And we're going to make you feel whatever it takes to get you to do what I want with it. Get it?" He moves his hand back to my arm, sinking his fingers into my thin layer of muscle.

I reach for his hand, prying away those fingers. He startles at my touch, then his own, and softens his hold on me.

"And how might you do that?" I ask.

"A series of triggers to try and wake up your Hollow ability—pain, fear, isolation, starvation—things like that," Sypher says, glaring at Eli's hand on my arm.

Pain? Like from crushing, skin-splitting rocks?

I take ragged breaths. "So you're going to do the same thing as the Centress?" My mind tells me to run, but my body is nothing but tingles inside a sack of skin, held up by bones. It won't move.

"Not quite," Eli says. "We'll start with fear."

I expel the last of the air in me.

Eli crashes two more light stones together, illuminating his face. The three of them leave me in the center of the clearing, trembling and frozen in place while they situate the four light stones around the edges.

Solemn features and a tight jaw take over Eli's bruised face when he returns. He leans close. An earthy scent surrounds me as his lightness evaporates, and I lick my lips at the taste of blood. I'm getting used to his darkness.

His cheek grazes mine, lips to my ear. "Get ready to run, little prisoner. It's the only time I'll let you."

CHAPTER 16

S ypher returns from the darkness beyond the edges of the clearing with a wire cage. Inside, a creature thrashes its wings. It stands on two hind paws while its front ones lean against the wires, curved claws protruding. It ruffles its hybrid of fur and feathers, constellations of orange and brown and gold on a satiny black canvas, its head almost like a penguin—small with a long, pointed beak and the same amount of regalness.

"What is that thing? I've never seen anything like it." I can barely spit the words out.

"That's because you only have non-magical creatures in Caldera," Milo says. "Magical creatures used to be all over the land, but that changed when the border was created around Sonnet. The Separation pushed non-magical creatures out of Sonnet with the Hollows, and all the magical creatures were forced to relocate here with the Vaile."

Of course, more magic.

Sypher looks affectionately at the cage—a rare glimpse of his face without the scowl he only seems to lose while staring at Eli. "It's a blitzer. Wild and fast, not quite lethal."

"Not quite?" His description only adds to the forceful thumping of my blood. I add magical creatures to my denial list. "And what? You're going to set that thing loose to make me afraid?" I lock my sweaty palms into fists. The blitzer's owl-like eyes search mine—mirrors, full of pain.

"Yes, but you're already afraid," Eli says. "And it knows it."

I'm torn between fear and fury.

Eli releases the bolt on the cage door, and the blitzer launches into the air, a majestic threat hugging the treetops.

I run for the sake of running, not knowing if I'm going toward or away from the damn thing. I search the sky above. Trees and dark swirling clouds close in. No blitzer.

Eli, Sypher and Milo scatter to the edges of the clearing to watch. Fear steers through me, and I hear it—a screeching roar—and with a turn of my jaw, I see the sprawling wings of night coming straight for me.

Running again, the cold night air sweeps over my face. The sound of wings behind me forces my legs to move faster. The flaps get closer, and the injustice-fueled fire grows inside me.

I duck down, yet the impact still comes—the whack of a beak at my neck, then another and another, beating away my strength, my barely-existent confidence. I smack the blitzer away, and it sinks its claws into my back, all four paws claiming me as their prize. The shock drops me to my knees, and the wind rushes in low and hard as if to break my fall. I pretend the pain is nothing more than a vision.

Claws drag along my back, determined to dig deeper, to tear me apart. I reach behind me and rip the creature off. Its beak goes for my arms as it flails in my grasp, clawing at anything within reach. I put all my weight into a spin and hurl it away. The blitzer flips in the air and lands on all fours.

Run. The wind picks up, bashing against me from all sides, strong enough to send me off course. My hair flies in my face, and I swivel my head, catching a glimpse of the blitzer gliding my way. It sails over the cage, howling. I'm pumping with terror when the forest has always brought me comfort. Rage rampages my insides. I won't let them take that from me.

I yell out into the night, not quite sure at who or what, "What do you have against *me?*" My voice is lost in a violent rush of wind. The blitzer's eyes come back to me, pulsing in my mind, blocking my vision. "Why the fuck are you so angry?"

I risk a glance behind me. It's gaining, its paws dangling uselessly in the air. I make a sharp turn. It turns too, overshooting my path and gliding in a wide arc. I gain some distance. I turn again and again, sharp turns that destroy my knees, each one creating more distance and taking me farther from home, from who I am, from answers. I weave through the clearing, keeping out of the blitzer's reach.

Each breath is a burning pain. I can't tell if it's my lungs or the fire raging inside me. I turn again. The wind wreaths roughly around my legs, threatening to topple me.

I'm done. Please let me be done.

The blitzer screeches again, a sound of pure agony. It calls to me, pleading. I feel it, the severed connection with nature, like lines on a map torn down the middle. I suck in a gravelly breath. I know what it wants.

"I hear you!" My heart flutters. *Me too.*

I pivot again, racing toward the light stone on the opposite side of the clearing, zigzagging as I go. The ground flies at me as I dive and slide toward the stone. I pick it up and run, my heart walloping in my ears, worsening the ache from the cold. I dive for another stone. The blitzer hoots and howls above me, circling its cage.

This is for you, Kelter. I dart across the clearing, a stone in each hand, wing beats close behind. Reaching the cage, I drop to my knees, raise the stones above my head and bring them down, bashing and smashing it into a tangled mess of wires. I pummel the cage, lights flashing, the clashing, clattering sound carried away on the wind and the mangled wire slicing red into my arms until the cube shape of the cage is unrecognizable.

The wind dies down to a swirling breeze, and the blitzer glides in for a landing at my side. I don't bother flinching. It lifts its front paws onto my thigh and lowers its head, its beak bumping me gently.

"Go home," I say, and it takes off into the night, its wings sparkling like stars.

Eli walks toward me with a light stone in hand, Milo at his heels, his cloak of darkness manifesting as chills down my back.

Sypher closes in from the opposite side and is first to speak as I rise, his light stone like a piece of a moon in his hands, casting his face into light and shadow.

"What did you do?" His words are frosty. Perhaps he was hoping the blitzer would leave me in shreds.

The fire crackles in my chest.

Sypher gazes into the sky. "You let her go. She was bound to that cage."

"You weren't supposed to let it get you," Milo says, "and hurt you—only run and climb a tree, trigger fear." He trudges away, a solacing hand on Sypher's back.

"Climb a fucking tree? And then what? Get torn to bloody

chunks?" I shout after them, then turn to Eli. "What in the holy son of a prick's asshole were you thinking?"

His brows elevate. "What did you say?"

"I don't fucking know!" Warm blood streams down my bare arms, shielding me from the cold of Eli's stare. "Look what you did to me!"

"Down. Try it now." He points to the ground.

"*You* get on your fucking knees!" I yell.

"Later, greedy little one. I said down."

My shoulders rise and fall with rage-filled breaths. I lower to my knees. My arms drip, painting the ground a beautiful red. I curl my hands into fists around the blood-soaked plants.

"Nothing. Look—" I say. "No magic. You're all losing your damn minds." *Like me.* I don't know what's real anymore. How could this place really exist? These people? That creature?

I'm gasping now, one lungful at a time, in and out, longer and harder. I'm not sure if the panic or the pain is worse. My hands squeeze tighter. I rip the sprouts from the ground and sit back on my heels, the blood-free roots breathing in the night air.

Eli sets down the light stone and kneels before me, my blood seeping into the knees of his jumpsuit. I lean away as he reaches for me. His hand swipes my arm, leaving smudges on my bloody armor. I stare up at him, pain igniting my nerves. Studying me with those cavernous eyes, he rubs his fingers together, a part of me slipping and sliding between them, finding every ridge and groove of his fingerprints.

"You understood the blitzer, its suffering," Eli says, too quietly for comfort, an admiration in his wide eyes that I don't want to accept.

I match his stillness except for my heaving breaths. He takes those wet fingers and touches them to my neck where the blitzer's beak left welts and craters. I flinch, moving too quickly while lightheaded. The ground shifts and spins. His hand stays, his fingers gentle over my open wounds. He smears the blood to my collarbone, a single finger trailing down. My throat closes. Pressure builds, confusion kindling a flame.

"It's so... red." His voice is stretched tight.

The fire erupts, destroying every wall inside and consuming me from within. I jump to my feet. He follows my off-kilter movement, and I shove him. It's like hitting a wall. He doesn't budge. My open cuts and claw wounds punish me for the sudden motion.

"Of course it's red, jackass. It's my damn blood, and you spilled it." The words spurt from my mouth like a crimson fountain from a fatal wound.

His hands clamp around my wrists. The stone glows from the ground between us, the only light in all the darkness. I cry out, twisting my body and yanking my arms, but his grip is solid, even with the wet blood cooling at his touch. His fingers spread, and he slides his hands up the length of my arms, so tight that he milks my wounds for more.

I groan, and my knees bend at the mind-cracking pain. He holds me up, the gushing blood covering his hands. I tilt my head back—way back—to find him, to plead for him to stop, and I catch his eyes, more black than brown in the dim glow, and gleaming. And like the mirroring eyes of the blitzer, he looks back at me with the same horror, the same fury, the same uncertainty coursing through me.

But I'm all out of empathy. I reach for that buried part of me he brings out so easily, and I plant my knee between his legs, swift and mighty. His eyes blow up, wide and wild. His mouth parts, and he crumples to the ground with a groan louder than mine, bloody hands consoling his crotch.

And it's so fucking beautiful.

CHAPTER 17

A ll of me is hurting this morning. My skin pulls tight under the layers of dried blood when I move.

I hate him. I hate him with every bone in my body, every remaining drop of blood, my entire soul. But I wonder if something's there. Something that's made people cast him away in the past, like everyone does to me. And if it's possible to be so broken, one only knows how to break.

I lie on the floor, huddled against the wall of the cell, trying to force myself back into a less painful unconscious state. Each day, a tenuous moment exists between sleep and wakefulness in which I'm invulnerable, untouchable—not yet aware of the reality that awaits, but just beyond the home of nightmares. That's where I'd like to stay. But it never lasts.

I couldn't handle Eli's scent wrapped around me, so I left his blanket bunched up in the corner last night and opted for shivers. I refused a bar smelling of beans and curled myself into another lonely ball. I regret it now as my stomach growls with vengeance. Peeking at the dreadful light of day, I see a new pile waiting for me.

A traitorously curious part of me crawls toward it, wincing the whole way, and is rewarded when I find a tiny folded note between a fresh change of clothes and a cold bar—only blue lint this time. I clench my jaw, seething at my own foolishness, and unfold the note anyway. Dried flecks of blood from my fingers and rings flutter down, settling in the creases.

Never,
You fared better than the cage, which is beyond repair. Red is a good color on you, but use this on your cuts. They'll hurt less and heal faster. I need you to be functional... We're not done yet.
Eli

A thick green spike of oozing plant falls out of the note and onto the floor.

I breathe through the anger rising in my throat, but it spreads faster than I can reel it in. Every breath spears my fresh wounds. Is this some twisted attempt at kindness so I won't knee him in the balls again, spoiled with a threat and a compliment on how I look when bloody? Or is he clueless to the point of infuriation? I gather the clean shirt and pants, also reeking of him, hold them to my stomach and return to that familiar ball, tucking knees to forehead, heels to bottom. As small as I can get. It's never enough to disappear.

I force myself to face the pain—not just the physical torment of my body, but the pain of facing a reality that mocks my attempts to ignore and deny it—and blame my sanity, or lack thereof. How can I say the blitzer was in my head when its claw marks sting my back and my finger fits in the hole its beak left behind? How can I refute this?

I can't. Not anymore.

Which leaves me lost.

I drag the bucket of soapy water closer and dip my hands into the cold liquid. The first layer of blood turns the water pink. I pull my shirt over my head, tugging hard to unstick it from the wounds on my back, and splash water up my arms, over the chain of my necklace and down my spine. I'm exposed, my skin raw and open, marked and foreign.

Shivering from the air roaming over my wet skin, I scrub away layers and layers of blood and lies I told myself, and underneath all those layers, I make sure to wash away any lingering hope.

I clean my full upper half, even dunking my head and rinsing away the blood holding my hair in clumps, then replace the embroidered bra. My back nearly rips in half as I fumble with the stained strings, tying them behind me. I tuck the blue stone back inside and move to my bottom half. The water is a dark red-brown by the time I'm done, and I'm so cold that I shiver on the inside too.

The cuts burn and throb to the beat of the blitzer's wings sounding in my head, so I do what Eli says, begrudgingly, and smooth the gooey center of the plant over the punctures on my neck and the gashes and slashes on my back and arms, then I inch my way into the clean clothes. They cling to the cooling salve like a new layer of skin. Tougher skin.

The afternoon dawdles on, visions of violent deaths every hour or so. Maybe one will actually kill me someday, a single death to save me from all the rest.

Sypher arrives in the early evening with another bar. Oat and walnuts, I think. I can't tell from the texture. They're all the same— chalky and chewy with random bits that crunch and make me wonder what else is mixed in—but what was once an assault on my palate is now a pleasure to my senses, an escape from the stone walls and metal bars.

Like chasing a dream, Eli returns after I'm asleep and leaves in the morning before I wake up, the only trace of him a fleeting note in his overly tidy script. He disappears again the next day and the day after, for a week, only showing his face once, all broody and quiet, as if he still feels my knee smashing into his balls.

We haven't talked—about the blitzer, about my blood on his hands, the look in his eyes. Nothing. Not that we would. That's what life is like now. Dark walls, deep stares, blood and silence. I don't doubt he's avoiding me. Which is a problem. I need him to fulfill his end of the deal to rescue Kelter before it's too late… if it's not already. I haven't heard a word about anything outside these walls. Sypher ignores my questions, and Milo only grants me guilty grimaces, making the unknown even less bearable.

No bar this morning, but a folded note taunts me, resting so innocently on today's change of clothes with another oozing plant for my cuts. He's trying to wear me down, pretending to be nice so I'll give him what he wants. He can't fool me. I ignore the note, willing it to disappear.

Fifteen minutes later, to my disappointment, it's still there. I give in and unfold it.

Never,
Hope you're healing faster than me.
Eli

Eight words.
That's what it takes to send me into madness today.

I can't decide if I want to bash his head in or strangle him slowly, making it nice and personal. As if I could. I don't have it in me. I'm all rage and riot without fight or bite. I can't believe I hurt Eli, but when I'm with him, that fire, that violence hidden deep down inside me from visions of death seeping into my soul, it tries to rise.

I fold the note and add it to the collection I've started, tucked between the stool and the wall. There's nothing to do inside the cramped cell, and my racing thoughts take advantage of the quiet morning, thoughts of Kelt and why what we had in Caldera isn't enough for him to return to.

The first day we met was utterly unspectacular. Me, my usual self, plagued with visions and on a solid path to total isolation, and him—I didn't know who he was that first day. I passed him in the coffee shop where we exchanged nothing more than a hello from him and a fuck off from me. That was it, followed by weeks of me pushing him away and avoiding his curious questions, so unlike anyone else in Caldera. I sensed something in him, though, something broken like me, and I finally said hello back.

If it hadn't been for every day after, in which *hello* became *how are you?* which turned into last night's stories, then inside jokes and grew into perfectly comfortable silence, I'd never have remembered that first hello.

The pleasant memories envelop me, pushing my hunger and worries to the edge of my consciousness. I close my eyes and rest my head against the wall, Eli's blanket snug around me. The scrape and stomp of boots on stone yank me out of my thoughts. Eli rounds the corner from the hallway.

"What are you doing here?" I hiss, the shock flipping into anger simply at the notion of his presence. He's wearing a white shirt, and I hate the way it sticks to the muscles of his chest, outlining each one. His light aura is absent, leaving darkness to fill my mouth with the taste of fresh blood and my head with doubt.

"It's my castle." He grins at the gray walls.

"Don't you have a shift?"

He tosses himself onto the couch, sending it sliding back a foot and screeching over the stone. "I got it covered."

"Why?" *To set another creature loose on me?*

He leans back, so damn smug as he looks down at me, arms spread over the back of the couch and legs wide, a man on his throne—fitting for a castle. "I don't need a reason to stay home and guard my little prisoner."

"Are you going to leave me in here all day… and watch me?"

A smirk climbs his cheeks. "Maybe."

"Don't you have my underwear for entertainment?"

"Panties don't look at me like you just did." He sets a bar on the stone floor outside the cell and returns to the couch. "Eat. You have work to do."

I spin the black ring on my thumb, easing the anger from the sight of my food on the floor. I'm too hungry for stubbornness. I keep most of the curses in my head as I push away the blanket and crawl forward to grab the bar, then sit back against the wall, chewing and simmering over Eli's smug face.

Only one man comes close to his level of smugness: Maverick J. He thought I was broken enough to take anyone willing, and he was right. I'd been alone, avoiding people as much as possible for the four long years since I burned down Reggie Junior's house, but it was the muscles stretching the sleeves of his shirt and the dark hair that swept over his eyes that had me opening my door for him, not the shortage of company.

He would go on and on about the unfortunate lack of appreciation at his construction job, how he should have been made site manager years ago. He found his way from the sidewalk repairs outside the coffee shop to my room upstairs—and kept coming back. He brought dinner every night, just for himself, and moped while I crunched on dry cereal out of the box and wondered if I'd ever track down my parents.

When he was full of his take-out food, and the black hairs on his belly stood up from being so stuffed, he'd finally shut up and crawl onto my squeaky floor mattress. Then he'd strip off all his clothes except the orange vest and wait for me to notice with that smug look on his face, as if I were in for a damn treat. In an attempt to avoid the unpleasant gurgles between the moans and groans, I always stayed away long enough for his digestion to advance a bit, busying myself with drawing the cardinal directions on my map or preparing my backpack for the next day's hike.

But there was nothing else to do in that small room. Eventually, I had to face the naked, slightly too hairy man each night. He was as selfish in bed as he was with his food and emotions, but I had needs. So I let him ride me until he cried louder than the squeaky springs—from pleasure… or self-loathing. It wasn't always clear.

My body was all I was willing to give to Maverick J. He was perfect in that sense—an escape—never asking me a thing or paying enough attention to notice the "episodes" from my visions. I'm still numb to the memories. He was just another confirmation that no one could care about me, especially when he didn't come back one day, like everyone else. Except Kelter. He was the first and only person to step inside my room since Maverick J. last showed his face over two years earlier, and it was always about the company, nothing more.

I wipe the crumbs from my mouth and glance up at Eli. He's been sitting in silence, watching me pick at my bar for fourteen minutes. It should be weird, but it's not—it's fucking disturbing.

"He was moved," he says, finally breaking the silence.

"Kelter?"

"Kaleida was reassigned over a week ago. No one has seen him since."

"He's missing?" My heart stops, holding its beat along with my breath. I thought she was with him every day. "You have to go find him."

"Not yet." He stretches his legs out lazily. "I have my own little prisoner to keep track of."

"Don't you realize that if anything happens to him, I have no reason to go along with what you want?"

He stiffens, as if this hadn't occurred to him. "Don't worry. I'll make sure not to tell you if the Centress kills him."

"You—" I can't even spit out an insult. I don't know if he said that to be malicious, or if he actually believed it would be comforting. I hug my legs, rocking and trying to stop the images of all the things that could happen to Kelter. Tears fill the pockets of my eyes and cascade down my cheeks, eroding all the layers I've built to block my feelings, until it's only me at my core—underneath the anger, behind the violent visions and far deeper than a lifetime of rejection.

And that "me" I uncovered—she's close to hysterical. The thought of never seeing Kelter again aches more painfully in my soul than any of the thousands of tragic deaths my own mind has offered up. Each thought hits harder than the last, taking me over with gasping breaths.

Eli watches me from the couch, observing my teary face with prying eyes like endless tunnels of darkness. I can't read him, can't figure out his expressions, too many faces and feelings blended into one. Then he's on his feet, that tall body high above me at the door of the cell. He unlocks it and steps inside.

"What do you want?" I brace myself for what he might do.

He crouches in front of me, his dark scent strong, and positions the side of his hooked finger under my chin where all the tears gather and splatter onto my knees. His eyes narrow, his nose wrinkling enough to make me notice. "Do you know how loud you are when you do that?"

"Cry?" I sob, sniffing between every heaving breath.

"Yeah, that." He pulls his finger from my chin, wipes the tears from my cheeks in two sweeps and dries it on my shoulder. "Follow me."

He leaves the cell, reaching the side of the couch before he turns and sees that I'm not following him. I'm still sitting against the wall, every breath rolling through my body with such force that my hands and feet go numb. My lips tingle as tears dribble past.

Eli huffs a huge lungful of air and thunders back into the cell. I'm not fast enough to form a scream between gasps before his hands are around my ribs. He lifts me up and tosses me over his shoulder. My stomach collides with his hard muscles and bones, and he wraps a firm arm over my lower back. Only the back of his legs and the stone floor are visible as he marches me out of the cell and into the room closest to the stairs.

He plops me down on one of three wooden benches and locks us inside with the flick of a stone. "Don't move."

Chapter 18

Eli watches me closely as I take in the room, the edges blurring from my heavy breathing, the lack of blood in my brain. Light stones are set into the ceiling, illuminating the flowers that line all four walls. The stalks are taller than me, the blooms as big as my hand with a reflective yellow center wreathed with green and purple petals.

Twig baskets litter the floor, loaded with trimmings in all different stages of drying, from freshly cut to shriveled and lifeless. The scent of cloves saturates the air and burns my nose. It smells like him... or the other way around. The aroma fills me, sucked in with my ever-quickening breaths.

He sits at the opposite end of the bench, tucking in close to a wobbly three-legged table only large enough for one. His curls glimmer in the overhead light, catching in all the right places, the tips grazing his cheekbones and making it even harder to breathe.

Even through the gasps, the question lodges in my throat: How could someone so heartless pull me in, blotting out the doubt and the warnings coming from deep within? He pauses, his hands stilling, and glances my way, wearing such a vulnerable look. It's as though he owns that doubt in me and decides when to dole it out.

I'll pass out if I don't slow my panicked breathing, but I can't get Kelter out of my head. I can't forget that I'm not home, that I'm here... with Eli. I grip the splintery bench as the dizziness sets in, focusing on the movement of his hands to keep me from swaying. The surface of the table is hidden by a crispy layer of dried petals and piles of thin paper cut into squares. He arranges a few pinches of petals in the center of one of the squares, and his speedy fingers work in unison to roll the paper into a thin stick. His tongue glides across the edge of the paper. Once, twice and back once more, and he seals it.

I try to speak, to let him know the room is going black—because even *him* catching me would be better than smashing my head into stone—but I don't manage more than one incoherent syllable at a time.

He shushes me, a finger to his lips, and slides down the bench. He reaches his arm around my back, rising and falling with me as the lungfuls come and go. His hand appears near my mouth, holding the pale green roll. I should yell, push him away, but the blackness elbows its way in. In my last shrinking sphere of sight, his other hand comes around my front with a small black stone. He holds it to the end of the roll, and it lights in a dazzling red blaze. It's the last I see before the room goes dark.

He puts the tip of the roll in my mouth and lifts my chin, forcing my lips to seal around it just as I inhale deeply. My throat is on fire. The smoke burns all the way down. He pulls the roll away and seizes me with hands as cold and rigid as metal, covering my mouth and pinching my nose.

The smoke inside me demands to escape, demands the same freedom I seek. Freedom from this castle… this mind. Spicy metallic fumes tear at my lungs, threatening to burst them, to leave only fragments of the once life-supporting organ. I battle against his hands that hold us captive, the smoke and me, tortured and trapped.

At last he lets me go. I fall to the floor, freeing the smoke on my way down, deflating with a glorious *whoosh*. I cough from the deepest depths of my vengeful lungs, until my muscles ache and my ribs pose to crack. When I can finally breathe without breaking into the violent contractions of a coughing fit, I look up at Eli.

He slouches on the bench, toking away at the tiniest shred of remaining roll between his fingers, not a care in the fucking world.

"Better?" he asks, slowly releasing a puff of clove-scented purple smoke.

I'm not gasping anymore, but my head might float off my shoulders. Relief and contentment settle in my chest, and I'm… okay—furious, but okay—and much too calm to act on such a piddly thing as anger… which is melting away. I pull myself back up to the bench and mop away the tears forced out of me.

"I think so." I can't remember what was wrong, only that he took it away. "What was that?"

"Teva." He inspects the barely there roll. "It calms, and it'll have a stronger effect on you because you're not used to it."

His lightness is back, lowering my defenses against him even further. It doesn't seem to matter what he does or says; my body decides how to feel.

"You…" I squint at him, my mind slow.

"What?"

"You brought me in here because you care."

His head jerks in surprise. "No."

"Yes, I was crying and—"

"And it was annoying," he interrupts, his tone cold and composed.

A slow smile scales my cheeks, courtesy of the teva. "And you wanted to help."

"No." A slight panic mounts in his eyes, and he smothers it. "I brought you in here to shut you up. You're loud as fuck. I have enough in my head without that."

I wait for the rage to ripple over me. It doesn't. I slowly roll my head his way. "You wanted to make me feel better."

Eli inhales again and holds his breath, a shadow of a smirk on his closed mouth, then smoke billows out and disperses into wisps of purple clouds. "You have no idea how I could make you feel."

I cough, my face heating. He's all over the place. "Too bad you'll never—"

"No." He sends me a sharp look. "If you insist on talking, tell me something I can use as a trigger."

"Why would I do that?"

I get a raised eyebrow in return, and he slaps down another square of paper in front of him. "Because you want me to rescue your wimpy boyfriend."

"He is *not* my—do you even know what you're doing?"

"There are endless ways to trigger the right emotions to wake up your magic. I can try them all—or you can give me a hint."

I run my hands over the unfinished bench at my sides, my rings scraping. "Fine."

"Tell me what you're afraid of."

Of my own mind, serving up death after death. The answer comes easy, the feeling behind it muted and soft with the teva. Cam spent years coaching me not to say things like that, not to let on to the chaos within. *Stuff 'em deep, hun. Don't let them see.*

I give him something vague. "I'm afraid of… places." *In my head.*

He rolls another stick of teva, his dexterous fingers too busy not to watch, and I wonder, for a fleeting, foolish moment under the influence of the purple haze, what else those fingers are capable of.

He glances down the bench at me, the slightest rise in his brows. "What kind of places?"

He's prying at closed doors, but the teva keeps me talking. "The kind you won't find on any map."

"Helpful." He takes a long drag. His disembodied voice comes from behind a dense cloud. "And what would you find in these places?"

Death.

"Nothing," I say.

"How am I supposed to use that?"

I drop my gaze back to his hands, one shoulder rising in a half-shrug.

"You're not cooperating." He gives me a warning look and bounces the roll between his fingers. "Who would you find there?"

Pretty much everyone I know. They all end up in those dark places with me, dying. Eli could be there with me soon too. What would it feel like to watch him die? Would I cry like I do for Kelter?

Kelter. The rough bench fights against my tightening grip.

"Ow." I suck my finger into my mouth.

"Splinter?" Eli slides back down the bench to me, passing through the purple smoke.

I tuck my hands under my thighs, pain thrumming down my finger. "No. I'm fine."

Two fingers nudge my jaw, turning my head toward him until our eyes meet. "A thief *and* a liar?"

Yes and yes. "It's nothing." I whip my face out of his grasp.

"Let me see it." Sitting right next to me, thigh to thigh, he holds his hand flat, waiting for mine.

I wiggle my hands deeper. "No, you've seen enough of my blood."

"I won't get tired of seeing any part of you." He smacks his hand down onto my thigh, those delicate rolling fingers now jabbing into me. "Don't you want your precious Kelter back?"

"It's a fucking splinter. What does that have to do with Kelter? You can't hold him over my head for everything."

"Because he's not even here, and the little fucker had you crying on the floor."

"*You* had me on the floor, struggling to breathe." I glance down at his straining hand. I should pry it off me, I should. But the way it tremors... It's as though whatever is hidden inside him is trying to escape through his fingers.

"Struggling to breathe is better than having someone breathe for you." His palm pushes down, his grasp strengthening along with his harsh tone.

"What is your problem?"

"I'd rather rescue someone worth my time." The whole room is a purple haze. He frees my leg and flips his hand over. "Let me see."

It could be the teva, or the rain-scented breeze that kisses my cheeks, but I jigger my hand out from under me and put it in his, as cold as his eyes.

He holds my hand up to his face, inspecting the splinter in my throbbing finger.

"It's big." He gives me a sideways look.

"You tend to think things are bigger than they are." I roll my eyes to his lap. "Get on with it."

With another puff on the roll, he clamps his hands over mine, encasing it in cold stone. Holding my outstretched finger like a lethal spear before him, he brings it to his mouth. With animal-like quickness, he bares his teeth, presses them against my finger and draws out the fat splinter. He spits the sliver of wood onto the floor, my finger birthing a beautiful, round, swelling drop of blood before he sucks the whole thing into his mouth. His tongue compresses the open wound, and his teeth bite into my skin.

"What are you doing?" I shriek and pull, but I'm trapped. He elbows away the attack of my other hand and ducks out of reach, standing and dragging me around with him, refusing to release me. My finger pulses inside the wet rolling cave. He might bite the thing off, rings and all, and swallow it whole. "Let go!"

He doesn't. He sucks harder, cheeks caving in, jaw working. And my depraved little mind only sends me images of that same busy mouth between my legs.

"Stop!" I yell—at both of us.

The heat of his mouth radiates around my finger. The throbbing fades, and he rips it out with a pop and a swallow.

"What is going on in your head?" I scold him, not believing my eyes and backing away as I cradle my wrinkled finger to my chest. My anger fights against the lingering effect of the teva, but it's enough to send me running to the locked door.

"Let me out." I grab the metal handle, rattling it up and down in desperate yanks, apparently to remind myself that I'm trapped. I flip back around.

Purple smoke billows from his mouth again. He waves it away so he can see me, then wipes the blood from the corners of his mouth. *My* blood. "We're even now."

I stomp up to him and grab a fistful of his white shirt. "What the fuck is that supposed to mean?"

"A taste for a taste." He takes another toke, face relaxed, serene. So smug.

I could kill him. I don't have to wait for a vision to watch him die. I only need something sharp enough to get through his arrogant skin. I pull his shirt tighter, wishing I weren't full of empty threats. "My tongue on your hand is not the same as sucking my finger for fun."

"You're right. We're not even. You owe me now." He tosses a glance at my fist, then bites back a smirk.

Fuck that. "You wanted to taste me? I'm sure you could have picked something better than my finger, coward."

"Next time." He licks his lips and disappears behind a puff of purple smoke.

I hate this gorgeous man.

CHAPTER 19

Visions come throughout each day, and with so many hours locked up, I'm gifted with plenty of time to contemplate the possibilities of Kelt's situation—none close to rational.

I tear myself open with the images my mind conjures, then slowly, so slowly, rebuild my sanity, like my wounds. For days, the cuts from the blitzer ripped open again with a sudden movement, a fresh stab of pain destroying the fragile layer of new skin. Torn open and rebuilt, over and over. One layer after another, hiding what's inside.

My wounds are closed now, the new skin lustrous and striated, untouched by the slow roasting of the sun, healed in the dark of night as my body put itself back together while I slept.

But not my mind.

It's been the same dream every night since the blitzer—a beating sound, shaking my bed of stone and syncing with my pounding thoughts. I wake up in a cold sweat, the beat still drumming into my mind and body.

***

"Out." Eli opens the cell door in the late afternoon, mint and cloves sweeping over me. He's only been back at the castle for an hour, half of which he spent in the shower, the other half in the teva room with Sypher and Milo. It's been four days since I was in there with him, and I still feel his hand on my thigh and his mouth around my finger. I've hardly seen him. He hasn't tried new triggers, but he makes sure to leave a note each morning with a bar and a fresh set of his clothes.

"Good afternoon to you too," I mutter.

"Outside."

I step beyond the cell door, where he stands in all black, and lean my head back to find his face. "You could be polite about it."

His shifty eyes look me over.

"Yeah, I know—I'm a prisoner." My hand is on his arm, resting. I don't know how it got there. Eli's head turns, piercing eyes staring at the contact. I pull away. "I'm not running away from that thing again."

He lets out something akin to a snort and takes a step back from me. "It was a blitzer. We're not doing that again. It didn't work as a trigger, and you let it go."

"It was clearly unhappy."

"So are you, and I'm not letting you go." His face is pure defiance.

"You don't know how I feel."

"I know you're as curious as you are pissed," he says. "And whatever's in your head is worse than anything you've been through in Sonnet."

He startles at his own words, and my breath hitches. Maybe those eyes of his, with those riveting looks really do see as deeply as they feel. I look back at him, scrutinizing every crease and curve, every minuscule movement, and I swear a longing lurks behind that adamance.

Blinking away any trace of emotion, he adds, "Maybe if you weren't eye-fucking me all the time I wouldn't be able to read every damn look on your face."

I don't deny it. "You're the one claiming my body parts for yourself."

His arms cross, and he drags his gaze from my mess of hair to the toes of my boots in slow motion, tongue peeking out from between his lips. "I claim *all* of you. And you like it."

Why why why? I clamp my thighs and lock my knees to keep from squirming. "Look who's eye-fucking now. If you're not setting another blitzer loose on me, then what are we doing?" I glance at Sypher and Milo waiting behind the couch, listening to every word.

"Not *we*. You're going to sit in the dirt, and I'm going to practice my shots." He grabs a knotted mess of straps from the junk pile on the counter, picks it apart with those speedy fingers, works it over his shoulders and clamps it to his pants. The gnarled black straps cross in the back, and an extra strap with pockets crosses diagonally over the front of his shirt from shoulder to hip.

"Suspenders?" I slip my hand over my mouth to cover a laugh. My stomach twists into a knot at the look he gives me, loathing lining every angle of his jaw, but it doesn't stop me. "You look like an old man, but fuckable."

Milo bursts into laughter.

Two minutes later my ankles are cuffed and chained to a tree on the edge of the clearing outside the castle, and I'm sitting in mud. The crisp air forces itself into my awareness, whispering in my ears and biting my cheeks.

"What am I supposed to do here?" I look past Milo at the gray clouds hanging low and heavy in the sky.

He kneels at my side, muddying his cerulean jumpsuit and furiously rubbing his hands together. "Figure out how to pull magic from the plants."

Oh, just that. "I can't."

"Eli said he saw you do it once. Do it again." He leans closer. "I threatened to poison his teva plants if he didn't give you a week to try and figure it out before putting you through another trigger, so make it count."

"He chained me to a tree, Milo."

He smiles bright and makes a further mess of his hair by sending a hand through it. "You called him an old man. What did you expect to happen?"

"Get over here," Eli calls, and Milo squeezes my shoulder and runs off to join him and Sypher across the clearing as Kaleida appears through the woods in her blue jumpsuit.

She takes Milo's place at my side, squatting to avoid the mud. "What now?" She surveys the cuffs and chain. At least my hands are free.

"I told him he looked like an old man."

"Oh, I think we should keep you." She pats me on the head, her freckled face lit with joy.

Eli nears us and dumps out a bag of slingshots and marbles next to his foot. He squats down to rifle through the pile, nabbing a smoky-gray marble, then chooses a slingshot made of dark wood, so worn that it shines.

"That's what you're shooting with? A ten-year-old's back pocket toy?" I ask.

He stands and squints down at me, rolling his chosen marble between his fingers like a good luck charm. "*Lethal* toy."

"Wouldn't a bow and arrow make more sense? Or sword practice?"

"Those were forbidden after the Separation," Kaleida says. "The first Centress confiscated, destroyed and prohibited most weapons in fear of a rebellion, which is why you'll only see guards with clubs and sometimes knives."

"And slingshots," Eli adds.

"You three are the only man-boys that use them," she says, provoking a glare from Eli and making me clamp my lips shut to hold in another laugh.

I didn't think I had it in me after... everything. I control myself, bringing back the walls and anger and doubt—my safety. But the rebellious turning up of my lips doesn't go unnoticed by Eli.

"Why not use magic?" I ask before he can react. He's so set on me taking it, but nobody seems to use it.

"What makes you think I have magic?" Eli shoves ammo into the pockets of the diagonal strap on his suspenders.

Kaleida waves her hand in dismissal and sits on an exposed root. "We don't get magic until after maturation."

"You haven't matured?" My hand goes to my cheek as I assess Eli's stubble, the angles of his jaw, his broad chest, the bulk in his—dammit. There is nothing immature about this man's body. It's fine. I can hate a beautiful man. He makes it easy. "How so? Your balls haven't come in yet? Oh wait, my knee has already met them."

Eli crouches and puts his face in mine, one hand gripping my ear. "That mouth of yours seems awfully interested in my balls."

"Too bad I don't go for old men."

His fingers tug my ear, bringing us nose to nose. "You might be surprised, little prisoner." He rises and wags his slingshot at Kaleida. "Do what I asked."

Kaleida grins at him, extending her curvy legs and getting comfortable against the tree. "You know I will, now go away so we can talk more about your old man balls."

He shoots me a warning glare and takes off toward Sypher and Milo, already shooting marbles into the trees.

I run my fingers over the stems and leaves around me. At this point, I wish I could do what he wants so I can see Kelter again. I turn to Kaleida. "What did he ask you to do?"

CHAPTER 20

To make you believe," Kaleida says.

My nails stab into the mud, instant ire flaring. "In magic?"

"And the gods."

"Why does he care what I believe?"

"He probably thinks it will speed things along. I don't know, but Eli hasn't cared about anything in years."

I look away. I doubt he cares about anything now either. "How come you do what he wants?"

"He's Eli. I trust him with my life." Kaleida tilts her head, trying to catch my gaze. "You know, this is my family now. I lost everyone I had, and these guys only spent a year with their parents before being sent to live at school. We only have each other."

My eyes stick to the ground.

"I'll tell you the story. You choose what to believe."

I rub the mud off my hands while she speaks. I have no choice except to listen, but I don't mind a distraction.

"In the great expanse of nothing, where the waves didn't crash and the sun didn't rise, where the laughter never sounded and tears never fell—thought only belonged to one: Ametrine, goddess and creator of the land and those beyond. And she recognized, deep within her matterless existence, that being alone would be the end of her. Her purpose was to create, and it would have to be more than whipping colors and textures and patterns into existence and sitting back to admire her work. She had to create something that mirrored the inherent purpose inside her—life."

"Of course she did."

Kaleida points her dark brown finger at the mud and lets a smile push up her freckled cheeks. "First she created the dirt and dust and rocks of the lands, the salt and tides of the seas, the rising sun and falling stars and the toes and whiskers and beaks and stingers of all the creatures she filled her world with. Then she sat back for thousands of years, watching life unfold, watching the beauty and the creatures multiply, and the landscape evolve and change with the seasons. But she was lonely, still plagued with the call to create. So she created beings with the fiercest of hearts and delighted in watching them navigate the world—and abhorred the death that inevitably came. She made one after another, watching them live and die alone, improving her design each time, tweaking the intricacies inside and out, until one day, she created a being so perfectly imperfect—wonderfully flawed and passionate, matching the give-and-take world she had created—that she was drawn to him."

"The goddess fell for her creation?"

"Who doesn't love a love story?" She drops her chin into her hand, beaming. "Ametrine took on the physical form she spent so many centuries refining and joined him in the young world as a Vaile. They fell in love—the first love—and the idea of him wasting away to dust tore her apart so deeply that she shared her essence with him, making him immortal. A god, like her."

"Wait, her *essence*?"

She frowns at me. "You really haven't heard any of this? I thought Hollows would have maintained some knowledge after the Separation."

"I was told there are gods and that I should believe in them like everyone else."

Kaleida takes a long pitying look at me. "Her essence makes her who she is. It resides within, capturing what matters most to her." She stares at me until I nod, then continues. "Ametrine made two more Vaile and shared her essence again, creating two more gods as company for them. Her lover used a part of the essence he was given to bring to life the Hollows. They lived among the many more Vaile that Ametrine created. The Vaile and Hollows each had a role in maintaining balance and harmony in the world and completing the cycle of magic. Then—"

"Cycle?"

She gestures to the nature around us. "The gods gift magic to Vaile when we're born, it gets activated inside us when we mature and it goes into nature when we die so it can be gifted again."

"This isn't helping me believe. It's making it worse."

Kaleida laughs and pulls on one of her gathered curls. "He's right. You're difficult."

"Elivander said I'm difficult?"

"Actually, he said you're a pain in the ass." She seals her lips in a smile, eyes wide.

"Really?" I smile back. "Not a pain in his balls?"

She falls into a fit of giggles, and I twist around to glare at him. His back is to me, aiming his next shot. My insides itch from the rising heat, calling to that often dormant part of me that wants to fight.

I grab a beat-up slingshot he left behind, like the ones in Caldera, but the sling is made from a stretchy vine. I skim my hand over the pile of ammo and pick an unpolished marble with light streaks of pink through the gray, like sunset before a storm.

A child's toy. I got this. I stand and face the clearing, stepping forward until the chain pulls tight on my ankle cuffs. The heat settles in my chest. I load the marble, roll my neck and extend my arm out in front of me, slingshot in my mud-stained hand. With a stretch of the sling to my shoulder, I find my target.

"What are you doing?" Kaleida asks.

Hunting.

He's pacing now, waiting his turn. I follow him with my aim, gliding my arm back and forth, mirroring his movements. The clouds drop lower, restless and probing. With another pivot, he spies me hunting him. A quick pause, and he keeps moving. That sideways glance, that smirk—they kindle a furnace in me. Instinct trickles out of my pores. I'm aware of every shift. The encroaching clouds. Sypher turning to watch. Milo's anxious hands. The wind tossing Eli's hair. The waving leaves.

Eli stops pacing. He sets his gaze on me, his eyebrows taunting, his tapping fingers provoking, the thought of a marble colliding with his smirk so damn tempting. He gives me the slightest nod.

I squint and line up my shot. His stare penetrates the air around me, burning holes in my concentration. I blink him out of my thoughts, but sizzling fingers slip down my neck and back, his darkness reaching out to me. I release the sling, and the world slows down. The marble flies, rising into the air like a bird taking flight. I soar right along with it, straight into the besieging clouds, my heart thundering in my chest. I want to look away, but I can't. It makes contact—a solid *plunk*—with the ground.

Three feet in front of him.

Eli drops his head to the tragic marble in the dirt, then looks back at me, a glint of satisfaction in his eyes. I fall right out of the sky.

He snatches up my marble and strides toward me. My knees knock with each step he takes. Then he's in my face, my chin in his hand. Those distracting fingers dig in, holding my attention on him and only him.

Where else would it be?

"You think a little violence will wake up the magic in you?" His voice scrapes beneath the surface of my skin. His fingers pinch tighter.

I pull away, breathing hard. "Maybe I'll like the sight of your blood as much as you like mine."

"Maybe so, but no one sees me bleed." He hands me the marble. "Again."

I'm motionless, marble in one hand, slingshot in the other.

"Now." His command hammers through me.

I startle and move into position, arm out, sling pocket filled.

Eli signals to Milo and Sypher across the clearing. "Stay there."

He swoops in behind me like a cold shadow. I stiffen under his touch. He stretches his right arm over mine, a tingling trail of chills sliding down from shoulder to hand. His left arm follows my bent elbow. His fingers stroll until they ripple over my muddy rings, the sling in my grasp.

My hands disappear under his. He clamps down on them. I whimper at the tightness of his grasp, the seductive pain. The faint sound gets lost in the air whipping around us. The rub of the wood burns. The sling smashes into the creases of my palm, my own nails piercing my skin.

His hips and chest press into my back, blocking all the wind from behind. Each marble packed into the pockets across his chest digs into me. His legs spread outside of mine, bumping against the ankle cuffs. His grip unrelenting, he pulls my hand back, stretching the sling into position. The vines whine in my ear.

I stop breathing when he tucks his head in next to mine. The billowing clouds drop again, surrounding us in a mist and trapping me in his scent—the cool, damp air of an endless cave.

"You're a lefty too," he whispers, his words crawling down my spine, his fingers pressing harder.

I tighten every muscle to keep myself from shivering against him. "I'm both," I croak.

He adjusts my aim, the marble's path settling on Milo. *No.* I try to redirect, but his arms are solid over mine.

"What?" he purrs into my ear. "It's only me you want to hurt?"

Fuck. That voice. "You have no idea how much."

His chin nuzzles roughly into my neck. "Then what are you waiting for?"

"Are you *asking* me to knee you in the balls again?"

"Is that the only part of me you think about?"

"Basically." A cold sweat consumes me, my body torn between the fiery rage within and the icy wind against my skin. Metal coats my tongue. "Let go of me."

"I wish I could, but you're a little nightmare that I can't escape—your hair smells like old blood and you're covered in mud, and somehow I want to throw you down, mark you all over and add to the fucking mess."

"Not interested," I grind out, breathing through my twisted desire.

"Even better." His hiss floats past my ear, his body pressing closer.

I grunt and fight against his hold on me. It only tightens, veins roping over the backs of his hands.

"On three," he says, cheek pressed to mine.

"One."

I shake my head, his rough stubble scraping my skin. "Stop. Not at Milo."

His smile pushes against my cheek.

"Two."

He lets one hand go, the sling now pinched between my fingers. "I said stop!"

"Three."

My fingers are pried apart, and the marble soars, up and up and up, over Milo's head and straight out of the clearing.

His arms fall away, leaving me to collapse with relief, and the cold misty clouds hug me in his absence.

CHAPTER 21

I t was a nightmare. Not a dream. That's why I woke up breathing like that. That's why I see it all again, why I feel it when I close my eyes and try to make the image go away—lying on my mattress back home, Eli hovering over me. His strong hands were on my ribs, then my waist. Curls grazed my skin, and his lips found my belly. And slid over my hips, and lower, centering. A bite, then two more. Lower and lower. Then it faded. It darkened... to black. To nothing at all. No lips or teeth or tongue anywhere.

Shit.

I force my eyes open with my fingers. A nightmare for sure.

Never,
Thought you might want to keep this to remember our first shot. And Milo says hi.
Eli

I wrap the marble we sent soaring back inside the note, exactly how I found it a week ago—the day after the slingshot incident. Then I tuck it behind the stool with the others I just read again. I hate that I haven't ripped them to pieces. Him taking the time to leave one every day with a change of clothes and a bar has me questioning every word, every look. I thought it was another way of getting me to behave, but the way he folds it so small, the way he tucks the corner in so it stays closed, the way every letter runs into the next, so damn carefully as if he'd spent half the morning on it—I'm not sure anymore.

Eli comes out of the bathroom, slick wet curls dripping and the outline of his knife sheath in a pocket by his knee. I can't pry my eyes off him, not when he looks like *that*—pissed at the world with a body that could tear me to shreds in more ways than one. But his invisible light is out this evening, the breeze hitting me, and I wish it didn't because I don't want to be pulled in again. I can smell him from here, like wind and rain in a field of mint. Fresh, unlike me.

I'm rotting in this cell, putrid and rancid behind bars. Even without coffee, my brain never stops, and three weeks of the stone walls and metal bars of this cell has that constant flow of thoughts gurgling in place like a stifled swamp.

"Elivander." I grasp a bar with each hand and pull my face to the door.

He swivels to attention. "What now?"

I'm too defeated to snap back, but I love how easily I can annoy him with only his name—an accidental gift from him. "You said you would find Kelter."

"After you do your part."

I flatten my nose against one of the suffocating bars. "She's going to kill him." My pain multiplies.

"Your chance from Milo is up. I've taken you out every night for a week to pull magic, and you did nothing. Maybe getting Kelter back is not enough motivation for you. Thinking about him is holding you back." A smirk breaks loose. "Maybe if you'd focus on all the ways I could wake things up in you, we'd get somewhere." He sits on the couch and bends down to tie his boots.

I blush, thinking all the wrong things… and remembering his lips so close to my ear, his body up against mine. That dream—no, nightmare. Dammit. *Focus. New plan. Connect with him.* It's my only chance of getting him to rescue Kelter sooner and let me go. "Haven't you ever lost anyone?"

The fingers dancing with his laces go still. "Yes."

"Who?"

Confliction paints across his brow, pain bleeding through his eyes. "My father."

So the fucker has feelings.

But why is it so hard to respond to his pain? It's all over—the way he forces a swallow, the muscles tightening in his arms.

"And didn't it hurt?"

He finishes tying his laces and sits up, fingers twisting his earlobe. "It was confusing."

My heart jolts. Something real came out of his mouth. "And now?"

"It's annoying."

This is pointless. I push back from the bars. "Your father's death annoys you?"

The pain washes from his face, replaced with lowered lids and a grin. "Almost as much as you do."

"What part of your crooked brain ruptured and contaminated the rest?"

His upper lip twitches. "Look at you caring about me."

"That is *not* caring."

"Then what is?"

Those three words cripple my resolve. Responses tick through my mind, but only silence has the gall to hang blatantly in the air between us. He stands to go, but that swamp-bound piece of me can't bear to be alone. "Wait."

"Lonely?" he croons.

Yes, incredibly. "Why would you think I'd be lonely in a four-by-four foot cage all by my fucking self?"

"It's a nook. Should I shut myself in there with you for a little goodbye fuck before I go?"

How fucking thoughtful. He never fails to find a way to turn me on and piss me off at the same time. "Tempting"—*truly*—"but I'm miserable enough without an *impressive* two minutes of your extroverted cock inside me. Take me to the house upstairs." Maybe I won't have to spend another whole day behind bars that slowly drill through me, puncturing my being.

He frowns, every inch of his face turning me down. "No."

"Why not? I'm dying here."

His brow creases, genuine concern filling in the lines. "I give you a bar every day, sometimes two. You should have told me you were dying. I need to know these things."

"Because that would be inconvenient for you?"

"Yes." He grits it out as if he didn't want it to be the case, or maybe—*maybe* it's more than that. Maybe he'd miss having a "little prisoner" to tease… to come home to.

I huff and bite my lip. "Two bars isn't enough, but that's not what I meant. Take me up there. Let me out of this cell." *Let me see walls that don't smother and destroy.*

His eyes pin me in place. "No. It's just a house."

"I only want—"

He grabs the cell door, and his whole face threatens me with its sharpness, taking the words from my lips. Then he turns away, a wall of black. Black hair, black shirt, black pants and boots. Impenetrable.

"Take me upstairs tomorrow." I panic, and the words spill out. "I won't talk."

He stops.

"For the whole day," I add.

"Tomorrow then," he says, his back to me. "Your next trigger will be upstairs."

Never,
Looking forward to every minute of your silence tonight.
Don't think I won't know if you talk while I'm gone.
I will.
There will be consequences.
Eli

Right. He's *looking forward* to whatever trigger he plans to torture me with. I crumple the note into a ball and chuck it at the wall. Why did I agree to this? Why was it my idea? Is that how desperate I am to escape these walls? To escape myself?

Milo appears at the top of the stairs hours later, bright and droopy, like overworked sunshine. His cerulean jumpsuit hangs loose on him, a tad too short, exposing his ankles and wrists. He settles onto the ugly couch, long limbs all over and his golden hair rebelling in every direction.

"You know why I'm here, right?"

Does Eli really think he can send Milo as a spy and break me? He has no idea how many kids I've lived with. I'm a master of the silent game.

"You're not going to answer?"

I curl my tongue behind my teeth.

Milo sits up and leans forward, his imploring blue eyes like the sea. "So I'm supposed to talk to myself?"

Nope. Not going to fall for it. Of course he would tell Eli if I talk. Whatever consequences Eli's dreamed up, I won't be finding out about them.

"He made me bring you this." Milo produces a bar from his pack.

My mouth opens, and I snap it shut. Eli already left a bar for me this morning, and it's much too early for the evening bar.

"He said you were dying." His two blonde brows climb his forehead, giving me an accusing look before handing me the bar. "And that he'd rather not have to remove your corpse from the castle."

I roll my eyes.

Milo's rosy cheeks rise with his grin. "I've never heard him speak so fondly of anyone before."

I laugh through my nose and lean against the metal bars of the cell. He's giving me more than two bars a day to keep me alive... right? It's selfish, not thoughtful.

Milo eyes me pensively. "You're not afraid of him. But you don't trust him either."

Nope.

"It doesn't make sense. After all these years," he muses. "I see why he's fascinated with you."

Is that so?

"I trust Eli. I'd do anything for him." His fingers rap on his knees.

Why so loyal when he goes behind the Centress' back and drags you along with him?

"He's like family, you know?"

Not really. I have no idea what family is like.

"But you can't trust what you feel, as real as it seems—not that you can stop yourself. I know how it is. There's more to him than you think..." Milo drops his chin, eyes stern. "Just don't go looking for it."

Why not?

I think of that little girl he held in his arms, the depth of his eyes that harbor so much. What is he hiding behind his smirks and scowls?

Milo's tone shifts, a playful lilt to it. "And he has a message for you."

I twist my rings and force myself not to look at him, not to show any sign of curiosity.

He goes on anyway. "He wanted me to thank you."

Surprise sends my head whipping in his direction. So much for disinterest.

"For last night."

For what? It almost slips off my tongue.

"And he says next time…" Milo stretches his endless arms above his head. "He'd like to be on top."

I didn't—we never—the words roll up on my tongue like the crest of a wave, and they try to crash, to deny, to set right the claim, but I swallow them up.

He almost got me.

Milo tosses his head back, his laugh high and loud and free, like how a sunflower might sound if it were to laugh at your expense. "You're good," he says to my sealed lips and scowl. "He said you'd never last." He wipes away a crystal tear of jester's joy. "I don't know if I'd rather see him be wrong or see you break."

He reaches through the bars and tousles my unwashed hair. Pulling away, his laughter dissolves like the words I held on my tongue. Night falls on his ocean eyes. "If you drag him up there, then it's on you to watch after him."

I spend the rest of the afternoon stewing over the jerks I'm stuck with… and Milo's final words. Why would I need to watch after Eli? In his own home?

I'm so deep in thought when he stomps down the stairs in cobalt blue—pockets plinking with treasures and cuffs, and a pack on his shoulder—that I almost say something about the racket he makes. *Almost.*

He struts right up to the cell door and opens it, carrying the scent of wet trees and afternoon showers. "Let's get this over with."

He pinches my ear and tugs me along by it, guiding me as if he were holding my hand. He takes me from the castle hatchway, around to the front of the house and up the steps of the wooden porch. I tiptoe, avoiding the gaping holes lined with jagged wooden teeth. We reach the top step and land on a narrow deck with a leaning railing that skirts the house, and it groans, the planks of the deck flexing and stretching and yawning under my boots. I throw my hands out to steady myself.

Eli frees my ear and loops his hand around my wrist, pulling us off the grumbling deck and spinning me around until we stand face-to-face in front of the door. The deck lets loose a sleepy sigh and settles its planks down to rest.

My blood redistributes inside me, shifting to shock. My mouth goes dry, my breath shallow. What the fuck kind of magic is that? Terror clenches my existence, but quickly—much too quickly for my denial—curiosity presses in, subduing the panic pulsing in my veins.

"It likes you," Eli says, his voice gruff, and tosses me back my wrist.

I'd ask what *it* is and why he would say that, but I can't. The door hinges screech as they're spread wide open, and I take one look back at the deck and follow him inside.

CHAPTER 22

I t's ancient. I thought the outside looked old, but inside—the inside is older than time. Not in the way that the exterior is falling apart and wears its years in its cracks and rotting wood. No, it's old in the way that the breath of the past lifts me from the present, opening eyes I didn't know I had and spilling years of memories and tears and laughter into the air. It pulls me the same way Eli does, toward things I can't understand.

It's nothing like the castle below. Decked in warm brown and bronze, maroon and gold, three walls are busy and buzzing with gadgets on crooked shelves, wall-to-wall, floor-to-ceiling. The red wood of the shallow shelves matches the crimson carpet with fibers so long that I sink with each step. And coming up through the carpet are stumps of trees situated around a table with a sofa and chairs nearby. Apart from the strange choice of stumps for seating, the furniture is similar to what I've seen in Caldera, but fancier, almost antique. Hanging on the fourth wall are swords and bows and daggers, and I stare long enough to wonder why they weren't destroyed with the rest of the forbidden weapons after the Separation.

Four doors are among the knicknacks on the walls, all closed, leaving one giant entry room for my eyes to explore. No kitchen, not even windows, but a spiral staircase claims the right side of the room, railless and open, the golden steps practically floating.

Eli twitches at my side, his dark aura making its way to me. I look right at him, and the look he gives back is harsher and more blistering than I've ever seen—and daunted. He glistens with sweat in the old, cold house as if it's an effort to simply stand there. Maybe it is. I could ask… if I hadn't dealt away my voice.

Fingers scrape down the back of my head, my neck, my back, pulling away when they reach the bottom of my spine.

"Time to go." His temples pulse, one foot stepping toward the door. "I'll find a different trigger."

I slide in front of him, rebelling with my silence. This house. It's as though its roots grow up instead of down, driving through the soles of my feet and up through my body, twinging every nerve and twining around every muscle.

I need more.

He takes a step past me, closer to the door. The walls shudder, the trinkets clinking and pinging on the shelves.

"I got it," he barks at the house, and the walls snap into place, unmoving with an air of defiance.

I follow him, and the house purrs. The walls and shelves and floor, they hum, and my feet tingle. He turns to face me, nostrils flaring and teeth chattering with mine as the vibration builds. The purple stone of my necklace heats on my chest. I grab it in my fist, right through my shirt, a perfect fit in my palm.

"Enough," he yells with the flawless command of a man in charge. The house whines and goes still. His eyes dart to my chest.

My insides twist. *Not my necklace.*

"You don't need to hide it," he says, startling me with the reassuring words—only to remind me who he really is. "I already saw it when I undressed you."

My core stirs at the thought. Damn him.

His voice deepens, churning out one word at a time. "What did it do?"

Why ask when I can't answer? Still holding my necklace tight, I throw up my free hand, gesturing to the house, then out to the side in question. *What's going on with this place?*

He dismisses my silent inquiry. "Let me feel it."

His hand lands on my upper arm, overwhelming it with the spread of his grasp, the strength in it. I tense at his cold touch, my muscles bricking. He reaches for the hand on my chest, but I force my body into action and twist away, scolding and screaming at him with my eyes, tapering them to slits and burning through his harsh stare. He knows exactly what I want.

He balls up his fist and brings his knuckles to his lips as if he wanted to stop the words from leaving his mouth, anguish in his eyes. "I could pry your hand open."

I dare you.

He sighs, pulling that shaky fist from his mouth and looking away. "Okay, but you're showing me after I tell you."

I blink in response. He gave in.

"I haven't been up here since my father died four years ago." He looks around the room. "It was his house." He drudges toward the furniture, the walls now quiet and motionless, waiting. "And my grandfather's. And his father's. All the way back to the beginning."

No wonder it looks as though it's about to fall the fuck over.

He moves to the sofa, dragging his hand along the scalloped back, and if I trust my eyes, it arches into his touch. Tattered breaths fight their way in and out. He seizes two handfuls of curls.

More feelings.

"Most houses only have a little magic—or none—but this one is full of it. Any time one of my ancestors received a gift from the gods, especially a rare one, they used it to add to the house—to protect and hide it, or build onto it and give it personality. And all this stuff"—he gestures to the shelves—"is from before the Separation, when Vaile and Hollows still lived together. It's bound to the house. Everything else was pushed out of Sonnet or destroyed."

That's why it reminds me of stuff from Caldera and why the swords are still here—they've been hidden and protected for hundreds of years.

His chin rises as though he's trying to overcome a battle within, but pain leeches into the hardness of his face. An endearing touch of pride remains. I move toward the sofa, pulled by something too deep to acknowledge, and he schleps himself away with dragging steps to a shelf on the wall. I follow.

"And now it's mine. Your turn," he says.

I clutch the necklace over my heart, reluctant to let go. I've had it since I was a baby. His gaze settles on my hand, his eyes signaling what to do next. With a focused calm, like that quiet beat between songs, I open my hand. The necklace falls against the skin of my chest with a *thud,* still hidden by my shirt. I look at him, way up above me. My chest swirls with regret. I can't do this.

His demeanor shifts, a teasing smile spreading slowly across his face. "Do you need help?"

No. I suck in a breath, rip down the collar of my shirt and pull the necklace up and out, holding it by the chain. He studies the light purple stone, its transparency and jagged edges. Even in this windowless room, a current of air sighs over me. Just like that, I'm drawn to him, accepting blindly, opened and exposed. His eyes are wide and probing as he reaches out and takes hold of the stone—of that piece of me.

Then it's as though all the air of the realm is sucked into this one room, so thick with... *him* that I can hardly breathe. His scent, his presence, his being—they choke me.

He tightens all over, brown eyes gleaming black. They try to suck me in. They hold the whole night sky, the bottom of the sea and the darkest corners of my own mind. His jaw is clamped shut, his neck flexed and corded. I open my mouth to speak, or scream, and he puts a cold, sweaty finger over my lips and holds it there, my hot labored breath wreathing around it.

"Don't—" he says in a raspy whisper. "Don't let me win because you're afraid."

His finger falls away, and with the drop of my necklace back to my chest comes the heat, sweltering, dizzying heat. It radiates from the walls, steams up from the floor and smothers us from above. Fear rips apart my gut.

I grab Eli's arm, pulling with my entire body. He's stuck, staring at me, frozen in this inferno. My head wobbles and floats. The house grinds, and the wood swells and moans. Across the room to the door and we're out. But instead, I drop into a vision.

Flames surround me inside Reggie Junior's house. I can't escape the fiery beds, the smoking dresser, the cold floor now so hot as I lie on it. Flames crawl closer, wood crackling. I drift away with the stench of my skin melting, dripping, falling to that awful floor.

Panting now, tears welling from the vision, I pull again on Eli. It's all more intense after dying—the heat, the colors. My hands slip over his drenched arm.

Run, please run with me.

Hot air closes my throat. Nausea spools in my stomach, saliva puddling in my mouth.

Out out out.

I pull harder, wet skin sliding over wet skin. Salty sweat drips into my eyes.

"Elivander!" I scream, and it burns.

He spasms, shocked back to the moment, and we run. Smoke rises over the carpet. He hauls me along through the sticky, suffocating room, opens the door and hurls us outside. The porch bucks in response, and we leap down the stairs. The cold air strikes my sweat-soaked body.

My muscles lock, and my feet give out beneath me. I fall to my hands and knees and rest my head on the ground. Eli drops to my side and feathers his hand over my back, fingers climbing up and up the notches of my spine, like the ones I so often feel around him.

"Now try."

I close my spread fingers, trapping bits of life between them. I beg for them to do something at my touch, *anything*. If a house can buck and purr, then I can pull some damn magic out of a plant. *Please please please.*

Nothing.

Tears crowd their way past my restraint. "I can't!"

He moves his hand from my upper back to my skull, holding me in place against the ground. "You can. I *need* this." His quaking fingers dig through my hair, snagging as they meet knots. Tiny stones indent my cheek.

"I said I can't," I sob. Still holding the back of my head, he collapses next to me, lying on his side with his knees curled halfway up. I crumple to the ground too, rolling to face him. His hand slowly falls away, and we look at each other—me with pebbles embedded in my cheek and half my face covered in dirt stuck to a layer of sweat, and him with wet hair clinging to his forehead and a lingering look of derangement in his wild eyes.

But they soften, growing big and round. The golden specks try to take over the brown, and maybe I'm as far gone as I thought because I swear I'm looking into two pools deep with regret.

But my failure, the sting of my tears, the deep fall into his eyes—they plow through me. I push up onto my elbow and punch him in the gut, my petrified muscles like rock, hitting with a force beyond my own, a violence and a vengeance I didn't think could surface.

He curls into a ball, disbelief claiming his face, but not ten seconds pass before he puts a hand on my heated cheek and rubs the dirt and pebbles away, wide eyes blinking, saying so many things I can't decipher.

I retreat from his soft touch, confused and shaking, and tuck my necklace inside my shirt, hiding it away with the other bits of me I don't want to share. He can't scare me away with a little heat. That house strums with life, and with vision after vision of death after death, I could use a little life.

"I win," I say. Because at least I'm not in that cell, rotting.

CHAPTER 23

With every hour that passes, the pit in my stomach grows and churns along with my thoughts of Kelter, worsened after realizing I spent that entire day of silence *not* thinking about him, letting my mind center on waiting for Eli. I can't take the bars and the helplessness, the not knowing and the worrying. I'm done.

I go through the motions of breathing only to stay alive, but I'm not sure why I bother. Maybe for Kelt. Maybe out of habit. *Breath after death,* Cam would say, reminding me to go on with living after I died in my visions.

It's been four days since we ran out of the house upstairs, and the life inside those walls hasn't stopped calling to me. But now, I sit slumped against the stone wall of the cell, secret notes from Eli tucked safely behind my back as night falls around the castle, coating it in darkness save for the light stones scattered around the main room.

Eli's in his black shirt and pants, my own clothes matching his, and he sits next to Sypher on the floor, their backs to my cell door, the couch in front of them. The bars push into their rounded spines, arms slung around their knees. Sypher, wearing his blue jumpsuit, huddles close to Eli, so close that their elbows bump. Every time Eli scoots an inch away, Sypher follows.

Two new friends of Eli's slouch on the couch—Sola and Coen from what I've picked up, both distressingly tall. Coen surveys the room with unease despite the apparent casual gathering, the muscles padding his trim body never relaxing. He wears black pants and a loose gray shirt, so subdued compared to the bright clothes in Caldera. I don't miss them, but I do miss real food. And my mattress.

Sola's dark brown locks sling around her chin as she sits up and hands out glass bottles, each shaped differently—round, cylindrical or wavy—with a flat base and a cork in the top instead of a metal bottle cap. Coen sits close to her, his beige fingers drumming against her thigh and his other hand slicking his hair back over and over, only to have it settle in silky strips of black on his forehead again.

I'm a forgotten set of eyes as they open their drinks and chat—until Sola notices me, almost hidden under Eli's blanket in the corner and imagining a hot coffee mug in my hand.

"How's it going with the Hollow?" Sola asks Eli, fiddling with the delicate folds of her black dress, eyes on me—warm and golden like her skin, but with an unsettling mischief sparking in the upturned corners.

Eli glances over his shoulder at me and takes a swig of the red liquid, his light aura clinging to him. "None of the triggers have worked, and neither did Milo threatening me to let her figure it out herself."

"Why not try a little scarlet soda to wake things up?" She taps the bottle in her hand. "What do you think it'll do to a Hollow?"

"I have another trigger planned for her tomorrow."

"It's fine. It won't kill her. We all know you want to keep her. It'll only enhance anything good that's already there, and things might go better tomorrow." She hands her drink to Coen, a smile tearing across her angled face. "This is the strongest batch yet. It wakes me up in all sorts of ways, including my gift."

"No need." Eli sends more red liquid down his throat. Sola stands over him with her hand out, waiting. His head slides along the bars as he looks up at her. "She's staying in there."

"Let me have some fun with her. When will we have another Hollow to play with?" she says, the smirk on her lips capturing every bad intention.

I pull the blanket tighter, enveloping myself in his unbearable scent. If I could only disappear…

"She's not for playing with."

"Maybe not with you. You're no fun." She leans down and tousles his black curls. "What's the point of keeping your secret if you won't share?"

He looks my way again, and in response to her not-so-subtle threat, he parts his lips as though he's about to return one, then slaps a stone into her hand. He and Sypher move out of the path of the cell door, allowing her to open it.

"Don't take your eyes off her." Eli turns once more and snatches my gaze with such intensity that I pull the blanket up to my nose. He holds it through another sip. "She misbehaves."

"So do I, Eli." Sola steps inside the cell and reaches a hand down to me. "Come, Hollow. You'll like it."

All four sets of eyes are on me as I emerge from the safety of the blanket and step out of the cell. Sola places me between her and Coen on the couch, so much taller than me that I feel like a child. Eli's on the stone floor a few feet in front of me, Sypher at his side. It only crosses my mind for a second—the irony of my guard on the floor and me, his prisoner, on the couch, as shabby as it is. He looks livid, with a death grip on his bottle, and I can't tell if it's directed at Sola or me.

Sola throws her arm around my shoulders and yanks me backward into her lap, nestling me closer until she can reach around and hold my jaw despite my struggle. "Grab her arms," she says to Coen.

I go rigid. "No, no, I—"

Coen pins my hands in my lap, and Sola shoves the glass bottle into my mouth. "Drink, little Hollow."

The cold liquid glugs out, filling my mouth and forcing me to swallow. It burns all the way down. I thrash in her lap, and she squeezes me tighter, my jaw locked in her grasp. Coen puts his weight on my lower half, keeping me from kicking him and rolling away.

Bubbles swim the length of the bottle, frantic spheres trapped and searching for a way out of the red liquid, only finding my mouth as an escape. Sola pours and pours, and I swallow and swallow. The bubbles fill my shrunken stomach, but the liquid keeps coming, trekking down my throat uninvited. She tips the bottle back until every last drop is inside me. I ache with fullness, and tears run down my face into my ears.

"That's right." Sola removes the bottle and puts her face an inch from mine. "You're going to give Eli what he wants." She runs her finger down my cheek.

But Eli is far from pleased, jaw clenched so tight he trembles.

Sola holds me close until my body slackens in her embrace, my insides unknotting and setting me at ease. I turn my head, defeated and compliant, and rest my cheek against her arm. Coen releases my hands. I'm warm, tingling head to toe.

"I told you you'd like it, Hollow. Now tell me, what do you think of your guard?" Sola's motherly voice falls gently on my ears, disjointed with her suggestive grin and scheming eyes.

I roll my head back toward the cell, looking Eli over. He sits with his elbows resting on his spread knees, hands locked around the bottle, swirling it into a whirlpool. His fierce glare is still set on Sola. My eyes follow the swirls. They pull me in—like him. Sola pokes my cheek, bringing me back and pushing the words from my mouth. "He's a bloodthirsty grump."

Sola howls with laughter. "I like her, Eli. Bloodthirsty? What have you been doing with her?"

Eli downs the last of his bottle and uncorks another with his teeth, clearly pissed, but I don't think it has anything to do with what I said.

Sola fusses with my matted hair. "And what do you think of Sonnet?"

"I want to get my friend and go home." I say it, but the pain I expect isn't there, the ache and the longing. I'm numb, on the verge of escape.

"Friend… doesn't she know?" Sola says to Eli.

He tosses her a pointed look mid-sip.

"Know what?" I ask.

"Shush." She presses another bottle to my lips.

"Stop," I beg, but before the liquid comes rushing, Eli is standing over us with hardened fists.

He smacks the bottle, sending it crashing to the stone floor, sharp crystals in a pool of red. "She said fucking stop."

Sola laughs, glancing nervously at the pile of glass as he returns to his spot on the floor. "Fine, Eli. You don't have to waste it." She moves me to her other side, leaving me unrestrained on the couch, directly across from Eli.

The effects of the scarlet soda trickle through me, my fears and worries soaked up, and that constant simmering rage I know so well doused with red liquid. Bottles empty all around, and the tingle trekking through me slowly turns to heat.

"Where's Milo? Scarlet soda is *his* creation," Coen says, breaking the awkward silence.

"His sister turned sixteen. He's moving her into his house," Sypher says.

Coen sits up straight. "Another one? How does he have so many sisters when each and every one of us is a damn miracle?"

"Anyone could," Sypher argues. "His mother was willing to lose two babies for every one that survived. Most women aren't."

"Or maybe his mother was a—"

"Enough, Coen," Eli says, his voice like steel. "You don't talk about Milo or his dead mother."

"Lose two for every one?" I ask as I look Eli over, marveling at his loyalty.

Sola puts a hand on my thigh, immediately removing it with the threatening look Eli gives her. "Only one in three babies survive birth."

One in three? "Why?" It's the opposite in Caldera. So many babies are born and given up that families are only allowed to have one child. Any additional ones need to be taken from the growing pool of foster children.

"That's how it is." Sola goes for another bottle, and I find myself wanting more of the so-called scarlet soda, seeking an even deeper escape… like the teva roll that turned my rage and fear into puffs of purple smoke. Escape from this mind that never stops.

Coen takes a long swig, his trim, muscled arm raised, his neck moving with each swallow. He shoves Sola's chest back for an unobstructed view of me. "What's it like not to have links? Everyone fucks everyone?"

"Don't sound so excited about that," Sola says.

"What are links?" I ask, reaching for an unclaimed bottle near my foot.

"The end," Coen says, garnering a laugh from Sypher and a whack in the chest from Sola.

"I'll tell you—I like you," Sola says. "A link is your person, a deep connection. Everyone gets one, whether they want it or not, so they're not alone with the responsibility of receiving a gift."

Right. Magic and gods again. "So you all have links at birth?" I fumble with the cork jammed into the bottle.

"No, the link comes later. We're born with the gift of magic, and linking creates the emotion needed to activate it. It's just like the triggers.

They're designed to cause emotions strong enough to wake up magic. And linking is another layer of protection in the cycle. Magic is a lot to take on internally. We have to keep it balanced and flowing to prevent it from dying... or harming us. It's ours until we die, then it moves to the next part of the cycle, going into nature to be used again. Coen and I linked years ago, and I was gifted matter shifting. I can change the properties of things. It's a common gift—and limited—but at least I was able to help melt the ice last month."

She holds both golden hands up, though apart from their size, they look normal.

"Eli and Sypher are due to link any time now," she says. "Magic is in them, but they won't receive their gift and be able to use it until their links form, which they won't feel until maturation starts. Then they'll grow taller and stronger and stuff. Maturation, link *then* gift."

Eli even taller? I blink away the carnal image my mind offers up. "What does it feel like?"

"Intense. It just comes on, and you *know* who you're linking with. You crave their presence and become so intertwined and connected that your souls are practically one."

Coen leans around Sola. "Ignore her. It's miserable. You stop being able to fuck without consequences, and your options are narrowed down to one."

"Isn't doing *that* before linking forbidden anyway?" Sypher's eyes dart back and forth, showing his innocence.

Coen pops open another drink and circles the hissing mouth of the bottle with his finger. "Forbidden? Yes. On everyone's mind? Yes. Happening every day all around you? Yes." His finger slides inside the bottle, and he uncorks it with a wet *pop*. Heat trails down my thighs. Damn this drink.

Sypher's eyes grow full and round like the moons, and I wonder if Coen is just trying to make him squirm.

Sola settles into Coen's arms as she speaks to me, her cheeks blooming pink. "Pretty much everything is forbidden in Sonnet— staying out after hours, most weapons, large gatherings, music, dancing, drinking, smoking, fucking for fun... being happy." She reaches over her shoulder and snags Coen's chin, giving it a squeeze. "But that's what makes it feel so good when you do it anyway. I wouldn't want it any other way. We can be loyal to the Centress and Sonnet and still find some way to let go. Everyone does it."

Coen points the mouth of his bottle at Eli. "I think Eli's loyalty to the Centress is questionable at this point."

Sola chuckles, throws one leg over the other and turns to Eli. "True, yet somehow we're more loyal to you than the Centress. You want to have a Hollow as a pet? We're here for you."

Eli narrows his gaze to me, licking his lips with a particularly red tongue. "I have my reasons."

I can't pull my eyes away even as I speak, slow and listless. "You don't get to choose who you love?" I finally get the bottle open and pour bubbles down my throat as I try to wrap my head around the concept of linking. Eli glares at me, his breathing heavier by the second.

"It's not about love," Sola says, smoothing her black dress. "The link has nothing to do with that. Maturation is so intense and full of ramped up emotions and sex drive that it's hard *not* to be together. It has to be strong enough to trigger our gifts."

I swallow more red liquid, the lust constant now. Strong emotion— exactly what Eli's trying to force from me—so I can take the magic they wait years to be gifted. It doesn't make sense, and his friends go along with it, not caring. Whatever he truly *needs* from me can't be simply about stealing magic.

I slide my toasty body into a deep slouch, my legs outstretched and heavy in front of me, and a perfect view of Eli sipping at his bottle, his lips dyed red.

CHAPTER 24

S ola and Coen giggle next to me, hands wandering over each other. I scoot away, noting Sypher passed out on Eli, his head a deadweight on his shoulder. Eli lets him stay, as though he's not standoffish and unforgiving. Maybe he saves that for me.

My body sinks deeper into the lumpy couch, and Eli's eyes meet mine, devious and focused with every measured sip of scarlet soda, looking right past my lowered walls. I want to look away. I do. But this drink… it's breaking me down. And heating me up. The angles of his face. The muscles trapped by his shirt. The memory of his hands on me, his words—they have an inexplicable pull.

I go for another sip, and Eli moves in a flash of black. He breaks our locked eyes, slowing only to lower Sypher's sleeping body to the floor, then jumps to his feet. "Sola, put her back when you're done."

She slings her arm over my shoulders and tips me into her and Coen's embrace. "I will. I promise." Her hand slips to my neck, stroking my throat. "I'll be done with her soon."

"And don't touch what's mine," Eli snaps. Sola's hand falls from me in an instant.

Eli twists his mouth into a crooked frown, snatches the bottle from my hand and gives me one last unreadable look over his shoulder before turning down the hallway.

Coen pulls Sola closer, and I move away again. Their tangled tongues barely reach my awareness until their frantic hands and hips go searching despite their clothes, their soft breaths turning to moans of pleasure from the passionate kiss. A red, bubbly tingle fizzes its way through me, passing my abdomen, down to my inner thighs and all the way to my toes.

Whether it's the scarlet soda or their link that has them so distracted by each other, I have to get away. I unstick myself from the couch and stand. It takes the last rational bit of me to resist that pull and walk in the opposite direction from where Eli disappeared down the hallway. I sit on the bottom step, letting the lust pound through my system. The steady pitter-patter of rain surrounds me.

Even with my rising temperature, my thoughts are slow, entering like a gentle breeze instead of a hurricane, soft and flexible instead of urgent and jarring. I welcome the break. I never realized how wound up I've always been, every muscle flexed at the ready, every thought on a precipice.

I flop back onto the stairs, too relaxed to find it uncomfortable. My fingers land on something metal—a red marbled ring hanging from a strip of satiny blue fabric. I push it into the cup of my bra. Mine now. The moonlight shines through the crevice between the hatchway doors where rain trickles down toward the top step.

The hatchway.

A wave of dizziness hits me. Nothing stands between me and that hatchway, nobody watching, holding me back from finding Kelt. From going home.

I can leave.

The calming, red tingle in my body fights the urgency thundering through me. Then, as if in response to my noisy heart, it reaches my ears—a fast beat with a hard edge. I know that sound. I dreamed of it. It comes from down the hall. I look back at the hatchway. It blurs together. Handle into door, door into wall. Wall into stairs, stairs into me. But the sound is clear and crisp, skating through the folds of my mind and coaxing me to my feet.

I follow it.

Past the rhythmic embrace of Coen and Sola's kiss. Past the broken glass and red puddle. Down the hallway. Farther and farther from the hatchway. Toward the beat.

I stand outside the last door, looking in.

Eli's inside, his back to me. I count five walls, all angled inward as if the room were falling in upon itself. Four dim light stones on the floor brighten the windowless space. He sits on a little stool across from a bed and shambly nightstand, holding a smooth stick in each hand—barely visible at the speed with which they hit the drums before him. Drums that seem to be crafted straight from nature, veiny plants stretched tight around wooden frames and tied with vines.

His whole body moves, every muscle of his back and arms rippling at once and sending waves of darkness across the room—invisible darkness that brings blood to my lips, my tongue. His head bangs up and down, his feet thumping along. One with the summoning beat.

What I'd give to let go like that…

An unscratchable itch works its way through my body from head to toe, and I forget to breathe. My heart beats along with the chaotic tempo. That damn drink. My body has a mind of its own, reacting, wanting—no, *needing*.

And then—fuck this beautiful man—he sings, his voice like the horizon turned upside down, walking on air with the weight of the world above him. I hug the icy stone doorframe to tame the heat that consumes me.

> *There's not a step worth taking*
> *A breath worth holding*
> *A neck worth breaking*
> *If no one's waiting*
>
> *So why should you hold on?*
>
> *Branded with a lie*
> *Bound to lose and loosely bound*
> *Take it with you when you die*
> *Left alone and unknown*
> *Old bones colder than stone*
> *They only see what they want to*
> *Trust that it's not you*
>
> *So why should you hold on?*
>
> *Your shadow is your fist*
> *Blinding beating start on your heart*
> *Your weakness is a catalyst*

Suspended, upended
All the light expended
There's nothing left to spread but
Darkness in the red

So why should you hold on?

Only alive when you fall
Dead when you rise, lies in your eyes
It's worse, I recall
To live just to die, and lie
Try, cry, retry, die, never go to the sky
There's a whole lot more to give
If you die just to live

There's not a step worth taking
A breath worth holding
A neck worth breaking
If no one's waiting

So why should you hold on?

His intoxicating voice is a rough caress on my senses, reaching out to me, intertwining us from across the room. I see only red, bubbling up from within. I let out a whimper at the pulsing need inside me. What the fuck was in that drink?

He pivots at the sound that he couldn't possibly have heard, his captive eyes locking immediately with my desperate ones, sticks in the air, the beat ripped from the room. Dammit. I beg my legs to move, to walk away. It doesn't matter that he's gorgeous, that simply looking at him makes me wet—he's an asshole… an obnoxious, self-serving, underwear-stealing, irresistible-as-fuck asshole. *With feelings.*

My breaths are uneven. There's no blood left in my brain for decision making; it's all between my thighs. I've already walked away from a free pass out of here, and now, even worse, I silently beg for his embrace.

It must work because he drops the sticks on the floor with a clatter and prowls toward me. I squeeze my legs together, trying to stop the throbbing, but it makes it worse—or better. I don't know anymore, but I can't let this man touch me. I can't want someone who takes away my freedom. The same freedom I just left behind.

Eli's eyes remain locked with mine as he approaches. It takes everything in me not to tackle him to the floor once he's within reach. To hurt him… or feel him under me—one of those. And then I see it. The raw desire in his eyes, the black of his pupils eclipsing the brown. The hard angle of his tightened jaw. The twitch of his juicy, red-tinted lower lip.

Every thought betrays me.

All the back-and-forth in me goes flooding in one direction. I give in. I don't care about the darkness. Or that it's all physical and nothing more, that every thought and feeling is driven by redness. That's exactly what I need—to forget, to escape.

He steps closer, and my entire body is thirsty for him, utterly parched and withering without his hands on me, caressing, exploring, devouring my need.

He shoves me out the doorway, his arms outstretched, cold hands squeezing my shoulders, and drives me right straight across the hall and into the stone wall. I stifle a gasp. My face flushes, warmth crawling over my skin. Damn traitorous body, loving every fucking touch.

Whichever man writes me notes, aches for his father and plays the drums—he's long gone. And this man stands in his place, his gaze so intense it splits me apart. And I want that intensity. I want him up against me, taking me, breaking me.

His hands slide from my shoulders to my upper arms, flattening them against the rough stone. He tastes me with his eyes. All the suggestive talk suddenly feels too real. I don't dare say a word, don't dare break the spell. But he dares.

"What are you doing wandering the halls of my castle?"

"I…"

"Feeling a little *red*, are you?" He smirks knowingly.

You mean turned on? About to knock you down, tear off my clothes and grind on your face? Yes.

"No." I shake my head, maybe a little too vigorously. *Not a single bit of feeling. Or swelling. Or dripping down my thighs. No.*

152

"Even *this* is more real than the rest," he says, shades of bitterness behind each word.

"The rest of what?" I whisper.

"It doesn't matter. Everything you feel is a lie." He rolls his shoulder as if to rid himself of his own thoughts. His arms bend, and he's the closest yet. "I still owe you a consequence. And fuck do I want to give it to you right now."

Please do. "I didn't talk."

"No?" His brows quirk up.

"I screamed."

"You screamed my name, little prisoner."

My knees give out, and I hang in his grasp, pinned to the wall. Then his face shifts. Two little lines appear between his eyes, and my escape slips away. Fear and fury take over his desire. He steps back from me, throwing his hands behind his head and grabbing fistfuls of hair, torment etched across his face.

"Back to your nook." He leads me down the hall and around the corner by my ear, and without a glance at the dropped jaw on my dumbstruck face, he locks the cell door and stomps away, back to his dark, collapsing room.

I'm left panting, thirsty, empty—a bubbly red fool.

CHAPTER 25

I slide down the wall and hide my heated body under the blanket, breathing his scent in deep. I can't stop myself. Sypher stands outside the second door, a solemn, moonlit statue looking at me, arms crossed and scowling. He wants Eli? *Go ahead, have him.* I avoid his gaze, leaving only Sola and Coen's continued writhing kiss on the couch to view—or the closed hatchway I didn't leave through, taunting me.

In the minutes before I fall into a deep red sleep, I question my sanity. What would ever make me want him? That cursed bubbly drink. I give it all the blame.

Morning is a painful shock to my system, full of blinding light and recollection. I stuff the bar in my mouth and go for the note.

Never,
I have another trigger for you... try not to scream my name. Again.
See you tonight.
Eli

I'm still crumpling and unfolding the note repeatedly when Sypher shows up in the late afternoon and flops onto the couch.

"Where's Elivander?" I shove the note behind me.

"Late." His tone is worse than usual. "The Centress made him stay to talk to her."

"Do you know what tonight's trigger is?"

He pulls his short hair with two fists. "I don't really care."

"It looks like you do."

A bitterness takes hold of his face, crinkling it into a mask of slits for eyes and a drum-tight mouth. "I don't care what Eli does with you. If you would hurry up and do what he wants, we could get rid of you."

Harsh. "And if I were gone sooner?"

"Even better," he mumbles as he rises from the couch.

I stand slowly and near the cell bars, my thoughts falling in line faster than I can think them. "I could be."

He pulls a knife from his pocket, squints one eye and chucks it at the corkboard. It lands dead center.

"If you let me go," I add.

He turns on his heels, light brown eyes wide. "I can't do that."

"You could." I tap the bars, choosing my words. "And what you saw in the hallway last night would never happen again."

His face hardens. "That was nothing."

"I guess not... if being held to the wall with those big hands is nothing." Sypher swallows, a little twitch below his eye. I push him further. "Or if having his face so close that I taste him with every breath is nothing." Dammit. The memory has me squeezing my legs together again.

He retrieves his knife and stomps back across the room, his chest heaving as he aims his next throw. "You'd leave Sonnet for good?"

"Yes, or do you think I should stay?" I work his jealousy, pulling it to the surface. "I mean... stay for Elivander."

Sypher flinches and sends the knife flying again. "No. He doesn't need you."

"But he might *want* me." A lie. Every splash of desire in his eyes last night was tainted with scarlet soda.

He twists his hands together, white knuckles rolling like waves. "That's what you think? And did he tell you that your friend was moved?"

"Yes, weeks ago."

"So he must have also told you that the Centress promised whoever finds and delivers you to her gets the honors of doing whatever they want with your friend."

A cold sweat coats my skin with tiny glass beads.

"He skipped that?" Sypher feigns surprise. "The Centress even lifted the curfew. I don't see how he could forget to mention it," he mocks as he approaches the cell door. "All of Sonnet's been hunting you since then. Everyone's competing for the chance to kill a Hollow."

Hunting.

"You're lying," I say, even as my insides ignite. Eli knew. And didn't tell me. I grab my stomach to ease the flipping. Why would I even think he would?

"Go see for yourself." He slams a stone against the lock and swings open the cell door. His hand clamps around my wrist.

"What are you doing?"

"I'm letting you go." He says nothing more as he hauls me across the castle, up the stairs and out of the clearing. The clouds are high overhead, following us through the labyrinth of bark and leaves. His steps are fast and anxious, his path erratic.

I try to pull from his grasp. "Which way do I go?"

Sypher stops short and drops my wrist. I could run, but something about the way he grabs the side of his neck and pulls his gaze to the ground has me waiting for his response. "It doesn't really matter. You'll probably be found on any path you take. I'd turn you over to the Centress, but I can't do that without having to answer questions, so go for the border and get yourself caught." He scuffs his foot against the ground, anger tracing his bearded jaw. "If you mention you were with Eli or any of us, I swear he'll kill you."

I take a trembling step back. "I have to find Kelter," I say, more to myself than Sypher. Another step. Back and back. One last look at his conflicted face, and I run, closer to Kelter with every stride. Maybe. My map skills are useless when I don't know where I'm going.

Step after step, I don't tire, fueled by potent betrayal. *He could have told me.* I run until my legs are as light as air, until I'm the wind, and the ground rolls beneath me—then I run more. The faster I go, the less likely I am to surrender to the cold spreading through me and the deep, cutting guilt of walking away from the hatchway last night, from Kelter.

The high clouds make their way down, embracing the evening and adopting a grayish hue, as though they've grown older and wiser with the sun's absence. The trees are scarcer as I reach the edge of the woods. Voices stop me in my tracks. I slip behind a boulder and peek around the side. Vaile in jumpsuits that match the clouds mill about—no, they're hunting. For me. They smack clubs into their palms, yearning for violence.

With slow, silent steps, I retreat back into the thick of the woods. Darkness piles on with the rapid fall of night. I gather fallen branches still trimmed with leaves and lean them against a boulder near two tree trunks in the darkest, densest area I've found so far. I tuck myself into the angled space.

Even in the depths of the woods, I hear the murmur of voices coming closer, the crunch of footsteps, the nearing of my end. I curl up against the layer of moss on the boulder, avoiding the slices of moonlight cutting through the branches.

I'm coming for you, Kelt.

I don't know how, but I'll find him. I'll take him home and fix whatever hurt him, and I'll go back to searching for answers, for my parents. A tear rides down my cheek, and the clouds let loose above. Rain pelts the branches around me, drops trickling through and mixing with my tears, wetting my clothes.

I wait for the footsteps to fade, for the Vaile to leave and wait out the rain, but they don't. They circle closer, stirring fear in my gut. My heart says it all, clobbering my chest walls loud enough to give me away. I roll my body tight and rest my forehead on the ground of slippery leaves. I almost miss the stone walls and metal bars of the cell.

Water gushes from the dark sky rolling above me, and I fractionate into a million droplets cast in every direction. If I'm small, oh so very small, a drop of vicious rain, then maybe I can keep my feelings just as small. I try to let the water drown my thoughts as it reaches every inch of me, soaking me. My clothes hang heavy on my body. Drenched hair pulls at my scalp. The wetness, the voices, my own damn mind—they pull me into a vision.

Sypher drives his knife forward, but before the silver finds its mark in my chest, Eli launches in front of me. His groan is clipped and quiet as he collapses. I fall over him and hold on tight as warm blood soaks my knees. When I finally pull back and let go, it's no longer Eli with a knife embedded in his belly—it's Kelter.

Why? Why am I like this? I return to the wet ball I'm rolled into, the cold taking over my body with shivers and clacking teeth. Every sensation is heightened. The voices and stomping boots close in. *Go away go away go away.* Twigs snap in the other direction. I clench my jaw until my face aches, trying to keep my teeth quiet.

"Be right there, I'm going to check something out," a man's voice calls out, and one set of footsteps nears.

He sees me. I'm dead, and Kelter too. I make myself even smaller, one with the ground, the boulder, the branches, the rain—willing my body to disappear. But huge boots sink into the mud in front of my face, and the branches are pulled away. Freezing air tears over my sopping clothes, and every muscle I possess tightens under the assault. I whip my head to the side only to be slapped in the face by my wet locks, blinded. Rough arms lock around my ribs and lift, holding my back to a chest. My feet dangle. I yell, but it's smothered by an icy, wet hand.

"Look what I found," the man murmurs in my ear. "The Centress will be so pleased with me, but first—we'll have our own fun."

More cries are stifled by his hand, tears falling. My nose stuffs up, hindering each breath. I try to wiggle free, but he's one of the tall ones, easily holding me in place as I pull at his arms and kick my heels.

"Shut your mouth, Hollow, or my fist will. Nobody cares." He lets go of my mouth, flips me around and throws me over his shoulder, holding me in place with a massive hand on the back of my thigh.

My scream is hollowed from my throat, powerless, silenced. Not a word pushes past my lips, trapped with the terror in me. And with the rain pounding down, I'm back in the shower all those years ago, my foster father's voice cutting through me. *No one will ever care about you. You're a waste of space.*

I punch his back and thrash my hips, trying to wiggle off his shoulder. I need to get away. Down. Out of his grasp.

"Stop struggling." He works his hand higher up my thigh and shoves his thumb between my legs, crude fingers drilling into my ass cheek. He gives it a shake, a cruel laugh erupting from his chest as his thumb presses inward. "I'll throw you down right here and give you a real reason to move those hips."

A whimper falls short of making an actual sound when it slips from me, and I force my body to go slack, to stop fighting when all instinct tells me to do the opposite. My arms hang limply down his backside, blood gathering in my numb fingers. The man's shoulder digs into my middle with each step he takes, and the wet leaves and undergrowth of the woods go by, his heels lifting one after the other. This is it. He'll have his fucking way with me then trade me in for Kelt… and kill him.

And that's simply not okay.

I lift my free leg from his chest and slam my knee back down. He groans and clamps his hand tighter on my ass, so I do it again. And again. Until he wraps his arm around the backs of my knees, and I'm stuck.

"You little—" His body goes rigid, then sways. He grunts, and we fall from his great height, my stomach tumbling. But before we hit the ground, I'm scooped into arms.

I open my mouth to scream at the bloody knife in hand, but a cloth is rammed inside—wet and stiff and cold against the roof of my mouth. It's shoved in so far and tight that I can't spit it out. I scream anyway, a muffled cry lost in the folds of fabric. Still blinded by my hair, the arms hold me around my back and under my knees with my arms trapped, pressed to a chest as wet and cold as mine.

Before he speaks, I know him by his scent. "Quiet for once," Eli hisses. "You'll get yourself killed."

Even Eli's arms are a better option than the other man, or being on my own and hunted. I shake the hair from my eyes, and twist my neck to look back. The man lies on his stomach in the mud, a river of red running from his back, right where his heart would be. With all the loss of life in my visions, I expect the violence of a real death to hit the same, but no—it's soothing. Entrancing. Alluringly final. I shouldn't feel like this. I turn away and bury my face in Eli's chest.

He carries me through the dense trees, knife still in hand, pulling his arms so tight around me that a torrent of rainwater punches the ground, wrung from my clothes. I breathe through my nose, recovering from the fright and knowing I should still feel it even in his arms, but I don't.

"Don't you understand yet?" he scolds. I look up at him—his face dripping, curls flattened to his forehead, jaw tight. "You can't escape me."

And for this moment, that's okay if it means I'm safe.

He walks far enough that the only sound is the constant drum of rain, and the only signs of life are the beats of our hearts and breaths, rapping and riveting through me like his song.

I wiggle an arm loose. He lets me, knowing I can't get out of his hold, and trusting—I assume—I won't scream again. I pull the cloth from my mouth.

"I can walk."

His arms curl tighter around me. "I know."

My fist loosens on the cloth at his words. Does he *want* to carry me? The fabric unfolds, and it's not a cloth at all.

"You stuffed my underwear in my mouth?"

Even from this angle I can see the edges of a grin trying to surface. "I'm going to need that back."

This man. I swear. I don't know what to think.

Watching him closely, I reach my hand up to his face. He flinches, his wet brows furrowing in confusion, but he doesn't have a free arm to stop me. To keep him from tripping and sending me flying into a tree, I push the wet curls from his eyes—one side, then the other—running my fingers just above his brows. He glances at me for a mere second, drops streaking over his stubble, and I sink further into his chest with the rush of air he lets out.

He squeezes me tight again, my knee bones bumping, shoulders folding. "I could crush you." Fingers slide down my wet neck, darkness on my cheeks.

I pull his shirt snug in my fist. "Don't you understand yet?" He doesn't bother looking at me. He doesn't know that I die and die and die and always live to face another death, another vision. "I'm uncrushable."

CHAPTER 26
ELIVANDER

I carry Never's wet body, leaving the bleeding man behind us. Dead fucker. His fault for touching her.

She's mine.

My clothes cling to her soaked body. I hold her arms down to keep her from pulling the panties from her mouth. We'll be caught if she screams.

I already almost lost her.

And it terrified the fuck out of me.

Sypher was sitting on the couch, staring at her empty nook when I got to the castle. One look at his regretful face and I knew what he'd done. I've been searching the woods ever since. I didn't have to ask what she did. I know she used that perfect fucking mouth to push him over the edge, then ran. She left the castle—and me. Of course, her only thought was of Kelter. She ran to *him*.

Which is why I didn't tell her the Centress' plan for him. She would have done exactly this—find a way to leave me and nearly get herself killed. I'm not even going to punish her… though I have some tempting ideas. I only want her safely locked up so this can't happen again.

I won't let it. I need her.

She's my savior, my only chance to end this. And she hates me. Which is okay. Except every time she opens her dirty little mouth, I want to fill it. Since day one. And if she wanted it too, it would have been fine—fucking on the black floor of the cell. Up against the bars of the nook. Flipping her over the back of the couch. *That* I could handle. But this? Not a chance.

I've been a walking disaster for years. Nothing quiets the thoughts or dulls the memories. Every day I wished for true death, its permanence—until her. I've never felt so alive before. But I'm not the type of guy to give an actual fuck about a woman. Or inhale her sweet scent, fifty times more potent when she's turned on. I'll say anything to make her wet so I can breathe her in, watch her cheeks pinken over me. And I'm not the type to notice the way her teeth scrape her bottom lip for that split second when the word *fuck* comes out of her mouth, longer when she's pissed. But I do.

I refuse to look down as she tucks her face against me, nuzzling dangerously close to my heart. I swear it'll jump out of my chest to get to her. How is she feisty as fuck on the outside and soft on the inside? She grew up in Caldera, not here, where we're beaten and tortured as kids. She shouldn't be so... troubled. I want to split her open and patch every hole in her fragile little heart.

And it's not okay.

Why the fuck is she doing this to me? She's wrecking everything. It's not only that one look at her makes me hard with nowhere to put it. It's worse. She's got me wrapping her up in my arms under the guise of shooting a slingshot. And giving her teva to stop those pretty tears. And I never should have taken her upstairs, shown her my house, my past, my life from before.

Because I have to focus on finding the right trigger. *I have to.*

But she's such a godsdamn distraction.

I can barely remember what I'm supposed to be doing when she misbehaves—giving me that look, her little nose scrunched up, dead set on not doing what I say. She's so damn defiant... strong in ways no one else is.

And those eyes.

Shit.

I'm so fucked. I have one thing to do, one thing I need. *Her.*

But it's more than that.

It's the way she puts on a brave face for everything as though she's been through so much worse—fucking fearless. It's that faraway look in her eyes when she seems to disappear inside her mind, and how I can't turn away—how it feels like, if I just look long enough, she'll let me in. And it's the way she sees me like no one else does, how she talks back and tries so hard to stay mad, pretending she doesn't crave my cock, that she hates me as much as she believes I hate her. It's her determination, that fire in her… and how she smells my blanket when she thinks I'm not looking. That's what has me wanting to lock her up only for me and keep her forever.

No, I won't let her get away.

I'll wrap her in chains to ensure her safety—and for fun too. She'd love it. I'll do anything. I grip my knife and squeeze her tight. *Anything.*

"Don't you understand yet?" I say, raindrops sliding into my mouth. She unburies her face to look up at me with stunning eyes, not a lick of fear in them. "You can't escape me." *Because I couldn't handle it.*

Her body relaxes against mine, motionless, except for her tiny shivers. I hold her close, so close, as I walk on and on in the pouring rain.

We're deep into the woods when she tugs one arm loose and removes the panties from her mouth. She won't scream again. She may not be too pleased with me, but she doesn't want to end up back in the Centress' hands.

"I can walk," she says, her voice soft, a hint of that defiance.

I pull her even closer. "I know." *But I can't seem to let go.*

From the corner of my eye, I see her—watching me much too closely. A curious look, those indigo eyes wide, wet lashes framing them. Maybe I gave away too much with two words. I continue on, the speechless seconds heavy and foreign without her usual backtalk—until I'm caught.

"You stuffed my underwear in my mouth?"

It's hardly the fierce tone I'd expect… almost amused. I smile. She's so tired she forgot to act pissed. I grow harder at the thought of pumping my cock with her spit-soaked panties. "I'm going to need that back."

I lift my chin, set on holding back all emotion, but then her hand is on my face. I startle and look straight ahead. *Don't react. It's for the best.* But her fingers run over my eyebrows, dragging the curls from either side of my forehead, and I crack.

I look at her. Our eyes catch. Only one second and my breath is taken from me.

Godsdammit.

She's breaking me. I hug her tight. Doesn't she see that I can't control my own hands, my own strength?

"I could crush you," I say, barely able to breathe. I would never.

But I can't let her want me. I can't want her. It's too risky.

And too late.

I haven't had a reason to breathe for years, and I sure as fuck haven't so much as mentioned my father to anyone else since... that day. But there's something about her I can't resist. Something that makes me want to strangle anyone that breathes near her. And it's something more than wanting to strip her down and throw her on my bed, ass in the air, and make her scream my name and claw the sheets while I devour her from behind—though that too.

I see the way she looks at me, hear her heart fighting in her chest. And all that sweet talk, every swear word that rolls off her tempting little tongue... I know she'd want me to do all the things to her that I've imagined. And that's the problem. I can't get her out of my head. And I hate it. She destroys me, like a fucking tumor taking over my heart.

I spend too many hours watching her sleep and picturing myself kissing away her tiny tears and holding her through the nightmares. And worst of all, I wonder what it would be like if she cared about me, if she craved my company, my arms. And if it wasn't a lie. But she can't know what she does to me, the obsession she's become. It has to stay in my head with all the other shit I have to hide.

It's simple. I stick with the triggers, and I force her to figure it out. She *will* obey me—I own her, every impeccable inch.

And I fight this. I don't let her in, don't let her know *she's* the one who owns *me*. I push her away, make her hate me more—keeping my distance, pissing her off... and letting whatever's left of my conscience go black to match what's inside.

So I've got issues.

But I'd spend a million lifetimes fighting for her, making her mine over and over—if it wouldn't ruin us both.

I'm hanging on her every breath when she works my wet shirt into her fist, pulling it to her chest. "Don't you understand yet?" she says.

I can't look at her again. I might do something I'll regret. Something like I almost did last night while holding her against the wall, her face flushed and heated, lips red.

I feel her eyes on me as she tightens her grip on my shirt. "I'm uncrushable."

Maybe so, little Never, but I won't let a single fucker touch you and find out.

CHAPTER 27
EVER

Over six weeks without coffee, without looking in a mirror. I haven't seen the scar across my throat, marking my arrival in Sonnet, or the ones on my neck and back, the blitzer's final lashing before freedom. What would I see if I did have a mirror? Rosy nose and cheeks from the constant cold? A stranger peering back at me, my indigo eyes no longer mine? Is this foreign feeling that lurks beneath my skin and seeps out my pores visible on my face, coating my skin with a mask that others mistake for me?

Eli refuses to rescue Kelter and is even less willing to turn me over in exchange for him. He won't let me go—not when I haven't pulled magic like he wants. He carried me all the way back to the castle from the woods, his protective arms never tiring, walked me straight into his five-walled bedroom and set my wet body on his bed. *You'll sleep here*, he said, *where no one can get to you but me*, then plucked the underwear from my hand and pocketed it. He gave me a dry shirt and a pair of his pants and assured me nobody else had a lock stone for his room, that I was safe. I looked at him for a long time, so long that I could see panic multiplying in his eyes with every passing second, then he turned away. I changed out of my wet clothes while he stared at the dark wall.

Every night this past week, he sat against his locked bedroom door, flipping his lucky stone and guarding, like in the black room. On the fourth night, I lay awake, waiting, eyes open only a sliver. I curled my toes to keep my feet from bouncing. A single light stone in the far corner granted a dim glow to the room. Two hours of silence passed, and he hadn't so much as yawned, but his eyes remained open... and on me. I made sure not to move, letting him think I had fallen asleep.

Are you going to stare at me all night? he asked.

Damn. How could he tell? *I'm waiting to see what you do with my underwear,* I admitted. He stood up and left the room, slamming the door behind him. His body smacked into it a second later, followed by a sliding sound over the stone, and I could almost see him through the door—sitting in the hallway, guarding grumpily and reaching for his pocket.

But most nights he played his drums through the late hours, loose and free, the words to his songs rocking me to sleep and the frenzied beat working its way into my dreams. Every morning, he left me locked safely inside, fast asleep and sinking deep into his giant bed with black pillows and blankets around me like a nest. I've never slept in anything this nice before—it even has a sheet. And the whole thing smells like his blanket. Like him.

Then I woke up to a bucket of soapy water, fresh clothes and a pile of ten bars of different flavors to choose from. And a note. Always a note. I might, maybe, possibly think he's trying to be nice—not simply keep me alive.

But despite the new comforts, he took me out to the clearing in the evenings, trying new tactics to trigger my supposed ability to take magic from plants. Each night ended in my failure to make anything happen—and his heavy sighs and stomping boots.

He's been irritable since I was let go. I'm not sure what he said to him, but Sypher won't even glance at me and has a scared look on his face when Eli walks me down the hallway, through the main room and out the hatchway to the clearing each evening. Sypher spends his time throwing knives while Milo keeps himself occupied by lying on the castle floor and staring at the unfinished ceiling for hours—except the days that he paces in infinite circles, rubbing his hands together and murmuring about his sisters.

Kaleida comes by every day and tells me stories about Sonnet and Vaile from before the Separation, always harping on the flow and balance of magic and incorporating something about the gods to sway my disbelieving mind. She shares her predictions for the gifts each of them will receive and who she thinks will link with who, and I listen, whether I want to or not, sitting with her in the clearing before facing my triggers. She seems harmless, even nice, but that's not enough to thaw a hint of trust in me.

166

I spent the week moody, off-kilter from the unexplained bed and piles of bars, and worried about Kelter. I tried to ignore the rising rage every time I thought of how Eli didn't bother to tell me about him being offered as a reward for my capture. That's probably what Sola meant by *doesn't she know?*

They all knew.

The hours we spend together and the luxury of a bed don't change the reality that I'm a prisoner.

I've started a new collection of notes in Eli's bedroom, a messy stack on his nightstand. I stare at the latest addition atop the change of clothes and pile of bars on the end of the bed. Not once have I had it in me not to read it. Today is no exception.

Never,
Use it... before it gets cold. I'll be back for you soon.
Eli

Use what? But I find out soon enough when I dip my hands into the water bucket. It's warm, teeming with light green soap bubbles.

He actually took the time to give me warm water.

Unable to contain myself a second longer, I strip, removing the ring and blue stone from my bra and setting them on the nightstand. I'm lost in the decadence, washing from head to toe. The cold hits seconds after, but it's worth it. Shivering, I pick up the dry outfit, and a wooden comb falls to the floor, landing in front of my bare knees. I have to poke my finger on each fat tooth to believe it's real. Swimming in the excess fabric of his clothes, I wash my underwear, socks and bra and drape them over his drums to dry.

Eli arrives after his shift, unbuttoning his blue jumpsuit as he assesses the room. A breeze circles my body and swirls down my legs, fresh like the dew of dawn, invisible lightness emanating from him. He stares at me, sitting on the edge of his bed and working through the tangles in my hair, then his eyes travel to my underclothes taking over his drum set. He raises a hand to his ear, tugging and twisting the lobe with anxious fingers.

I lower the comb and slide off the bed, stepping closer to him, to this man who has me puzzling over him. "What's waiting for me in the clearing tonight?"

He glances down at my braless chest and quickly finds the floor to look at instead—no smirk, no lewd comment, no attempt to claim a second pair of underwear.

Something's wrong.

"Nothing. Put your *things* back on. We're going up to the house." He grabs a white shirt, pants and something like boxers for himself and closes me inside his room.

I put my damp clothes on under the dry ones and return to the nightstand for my treasures, sneaking a jade button out of his drawer and tucking it into my bra.

He opens the door and shoves a bar at me. "Eat on the way."

We stand in the grand shelf-lined room again, the house motionless and quiet, the unspoken stories written on the walls as heated and charged as the air between us. I still can't look at him without thinking of Kelter. And his hand on my bloody neck. The scarlet soda's forced desire. His song that stole my escape. And feeling and seeing and hearing all that at once—it paralyzes me. So I try not to look.

Eli circles the room, head dipped, watching me. His white shirt takes on the warm tones of the room, and the remaining daylight slips through the missing shingles on the roof.

"Aren't we going to start?" I ask, my breaths stumbling with nerves over the next trigger.

"Patience, my little prisoner. I'm waiting for something."

Great. Very specific. Such an impressive tolerance for the torturously slow passage of time.

My damp socks make my feet cold inside my boots, so I take them off, gambling on the room not turning into a furnace again, and dig my toes into the carpet. The fibers tickle and rub against that rarely touched skin as I follow the shelves, inspecting the trinkets on the walls. I arch and roll my feet every time I stop to pick up a new item, turning it over in my hands and poking at buttons and springs and knobs and gears that remind me of Caldera. Then I spot a tiny silver key—a real one, not a stone. And simply to have a little piece of home, I wait until the staircase is between us and add it to my treasures.

After four laps he calls to me from across the expanse of the room. "Is that a Hollow thing?"

"What?" *Did he see me?*

"Your feet."

It comes back to me with such ease that I startle at the memory—my bare feet slapping the stretch of sidewalk between Kelter's place and mine, rough and cold and puddled from the night rain, my arms outstretched, fingers tapping the glass store windows on my way by. *You're wild,* he told me with a grin when I showed up at his door, toes exposed and wet to my knees, windswept hair. I hid his shoes and dragged him out the door, his jeans cuffed much too high above his ankles. Anyone else in Caldera would have been appalled. Not Kelter.

"Maybe. Try it." I trace my finger along the shelf, focusing on anything but him and avoiding the surge of thoughts. It's strange to walk freely like this after so much time locked up, cuffed or held tight in his grasp.

"No." His jaw falls open a notch. "I don't go barefoot." He crosses the room, and the sofa sighs under him as he sits—stiff, back straight, knees at ninety degree angles.

"You could." I flop down on the opposite end of the sofa. "Are we just going to sit here?"

"For the moment."

My knees bounce, hands squirming in my lap. The room dims as night approaches. Pink-orange rays of dusk beam into the room from the shambly ceiling above, but Eli carries that light aura tonight, warming the space.

"Why are you sitting like that?" I ask, holding my hair down as that breeze of his sweeps over me.

"Like what?" He looks down, then at me, and I make the mistake of looking back. It all comes rushing in—the blood, the desire, the song. I can't move on the sofa, even as the cushions ripple under my bottom and up my back.

His hand raps his thigh, soft, ceaseless taps.

"Like you're in pain."

He sits there quite the same, tight and stuck, tapping away, so I sit here too, unable to move, long enough to notice the tapping is a beat, a drum, a song without words, and slowly—*slowly*, it unfreezes me.

It could be because he carried me away from that awful man and the Vaile hunting me, or the way he held that girl through her final moments, or the bed and buckets and bars, or it could be that it hurts to look at pain, even his. Like a chisel driving slowly through my chest, closer to cracking with every strike. It could be that, or the inexplicable lightness pulling me toward him—or not—but something quiet and fearless shifts in me. I rise from the sofa, my movements smooth like a flower unfolding in the dead of night.

He watches me, side-eyed, glaring at my every step.

"You're stiffer than an old man." I push him down against the corner of the sofa, my hands on his chest not my own—I'd never. "Like you haven't gotten off in years… but we know that's not the case."

His eyes flicker and widen, and I don't miss the relocation of his hand, the light squeeze of the fabric bulge in his pocket.

"What are you doing?" he growls, but lets himself fall back.

"It's painful to look at you." I tuck my hands behind his calves and lift his legs onto the length of the sofa.

His eyes dart around, surprise stealing any chance of resistance. I sit down next to his feet. "What was your father like?" As if my hands don't belong to me, I pull at the laces of his boots.

His forehead creases. "Like me."

"And your mother?"

"No."

"No?"

He doesn't answer, so I move on. "Then tell me why you need me to take magic. Aren't you going to get a link and a gift of your own magic soon?" I untie the laces, wiggle off his boots and toss them to the carpet. He glances my way, two ruinous brown eyes, so ruinous that I slide under his feet and plop them onto my lap.

His whole body jerks in response. His hands grip the sofa, and the shelves quake, a single jolt gone so fast, leaving only the lingering clangor of metal parts.

"You're misbehaving." His voice is gravelly and forced, full of warning and threat, but his legs stay right on top of my lap. The room darkens another shade.

"Are you going to stop me?" I reach inside his pant leg, ease my fingers under the edge of his sock and inch it downward.

Every muscle in his leg contracts, tightening into rock-hard swells and divots against the feathering of my ringed fingers. He sits forward, terror all over his face, the angles sharp enough to slice me open.

I peel off a sock and chuck it over my shoulder.

His chest fills and empties, deeper and deeper. "Don't make me," he says with the threat of a storm. The shelves and doors and furniture become mere shadows around us as night slinks its way across the room.

"Make you what?"

I fling his other sock behind the sofa.

This man—*this man* who is always ready, always dressed, pockets full, knife sheathed, boots on all night guarding the door—his bare feet on my lap, his skin, the veins, that ankle bone. Maybe it breaks something in me.

I blow on his toes.

Then something cracks in him too.

He slams his feet back down to the floor, and he's up, towering above me, his face bent with fury. He lifts me, hands under my arms, turns us around and propels us toward the wall. My feet slide and stumble over the carpet, trying to keep up with his long strides. It's only seconds before my back smacks flat against a wooden door between the shelves.

His arms cage me, his chest heaving in my face. My heart stutters, and I tilt my head back and look up at him. His eyes—deeper than invisible scars. He looks straight into me, *seeing* me.

I should be afraid of this man, of his temper, his hands. But no. I want to know more. So slowly, I creep my big toes into his, the tips touching. Our breath mingles. We look down at our barely visible toes, at the contact, at the shrunken space between us.

He drops one arm from the door and his fingers brush my cheek, so forcibly soft and trembling, as though he's afraid of his own touch.

His nose wrinkles in the most perfect way. "My toes itch."

I'm about to laugh when he looks up at the last of the dim light being consumed by the night, as if he were waiting for it this whole time, and that's it. He flips. His fingers sink into my arm. He yanks me away from the door, throws it open and thrusts me inside. Remorse flashes across his face, only a twinge before—

"Trigger time." He slams the door shut. Me inside. Him outside.

Chapter 28

The lock clicks, and pitch darkness crowds me. I blink to make sure my eyes are open. Still dark. So, so dark. It smells like wet, rotting wood and mold. I feel the walls—smooth to my left and right, and rough like the bark of a tree behind me—only inches away. I can't spread my elbows out at my sides. A damn closet. With no way out. No light. No end. My control unravels, spiraling me into a vision. A vision without sight.

Darkness walks up me, cold and damp on bare skin. Wet, deathly kisses. All the way up my legs, my belly, my chest, my neck—then pure blackness pries open my mouth and crams itself down my throat. It spreads like roots, growing until it reaches my mind, an inescapable insistence with a silent, cruel laugh, leaking into every thought. And destroying me.

I scream.

Life slams back into me, thickening the darkness and tingling over my skin.

I bang my hands flat on the door.

"Elivander!"

My fists pound.

"Let me out!"

Only silence answers, and I can't stop the memories from surfacing.

The small dark pantry. The hours I spent there.

The threats. *You go into that forest one more time, you'll be in here for a week.*

The judgments. *What's wrong with you, child? Always asking questions. Always wandering off. Don't you understand there's nothing out there?*

The cries, *my* cries. Unanswered.

"Elivander, damn you. Open the fucking door!"

He could be gone. Back underground in the castle. He could leave me here as long as he wants.

I drop to the floor, wooden planks with notches and splinters that poke through my pants. Sitting with my knees tucked and my back to a side wall, I hold my necklace and count. Out loud. Like I did as a little girl in that pantry, locked away by my foster mother. I count to a thousand, endless strings of numbers, over and over, losing track of how many times.

Hours pass.

Then I hear it. A *creak* outside the closet.

"Open this door!" I cry.

I stand up and kick it with my bare foot. Pain rips through my toes, and I kick it again. And again and again. The door rattles against the frame.

My foot stills, and my voice quiets. The dank darkness wraps me up tighter in its wispy tendrils, breathing with me.

So softly I whisper, "It's dark in here." Hot tears fall, and I sob. I'm so fucking sick of crying, sick of the dark and the pain and the locked doors.

"It's dark out here too." Eli's voice drifts under the slightest sliver of space beneath the door, a consoling tone cracking with regret, with pain.

My chest collapses, and I wonder if that look on his face while waiting on the sofa was the pain of knowing what he was about to do, if a part of him was fighting it.

"What do you want from me?" I ask.

The softness is gone. His words strike me. "You want light? Make it." His body flattens against the door with a swish of fabric, a whine of wood. "Use the tree."

It *is* a tree. The house is built right up against it, one with nature.

He smacks the door, and the sound claps into the black around me. And as if to keep me from feeling alone, those fingers, those cold, probing fingers find the nape of my neck and every bone of my spine. They spread out, following my ribs, mapping their way around me, hugging and holding me, and I don't shiver. I don't shudder. I relax into them, my head against the tree.

I move my hands to my sides and press them to the bark. And I try. For me, for him—I don't know, but I really try. I lay out a blank canvas in my mind, like the start of a new map, and search for new paths, connections, a surge of life—anything between the tree and me.

I can almost feel them, stretching and searching, splitting and splicing anew. The comfort of my forest back home reaches for me, the pine on the wind, the snapping of branches, but walls stand between us—walls constructed with bricks of betrayal, layered with rejection, coated in pain and dusted with shame—and I can't get through. I can't make light in the dark, can't pull magic past my walls. I stab my fingers into the tree. I try over and over.

Nothing. Not a glimmer of light.

I push myself away from the tree and into the door, the side of my head flush with the wood. "I can't do it. Let me out."

The vibrations of his deep voice roll through my ear pressed to the door. "We have all night. Try again."

My blood heats and hurtles through me. "I'm done!" I scream and punch the door. Pain cleaves through my knuckles. "I'm not trying again. You're getting nothing from me. You push and you push, and you give me nothing. You tell me nothing. I have no reason to do anything for you." *Give me a fucking reason because maybe*—just maybe—*I might want to help.*

A growl grazes my cheek through the wood. "And what about your friend?"

How dare he?

"Let him die," I bluff and spin my rings, letting him think he's lost the only control over me. "There isn't a chance anyway. They'll kill us both." And that part feels real. Too real.

The door moans under the force of his body slamming into it. "You are *not* done trying. Friend or not, you'll do what I say."

"*You* don't decide. You can rip me open, take my blood and pump me with fear, and I still don't have to do what you say." I can hardly hear myself screaming over the crashing beat in my ears. Darkness tramples me from all directions. I throw myself into the door. "You control where I am, who I see, my food, the damn fabric that covers my ass"—I lower my scream to a whisper—"but you don't control *me*, Elivander."

The door flings open. Eli stands before me, basking in the moonbeams, so bright compared to the pitch-black closet.

I don't know which one of us attacks first. Our bodies collide and spill to the crimson carpet, his back flat to the floor and my body stretched over him, legs between his. I scowl down and ram my hands into his chest, my elbows locked. "*You.*"

My fingers curl, nails digging into his shirt. I put all my strength into it, and as though I'm no more than a slight nuisance, he moves his hands to my wrists and slowly lifts them away from his rolling chest before I draw blood. Fuck. I *want* him to bleed, to be vulnerable to my touch. I want to do to him what he claims no one can, exposing that hidden piece of him and taking it for myself.

"*You,*" he says, holding me suspended over him. Despite his labored breathing, his expression is tight, controlled. Every feature of mine, raging with emotion, is locked in place on his face, but he doesn't have to show his fury—I can feel it. In the solid muscles beneath me, in the way he pinches my wrists, the squeeze of his legs on mine.

"Fuck, Never, I'm trying," he forces out. "But it's pointless. You can't see... you never will. And I don't know what I'm supposed to say to you, how to do this. I only—"

He stops mid-sentence with a heaving breath, and I'm not sure if those vulnerable words are about triggers... or something else. My arms wobble with fatigue, and I crumple down onto him, panting, my cheek pressed against the cool white shirt on his chest. He releases my wrists upon impact, and my hands fall loose at his shoulders. Defeated. Wrecked by rage. And so fucking confused. My body rises and falls with the air he breathes in a comforting rhythm I can't explain.

"It's *Ever,*" I seethe through the hair on my face, trying to hold on to my anger.

He's still for the longest time, or maybe only seconds. Maybe time stopped. Then his hands are at my sides, cold and broad, encompassing so much of me. In a single effortless roll, I'm flipped on my back and he's on top of me, arms locked, hands above my shoulders.

Our hip bones kiss.

He looks down at me with those soul-stealing eyes, taking me in, hair strewn across my face. His lips squinch into a rosy ring, and a breeze travels over my heated features, taking the hair away with it—a real breeze. He's too bloody gentle, the caress of air too soothing to escape.

"I only know I need you," he says, low and breathy. His hips slide higher, and with the movement comes pressure, right between my legs, his hard length dragging against me.

My full body reacts, betraying me, flooded with sensation—hot and racing—and I focus all my effort on not pushing my hips up into his. But I can't stop my legs from parting, my thighs moving to either side of him as his body drops between them.

He folds himself over me and slides my arms straight above my head, pinning them down, pressing until my muscles rearrange against the bones. He has my body accommodating for him, needing him, craving his harsh touch. His chest mounts and crashes like a wave, shoving all the air out of me and giving me his. *I'm mad at this man*, I remind myself, but it does nothing to prevent my back from arching, pressing me into him.

His face is an inch away, eyes overflowing with desire. A small smirk surrounded by stubble finds its way to his mouth before he tucks his head next to mine.

"Are you going to stop me?" he rasps into my ear, using my words against me.

My lips part, but my voice fails to surface.

"I didn't think so." He rolls his hips into me, his cock smashing between my lower lips and sending me into a fit of unchecked rapture.

"Fuck," I whisper, long and drawn out like the spell of euphoria still resonating through my core, wetting me so thoroughly.

Now my voice works?

He manifests the lowest chuckle from deep in his chest, reveling in the way he has me at his mercy. I convince myself I don't feel teeth tugging at my earlobe, frosty lips dragging down my cheek. I can't do the same when his slow motion and long breaths shift into the sudden angling of his head. He bites my jaw like a starved beast, teeth and tongue on my skin. Pain and pleasure collide and anchor at my slick center.

His scent pulls me into the darkest depths of the earth, burying me in him. I let out an awful sound, somewhere between a moan and a squeal, all command of myself lost in lust. I'm light and heavy at once, desire and denial battling for the upper hand. Then his lips hover over my mouth.

And it's excruciating. "Are you going to kiss me or bite me again? Pick one and get the fuck on with it."

He smashes his palms into my arms. "Give me a godsdamn minute."

His cagey eyes fixed on mine, he drops lower, his closeness pushing past the loneliness, filling the holes in my heart and mending the scars on my soul. My thighs squeeze his sides, and I clutch the carpet fibers in my fists.

A minute is a fucking eternity.

Hot air warms my face. Shaky, hungry breaths. His lips brush mine, the lightest touch of skin on skin, of him and me.

Then something inside him snaps. He pulls back, eyes flaring.

I stare into his growing pupils until his words seep into my consciousness, tearing me away from the false escape. His face contorts with alarm. "Get your boots. We're going."

"Are you fucking kidding me?"

He releases my arms and climbs off, his bare feet brushing over my bruised toes. A rush of cold air cushions the blow. Confusion and anger crisscross his forehead. His huge figure stands over me, one hand adjusting his stiff cock. "Now."

I stay flat on the floor, breathing through the internal chaos and trying to calm my dueling heart while Eli paces around the room, hands laced atop his head.

Chapter 29

The polished moons give off more light than made it through the shingles of the house. We work our way through the dense trees, moving southeast. The night air numbs my nose and ears, and the wind picks up, swirling around me while I run through the earlier events.

I'm not surprised that Eli acts like he wants me, only to pull away and toss me aside. That's what happens once someone gets a glimpse of the real me. *Put up your walls, hun,* Cam would say. *No one wants to see what's behind them.*

But I don't know what possessed me to take off that man's boots, or what part of me insists on noticing every shift in his face, every ripple of muscle. What part makes me want to take him apart and know everything about him.

Milo, Kaleida and Sypher were in the castle when we returned from the house, red-faced and out of breath. They walk with us now, all in their jumpsuits and boots.

"You should have left her at the castle. It's not safe," Milo says, his long legs easily keeping up with Eli's pace. "Someone could see her."

"Nobody ever crosses the ravine," Eli says, pulling me along by my arm.

"But they could." Kaleida places a hand on his broad shoulder, an affectionate touch. "We're not under the protection of your house anymore."

"I know," he says. "I need a godsdamn break from that place and that fucking clearing."

For once, I agree with him, despite the painful steps that make me regret kicking the door.

Milo pushes forward and steps in front of Eli. The usual softness of his face is gone, his golden brows angled, lips thin. "Take her back, Eli. You'll regret this."

Eli tugs me to his side. "I'm not leaving her behind for someone to let loose again." He gives Sypher a pointed look with the darkest of eyes and shoves past Milo.

No one questions him again.

A half hour later, Eli passes me off to Kaleida, and I peer over the edge of a ravine. Trees on both sides lean inward, branches and foliage overlapping in the center and creating a ceiling along the length of the ravine as far as I can see. A frothy torrent claps against the steep banks below. It's breathtaking—and a tad terrifying after only seeing city streets and the forest my whole life.

"Eli may be reckless, as usual, but at least you're getting out," Kaleida says, surveying the view.

"He doesn't seem reckless to me, more… calculated." I look up at the stars, and Kelter invades my thoughts. How many nights did we climb the metal ladder to the roof of my room and curse at the stars? How many nights has it been since he's seen them? Will I ever see him again?

"He has no regard for his life and makes rash decisions, like stealing a prisoner without a plan."

"And you go along with it."

"He's Eli." Kaleida catches me staring up at the night sky, and her tone softens. "I'm glad you're with us, and not the Centress."

My gaze drops from the sky to her, then I turn away, not knowing how to respond, and there's Eli—white shirt and black pants, suspenders fastened and slingshot hanging out of his back pocket—scaling a tree like a child. He's fearless. He climbs fifteen feet to the first large limb extending out over the gaping emptiness and proceeds to slink out onto it, reaching all the way to the center of the ravine before returning to the trunk of the tree and shimmying down with a hefty rope in his hand, braided and frayed.

"Who's first?" he says, catching my eye.

"Oh, that's me." Milo steps forward and wraps his legs around the fat triple knot at the end of the rope.

"What is he *doing*?" I hiss at Kaleida.

"Crossing."

My stomach clenches at the thought of sailing over the death drop below. Eli pulls the rope as far back from the edge as he can, holding it by a thinner rope tied around the knot. Step after step, he moves deeper into the thick of the trees, then releases it. The rope sails out over the ravine with Milo clinging to it and howling into the night, the thinner rope whipping in the wind. He reaches the opposite side and lets go, free falling into the darkness behind the line of trees.

I let out the breath that I was holding, the thrill rushing over me despite my two feet planted safely on the ground.

"Who's next?" Eli says, grinning as he reels in the smaller rope until the knot is back within reach.

Sypher goes next, then Kaleida after handing me back to Eli. Their successful trips don't calm the even fatter knot tying in my stomach.

Eli holds the rope out to me. "You're up."

"I'm not getting on that thing." With all the visions of falling to my death over the years, nothing could make me clamp my legs around that rope.

"Yes, you are. Sypher is terrified of heights, and he does it." He lowers his voice a notch. "I mean, it took him three years to work up the balls, but…" He trails off when he sees the look on my face, a hint of a smirk jesting at the side of his mouth.

"I will not be working up any *balls* tonight."

"Not even mine?" He straddles the knot, one hand holding the rope, the other pulling me toward him.

"No, you—" I lose sensation. A vision hits, flashing and slashing through my brain.

My fingers slipping. My silent scream. The rushing air deafening me. The ground nearing with sickening speed. The tumbling and diving of my stomach.

More visions hit fast, one after another. Eli frees my arm and swoops his own around my waist. The feel of his hand flexing on my side calls me back. I shred through the vision and open my eyes to find him inches from my face. But it fights its way back in. I slip away again, watching myself from above.

Impact. Bones cracking. Air forced from me. My mangled body in the rocky river. My eyes staring into nothingness, staring at me. Then Kelt appears, doubled over in grief.

I grip Eli's hand on my waist, harder and harder, trying to squeeze the vision from my mind. I keep his eyes captive until the remaining flashes let up. He stares back, unblinking.

And I'm not alone.

Life after death—I feel everything. My senses attack. Eli releases the rope and raises a hand to my face. I jerk my head back, but his slow advance is unfaltering, space slipping away inch by inch. He runs a cold thumb down my cheek then pulls it away, inspecting the wetness.

A tear.

He sucks his thumb into his mouth and pops it back out. "Hold me tight," he whispers, then grabs the rope, backs up and launches us over the ravine.

I hike my legs up and around his waist, anchoring them in place with crossed ankles, and hurl my arms around his shoulders. He's as cold as the night air biting my face. Here, with one arm wrapped around me—one that held my arms above my head only hours ago—soaring over a lethal drop, clinging to as much of him as I can, I'm torn. I'm torn between an illogical sense of safety and freedom, and fear and shame for the way he cracks me open… and the way I embrace every splintering strike. I bury my head in the crook of his neck and curse at him as my stomach somersaults all the way across.

"Let go," he yells.

The words make it past the wind lashing at my ears, and I coerce my limbs to surrender the body they cling to. Eli unravels himself from the rope, and we fall together, landing on our feet. I open my eyes. Kaleida, Milo and Sypher are in front of me, the latter ripping me apart with his glare.

Eli turns to whisper in my ear, "You're on your own on the way back." My stomach plummets.

"I've never heard that many curse words strung together before," Milo says with one of his all-consuming smiles. He ties the rope to a nearby tree, and Eli guides us deeper into the woods, his arm still tight around my waist.

Kaleida and Sypher walk ahead, and Milo takes up Eli's other side, smoking a roll and hopping about as he walks.

"You should know…" he says to Eli in a cautious tone. "They're sending me to the teva fields almost every day now."

"You're still working on the new elixir?"

"No. It's ready."

"Then what do they have you doing in the fields?"

Milo is quiet for a long moment. "Mass production."

Eli's hand tightens on my arm. "I thought it was only for emergencies."

"That was what the Centress said, but the storage huts are full and they've started filling the overflow storage too." Milo hands the lit roll to Eli.

"They're going to make the switch at Caldera Falls," Eli says, a harsh breath leaving his lungs before inhaling the teva.

"Switch what?" I ask. The falls are Caldera's water source and shouldn't have anything to do with Sonnet.

"That's the only explanation. They have more than they've ever stored before. I thought you'd want to know because of…" Milo leans forward and tilts his head at me, not at all discreetly.

"How strong is it?" Eli asks, letting out a puff of purple that rises into the gray sky.

"Potent."

"How potent?"

"At least ten times stronger." Milo hesitates. "I tried it on Sypher."

"You drugged Sypher?"

"Only a couple times. I had to give him a ton to get it to work at the same level as it would for a Hollow."

"What elixir, and what about the falls?" I ask. Eli's lightness is back again, pulling me in and letting the questions roll off my tongue.

"Can't she walk ahead of us for a bit?" Milo asks under his breath. He takes the roll back from Eli, finishing it off with a deep inhalation.

"No, she'll run off. She doesn't obey me at all."

"But you had to bring her instead of leaving her locked up?" Milo mocks, obscured behind a cloud of purple.

"Yes."

"Stop ignoring me," I yell.

Milo twists his mouth to the side, his nose scrunching. "Maybe she shouldn't hear this. She seems a bit fragile."

Eli serves a quick glance in my direction. "She's not. At all."

"I see. You know you have to be careful with—"

"That's not a problem." Eli tilts his head, grabbing his ear. "I have it under control."

"You can only control your side," Milo says, stopping and gripping Eli's upper arm. "If she falls, her blood's on you. And clearly she sees—"

Eli pulls out of Milo's grasp and faces him. "She won't."

"I won't what? Fall from the rope?" I ask, trying to pull away from Eli. "What's happening at Caldera Falls?"

They look at one another, then back at me, Eli's face crimped with indecision.

"It's not like she can go back home after all this and say something," Milo says.

I nearly faint. Of course I've seen too much, but hearing him say it, knowing I'll never be allowed to return to Caldera, never find my parents, that I'll probably end up dead within a month—it's too much for my cracking mind.

Eli tugs up on my arm to keep me from collapsing and gives Milo a nod of permission.

He paces in circles around us. "The Centress is going to replace the current elixir used in the falls with my invention of a freewill sedative made from the core of teva flowers. It was supposed to be an elixir for emergency medical procedures only, but she's having us produce much more than that."

I can barely process his words. "What current elixir?"

"We've used a simple elixir in the Calderan water supply since the Separation. The dose is sent to the falls every day in a carriage to keep the level high enough. It dulls Hollows' curiosity and promotes ignorant obedience, the usual, but this new elixir is something else. There won't be any awareness left."

My past slips out from under me as I choke out words. "You've been drugging us through our water supply for hundreds of years?"

"Not us." Milo holds up his hands in innocence. "The centresses over the years, to keep Hollows from getting curious enough to wander across the border and drain Sonnet of its magic."

I turn to Eli. "Like me?"

"I suppose."

He *supposes*? "Do you realize how fucking terrible that is? I've been drugged into complacency my whole life and forced to cooperate with whatever the Centress wants?"

Eli raises two dark brows at me from beneath his ringlets. "You are anything but cooperative."

"And it's the same as the rolls? You gave it to me to control me?"

Milo gives me a big smile on his way by, still circling. "No, no. The rolls are made with teva petals, not the core."

"And now she's going to give us something even stronger? What for?" I ask, dizzied by Milo's incessant pacing.

"I've heard rumors that they're changing it because the Centress doesn't want this happening again, but the stockpiling started before the intrusion," Milo says.

"You mean my abduction and imprisonment in a foreign realm?" Neither of them respond. "Doesn't the Calderan water make it back to Sonnet?"

"So many questions. You must love that." Milo slaps Eli on the shoulder.

A smile hides behind his scowl. "It does make it back to Sonnet, but it would take more than twenty times the potency to even start to have an effect on Vaile."

"That's why it's for emergency use," Milo adds. "It takes an extremely concentrated dose to work on us because of the magic we hold. We're almost resistant."

I try to speak, but the thought of me and everyone I've ever known living behind a facade my entire life pulls me under, along with the realization that Kelter and I still drink that tainted water, even here in Sonnet.

Is every action I take controlled by the elixir? Not a fate of my own? I feel like I'm choosing, but how much more could I have done if my mind were fully mine?

Or maybe it doesn't work on my vision-afflicted, broken mind. Maybe this is why I was the only foster child interested in finding my parents, why I couldn't stay away from the forest, curious enough to question what lies beyond Caldera.

CHAPTER 30

I've never seen a lake. I told Kelter a million times how I plan to explore beyond the forest and find the edges of the land, and he promised I would one day. I made it out of Caldera, but now I'm stuck here. Kaleida, Sypher and Milo swim in the lake I face, splashing and laughing and dunking each other's heads beneath the dark surface, as if they didn't live here... where everything is forbidden and nothing is their choice.

I pull my arm from Eli's grasp, unsuccessfully. "Are you going to tote me around like an appendage all night?"

His eyes turn to slits. "Yes."

"You really think I can outrun any of you?" I set my gaze on the large rocks on the shore that would certainly break my ankles if I tried to run, then on the shadowy woods behind me.

"Are you suggesting I chase you and find out? Maybe you'd like to see what happens when I catch you."

I breathe away the scandalous thoughts his words give rise to... him tackling me to the ground, my body pinned, those vengeful hands claiming triumph over every inch of me. *Stop stop stop.* I channel all my anger from learning about the elixir and hurl it at him. "I want one minute without your fucking hands on me."

Eli lowers his lips to my ear, my elbow pulled against his abdomen. "That's not what it sounded like earlier."

I can't stop it. Warmth spreads through me from cheeks to thighs with the memory of his hips pressing into mine, how hard he was sliding over me, the deplorable noise that escaped my lips. That almost kiss. Dammit. Why does he do this to me? I release my pent-up steam with a long exhalation just as the wind brings in a cold rain from the dark gray clouds above.

Goosebumps cover my skin, and I cross my free arm over my chest to hide my hardening nipples. We stand in heated silence, watching the reflection of the moonlight fracture on the lake's surface with the splattering of rain. The boulders on the shore darken, and I try really hard not to notice Eli's white shirt getting soaked and sticking to his body.

"Come on," he says out of nowhere, tugging on me.

"What?" I throttle the cravings for him and explode. "You want to drag me around again? And I'll *cooperate* because I've spent my life drugged?!"

Calm and fierce, he says, "You'll cooperate because I'll make you." His hand slides from my arm to my wrist, and he yanks me toward the lake.

I plant my feet, resisting his pull—and failing. My feet drag over the rocks as I yell at him. "What's the Centress going to do once the new elixir is in the water? What will she *make* me do?"

He stops and turns to me. "She won't make you do anything. I won't let her."

My head rises from my toes to his face. He'll protect me?

He brushes his knuckles over the scars on my neck with his free hand, his cold fingers deceptively warm grazing my frozen skin. I fidget and pull away from his touch, swishing around the taste of blood in my mouth.

His eyes meet mine. "Only *I* get to control you."

Oh. He grabs me by the waist and carries me across the shore under one arm. I scratch his thigh, clawing at him, as if that might make a difference. "What are you doing? Put me down!"

"Swimming."

"You're fucking mad. It's freezing."

We reach the crisp water's edge where the lake licks the rocks.

"I still have my boots on," I yell, one last attempt to stop him.

"That's so you don't step on a sole-ripper." He splashes into the water, fully clothed.

I kick and squirm, the surface closer and closer as he walks out toward the expanse of the lake, holding me above it. "What's a sole-ripper?"

"You don't want to know." He flips me head up and drops me in the water.

It surrounds me, rushing under my clothes and forcing its way into my boots, and it's… warm. I sink down until the water laps at my neck, my anger dispersing. "It's not cold."

Eli grins—not a grin at my expense, but at *me*, with something like happiness behind it. My heart jumps, and the black-blue water ripples around us, the only evidence it's not a mirror of the sky.

Kaleida tips over, crashing down from Sypher's shoulders with a splash. She swims back to him, grabs his head and shoves his face underwater. "You weren't supposed to let me fall," she squeals when he surfaces, gasping and already reaching to retaliate.

But their laughter fades when they notice Milo staring in our direction, treading water, his face hard in silent warning.

Eli turns his back to Milo and pulls me around with him, a foreign warmth in his eyes. "Can you swim?"

"Is this another trigger?"

He steps into me. "It could be."

"I can swim," I lie. Maybe he won't try to drown me.

"Come." He finds my wrist under the surface and pulls me along as he walks deeper and farther out and around a bend, away from the rocky shore and the prying moons overhead.

My clothes drag me down, my boots tiring out my legs. On the other side of the bend, Eli releases me. We enter a circular inlet about ten feet across, surrounded by a steep muddy bank with trees beyond it. Leafy vines invade the trunks, creeping up, wreathing branches and hanging down over the water in curtains of black and white flowers. The rare white petals twinkle against the endless black blooms like a starry night sky.

It's a perfect place to push my limits with a trigger and test me with the plants right after. With another step forward I hit a dip, and the lake floor drops away beneath me. I slip underwater, kicking my feet in search of solid ground, but I only sink deeper. Seconds pass, so many that it feels like minutes as panic surges through me, bringing me back to the courtyard where the guard held me underwater. Finally, Eli pulls me up by my arm and into a shallower area. He sets me down in front of him, the water now hugging my neck, frigid air on my soaked face.

"Liar," he says.

My oversized shirt floats up in bunches around me, and I wrestle it back down. "Maybe."

His body inches away, I fight the urge to look up at him—and lose.

"What do you think?" He fingers his earlobe, his face strangely unguarded with soft lines and wide eyes.

"It's hideous." Another lie.

His eyes sharpen. "I find you difficult, Never."

"Do you expect me to bend to your every whim?"

He tries to hold his face neutral, failing beautifully. A shadow of a smile dusts his lips and pools in his eyes. "I'll bend you any way I need to."

"You'll what?" I mean to sound upset, but it comes out breathy, my mind wandering to all the possible ways he meant that, lingering on ones it shouldn't. The ones that have me folded in half and him behind me. *What's wrong with me?*

The night air stings my skin, and rain trickles past the branches and flowered vines above, striking my face. I wipe it away, and my shirt billows up again.

He stares at me, swallow after nervous swallow.

Are we here for a trigger... or to finish what his hips started earlier? I avoid his eyes, and he locks a hand onto my face. "Look at me."

I squeeze my lids shut, the urge to disobey too strong to resist.

"I want to know what you see," he says softly, despite his tight hold, "underneath."

A loyal friend? An underwear thief? A man with a heart in so many pieces it can't find its beat?

His fingers sink into my cheeks. "Open those beautiful fucking eyes."

Well fuck.

I let his infinite gaze find mine, and the worst of thoughts hit me. Thoughts of taking hold of those stupid suspenders and letting our hips meet again. Thoughts of running my hands down his back, exploring every ridge while he fills me. Thoughts of wrapping my legs around him, tighter and tighter, smothering every bit of space between us.

Desire pumps through my core, and I don't want to fight it anymore. I want to escape—from myself, my thoughts, my past. It's lust, nothing more. Just for a little while, I want to forget about Caldera and

Kelter and elixirs and magic and never going home—and get lost in his arms.

"Tell me what you see," he demands.

"Just you."

His expression softens. Letting my face go, he slowly takes the edge of my floating shirt and pulls it underwater. Two slippery fingers tuck it into the waistband of my pants, inches below my belly button, his eyes never leaving mine. Then those fingers dip lower, oh so low. His other hand comes to rest on the bare skin of my hip, then tightens. I groan in pleasure at his firm grasp and fall forward, clutching his arms. Small waves crash between us.

He wiggles down farther, eyes growing round and glossy, mouth open. A forced breath leaves me, and his hand pinches my side, harder with every viciously slow swipe of his fingertips across my mound.

I might die, but I keep our gazes locked—even when he licks his lips.

Kiss me, you idiot.

The burn is unbearable, his touch blazing through me, the strength of his grip, the sensation of his skin on mine. I can't keep doing nothing. Not escaping, not fighting, not finding answers. I want to make my own choices, to fight against the elixir.

I lean in toward him, tippy-toed, reaching for those suspenders to pull him low enough. My head tilts, and I go for his lips, those sharp bowed lines. But before I feel our lips melding into one, his hand flies out of my pants and he's pushing us apart. Water rushes in, crushing in ways his arms never could.

Every damn emotion is painted across his tempting rain-kissed face, as though he were a thousand men in one—sinking regret mixed up with unmistakable longing, creases of confusion, restraint in every quivering muscle—and through those cryptic brown irises, he's trying to tell me everything and nothing at once.

He holds me at arm's length, his trembling fingers digging into my shoulders. "What do you think you're doing?"

"Was it not obvious? What in the mad fuck is wrong with you? You'll stick your hand down my pants, but you won't kiss me?"

He forces a cruel mask of spite onto his face, concealing the jumbled muck of emotions he let through. "Yes."

It's like a kick to the throat. I shove his chest, splashing water onto our faces. "*You* brought me here. *You* got close. *You* touched me." But what does it matter? This was an escape, two bodies, no feeling.

"Malachite." The force of his grip doubles, and he drives me backward and slams me into a nest of slimy roots forming the eroded bank of the inlet, his eyes set on the woods behind me. "Guards."

"The Centress' guards? How did they get across the ravine?" I whisper, fear winning out over the fire in me. Milo tied the rope on this side for us to get back.

"The bridge."

"There's a fucking *bridge*?"

He holds his thumb to my lips and sneaks a glance down at me, smirking. "There's always a bridge." The roots creak as he presses closer. "Stay low, don't speak and don't move." He backs away from the bank into the center of the inlet, leaving me holding on to the roots, rejected and forcibly drowning my desire.

CHAPTER 31

Who's with you, Eli?" A man's voice booms from the tree-lined bank behind me.

"No one, Poett. What are you even doing in this area?" Eli asks. He's six feet away, treading water in the middle of the inlet where it's deepest, avoiding looking at me.

"I saw her."

"None of your business who I fuck at the lake," Eli says, fast and pissed.

"It is when the only reason we're allowed to be out past curfew is to find the missing Hollow."

"Right. I'm leaving."

"Show me her face." The voice moves closer.

No no no.

Rain streaks down Eli's shifting jaw. "You can't be serious."

"What's there to hide?" The guard he called Poett is almost above me.

Eli swims two feet closer. "Just giving her privacy."

"Since when do you give a fuck about anyone?" Poett snatches a fistful of my wet hair and pulls me up and back, holding my head against the edge of the muddy bank. His sunken pale cheeks and black eyes loom over me, brown hair tied back into a tail that falls over the shoulder of his black jumpsuit—one of the Centress' guards from the school. He jerks my head back harder upon seeing my face. "It's her. Get over here, Jace."

Eli lunges forward, plants a foot on the tangled underwater roots and launches himself up onto the bank. With a punch and a *smack* of wet flesh against flesh, my hair is freed. Eli hurls Poett over my head by his hair. His body slaps the water, and Eli jumps onto him, throws an arm around his neck and wrenches it back. "Do *not* touch her again."

I clutch my flaming scalp. Screams and splashes come from the rocky shore where we left Kaleida, Sypher and Milo. How many more guards are there?

Poett wedges his fingers between his neck and Eli's arm, thrashing and trying to break free. "You're fucking the Hollow, Eli? That's where she's been all this time? Under you?"

Eli tightens his grip, forcing a grunt from Poett.

"We should have known no one would have been able to get past you to take her from the prison cell. You had us all fooled while you helped look for her and the traitor every damn day. Where'd you get the bruises?" Poett rasps every word while he tries to escape Eli's crushing hold on his neck. "Did you get off on letting her beat you while you rammed into her? Or did Sypher do that when he realized you'd rather have another species over him?"

Eli groans and thrusts Poett underwater. A muffled scream travels below the surface. I've seen enough death for a thousand lifetimes, but I can't look away. Rain-soaked hands latch onto my arms from behind and pull me out of the water. The onslaught of cold air strikes my entire body.

"Elivander," I scream.

He flips around, shoves Poett's body deeper underwater and swims for the bank, heavy boots slapping the surface of the lake with the few kicks it takes.

"That's the second time I've pulled you out of water, Hollow. You should have been killed that first day." The guard from the courtyard who almost drowned me—she adjusts her grip and grabs me around my ribs, dragging me away from the inlet… away from Eli. He's at the bank, climbing out after me, but Poett leaps onto his back and drags him into the water by his suspenders.

"Go, Jace," Poett yells to the guard holding me. My nails scrape uselessly over her jumpsuit.

Eli lands a punch to Poett's jaw combined with an underwater move that makes his face scrunch up in agony—a blow to the balls, likely. He lets out a gurgle audible from here, and Eli leaves him, swimming for the bank again.

The guard holding me, Jace apparently, whips me side to side in response to my thrashing. She's all muscles and speed. "The only reason I'm not strangling you right now is because the Centress wants you delivered alive."

Another guard appears through the trees, schlepping Milo along. I recognize the guard from the school in the village too—dark brown skin and tight curls with bright eyes. He's at least six inches shorter than Milo, but manages to drag him next to Jace. Milo's lip is split and swelling. His shirt is ripped, and shiny bruises obscure his normally rosy cheeks. How could they? He's not like them. Milo's gentle. I fight harder against Jace's hold.

Following the sound of grunts and yells, I crane my neck to see the shore through the trees. Kaleida and Sypher fend off a huge guard in a black jumpsuit. He's slow and unfocused, but so solid that their advances bounce off him. Kaleida fights with her elbows, jabbing every which way and targeting sensitive areas. Sypher leverages brute force with punches to the stomach and face. Even two-on-one, they're barely standing.

"I'm taking her in," Jace tells the guard struggling with Milo.

"The Centress is gone for the night," he says.

"It's fine. Bring him too." Jace signals to Milo with a jut of her chin. "The Centress will want to kill him herself."

"Eli!" I yell to him again as they drag us away. He doesn't turn around this time. Poett elbows him in the face and drives him underwater. *No.*

"You think a Vaile will help?" Jace says in my ear. "No one—especially not Eli—cares about you. That man broke after his father died. He doesn't care about a single soul but his own."

Ten, twenty, thirty seconds… still under. Raindrops smack the surface. A shadowy form dips and dives below. Eli's head pops back up. Then his hand. And his knife. He swings it around, searching for Poett, but he's feet away, ducking back under. Eli swims backward toward the bank, turns and pulls himself up and out. Squelching boots and soggy, dripping clothes don't hinder his nimbleness as he springs toward the guard holding Milo and stabs his thigh. I don't hear the rip of flesh over the rain, but the blow of blade on bone is unmistakable.

The guard wails and releases Milo. He crumples to the ground, clutching his leg and groaning. Blood streams over the raised veins and tight knuckles of his hands, turning pink in the rain. Milo staggers back, stunned, and ducks behind a tree. He's trained like the rest of them, but clearly wants nothing to do with fighting. Eli climbs on top of the guard, and with two hands around the wet handle and a perfect face of murderous malice, he drives the blade through his heart and pulls it out just as fast, like a vision of death coming to life in the most alluring way.

Then he's a step in front of me, bloody knife in hand. "Hand her over, Jace. You touched her, you're next."

He won't let her take me from him. He won't.

"Back off, Eli." Jace loosens her grip on me long enough to produce a club from her back and slip it across my throat. "You're already a dead man."

Poett emerges from the water behind Eli, strands of hair wrapping around his neck and crossing his face.

"Behind you," I screech, and Jace tugs the metal club in and up, squashing my throat.

Eli spins around and elbows Poett in the neck. Poett bends in half, wheezing, breath crackling. Eli helps him fall to the ground and sends a knee into his stomach with all his weight. I have to look away after he curls into a ball and vomits chunks of brown bar and blood. I gag against the club from the sour stench.

Eli's about to bury the knife in the back of his neck when Kaleida shrieks. I turn my head to see her collapse against a tree near the shore. The enormous guard stomps on her limp figure. Sypher kicks the back of his knees, but fails to bring him down. Jace takes the moment to attempt to slip away with me.

Eli hurls himself forward, knocking Jace on her back with me on top of her. She pulls the club tighter. My throat gargles and groans. Eli sits on top of my hips, his wet weight squashing me against Jace. He raises his knife, aiming it dangerously close to my face, but she swings the club away from my neck and into his wrist. The knife flies from his hand. I suck in as much air as I can, coughing and gasping.

Eli lifts his hips and rolls me to the side, off of Jace and out from between them. She reaches for me, trying to gather me back up as her shield. Eli's fist soars past me and into her face.

"Go," he says. I roll once more, smacking into the dead guard that held

Milo. Poett pushes up out of his pile of vomit and reaches for me. His hand snags my hair as I scurry backward on my hands and feet, my bottom scraping the ground. I squeal, pivot and jab my booted heel into his ribs.

"Oh shit." I stare at my leg as if it weren't mine. Poett releases my hair, and I catch Eli's eyes on me while I push myself up, blood and mud squishing between my fingers.

I run to where Milo disappeared behind the trees, spinning in search of him—only to spot the little boy from the forest slipping behind a trunk. As I reach the tree, a hand finds my wrist, and I'm hauled to the ground and into Milo's arms. No little boy.

"It's you." I let out a relieved breath, my heart clamoring for a way out.

Milo pulls me sideways into his lap and wraps himself around me. He's wet, but somehow warm like Kelter, and he still smells like cloves—reminding me of Eli. "Are you hurt?"

I'm not sure I can even feel my body. My hands move to my throat. "I-I'm—no."

Milo turns my head toward him, his fingers inspecting me and wiping rain from my face, even as it continues to fall. His bruises are already blackening, and his golden hair looks dark, drenched and flattened to his forehead. "Come on, we have to get you back to the castle. It's going to be okay." He slides me off his lap and stands.

"What about Elivander? And Sypher and Kaleida?" I peer around the tree. Eli is still wrestling with Jace, each of them throwing punches. She somehow competes with his strength.

"*You* are Eli's priority. He's told me over and over. Let's go." Milo tugs at my arm.

Poett stumbles his way to where Jace now sits on Eli, grabs her club and slams it against Eli's throat.

"Eli!" It hurts as if the club were on *my* throat, stealing *my* air.

Milo leans down behind me and throws a hand over my mouth. "Let's go," he hisses.

My fingers rip his hand away. "No, go help him!" I drop to my hands and knees, fists curling around the lush undergrowth. A vision strikes me, images blasting through my mind.

Knife after knife in Eli's body, blades buried, handles gleaming, limbs speared to the ground.

"He'll be fine. He can get out of anything." Milo tugs at my waist, trying to pull me up. I resist, holding tight to the foliage and blinking through the lingering flashes of the vision.

Eli struggles, his hands locked on either side of the club and pushing upward, preventing it from cutting off all air. Jace, straddling his stomach, leans forward, hands on his chest, and spits in his face.

Oh, fuck no. My whole body ignites. My throat flattens with his. Every drop of blood in me boils, rushing through the tiny rivers of my veins, spreading and marking their path like ink spilling over a map. My ears fill with roiling, rioting blood, drowning out all other sounds.

Eli's legs jerk. His hands fight the wet club at his neck. Poett props his knee on Eli's head and with the crack of his knuckles in preparation, he forces his weight down.

The surge of rage reaches my hands, navigates down my fingers and out through the tips. And with the outpouring of emotion, energy rushes into me, a tidal wave of sensation, and staggering, bright white light splashes on the ground, moving from my fists and out and out and out.

I stare down, not trusting my eyes. I know they said magic exists. I know I've seen it, but experiencing the flip of impossible to possible in my own hands, the world waking up inside me, the reordering of reality—it's different than knowing or seeing. It's believing.

"You're doing it." Milo panics, his hands slipping from my waist.

The wave of white illuminates the night. The two guards and Eli are blasted into the air. Their bodies soar ten feet off the ground, flailing and twisting, turning and cursing. They land with heavy thuds. The glowing stems and flora and bits of grass sweep beneath them and beyond. In a sea of white, Eli lifts his head and finds me, and I'm looking right back at him, breathless. Magic bursts from every plant and root below and shovels into me.

"Run!" he shouts, and Jace appears behind him.

"Look what you let happen." She knocks his head down. Face to ground, smashed into the mud and luminous leaves below. "Your Hollow is stealing our magic."

"Stop, not here!" Milo forces me to my feet.

The light fades, and only fistfuls of uprooted sprouts are left in my hands. He pulls me through the dripping trees, ducking under branches, weaving through trunks, hurtling forward. Traces of white energy trickle through me. I propel myself onward through the trees and the rain, hand in hand with Milo, step after step after step in my wet, heavy boots—

Right into the massive chest of a guard, the one who left Kaleida in a heap, and probably Sypher too. My nose crunches against his damp jumpsuit, filling my nostrils with the scent of blood and rain and sweat. Crooked teeth on a dark face grin down at me. Then his fist clobbers my head—and all goes black.

CHAPTER 32

I can't listen to another one, Milo." I clamp my hands over my ears
as yet another woman sucks in long breaths between moans.

"Me either." Milo rolls away from the foot-wide grate along
the bottom of the door that we're taking turns watching through, lying
on our bellies on the floor. I hear him right through the pointless
covering of my ears, along with the steady tap of rain and all the
miserable sounds—the screams and groans and roars of labor that we've
been listening to since late last night. And now it's dark again.

I woke up from the blow to my head inside a wooden carriage with
Milo, pitching through the woods. I tried to convince myself the
memory of a white sea of magic was the result of a concussion as the
guard sat on a bench with a foot on each of our backs, pinning us to the
cabin floor until we reached the round building—the Ring, as Milo told
me, where women come to give birth.

We were dragged through the double marble doors at the entrance,
the only exterior part of the structure not covered in leafy vines, and
locked inside this room. The huge guard passed canteens and stale bars
to us through the grate early this morning before leaving us unguarded
with no way out. At first I refused to drink, with the whole land's water
tainted by the elixir, but I didn't have a choice.

I uncover my ears, take Milo's spot on the floor and look through
the grate, unable to stay away. It's better than staring at the four blank
walls that surround us or the narrow bed raised to waist-height and
sitting on a silver post in the center of the room. It's similar to a hospital
bed with a pedal for adjusting the height, metal rails lining the long sides
and a thin mattress covered by a white sheet. Except the sheet is more

pink than white, stained with faded blood, and four sets of chains and cuffs dangle from the rails.

On the other side of the grate, the walls form a ring, enclosing an open-sky atrium with doors all around. I can see into almost all of them from here, mostly more rooms like this one with a single bed. Thousands of white stepping stones are built into meandering, looping pathways on the atrium ground, and green moss pecked with teensy red flowers fills the crevices between them.

I wait for the woman's contraction to ease before whispering, though our voices go undetected with all the sounds of labor. "Are you sure Elivander is okay?"

My stomach tightens against the cold marble floor, and I see Eli again, telling me to go, to escape... without him. I should be grateful he stopped me from making the mistake of kissing him, grateful for the rejection, but I hurt.

Milo puts his hand on mine. "I'm positive. Eli survives everything."

"Will he come for us?"

"He won't stop looking," he says, resting his head on his folded arms. "But he has no idea we're at the Ring."

"Do you think Kelter is here?"

"Your friend? I'm not sure."

I turn my attention back to the grate. An overly tall woman in a gray jumpsuit speedwalks across the atrium, rounding the many winding turns of the stone pathway that lead her to the door of the moaning woman. She wears her light brown hair in a neat bun on the back of her head, and her legs seem too thin to hold up her voluptuous upper half, but she manages.

"Only a while longer now," the woman in the jumpsuit says from the doorway.

A woman lies on the bed, wrists and ankles chained to the metal rails, her pregnant belly exposed and her bare knees spread. A gray shirt covers her breasts.

"Ash, don't leave me, please. I can't lose this one too," she says through heavy breaths. The worker she called Ash enters, hushing her cries and holding her chained hand.

This is at least the tenth woman we've watched go through labor. Milo explained that Ash is part of the Life Cycle Sphere, which handles life, death and any injuries or illnesses in between, like nurses in Caldera, but they do it all.

"Why are they chained to the beds?" I ask. I hadn't actually seen a woman go through labor before today, but of the few home births I heard through the walls over the years, none included the clink and chink of chains between the guttural groans and excessive cursing. I knew I'd be seeing Cam soon after. No one ever wanted *me* around a baby, not with my "episodes."

"I don't know. It's not like I've been here before or done *that*. But with that much pain, I'd expect punching is common," Milo muses.

Minutes later, Ash is positioned between the woman's raised knees. Somehow the sight of her trembling legs makes it real. The raw screams coming from that little room cut right through me. After the most jarring wail of them all, a silence spills into the moment, and the high-pitched cry of a newborn sends it on its way.

"This is excellent contraception," I say to Milo, shoving my shoulder into his and swallowing down the rising nausea.

"I'm never sleeping with anyone after I link." Milo stares at the wall, dead-eyed.

I scoff. "But now you would?"

"It doesn't matter *now*. It won't end up with someone screaming like that and blaming me after."

"It only takes one time," I remind him.

"Yeah, *after* linking. We're infertile until then." His head rolls to the side to meet my stare. "When do Hollows become fertile since they don't link?"

"Usually around thirteen years." I don't tell him that wasn't the case for me, especially with his gaping stare. How could we look so similar, but have such differences on the inside?

Like after the other births, Ash scuttles out of the room holding a blanketed bundle.

"Where are you taking him? Is something wrong?" The new mother's desperation slashes through my heart. Chained and alone.

"Why don't they leave the babies with the mothers?" I ask.

"There's probably something wrong with him," Milo says. "He's not one of the one in three that survive. Most of these women will leave the Ring without a baby once they recover."

Hearing it was one thing, but seeing the loss in action—that's something else, something much too painful for words.

Over the next hour, the women who gave birth earlier in the day begin to stir with worry as they wait for the return of their baby, fearing that their newborn isn't a survivor.

Ash attends to a red-haired woman jangling her chains. Blood cakes her legs, a red puddle on the floor. "When can I see her? It's been hours. Is she alright?"

With one leg out the door, Ash calls out, "Tea, suite four."

"I don't want tea! I need to see her," the red-head yells, thrashing her naked hips up and down.

Milo shoves in next to me, sharing the view through the grate, our shoulders smashed together. He tips his head against mine, his fair hair brushing my forehead.

A scrawny man in a gray jumpsuit makes his way out one door and across the atrium, pushing a wooden cart stocked with tea cups and a teapot, clattering and clunking over the uneven stones. A gray drape hangs from the edges of the cart down to the wheels below. The man moves slowly, following the unnecessary stone path despite the urgency in Ash's call, licking his lips every other step. He parks the cart, squats and pulls open the drape, revealing a row of sacks on the lower level of the cart.

"Malachite!" Milo inhales sharply. "That's the new elixir. I recognize the sacks. I packed them myself."

With heaping spoonfuls of yellow powder, the worker distributes the contents of the sack among the teacups, following with steaming water and the swirl of a metal stirring rod that mixes the falling rain in too.

Ash takes a teacup off the cart, grabs the woman's chin and forces open her screaming mouth, pouring the tea down her throat while she fights against the chains. In under a minute, the woman's crying stops. Her body droops. Her thighs fall to the side, mouth hanging open.

"Why would they give the elixir to her? I thought it didn't work on Vaile," I ask.

"It's supposed to be used for medical emergencies, not to shut up women who want to hold their newborns. They gave her enough to put five hundred Hollows into a stupor."

We watch as every woman is forced to drink the tea, becoming limp and lifeless, drugged into submission. The picture is clear—following every ear-splitting birth, the babies are severed from their mother's arms before the silence-inducing elixir tea is given.

This isn't right. Even if the babies are dying, the mothers aren't given a chance to say goodbye, to feel, no matter how painful.

"We have to stop this." Bands of injustice tighten around me.

"Ever…" Milo nudges my shoulder with his. "We can't do anything right now. We're locked up and wanted dead."

Like Kelt. My top priority. I bury my head in my arms.

A late-hour lull settles around us. The women are quiet, pacified despite their empty arms. The double doors open, and the Centress sweeps straight across the atrium with a handful of guards in black jumpsuits behind her. She ignores the stone pathways, leaving a trail of mangled red flowers and trampled moss in her wake. Her hair follows her in black waves down the back of her forest-green dress. It sticks to her trim middle and wide hips, flaring out from her thighs down. The rain rolls right off it.

"She came." I shut my eyes, trying to get the memories and pain of that day at the temporary school out of my head.

Milo taps his fingers in the rainwater now overflowing from the gap under the door and into the room where we lie belly-down on the floor, watching through the grate again. She'll probably kill him for helping Eli hide me.

The Centress scans the atrium. "Where did you put them?"

"They're locked in a birthing room," a guard says.

"Take me to them."

I reach for Milo's hand and squeeze it.

"Centress Oreyla—" Ash, in the blood-splattered gray jumpsuit, steps forward and dips her head. "The carriage will be leaving soon. We need you to choose the babies first so there's time to load them up. And one more is coming."

The Centress stops, reluctant fists at her sides. "Right. Remove the blankets. Let's get on with it."

Ash enters a room behind her. Each baby taken from its mother is in a nest of blankets inside a basket and lined up in a row on the floor.

"Only four will be returned as surviving babies tonight. Take the rest of them to the carriage and inform each mother their baby didn't make it," the Centress says.

Ash nods and leans over the first baby, blocking our view. When she pulls back, the swaddle is loose, exposing its tiny chest. The Centress reaches up to the collar of her dress, tucks her hand inside and produces a necklace. She squats in front of the first basket, dress puddling around her, and stays there, her back to us while the baby wails.

Then all the babies cry.

Minutes pass, and the Centress rises, necklace still clutched in her hand. We can't hear anything except each other over the ceaseless cries of all the babies at once. We can only watch as she moves on to the next one with her necklace, emotionless. Ash whisks the first basket away, a loaded syringe in hand.

"What is she doing with her necklace... and why a syringe?" I ask, wrapping a hand around my own necklace, the other still holding tight to Milo.

"I don't know. The carriages go to the falls and dump the elixir into the water supply. Why would she put babies in them?"

"I'm not the one to ask, Milo. But they're lying to the mothers about their babies dying."

Ash disappears into one of the suites and rushes out a minute later, chased by a soul-shattering cry, louder than the babies'. The gaunt man in the gray jumpsuit enters with a teacup in hand. He forces the liquid into the woman's mouth. She puts up a fight in the chains, turning her head side to side, but fingers pry at her jaw with ease. An empty teacup shatters on the floor, shards scattering over marble and blood. The mother's cries deteriorate into an unnatural hush, her mourning silenced with the elixir.

I'm transfixed on the ruined futures unfolding before me—of a childless mother and a parentless child, of the years of seeking answers that won't be found. My past and present rushes into the baby. It never had a chance.

I hold back a sob. Milo releases my hand and throws his arm around my back. A thud sounds behind us, barely heard over the constant shrill screams of the infants and the pounding rain. We both flip around, and Eli drops through a smoking hole in the ceiling.

CHAPTER 33

Eli jumps from the bed and slips a black stone into his pocket as the flame flickers out. He looks down at us, lying on our stomachs with our upper bodies twisted to see him.

"Took you long enough," Milo says, letting go of me and sitting up against the wall. "How many holes into half naked laboring women's rooms did you have to burn to find us, or were you lying on the roof waiting?" He signals to the ceiling with a quiet laugh and rests his head back in relief. "Good timing though, they're all in that room now, busy with some sort of scheme, and nobody can hear a thing with the babies screaming out there."

Eli's eyes are only on me. "Get up."

I sit up in response to the venom in his voice and disguise the pain of him pushing me away with an equally toxic tone. "Don't tell me what to do."

"On your feet." He's soaked, all in black, suspenders gone and fabric clinging to every muscle again. Dammit. It's as if he plans it. I can't look away. Rain falls through the hole in the ceiling around him, his personal storm.

I don't want to. I really don't want to give in, but I get my feet under me and push up slowly, sore all over.

"Come to me." Raindrops roll off his chest with each breath. His gaze is merciless, dark eyes shadowed by his brows. He might tear me apart with that look when I reach him, but I take a step forward, and another, pulled by something I can't see or name or control. A warm breeze passes over my cold nose and cheeks. Another step and I'm in front of him, surrounded by his light aura, rain smacking my face.

Rage coils in his bruised features, and he takes out his knife. His voice is a low, rumbling threat. "Tell me they didn't fucking hurt you."

Surprise sends me back a half step, both at the knife and his command, but he brings me close again, sliding his fingers up my neck and through my hair and holding me in place with a tight fist. "Did they put their godsdamn hands on you?"

"*You* have your hands on me."

He drops my hair, and his freezing wet hand goes to each side of my neck, shoving my head back and forth. He lifts my arms and twists to see every angle.

"What are you doing?" I pull back, but he grabs my hip and turns me around, raising my shirt and exposing my back. His hand rides up over the blitzer scars and back down, inspecting, and I stifle a shout at his cold touch. He turns me and lifts the fabric again, icy fingers on my belly. I squeal and smash my hands down on top of his, trapping it under my shirt.

"You can't do whatever the fuck you want, Eli." I hold his hand away from my skin, still wrapped up in the damp black fabric.

The knife hangs between the fingers of his other hand, the blade grazing my arm. "You're my little prisoner."

I squeeze the ball of shirt around his fist. "You keep saying that, but it means nothing."

"It means..." He pulls the hand in my shirt closer, my whole body following until we're a breath apart, rain streaming down our faces. "That you belong to me."

His scent. The closeness. His words. My stupid insides blush with want. He stares so damn hard with those eyes, as if he actually sees me. Air is shoved from my lungs, my heart cramping. Then the anger comes, rolling waves mixing with the heat of desire—anger at the rejection, at using Kelt, at the way he dares shatter my illusion of hatred for him. I'm not sure if I want to fuck him or fight him. Maybe both at once.

His reflection glints on the blade as it totters between his distracted fingers. I release his fist, snatch the knife and step back out of the rain, silver blade wobbling, pointed at him. My mind floods with every moment spent with this devastating man—the tug of my ear, my hand in his pocket, the touch of our toes, water up to my neck. Too many tiny moments pulling me into him when I should be running away.

An angsty hand migrates to his ear, and damn him—he smiles, looking me up and down, the knife wavering inches from his heart.

"Go ahead." He steps forward until the tip snags on his shirt.

My hand is far from stable, the blade scraping chaotic circles over his heart. "I'll do it."

He nods, smirking.

"Uh, guys?" Milo clears his throat. "Shouldn't we get out of here?"

"Kind of busy here, Milo." Eli's boot taps the growing puddle of rainwater and old blood below us, unheard with the babies' unending cries.

"You don't get to say that I belong to you." Tears prick my eyes. "You don't get to act like I'm *something*. Not now."

Invisible darkness rushes over him and curls around me, leaving me shivering and forced to take in his musky scent. He loses his smirk. "Because I make you want things you wish you didn't?"

You, in particular.

"And lock you up so I can keep you for myself?"

The knife slips in my wet grasp.

"And hold you so fucking tight?"

Oh so tight. I close my eyes and savor the taste of blood behind my lips, shuddering at the fingers whispering down my spine.

"And you don't like that?" He slides a hand down my arm and over my wrist, my eyes opening as he gently twists the knife and points it to the side. Then he presses my hand to his chest, running it up and up until the blade meets his neck. His blood pumps beneath my trembling fingers.

"I don't," I lie. To him, to myself.

He swallows against the blade. "Then do it. Kill me."

"Umm—" Milo starts.

"I swear to the fucking gods, Milo, join us or get out," Eli says.

I can't look away from those eyes of his, alight with darkness. He's teeming with lust, but it's the trace of panic, the indecision on his face that bottoms out my soul, and it has nothing to do with the metal pressing into his throat—he's going to push me away again.

Tears threaten to spill out... for the beautiful knife at his neck, for letting him live and for wanting to escape so badly that I tried to kiss him. Each breath is a damn chore. He lowers his head, his soulful eyes questioning. So I answer.

"I can't fucking kill you."

He pries the knife from my fingers and charges me through the falling rain, right smack into the wall, sliding his arms around my back in time to keep me from hitting the cold marble. His hips roll and slam into me. Pleasure jolts through my belly.

I lift my hands to his heaving chest, rain dripping from the tips of his wet curls down onto my fingers. "But I will if you panic again."

"Fuck." He sucks in the deepest breath, holding it far too long as his hands creep up and cradle my face, then lets it all out along with the last of his self-control. And with one final, pained look, pleading for me to stop him, he crashes his lips onto mine, hard and insistent—not at all optional. Yet soft and inviting. And rough and stubbly.

Heat floods through me at the contact, the press of our lips, every muscle of his flexed, flattening me against the wall. His hands tighten on my face, a slight quiver in every finger. And somehow—our faces so close, noses side by side, lips sealed—it's more intimate than the gliding of tongue on tongue. Too intimate. Torturous, actually.

I gather his shirt into my fists. *Don't fucking stop.* Cold steel presses against my cheek as he curls his fingers in my hair, his eyes wide open and blistering with fear. He blinks—four times that feel like four thousand—locked in place, kissing me.

I blink back.

Then those eyes shrink to dark slits, and he pulls away, lips poised a breath from mine. "Look what you made me do, little Never."

The door opens, leaving me no time to throw the blame at him— nor pull him back for more. *That wasn't enough.*

Milo yelps and jumps up, sending himself sliding along the wall and into me. A guard stands in the doorway, gray eyes and ashy hair, muscles barely contained by his black jumpsuit. He looks up at the hole in the ceiling, then at us, and storms forward.

"Give her up, Eli."

Eli shoves me behind him and braces for attack, but before the guard's bulky body collides with his knife, Milo dives between them in a flash of blue and blonde. I hold onto Eli's waist and peek around him. Milo is squashed beneath the guard on the floor, every limb triple his size.

With a hand on my chest, Eli pushes me into the wall. "Stay back."

Not a beat later, he leaps onto the guard and punches the back of his head. Dazed, head rolling, the guard loosens his grip. Milo crawls out from under him and scrambles to his feet, patting himself down with those fidgety hands of his, searching for damage. Eli kneels on the guard's back and slides the knife into the side of his neck with a stunning smoothness, no hesitation, like a key into a lock. No amount of scrabbling for a hold on reality makes the corpse vanish. Because it's not a vision.

"You could have cuffed him," Milo says, stepping out of the red puddle.

Eli climbs off him, his upper lip curling. "He wanted to take her."

"They *all* do."

I find no security in the solidity of the wall behind me at Milo's words, not like I do in Eli's arms.

It takes Milo and Eli dragging the guard by his ankles to maneuver him through the doorway, leaving a guard-sized smear of blood on the marble floor. I move to follow, and as if Eli heard the sole of my boot tap the wet ground over the pouring rain, he spins around and finds my uneasy eyes. "Wait behind the door."

Please don't leave me here. But he turns away, not catching my rising panic over losing his protection again. I halt in place. I can't go out there, not when the only fighting I know how to do is battle my own mind, and the sharpest thing I have is my tongue.

Eli and Milo run across the atrium and jump into a tangled mess of fighting guards in blue and black jumpsuits. I can't keep track of the wet bodies and swinging clubs and barely catch the flashes of faces, but the equal amount of blue and black fabric has me on my toes, ready to run. *We're getting out of here.*

I slide between the wall and the open door of the birthing room and watch the brutal bashing through the crack next to the doorframe. To the side of the brawl, the two Life Cycle Sphere workers huddle against the wall of the atrium, no babies in sight… and no more crying. I search for the Centress through the sheets of rain and the fist-flinging guards, but don't find her either.

"I thought I left you dead at the lake," Jace says to Eli, scowling up at him from her knees while Coen holds her arms behind her. Eli doesn't bother with a response. He simply readies that knife of his.

"Put that thing away. I'll handle this," Sola says, swooping between them. She lowers Eli's muscled arm and grants him a pat on the hand, then flips around and kneels before Coen's captive. Her slender fingers brush the hair from Jace's eyes. "I hear you weren't very nice to Eli and his plaything."

Jace's face twists with rage. "She's a Hollow, and he's a traitor."

"Well, unfortunately for you, I am too." Sola cups her face, leaving Jace screeching and arching her neck in agony. When she steps back, two blue-gray handprints span Jace's cheeks as though her skin turned to ash, or froze, or became something else completely. Coen releases Jace with a disgusted shove, and she curls into a ball, holding her face and screaming.

Feet away, Eli holds a guard to the ground, stabbing limbs to pacify him. He manages to shift the guard just enough for Kaleida to jab a boot into his throat. She jumps into the air with a satisfied smile, celebrating. "Did you see that?"

Eli claps her on the shoulder and returns to the fray, hair and blood and fists and feet all over.

"Die already, you worthless shit," Poett yells as he tackles Eli and clamps two hands around his throat, his hair like a wet tail down his back.

Sypher grabs an unclaimed club rolling over the stepping stones, and with a bellow and a leap, he whacks it into the side of Poett's face. I turn away, but the cracking sound is worse than the sight of the impact. With the amount of blood that went flying, he's soon to be crawling on the ground searching for his teeth. Or unconscious. The whole scene is too much like my visions. I lean into the wall at my back and close my eyes. We'll make it out—*alive*—then we only need to get the babies from the carriage, return them to their mothers and look for Kelt. Simple.

The door creaks, and I lift my lashes... to see the Centress in my face.

CHAPTER 34

"Here you are." The Centress runs the back of her deathly finger down my cheek, then kicks the door shut. Her dark green dress flutters around her.

I freeze, all the pain she put me through returning in instant waves of nausea. The rain falling through the hole in the ceiling turns to hail, forming a small mountain of white stones where I stood and held a knife to Eli's chest minutes ago.

"I already knew you were different, but with only one session, I saw what's inside you." She strokes my face with her gentle touch, something much worse pulsing beneath her fingertips.

"I didn't steal your magic."

"Oh I know, dear. It was given to you."

She can't even keep her accusations straight. "Nobody gave me anything." I take a deep breath, attempting to fill myself with courage— or anything that will keep me from passing out. "Get the fuck away from me. I know you're taking babies from their mothers and telling them they're dead, and you're drugging Calderans to keep them from entering Sonnet."

"You make it sound so awful." She chuckles, a rare emotion on her frosty face. "I *have* to keep the Hollows out of Sonnet. And we're short on magic. I'm forced to take it from the babies—"

"You took the babies' magic? How? With that necklace?"

"Where else am I going to get it? Magic is woven too tightly in adults to use the necklace on them. If I don't take the babies' magic and put it back into the cycle, the supply will get too low. Nobody can know the magic is dying. And the babies can't stay here, panicking the people when they see they don't receive a gift in the future. They have to be sent to Caldera. It's harmless. They grow up not knowing what they're missing."

I can hardly breathe. "They grow up without mothers." *Like me.*

"I'm simply saving the land from destruction. You think boulders of ice falling from the sky is a problem? We would see weather a hundred times more terrifying if I let the magic continue to diminish and throw nature out of balance."

"I don't care what bullshit reason you come up with—you're separating infants from their mothers. There has to be another way."

She coils her fingers beneath my chin and serves me a forced frown of sympathy. "*You* are the way."

She wants to mess with my mind, break me, but I hold myself together. "Where are you keeping my friend?" I make a sudden move, slipping out from between her and the wall, and advance a whole two steps before she grabs my arm.

"It doesn't matter now, Everielle. Saving the land, replenishing the magic—none of it matters now that you're here."

"How do you know my full name?" The hailstones grow in size, pelting the floor and bouncing off the surrounding marble. I choose to watch them instead of braving a glance at her face. Did Kelter tell her my name? Did she force it out of him? Torture him?

She tips my chin up. "I know everything I need to know about you. And soon, I'll have every moment too. I won't ever have to be apart from him again."

"From who? What are you talking about?"

"I'm your mother, Everielle."

The hail pauses outside, ceasing to fall for a beat, as though caught on her words.

No... no. That's not right.

My mother is not the leader of a magical realm full of people who want me dead.

My mother did not imprison and torture me.

"You're lying." *Please be lying.*

"I can give you the answers you've been searching for." She sweeps her hand over my cheek, warm and soft and dreadful.

"I could never be related to you."

She sighs and leans forward, her hand maneuvering into the high neck of her green dress, then pulls out her necklace and dangles it over her chest. It looks a lot like mine—one raw broken edge. Pale yellow instead of purple. Identical chain.

It means nothing, but I can't look away.

"It's the other half of your stone. I would know, I'm your mother." She repeats that awful word, her hands riding down the front of her dress and out to her hips as she watches me fumble for a response.

"I'm from Caldera. I-I grew up there."

"But you weren't born there." Not one bit of feeling feeds her features. "I knew it was you the second I saw your eyes. I remember the first time I held you, how you opened them and looked up at me. That color, that brightness—unforgettable." She flashes her lashes, a dead stare behind them. "I can tell you why you don't know when you were born and why your birth documents are blank except for your name. I can tell you everything."

My body ceases to feel, struck so hard by her words that it's no longer part of me for this moment.

"You are not a Hollow, love."

A foul taste rises in my throat, the disgust trying to escape me. *She's the mother I've searched for my whole life?*

"How is this possible?" My voice falls to a whisper. "I'm not like you." I regain feeling and slide my arm across my middle, wanting to endlessly fold myself in half until I'm not here anymore. "I take magic. That's what I do, what Hollows do." That's what they told me, over and over. That's what *Eli* told me.

"Hollows don't actually take magic from plants—or anything else. And Vaile can't either, of course."

"Then why—"

"It's a centuries-old lie to keep Vaile afraid of Hollows. Only the Centress carries the truth and passes it on to her successor. I have to perpetuate the lie in order to maintain the Separation. I need every Vaile to believe that Hollows from Caldera can take magic and will let it die with them, slowly depleting it. They must fear Hollows and be motivated to protect the border and produce the elixir. If I let Hollows return to Sonnet, they'll eliminate our people. If it weren't for the Separation, all Vaile would have been erased by now."

"What? How? Why are you telling me all this if it's such a secret?"

"Oh, don't worry about that. You won't remember a word I've said once I take all your lovely memories away. Then I'll have what should have been mine from the start."

Lovely? Not quite.

"Take my memories?" That's impossible. I scan the room, frantic for a sense of security, but reality cracks all around me "What should have been yours?"

She doesn't answer. Her ghostly hands grab my shoulders, sending pain searing through me, reaching my insides and bubbling back up to my skin. My body transforms into a mass of agony. Her eyes close, head tilting back—the last I see before my vision goes and screams tear their way up my throat.

Darkness fills my mind as I try to hide from the pain. Visions hit me in blinding flashes. *The messy, gory death of everyone I've ever known, the afflicted cries of torment, the life fading from their pleading eyes, a gaping hole in my heart with every loss.*

Mixed between the visions of death comes the sensation of pulling, a tug at the fabric of my being, an attempt to unravel me. It strengthens, slipping among memories, all the moments that make me who I am, tethering them to the Centress.

She's actually going to take my memories.

She pulls and pulls and pulls. I try to tie them down, root them inside of me, etch them into the map within.

You can't take away who I am before I've even figured it out.

But the pain, it makes it so hard to fight. I scour the depths of my mind for an escape. *Let her kill me. Make it stop.*

"She's mine." Eli's stone-hard voice comes from behind me, then a cool tenderness wisps over my arms, tightening into an embrace. He traps me between the Centress and him. A shadow cuts into me, taking as it pleases, digging for parts of me much deeper than memories.

His lips skim my ear. "I got you." Those words—a confusing comfort. Kelter whispered them to me inside the sack.

Eli's head tucks in against my cheek, his cold chin nestling into the skin where my shoulder meets my neck. The battering on my nerves dissipates into the fleeting flashes of a nightmare upon awakening. Awareness crawls back and lets me open my eyes. Feeling returns to my limbs. The pain is gone despite the Centress' fighting grasp on me.

Milo drops to the bed from the hole in the ceiling, a slingshot aimed at the Centress' face. With the release of the sling, he lets a large stone fly the short distance to her forehead. She stumbles back at the impact, releasing me and reaching to soothe the dent in her flawless face. Milo jumps off the bed in a flare of cerulean blue. Hailstones crunch beneath his boots as he nears the Centress, pulling a club from a back pocket of his jumpsuit. He smashes it down over her head and watches her crumple to the ground.

"What did I just do?" The club slips from Milo's hand to the floor. His pale face turns white, his blue eyes round.

"The right thing." Eli pulls out his knife and grips a handful of hair atop her head, wrenching it back to expose her neck.

"No!" Milo and I shout together.

"You can't kill her," I beg, breathless. *She has all the answers.*

"She fucking touched you." He looks at me, fingers tightening, the line of his jaw so sharp that I step closer to Milo. His next words appear painful. "She hurt you."

Please. I try to puncture that hostile gaze with desperation in my own. Eli's shoulders drop, his body conceding, the internal struggle still all over his face. He drags her unconscious body to the foot of the bed, the familiar clink of chains sounding as he slaps the hanging cuffs around her wrists.

"Sh-she tried to take my memories," I mutter, still adjusting to the lack of pain.

"That's her gift—memory stealing," Eli says, guiding me out of the room with a hand latched tight onto my waist.

Milo looks back at the birthing room with a grimace. "It's a painful process, and it's why the last Centress chose her as successor."

I know. I felt it.

In the atrium, Sola and Coen hold Jace and Poett's faces to the ground and keep eyes on the Life Cycle workers as the hail beats against the white stepping stones, now a full-blown storm. Sypher and Kaleida have another two guards pinned among the bodies. The mothers are still silent, drugged.

"Take her back to the castle." Eli shoves me toward Milo, and he nods in understanding. "I'll take care of the rest of them, then we'll be right behind you."

Milo points a finger at Eli. "Cuffs only."

"We'll see." He twirls his knife in his fingers and takes off.

"Follow me," Milo says, and I run after him, my legs weak, yet functional.

We pass through the room where the babies screamed from their baskets and continue straight through an exit at the exterior of the Ring. The round outer walls curve left and right. Milo veers right, and I ready my feet to follow, but a decrepit wooden carriage with a cover is parked off to the left, loaded with baskets balancing on top of sacks crammed along the floor, like the ones used to make the tea.

The babies. They'll be sent away, separated from their mothers. I refuse to leave them to live out my same past, to grow up searching, wondering, *hoping...* until they lose that too.

I dash left, hugging the edge of the building, my boots barely skidding over the hailstones with each soaring step. I only need to take the babies back inside. But the carriage doors slam shut, and the wheels turn, gaining enough traction to send the carriage bumping away after a violent lurch. And it's gone. I glance behind me. Milo's gone too.

I'm alone.

I reach the spot where the carriage had been moments before and sprint after the wheel tracks, unbothered by the sting of cold and hail on my cheeks. I only feel the mounting storm within.

I bolt past trees and leap over roots, hailstones smacking me in the face and pelting my arms and legs. Broken branches crash to the ground. Every parentless moment of my life drives me forward, the memory of the babies' screams scarring my heart. The scrawny figure of a young boy flashes to my right, running with me. I look again, and he's gone. I run as if I were the storm, teeming with wrath and destruction, vengeance and justice.

It's not enough.

The carriage escapes, and the hailstones grow even larger. I reach a bank and tuck myself under the ledge of dirt and tangled roots, fearing they'll reach the size of the life-ending boulders that fell through the roof of the school. Hail pummels the ground in a calming, sporadic rhythm.

I hide my face in the bank and clutch the roots. As the storm finally loses steam, a gentle quiver of energy trickles through me. The final hailstones plunk to the ground.

I can't ignore how the energy pulls at me, an inaudible whisper urging me along. It's different from what happened near the lake, which I still can't align with reality. Instead of a chaotic scramble of panicked light hurtling its way toward Eli while energy—no, while *magic* barreled up my arms and into my body, this time, it guides me.

My feet obey, and I crunch my way through the aftermath of the storm, studying my mental map, but all the sharp turns following the carriage have me disoriented. I only have the guidance below my feet, transferring from the roots of one tree to the next. I run above the tugging energy, a puppet on the end of its strings. My legs lift and fall, boots gliding and vaulting until the roots run me straight into the runaway carriage.

I don't understand how the magic found it, but here it is. Relief surges through me. I can bring the babies back to their mothers at the Ring.

The back wheels of the carriage are stuck in a muddy trench, spinning and splattering mud droplets on my face. I climb up and peek inside the cabin. The babies are still deep asleep—which is concerning. Babies don't sleep through hail storms. It's only now that I realize nothing was pulling or powering the carriage—no horse, no motor, only... magic. Like what Sola used on Jace's face. She told me she received her gift after linking, that she could somehow shift matter, but I didn't believe those same hands—hands that were all over my face, forcing scarlet soda down my throat—were so dangerous. Maybe because the use of magic is almost as sparse as good food around here.

Exhaustion catches up with me, and I slide to the hail-studded ground. I sink into the bliss of success at finding the carriage. My limp and lavished body ties me to the ground along with the truth in the Centress' words. *She's my mother.*

Deep in the woods, with her and the guards defeated and cuffed at the Ring, I prepare for a long, cold night and hide under another bank of roots beneath an aging tree.

My eyes are still fighting sleep not twenty minutes later when footsteps approach and faces appear in a half circle overhead.

CHAPTER 35

E li drops to his knees in front of me, grabbing my shoulders and pinning me to the roots at my back. "What the fuck were you thinking? You were supposed to follow Milo." His wide eyes flare with fear, not with the anger spearing over the rest of his bruised face.

I can't stop the heat from rising in me and diffusing across my cheeks from simply looking at him. His stubble is a shade darker beneath the late-hour moons, accentuating his angles and framing those ripe lips, the ones he had against mine. But it's his concern for me that has me staring at his face, an even deeper heat settling in my chest.

"Calm down, Eli," Milo says, pulling back on his arm. Eli growls and shakes him off. Coen, Sola, Kaleida and Sypher stand behind them, all peering down at me.

"How did you find me so fast?" I ask, but my focus snags on the way his hands grip my shoulders, that scar on his jaw and the earthy cave scent of his darkness, telling me to get as far away from him as possible. I breathe it in. "I must have run for miles."

"I know the carriage route used for the elixir, but I didn't know she was putting babies in them too." Milo shrinks down to a crouch next to Eli in his wet jumpsuit. His bright eyes inspect me from head to toe, but besides being sore, exhausted, hungry, cold and wet, I'm physically fine. It's my mind that's reeling and coming undone—the babies, the magic, the Centress. *That kiss.*

I scan the faces above me. Sypher and Kaleida are covered in black-and-blue bruises from the lake, now with fresh red welts added to the mix. Sola and Coen are equally battered.

Kaleida kneels next to Milo, her tight curls frizzy and escaping the tie holding them atop her head. Her dark brown eyes are full of warmth. "Are you okay?"

Am I okay? My baby-stealing mother tried to take my memories, and tree roots guided me through the woods. No, I'm not okay. I nod. And lie. "I'm fine."

"We would have made it to the Ring sooner, but it took Eli a while to find Coen and me—and to convince us to join him as traitors to the Centress—but here we are," Sola says, as though it's no big deal.

But it is. Why would they help him? And ruin their futures and risk their lives?

To save Milo—it's the only explanation.

"What were you thinking?" Eli says again, still holding me against the roots.

"I'm taking these babies back to their mothers then searching for Kelt." *Then curling up in a ball and crying over my mother.* I hold my head high, my voice only wavering slightly.

"No. You're going back to the castle, and I'm locking you in my room where you can't run away and get yourself killed." Eli lifts me to my feet, hardly giving me time to drop my jaw.

"You'd kiss me then lock me up?"

He doesn't so much as glance at his friends shifting awkwardly behind him, his night eyes glued on me. "Of course." My fists are as tight as my legs are weak with what he's willing to do to keep me safe.

"She went through the trouble of following the carriage. Let's at least get the babies out of the woods," Sola says, holding the open gash on her arm and peering at me with a swollen eye. "Milo explained everything. We need to expose the Centress for what she's doing. Nobody has any idea she's lying about them dying, and I'm sure she takes the memories from anyone helping her. She can get away with anything."

"Expose her to who?" Coen counters. "To all her loyal devoted followers? She's the Centress. They'll follow her no matter what. She's nothing special beyond her gift, but it's all about the title. She could lose her magic, and they'd still line up to serve. I know because that was us earlier today—until Eli asked for our help."

That's it? He asked for help and they gave up their loyalty to the Centress? It's as though they'll do anything for him, while others hate him with a passion.

"But no one will believe us," Coen continues. "And even if they do believe she's taking babies from their mothers, they'll also believe whatever lie she feeds them to justify it."

Kaleida massages a dislocated finger as if she is trying to slip it back into place. "I swear this all has to do with the Centress' missing lover. The stories say he showed up out of nowhere and disappeared just as suddenly. Why else would she risk turning Vaile against her? Everything comes back to love."

"Maybe, but we still need to get them back." Sola looks warily at the carriage.

"Maybe she killed him," Sypher offers.

"I said love, not murder." Kaleida gives him a soft shove.

Coen reaches for Sola, taking her waist. "We can't simply walk back into the Ring and hand the babies over. Or walk anywhere after dawn. No one is out searching for the Hollow because they know she was caught at the lake, and the Centress only sent her guards to track down Eli, Sypher and Kaleida. But we need to be well hidden by the time the next shift of Life Cycle workers arrives at the Ring in the morning."

"I shouldn't have listened to you and left them alive," Eli mutters, then looks up at Coen and Sola, each a head taller than him. "You can stay at the castle. It's protected. No one can find us there."

"But what happens after that? None of us are safe since you were seen at the lake with *her*. We can't go back to our shifts," Coen snaps.

Or their lives. I drop my head. I know what that's like.

Kaleida squeezes my shoulder.

"Calm the fuck down. I'll figure it out," Eli says. He pulls my back against his stomach, sliding his arm around my neck and locking me in place as if I might try to run away. I don't fight him, not when I can feel every muscle down his front pressing into me.

"What's she doing with the babies?" Sola asks quietly, her hand finding Coen's and making me wonder if she's been in the Ring before. In one of those bloody beds. Forced to drink tea.

"She must be drugging them." Milo gestures toward the noiseless carriage, and no one has a response. The syringes prick back to mind. They were for the babies, to subdue them like their mothers, like Calderans.

I take in the solemn faces around me, raise my hands to Eli's arm and tug it down over my chest. Then I repeat what the Centress told me

220

about using her necklace to take magic from the babies and sending them to Caldera because they won't ever get a gift, all to make sure the supply of magic doesn't get too low and cause even more extreme weather—everything she told me thinking my memories would be gone.

Except the part about her being my mother… and the lie they've been fed their whole lives about Hollows taking magic from plants. I can't risk them blaming me or thinking I'm like her. Or risk revealing to Eli that I'm not a Hollow. Would he still want my magic if he knew? Have a reason to keep me alive?

"But why is the magic diminishing to begin with? What's changed in the cycle after hundreds of thousands of years?" Sypher asks after I've answered a dozen other questions, all with unhelpful responses.

Milo steeples his fingers below his chin, looking at me instead of Sypher. "Our gifts of magic are returned to the plants when we die, and the gods pass them on to the newborn Vaile. It doesn't make sense. Stealing it from the babies doesn't create more magic. It can't replace what's been lost. She's taking it from one part of the cycle and moving it to another."

"It's a temporary fix," Kaleida adds.

But no one can answer Sypher's questions.

Eli tightens his arm around me and changes the subject. "Find a tree and rest while Milo patches up wounds. Coen brought supplies. Sleep a couple hours if you can."

He takes command with such ease, and despite his guarded nature and dubious decisions, he cares for his friends, guides them.

"Then we'll take the runts and leave them in the village before dawn," he adds, sabotaging my positive thoughts of him.

"You can't abandon babies," I argue as Eli drags me away, leaving behind the others already following his order. He doesn't understand. Maybe *I* was one of those babies long ago.

"Better the village than alone in the woods. We're not going back to the Ring."

"*I* am."

He stops in a small clearing a few minutes later and turns to face me. "I'm starting to think you *want* to see what happens if you misbehave. You've run away twice now. I'm not letting your little ass out of my sight again." With a stern look and a press of my shoulders, he sits me down in front of a smooth-trunked tree, the smell of soggy leaves intensifying in the still night air, the ground cold and wet.

I pull my knees to my chest. "I don't see how that's going to work." I glare up at his tall frame, even as I imagine us locked inside his room, his bed ramming into those slanted walls with every violent thrust. I'm so conflicted.

He drops to a kneel in front of me, his hands finding the sides of my thighs. The touch sends warmth rushing to my legs despite the cold of his skin passing through the fabric. He leans in close, a tempting smile on his face. "You're right. You never shut your mouth. I'll lose my damn mind."

Fuck him—he smells better than coffee. I don't want to endure the pain that comes with my thoughts, only remember his arms around me, his lips pressed so forcefully into mine... to feel that again. "You didn't seem to mind my mouth earlier."

He moves fast, snatching my face in his hand, a vicious smile surfacing. I wince and stretch my jaw against his fingers.

His smile vanishes, and he pulls in a sharp breath at my reaction, letting go as quickly as he had me in his grasp, as if surprised at the strength of his own hand. And that look on his face, that angry, lost look, that tender ferocity—it's too much like the swarm of feelings inside me. And I can't hold myself together anymore.

Tears fall down my mud-splattered face.

He sits back on his heels, looking me over, his lightness filling in around us. Then, one swift motion has him on his bottom, his legs on either side of my tucked body. He takes my ankle and unfolds my leg, drawing it over his knee, then the other, outstretching my legs over his.

I can only feel the tears, the struggle of my heart trying to keep itself in one piece as he holds my waist and pulls me closer. And closer. Until I'm in his lap. Until my legs hug him. Until his arms so tentatively find their way around my back. Until breathing is a burden. And he looks at me. With those eyes. At every falling tear. He simply tugs me nearer when my legs tighten around him, when my tears wet his shirt.

I can't take the silence, the depth of his stare. I punch two fists into his chest, into that tiny space between us, right over his heart, my face crumpling. "She's my mother," I sob.

CHAPTER 36

One dark brow rises.

It's the only sign he heard me mention my mother. He doesn't ask who, doesn't question my tears, doesn't take one look at my knuckles digging into his chest. He goes for his knife instead, pulling it from his pocket, and brings it to my face. His eyes soften as though the heaviness in my heart were his, but somehow they hold on to their sharpness, that edgy glint catching the moonlight.

One side after the other, stroke after stroke, he scrapes the cold blade over my cheeks and down my jaw, wiping away my tears before licking the metal clean. He holds my gaze, watching me sniffle. My shoulders quake, my lip tight between my teeth as I try to stop the salty streams. His tongue slides over the knife's surface until not a tear falls, my breath fogging the silver as he pulls it away one last time.

I stumble through the act of breathing, addled by his gentle touch and the way he takes those little jewels of sadness from me and makes them part of him. "What are you—"

"Don't." He shoves the handle of his knife longways into my mouth, pressing on it so I can't spit it out. His thumb taps the metal. One, two, three times, and he leans in so close our noses touch. "Don't let me do this," he warns, his voice uneven, pained.

His pinky strokes my temple, and with his quiet, steely words and trembling touch, something hard has me biting down on that knife—*him*, his cock crowding between us, growing.

Despite his words, his free hand goes to my ear, thumbing and stroking its shell. He dips a finger inside, and I squirm in his lap, my hips sliding forward. He lets out a fast breath at the movement, and grips my ear tighter. Saliva dribbles down my chin. One more tap, and he pulls the knife from my mouth and slips it under a lock of hair in my face, guiding it away.

I can't move my hands from where they rest on my legs, can't let myself take hold of this man and can't—not even if I dredge up every maddening moment—bring myself to push him away. I look at his beat-up face, the heat he spews from every pore, and I beg with my eyes. I beg him not to do the things I want him to do while I speak in the most hushed of tones, fighting each word. "Don't do it."

He groans, desire and the rigor of restraint rising in his throat like faint thunder.

"Stop?" I offer, but my breathless attempt at resistance screams the opposite.

Another sound makes its way from his chest, more primal than the last. He shakes beneath me.

I swallow. *Hard.* "No?" It's excruciating, the word leaving me.

Another groan, and that control, that tightly coiled band holding him back—it snaps. He's free, and even the air around us changes, raw and possessive, biting cold. His lips graze my cheek, so lightly I might be imagining it.

I don't dare move, not even when he flattens his tongue and licks the trail of saliva from my face, terribly close to my open mouth, my lips. Warmth spreads over my cheeks and down, flushing through my chest, and down again. To my belly. And down, *so far down.* I shudder, an uncontrollable ripple of pleasure at the warm wetness, at what he does to me.

And if I make a sound as my neck arches back, my hips and chest seeking him out, I can't hear it over the firing up of my senses, the blaze now roaring at my core. He snatches my jaw and forces it back down. Every inch of me is screeching—shrieking no, shouting yes, my body pulling me in two, doubt and desire rampaging through me. My moral compass spins out of control, round and round until it marks its point, finds home.

I want him.

His wide eyes dart back and forth, such a panic in them, such hunger that I dig my fingers into my legs, holding my hands back from acting on those same feelings.

"Fuck, Never." His throaty voice rumbles through me. "Stop me before I fucking devour you."

My arms finally move, unbearable desire forcing them into action, giving him what he wants.

I shove his chest and yell. "Get the fuck away." I freeze, remembering the knife in his hand. He pokes the point into my cheek and moves closer. I flinch. A warm drop of blood slides down to my jaw.

"Fight me, Never."

I push him again.

"Harder," he says, blade still to my skin. "Godsdammit, now's your chance. Fucking fight me. Stop me."

"I can't," I scream and throw a fist at his face, only to be caught midair by his palm.

"Why the fuck not?" he roars, as if he's truly outraged that I can't overpower his massive body.

The knife moves with my panting breaths, drawing more blood. I whimper. I'm dripping wet over how he doesn't want to want me and can't help it.

"Why," he demands.

I give in. "Because I don't want you to stop!"

He smashes his lips into mine. Skin to skin, hot breath from our noses like steam between us. I'm stuck in this moment, pinned between lust and logic. He parts his mouth and nudges his tongue at my lips, hot wetness sliding along the seal, but that heat goes *everywhere*. I hold my lips shut, locked tight. I revel in punishing him—for pushing me away at the lake, for making me want him, for being so obnoxiously irresistible—but I can barely last.

His darkness crawls over my skin, and he tugs my hair to the side and pulls his mouth away, moving the knife tip under my chin. "Let me in, or my cock will split those pretty pink lips wide open. You'll like it either way."

That little smile, the heat it riles in me… I would have given in anyway, but much faster with that image in my head. "If only your cock were as big as your ego, I'd—"

He takes advantage of my parted lips, his tongue gliding inside, hot and slippery, waking up all my nerves.

And the whole world stops. I'm sure of it. It's only the two of us, and never have I wanted to be conscious more than I do now, to be present in a single moment and never let it slip away. He's so close, his touch gathering me up, hauling me in, immersing him in me, me in him. I grip the corded muscles of his arms tighter and tighter until my fingers ache.

He explores the depths of my mouth, tangling his tongue with mine. Like the darkness and lightness that come and go, the push and pull between us, he draws out slowly, the tip of his tongue tracing the roof of my mouth, then angles my head and thrusts back inside, so deep that I don't know where he stops and I begin.

I can't keep my hips still as he sucks my tongue inside of him, as if he needs me closer—needs a piece of me. *Fucking take it.* He bites down, trapping me with his teeth. I rock against him, the rhythmic pressure hardly sating the craving to be filled to the point of pain.

I whine into his mouth, destroyed with need. *Years* of need. I tried to resist. I did, but now that I've tasted him, felt him, I want more. His cock rubs between us with the movements of the deepening kiss, and I fall apart, hurting for every inch of this man.

He breaks the kiss and pushes us apart, gasping, still grasping my hair. I miss his touch immediately, the air we shared. An untamed look carves his face into nothing but angles and hard-cut gems for eyes.

My arms lift on their own accord, draping over his shoulders. I let the trace of a smile cast my mouth upward on one side. "Change your mind again?"

He tightens his fist around my hair and yanks my head back until I'm looking straight up at his lustful face. And as if he ripped it from me with that look, my breath is gone. He kisses my neck, his deep voice vibrating through me. "Always misbehaving, aren't you?"

Always. I slide my fingers up his neck and grab a handful of curls on the back of his head, as soft and devastating as I imagined. "I can't fucking stand you," I whisper and pull his hair with all my might.

"Perfect," he growls and dives his tongue back inside my mouth.

His fingertips skip along my lower back, two hands and a knife roaming under my shirt, every whisper of his touch haunting my skin.

This one escape. This one time.

I force his head closer and curl my tongue against his, over and over, deep inside. Until my tongue aches and my gums tingle. Until I'm breathless. Until I jerk away, gasping for air. And that sudden movement has his knife scraping a shallow cut along my back, leaving a stinging trail. He brings the bloody knife between us, then slides it along his tongue.

"You sick beautiful fuck," I say, watching him lick it clean, one side, then the other. "Want seconds?"

"I want every fucking drop of you." He tosses the knife aside and hauls me back to his lips for more. His hands caress my lower back, fingers wet with my blood, slipping and sliding like the passage of time, trespassing downward and wriggling under the crimps of my waistband, his kiss unrelenting. I flinch at his touch—cold, even covered in my warm blood. My hands grip his ringlets.

It feels unfairly good to be wrapped up in his arms—the last place I should be.

I rub my thumbs behind his ears, stirring a low rumble in his chest. Everything else falls away. No regrets. Only freedom from the hurt and pain and fear and death.

But he pulls back again, putting the cruelest inch between us. Then more inches.

"Please," I say.

And his face is back in mine, bruises shining, eyes tunneling into me. "That's not how this works."

Fingers still dipped below my waistband, he bends down and unleashes his tongue on my neck, licking my collarbone, my throat, my jaw and all the way to my earlobe, and that little part of me—he sucks it into his mouth. I gather up as much of his hair as I can and tighten my grasp so he'll never pull away again.

But he does.

Then returns to whisper in my ear. "I'll tell you when I want you to beg."

Dammit, I need him. And I want to hate him. That wetness low down gushes again. My hips meet his, and I work my hands down his back, cherishing his form, every muscle and bone and the give of flesh under his damp shirt. My ear is back in his hot mouth as my hands find their way around his sides, tucking between our bodies and inching down the ridges of his abdomen to the sliding angles of a V, following them down and down and—

He recoils and hardens all over, eyes darkening. His hand slides from my pants and into his pocket. In a split second filled with the clang of metal and the silent sinking of my soul, he grabs my arms, and this man who just kissed me cuffs my wrists behind my back.

"You won't be running from me again unless I'm chasing you," he says, tightening them, then smacks a kiss on my lips. I'm stunned, mouth open as he pushes me off his lap, bends my knees and cuffs my ankles.

Finally, words surface. "What in the raging fuck are you doing?"

Kneeling before me, he looks down at me with those beautiful brown eyes, full of the same hesitation that nags at me, and so clearly wanting, longing, *needing*... and resisting.

"I can't—fuck—I can't do this." His fingers tug at my ear, an affectionate touch, his eyes falling shut for the time it takes my heart to remember to beat, then he backs away.

I'm speechless, still dizzy with desire, wet and swollen and distracted as he collects his knife with a blood-soaked hand. Eyes heavy with regret and a pain I know all too well, he admires the blade up close before wiping the remaining smears of blood on his thigh—and walking away.

CHAPTER 37

The whispers of the trees dissolve into silence after the rush of life following another vision fades away. I can't give way to sleep after the eventful night, much less with the shiver in my bones and the tangled net of thoughts tightening around my head. Kelter, screaming babies, my mother's painful touch… and Eli, how he somehow took away the pain, the way he kissed me, the way his cock rubbed—

No. Not going there. I lick my lips. I can still taste the metallic tang of blood from his dark aura like a lingering kiss. But I only want him because I'm hurting, because my mother is worse than any version of her I concocted during recent years to convince myself I wasn't missing anything. And because I don't know who I am… or what I am.

I thought the elixir chose my life for me, imprisoning my mind, but I chose it—every path, every direction, every landmark on my map leading to this moment. And I get to keep choosing. What to believe. Who to trust.

And I choose to ignore the man sitting on the other side of the clearing, watching me. It doesn't matter that he saved me at the lake, that he wiped away my tears or how good it felt when he forced his tongue so deep. Those very same hands that wandered over me locked me in cuffs right after. Then he walked away.

I'm just a mistake to him.

Focus. I have to find Kelter. I have to go home.

I pinch my eyes shut and roll my head back against the tree, counting minute after minute until the thoughts fall away.

A rapping sound rides on the wind, low and steady, occupying the edges of my half-asleep mind. The boomy pulse quickens, and my heart mimics the anxious beat. My eyes pop open. A peppery scent fills the air.

Eli is kneeling in the center of the clearing, bent over a wide tree stump with a cluster of flat rocks arranged into a drum set atop it. He raps them with the length of his fingers, whacking them in a fluid pattern of blurry hands. Skin on rock. Rock on skin. Slapping and tapping. His eyes are closed, his movements exaggerated as though the music in his head flows from the looseness in his elbows, the dancing hills of his shoulders. Somehow he's mastered the art of escape, found a peace in this realm, one he can reach for even in the woods at night. He's a completely different man from the rigid, rankled one I see so often.

And that choice to ignore him slips deep into the depths of my mind. I stand up and take one tiny cuffed step toward him at a time. The beat loudens, pulsing through me in violent waves.

He's beautiful, there in the dark, the moons illuminating him from behind and casting a deviant shadow across the clearing. It lunges toward me with sweeping, drumming motions, pulling me closer and dragging me into his spell. A soft wind flows over my body, taking away the cold of my damp clothes and warming me, though not a single leaf rustles in the trees.

His eyes open a slit, and a twitch of awareness confirms he sees me. He doesn't stop. One hand reaches to his side and picks up a burning roll of teva. He tucks it between his tightened lips and inhales deep, his other hand thumping away at the rocks, his body rolling. He extends his arm toward me, the roll resting between two fingers.

An escape.

But it's not what he offers in his hand that makes my cuffed feet pick up one after the other, or the way he moves, or his sculpted face. And it's not the memory of his lips on mine.

It's something dangerously infectious… yet irresistible. Something that wakes up inside me when we're near, something that strums to life amidst all the death in my head.

I cross the clearing and kneel at his side in the melted hail and dirt, wrists still cuffed behind my back. He lets the air loose from his swollen chest, a cloud of clove-scented purple smoke escaping from his mouth.

I don't think twice. I don't think at all. My lips part, and he slides the roll between them. I take a long, delicious hit, watching the ember drag upward until my lungs ache with fullness and my cheeks puff out. His eyes are on me as he assaults the drums, his movements looser, his blows harder. I hold in the spicy smoke until I explode from within, seized by a coughing fit. Unphased, he bangs away. The goodness travels straight to my brain, cutting through all the knots and ties I can't undo, and my thoughts run loose, lost in the haze.

He watches me closely, my eyes teary from coughing, and brings the roll back to my lips for another hit. I suck in the smoky escape, the red glow almost reaching his fingertips. I cough again, less this time. His eyes close, the roll now on his lips, and he inhales until there's nothing left to burn. Such intensity, such devotion. I want him to inhale me like that—until there's nothing left.

I bend into a slouch. The very last of my worries whisper away with the thick smoke, swirling higher, dispersing into the night. Eli pulls at my waist, a wrenching movement, sending me falling without hands to catch myself. But he catches me... and sweeps me in front of him. Urgency crashes through me, my body craving the undeniable attraction—and fighting it, denying the heat sprinting through my veins, the swelling between my legs, the tingle of my skin under his rough hands.

I kneel in the slush, wedged between his thighs and sitting on my cuffed ankles. My back and arms are to his chest, and it takes only a second for him to wrap his arms around me, crossing them over my front and tightening. His chest presses against me, tearing the breath from my lungs. The metal on my wrists pushes into my lower back.

I can't get enough of his hands on me. I hate that I crave his touch, the lure of his gaze. Everything I think I loathe about him is drowned out by those eyes that let me in deep, let me see past it all, yet nothing at all. Without even setting sight on those brown irises, I sink into them.

"It took every fucking scrap of strength in me to walk away from you, and you come to me?" He hugs me tighter, a struggle evident in his shaky embrace. "You're going to ruin everything."

"How?" When he doesn't answer, I confess, "I don't want to feel right now."

He scoffs. "If you're looking not to feel anything, you're in the wrong arms."

I rest my head back on him. "I don't want to hurt."

"Also the wrong arms."

"Fuck, Elivander. The cuffs. Take off the cuffs," I say, my breathing rapid.

He speaks into the back of my hair, his hot breath on my scalp. "Why would I take them off when I like them so much?"

Maybe I should be appalled. I try to make my voice sound like I am. "You *like* them?"

He purrs as he speaks, words dribbling over me. "I like the hard metal against your skin, the little red marks that take days to fade, the sound they make banging into each other when you fight back—and most of all..." His breath warms my ear, and I snap my head to the side to escape the sensation. "I like that you can't get away."

Yes, yes... appalled was right, but my body reacts in quite the opposite way. Maybe I like being at his mercy and given the chance to defy without fear, to resist without ridicule. I wiggle my hands at his crotch, metal clinking. "Then you might as well tighten them, make it worth my fight."

He groans, flustered, and sets his chin on my shoulder. It presses into me with every syllable. "I told you not to let me do this. I told you."

"Then shoved your tongue in my mouth."

His arms squeeze tighter. "I fucking tried. But now—it's too late to stop me."

My voice cracks, letting out only soft, scratchy words. "Stop you from what?"

"What I'm about to do..." He licks my ear, a long hot stroke from lobe to tip. "To you."

CHAPTER 38

My insides heat at Eli's voice, his words, his tongue on my skin. I can't decide if I want to lean into his wet warmth or pull away and slap him. "I thought you couldn't do this."

"I can't."

"You're not making sense."

"You hate me, don't you?" he asks.

A little. A lot... maybe not at all. This isn't about the tenderness I know was behind his forceful kiss. Or what I see in him. Or the man I want to take apart and map his every thought and feeling so I can follow along. I can't let him think I want anything more than he wants—to simply fuck away the feelings. It'll scare him off. And I *need* this. I angle my head, trying to look up at him. "So much. This means nothing."

He lets out a strained breath with a controlled tremble to it, as though he's holding back things I can't imagine. "Nothing."

Keeping me tucked tight against him, he uncrosses his arms and plays the stone drums on the stump in front of us, smacking and building a rhythm. Our bodies move together—his hips rolling with mine, his chest becoming my own, my breath, his breath—until I can't tell the difference, the beat as fast as our drumming hearts.

No warning strikes before the rhythm stops and he leans back, pulling me with him and wrapping me up. His lips clamp onto my neck, sucking, my skin drawn into his eager mouth, teeth scraping, tongue rolling. Then nothing. Only the scorching air from his lungs whisking over me, cold on my wet skin.

"This is how it's going to go," he lectures. "I'm going to fuck you until I don't want to anymore, until I don't spend every minute thinking of me inside you, until I don't see your face when I close my eyes, and you're not a constant fucking distraction with every godsdamn breath I take."

"Careful… I might think you care."

He only takes a deep, measured breath and continues. "Then I'm going to do it again. In every position. Every tight little hole will be for me. And I'll take you home, little Never. I'll lock you up and keep you as mine forever, and you just go on hating me. Can you do that for me?"

Lust flips my stomach and wets my core. "I hate you." *But I don't.*

"Just like that," he murmurs. "Good girl."

"Fuck you."

"Patience. First, I'm going to make you squirm."

A quiet gasp leaves me. "No."

"No? You don't want me to do this?" His mouth is on me again, exploring, tasting, his tongue slipping under my shirt collar.

Yes, I do.

The slick heat blasts me with need, a deep, demanding need, but with a foggy purple patience I've never known before. I look around at the towering trees lining the clearing, the dark shadows living and breathing between them, trying desperately to resist the steep incline toward feverish bliss.

"Not at all," I mumble.

His lips abandon me, his tight embrace easing, as if he believed my words.

I push my head back against him in protest. "Don't stop."

"Not even if—"

"Whatever I say, don't fucking stop."

I sense his relief, the smile over my shoulder, and I'm unable to tame the upward curl of my own lips. He understands my need for resistance—and for him. The semblance of hatred is our buffer, preventing other feelings from crashing into each other.

He slides his hand over my necklace, leaving my chest burning, and up my throat, tipping my head back and wrapping his fingers around my neck. Then those fingers compress, harder and harder, my life in his hands. I'm still not scared of him. He wants me alive. He saved me.

I trust him.

The realization takes my breath away, more than his hand ever could. But trust is the path to betrayal. To pain. To loss.

"And don't do this?" Darkness drips from him. Still holding my throat, he slides my shirt off my shoulder and fastens his teeth on the newly bared skin, biting—a whisper between each pinch.

"Never. Ever. Never. Ever..."

I let slip a strangled moan, and he releases me. His nose nudges my jaw until my head rolls to the other side, exposing a pathway down my neck. He follows with more bites that build in force with his breaths.

"Never. Ever. Going... to let... you go."

His teeth sink into the sweet spot in the crook of my neck, hard enough to pierce the skin. The anger mounting in me only amplifies the pleasure. I want to feel alive. I want to be craved so fucking hard that a beast awakens, primed to hunt, to catch, to feast... on me.

I hold in a needy groan, but he smacks a rough kiss on my throat as if he heard it forming there. "Only *I* taste you, Never. If anyone else makes you bleed, I'll slice them open and drown them in their blood." He latches his mouth onto the fresh marks, easing the slight sting with circles of his tongue.

I've never felt safer. My head falls back against him. Not a cloud remains, and I swear the stars shine brighter than ever before, damn near blinding. They remind me of Kelter.

What am I doing?

"What else don't you want?" Eli murmurs in my ear.

My mouth betrays me, letting out a soft whine, but I search for self-restraint, something to reel me back to the moment, out of the purple haze and back to the facts. "I don't want your hands on me," I grit out, much too breathily—my biggest lie yet. I fight his grasp.

"Like this?" he says, ignoring my thrashing. His arms unwind from around my middle, and he drags the firm grip of his hands over my knees and up my inner thighs, stilling me.

"Or like this?" He takes the soft pouch of my belly in his grasp then rides up the ridges of my ribs, dipping between each one, feeling them through my shirt, higher and higher, then in. His palms slide onto my breasts, and fingers drill into my soft flesh. A rush of hot breath hits my neck. My back arches, pushing my chest into his touch.

"Dammit."

"What else?" His fingers dig deeper, and my body trembles at all he holds back. "Let me hear it."

The things I don't want? Like every inch of me explored? To feel those hands under my clothes? To be pleasured into madness? But it's all in my mind, my private, troubled mind. Hiding.

"I thought all you wanted was for me to shut up, and now you're asking me to talk?"

He shoves his fingers into my mouth, pulling my jaw open. "What this little mouth does is up to me." I bite down. He grunts and rips his fingers away with a laugh. "You can't get enough. Tell me what else."

I can't play his game. I can't form the words he wants, bring those thoughts to life. They're mine. "Does it really take you this long to get hard? Hurry up and fuck me already."

"I've waited too long for this not to play first." He pinches my nipples through my shirt, fingers like clamps. "What first?"

I exhale, a sound of ecstasy escaping me. Nothing else seems to matter—the before, the after, the what-ifs or the how comes. It's me and him and the heat between us. "Shit… everything."

"That's cheating." His arms trap me in place, inescapable.

"I-I want…" Desire chokes the words from me. "I can't."

He hugs me closer. "I guarantee whatever dirty little thought is in your head, I have it too. I want it too. I want it more. I'll fuck you deeper and harder than you can imagine—after you come on my hand. That's what I want—your juices dripping all the way down to my elbow."

Oh, *this man*.

He slides his tongue into my ear and back out—an unwelcome invasion of warmth and fullness, forbidden sensations. "You think you can run from me? Go ahead and try, misbehave," he hisses. "I'll track you down and chain you up, and we'll do this again and again until every perfect bit of you accepts that you're mine."

Why do I want him to do exactly that so I can fight him over it, defend myself, have the voice and strength he brings out in me? *Then* fuck him. I whimper and attempt to pull myself together, studying the tree rings on the stump in front of me and shifting my knees on the cold ground before I speak. "You're a fucking fool if you think that'll scare me into behaving."

But I only see a man finally letting go of all his pain for a minute— being himself. *With me.*

"And this means nothing," I remind him, wanting him to negate it, to admit I'm more than a find-and-fuck fling.

"Nothing," he assures me again, locating the bottom hem of my shirt and slipping his hand inside. My abdomen shudders at his touch, and he probes further, his fingers walking up and up. He pauses. "And now what?"

I squirm at the pulsing between my legs, at the way he wants me all to himself, what he'll do to have me, his raw scent, the things I don't want to say—the things he *won't* say. But his hovering, waiting, teasing hands have all the control, and I need them.

"Fucking touch me already."

He runs his fingers along the bottom of my bra, my heart skipping every other beat. "Never"—a nibble on my neck—"you're going to have to be a little more specific."

"You're going to have to go fuck yourself."

"I have you for that." He traces the curve of my breasts and tucks his fingers between my legs, curling and prodding over my pants. Every inch of me awakens beneath his touch—the ache of desire and the burn of fury mixing and melding into a single pending explosion, unchecked, my mind wrecked and raw. And I cave.

CHAPTER 39

P ut your damn hands on me, in me, everywhere. I want my nipples between your teeth. Your tongue on my stomach. Your head between my thighs." My body folds in on itself at the image that hits me, and as though someone else were drawing the thoughts from the marrow of my mind and putting them into words that aren't my own, I say, "I want to suck you then fuck you until I come so hard I cry."

I slam my mouth shut.

He broke me. "I didn't…" The pending lie fights my tongue.

Eli's groan thunders against my back. I'm a hot, throbbing, humiliated mess when he slides his hand inside my bra, cupping my breast, his fingers above the hidden treasures tucked inside. But his hand retreats just as quickly as it slid in.

"One thing at a time." He exhales and pulls my hips into him, anchoring himself to me, his hard cock pressing against my ass and his palm smashing my mound. Knowing, feeling that he wants me like that—it destroys me.

He growls in my ear. "Spread your legs for me, little Never."

I freeze, his words as pleasurable as his touch. "No," I say, to hear them again. He hesitates, unmoving. "Do not make me wait," I hiss, spurring him to release a breath.

"I said spread them." He forces my thighs apart, two rough palms pressing outward. I try to shut them tight, but he holds me open and slips a hand under my waistband. It's cold. Goosebumps crawl over my skin as he shoves his finger inside me. I cry out at the icy pleasure, my hips bucking forward, my knees parting.

"That's it, wide fucking open for me. I told you this was my pussy," he says. "It's like coming home."

"Can't the others hear us?" I ask, panting, my eyes darting from tree to tree.

He curls his finger inside me. "Every sound."

Ugh. I don't even care.

"We can hurry things along if it bothers you," he says with fake concern. "They won't hear a thing if my cock is in that loud little mouth."

I make more noise, nothing intelligible as I spread my legs wider and push upward, trying to force his finger deeper. His thumb finds my clit… and crushes it, rending another yell from me.

"You know, you're really fucking wet for someone who didn't want me touching her only minutes ago." His finger pulls out and taps over my entrance, a quiet, wet slap. "Still a liar."

"That is *not* my fault." I wriggle my hands on my lower back, cuffs clanking as I stretch my fingers down and grab his length through his pants. "This is to blame."

He gasps and bites my earlobe, then retaliates. His fingers sweep up my slit, scooping up juices, and he sticks those wet fingers up my shirt and back into my bra with a punishing quickness. He captures my nipple between his knuckles, pinching and slipping and sliding.

I buckle at the waist, escaping his touch and nearly banging my head into the stump. His palm presses the base of my spine and climbs all the way up, and he wraps his hand around my neck and yanks me back against him, my ass colliding with his cock. "No, no. You don't get to escape this."

"You're so fucking controlling."

"And you're so fucking stubborn." He reaches between our bodies, lowering the front of his pants. Then his scorching flesh is in my hands, tip dripping, skin so soft, and the rest so damn hard. My fingers tremble—at the heat, the size, the intimacy. I stroke him, as best I can with my bound hands, my rings sliding over the wetness I spread upward. His hips move into me, adding rhythm to my fumbling motions.

Reaching around to my front again, he slips both hands into my pants and runs them down my inner thighs and back up. He massages the creases on either side of my swollen lips and drags his fingers all over, circling around my core, touching everywhere but where I need, all the while humming the tune of his song in my ear, his chest vibrating against my back. I move my hands faster over his cock, imagining it filling me with those movements of his hips.

I suck in the night air, ripe with the scents of pine and bark and arousal. *How* am I letting this happen?

Finally, his finger dips back inside me. And it doesn't matter how. Nothing matters. His other hand grips my bare thigh.

"Don't fucking go gentle on me," I say.

A second finger slips in, softly stretching. *Harder, dammit.* I summon the pain of patience, forcing myself to ease into the pleasure, relax back into his touch, the rocking of our bodies, his wordless song. My eyes fall shut, only to fly open a second later as another finger rams inside of me, then a fourth.

I scream, pleasure and pain catapulting through me. My hands tighten around him, and he hitches forward. The tearing stretch, the ache of fullness, the wetness—fuck. When my hips should retreat from the attack, they don't. They push into his hand, seeking more.

His ragged voice sounds over our heavy breathing. "Just making room. For what's next."

I squeeze him tight at the thought as those four fingers ram into me again, inch after inch, in and out and out and in, as hard and dominating and unstoppable as my visions. Taking everything I am. Wrecking and consuming me over and over. His hand pounds against me, wet slaps mingling with the chink of metal with every shove inside.

He's vicious, and I love it.

I dare to look down. His hand moves fast, pumping inside the front of my pants, the waistband stretching and retracting, revealing flashes of skin and glistening fingers inside. And that's it, that sight, that fullness— I can't stop it.

"Go ahead, little Never. Hate me, fight me all you want, but don't fight this. Come for me."

"Not for you," I seethe, and with full-body breaths and unhindered moans growing louder and longer with every slamming entrance, my body rolls and rolls, meeting his hand, thrusting upward, and when that sweet release comes, I abandon all control. My walls crush his fingers in an uncontrollable rhythm, wetter and slicker by the second, and his fingers fuck me even harder. My cries are rabid, raw, downright riotous, escaping into the night with all the cursing.

"*Fuck fuck fuck.* You seductive prick, I won't come for you." My legs shake violently as my body seeks center, my hips jerking at random. I pant, limp in his grasp, conquered.

"Too late." A kiss lands on my neck. "Not so stubborn *now.*"

"Eli." I stretch his name into a moan and stare up at the black sky.

He twists his fingers as he pulls them out—a slippery spiral of knuckles—and watches the drops slide down his arm. Then he slaps his hand over my mouth, smearing my juices over my lips and cheeks and chin, careful to stay out of biting range.

"Say it again." His wet hand slides down my neck. And squeezes.

I give him nothing. I stay silent, loving his hand on me. He presses harder, my air gone. It's not until I'm lightheaded that I scrape out his name again.

He lets go and twists my neck back. "Is this the only way to make you behave?" Then he licks my face, tasting me, lapping up every bit that he slathered over me.

I smile. "Screw you."

His hands drop to my hips, yanking the back of my pants and underwear halfway down my ass. Then I feel it, his hot skin against mine as his cock slides into the pants, tucked tight inside the waistband. His stubbled cheek rubs against mine, then his lips, and they quirk into a smile. "Ready for me, my little Never?"

I push back into him with an impatient moan. "You take fucking forever. You'd better last just as long."

"Down." He kisses my temple, then his hand glides up my body to the back of my head. A sharp push bends me at the waist until my cheek smacks the stump. He's completely feral now, no sign of his gentle side left. And I don't miss it, even as I taste blood in my mouth, even as phantom fingers roam along my neck and back, his dark aura in full effect. I used to want to run, now I want nothing more than to stay here, with him.

One hand holding my head down with a fistful of hair, he tugs my pants lower with his other hand, exposing me to the cold night air. My knees grind into the ice cold dirt, my arms stretched down my back and meeting at my cuffed wrists. He pulls my hips back, and the head of his cock rubs against me, slick and hot.

He slides up and down my slippery soaked core, smacking my clit, teasing my entrance, then presses himself against my ass. Feeling his cock grind against me is enough to make me afraid of where else he might put it, and I pull my hips away. He hauls me back against him, spreading his fingers on either side of my ass where his cock is waiting.

"All mine," he whispers, then draws back with a deep groan. "I want to see every face you make while I fuck you." He lifts me up, turns me around, and like a trophy on display, he sits me on the stump, surrounded by the rock drums.

It's instant, not a split second passing. He holds my face and kisses my lips, his tongue slipping inside, and *the passion*—his frantic breaths, his needy touch, the way he gets as close as he possibly can. His hands ravish every inch of me, smoothing over my back, tracing the curves of my sides, thumbing my hard nipples through my shirt.

I need my hands on him, to feel his skin under my fingertips. I lean back, catching my first look at his cock, standing tall and so damn thick and hard that my stomach clenches and flutters.

"Take off the cuffs."

Terror captures the black and brown of his eyes, and he grabs my arms. "I'm not letting you get away from me again."

"My hands then. Let me feel you."

He grips my thighs tight, breathless and panicked, closes his eyes and reopens them with renewed desire. "Fuck it."

Still kneeling before me, he reaches into his pocket, pulls out a stone and frees my hands. The cuffs fall to the ground. The stone follows. I roll my wrists and reach for him, pulling him close and pinning his thighs between my knees. His eyes go straight to mine—a moment of hesitation for both of us. Face-to-face like this, my hands on him, it's another story. I search his eyes for an answer that only I have. Do I really want to let this man take me?

Then the moment ends as fast as it began, and I have my answer. I wrap my arms around him, claiming him for myself, but it's not enough. Not enough answers, not enough escape. I need more. Skin. Muscle. Contact. I pull his shirt over his head, past his molded arms, and toss it aside. Fuck, his chest is gorgeous, scarred and sculpted, scratched and bruised. A recent wound mars his belly. I place my hands on him, and everything intensifies—the urgency, the heat, the need, the speed with which he moves the rocks, making room for the coming collision of our bodies. He takes the last rock, turns and leans into the toss—and I see it.

And it's not the first time.

My heart flip-flops, my hands falter, and I suck in a long breath. *This* man. I slide forward off the stump, my knees touching his, and I rub my palms up his bare chest. My lips land below his collarbone, as high as I can get on his tall frame. And I kiss down, flicking my tongue over his nipple, and down again, scraping my teeth over his ribs, and down, sucking and licking the pack of solid muscles covering his abdomen. I move lower, kissing down that trail of hair below his belly button, bending my body as I go and lowering his boxers and pants to his knees.

He groans in anticipation, his hands finding my head, his fingers lacing through my hair. I reach to my side and pick up the discarded cuffs. He freezes, holding my head in place as I move the cuff to his wrist.

"You're misbehaving…"

"Do you trust me?"

He smiles down at me, a wretchedly beautiful, mind-melting smile. *"Never."*

"Good." I snap the metal over his wrist and pull down on the other hanging cuff. He responds with a low, sexy laugh, then lets go of my hair with the cuffed hand and allows me to lower him until he's sitting on his ankles, his knees spread before me, giving me all the access I need. My other hand moves to his balls, fondling, rolling, my fingers grazing that sensitive spot behind them. His cock twitches, taunting me.

"A taste for a taste. I believe I owe you," I say.

An incoherent response slurs past his lips. I lower myself over him, spilling hot breath onto his pink tip. The fingers of his free hand tighten in my hair, and a fat white drop comes out. I look up at him, and he's still looking down at me, licking his lips. So I stick my tongue out, curve it upward and scoop the drop from him. He lets out a roar and throws his head back.

My only chance.

I squeeze his balls as tight as I can, my nails digging into the soft, loose skin.

His next roar is one of fury. And pain. He releases my hair and falls forward. I wriggle my way out from under his shocked body, wrench his arm back and slam the other cuff around his ankle, shackling him hand to foot. Then I stand back, taking in his bare chest and low moans.

He turns his contorted, abused face up to me, confusion and agony written all over it. "What in the godsdamn fuck are you doing?" He heaves a breath and pulls at the cuffs, now fully realizing his situation.

I pick up the stone between us, uncuff my ankles and pocket it. Then I take another four steps back before I tell him—

"It was you."

PART 3

BETRAYED

CHAPTER 40

W hat was me?" Eli asks, trying to get up and stumbling with his wrist cuffed to his ankle.

"In the forest." I step back again. The ground spins beneath me. "In Caldera." A knife flashes.

His eyes flare with understanding, winning over the confusion he wore a moment ago. He parts his lips, but can't get anything out—not even a denial.

My eyes burn, but I threaten to gouge them out if a single tear escapes, and they comply. For now.

"H-how?"

That's what he manages to say? "Your back."

He slaps his free hand over the tattoo—two black towers etched on his back—and his face falls, then hardens.

A crushing pain settles in my chest. This is so much worse than him taking me away from the Centress' torture and keeping me for his own obsessions. He's the reason I'm separated from Kelter. He's the reason I'm in Sonnet and not home, searching for my parents... for the mother I never would have found there. He made the false report that I was taken on this side of the border.

He's it.

I let him grapple with the bleak silence between us, my endless supply of curse words suddenly spent, meaningless.

"Never..." He crouches next to the stump.

I retreat.

"I know you're... you, but I thought—" *I thought there was someone underneath all that pain, that toughened exterior, someone that saw me, yet still wanted me.*

"You could have at least told me, explained that you were working your shift at the border, doing what the Centress wanted. It's not like I thought you actually cared about me," I lie again. "I know you only keep me around for whatever you think is inside of me. From the first time I saw you—it's been so obvious. I didn't want to believe it." My face crumples, but my tears don't dare show themselves.

His brown eyes widen. "Believe what?"

"That you really are the bad guy here." Disgust bubbles under my skin. "And I let you put your hands all over me." *In me.*

He hobbles a few steps. "Get over here and uncuff me."

I walk backward. "Why would I when you like them so much?"

He growls, yanking his cuffed wrist. "You'll be back in the Centress' hands in a day. It's not safe. Come to me."

I search the clearing for the direction we entered from, orienting myself.

"Never, don't you run away from me again. There's nowhere you can go that I won't fucking find you." The ferocity in his words hits nowhere near as hard as the panic splashed across his face. "I'll *always* take you home with me." He drops to his knees, scuffing closer, thighs bare and cock out. "Don't make this difficult."

The sweet swears surface, along with a slew of other words I don't mean to say. "Fuck no. Not even in my nightmares would I let you put this back on me. You weren't the one inside a damn sack, taken from everything you knew in life, then blamed for it and imprisoned and attacked. And you know what the worst part is? How badly I want you to sweep me up in those stupid strong arms, wipe away the tears that are about to flood my face and tell me how fucking sorry you are. That I'm worth caring about. But that's not at all who you are, and wanting that, wanting you to be someone you're not—even for a second—is worse than you not doing any of it."

He stares up at me, his lightness and those dark eyes trying to pull me back to him.

Not this time.

I turn around and march away, leaving a shirtless man alone in the woods—a stranger.

Outside the small clearing, my eyes betray me. My tears evolve into sobs as I reach the carriage packed with eerily quiet babies, unaware of the fate they nearly met. Milo and the others are passed out too, slumped against the trees. I silence my sobs so I don't wake them up while reliving moment after moment—the fear, the pain, the danger—all the way up to this very night, wrapped in Eli's arms.

"I'm going to take you to your mothers where you belong. And they're going to love you," I assure the babies in a whisper. The only sign they're alive is the tiny puff of fog below each of their noses.

I'll push the carriage myself. I won't make them wait or leave them alone in the village. Powered by the pain within, I plow through the cold mud around the wheels, my hands like spades, driving downward, scooping and flinging until they're free from the stiff hold, and the carriage takes off.

Shit. I run after it, long, leaping strides. My hand catches the back, and I climb up. I find a gap between the wall of the carriage and the baskets and stuff myself inside. It careens along, swerving around trees and boulders. I hug myself tight through the sprinkling of rain. And I cry until I'm out of tears, my face streaked with salty, dry trails.

There's no chance Kelter would want to live in Sonnet after all this. Being born here doesn't mean this is where I belong. We'll find a way to stop the Centress from using the elixir on Calderans, then I'll take Kelter home.

I watch the scenery with swollen, burning eyes, a palette of brown and green brush strokes blurring by, then swaying golden grass. I'm all turned around. This doesn't look like the way back to the Ring—because it's not. Milo said the carriages take the elixir to the falls…

It steers along its predetermined path, splashing across a shallow stretch of river and weaving through woods at a sickening speed, putting more and more distance between Eli and me. There's a reason I chose never to drive in Caldera, apart from the sudden visions that would surely kill me behind the wheel—I can't handle the motion. Nausea wells in my gut. An hour or two must have passed by now. The pinks and purples of dawn play at the horizon.

Water roars in the distance, growing louder with the rickety clatter of the wheels. The same wheels laying against the wall in that stone room, the one that keeps coming back to me. Would Eli have really returned that morning if Kelter and I hadn't gone through the wooden door? Would he have taken me straight to the castle, and Kelter too, pushing us both to harness the magic he needs? Would things have been different?

Without warning, I'm crushed by the air—flattened, life sucked out of me, edgeless and blurry—then it's gone.

The border.

I have only seconds before we reach the waterfall outside the carriage window, but my useless mind chooses to spend the precious moments imagining my death instead of preventing it. The vision strikes just as the heavy mist rising from the falls sprays my face.

I'm falling, surrounded by the rushing cascade of elixir-tainted water, baskets at my side, blankets and babies floating free, all out of reach, waiting to meet the points of rocks below. They sleep, the sweet oblivion of magic on their lips as their tiny bodies make impact.

The carriage skids to a halt, and I'm pinched between the cabin wall and heavy bags of elixir, baskets sliding into my head, the vision becoming another nightmare memory, my senses awakened. I poke my head out the window and into the mist, then pull it right back in.

We're on the edge of the falls, and the drop is worse than my vision.

Dawn flips to morning. The sunshine pelts my skin with dreadful warm rays I haven't felt in a month and a half.

The Calderan sun.

CHAPTER 41

I t'll take forever to walk back to the southern part of Sonnet pushing the carriage, if I'm able. I can't carry the nine babies that are inside, but I'm not giving up on them. Or Kelter.

The air is brisk, the rising mist thick enough to taste the minerals in the cyan water as it endlessly gushes over the edge and coats my face. The sun beats down on the river's surface, and wildflowers line the banks leading up to the steep drop. The constant pounding of water on the rocks below drowns out any sounds of wildlife. Unlike Sonnet's lack of non-magical creatures, the birds and squirrels and deer of the Calderan forest are as much a part of it as the trees and the dirt.

I'm home.

And all I want to do is leave.

A pair of pale arms reach into the carriage and steal a basket.

"Hey!" I unbury myself and tumble out. The ground is foreign under my feet after the carriage ride. I run around the back in time to see Cam toss the basket—baby and all—over the falls.

This can't be real, but here she is—exactly the same, but older. Her rosy cheeks and pale skin. Her wavy midnight hair. My throat closes. I tear at the skin on my face.

Wake up wake up wake up.

I haven't seen her since I was sixteen, since I burned down that house. For every wall that fell—flames to embers to cinders—I built a new one up around me. For every shred of innocence taken from me, I forged new meaning for such things as love and hope, intimacy and pleasure. If I defined them as impossible and traitorous, then I couldn't be let down when they were exactly that. I didn't need Cam anymore, not with my walls up. I left her behind.

But now, I've messed up—caring about Kelt, letting Eli get close. I set myself up to hurt again.

"Everielle? What are you doing here?" Cam looks at me like she didn't just send an infant to its death. Like she hasn't spent decades finding families and homes for parentless children. "You're a mess. Are you wearing men's clothes?"

"Wh-what—?" I can only point at the falls, the rest of my body refusing to act.

"Gods, it's been years." She walks back to the carriage.

My feet won't cooperate.

"The Centress mentioned you were in Sonnet. She said I should keep an eye out for you, but I didn't take her seriously." She swipes three more baskets. My feet kick into gear, and I race after her, lunging to rip the baskets from her hands. She lets out a yelp and shoves me back with them. I fall on my ass in the lush, green Calderan grass, still stunned and unable to process the scene before me. She schleps the baskets to the water's edge and sends them sailing over the misty falls while I pull myself up again.

No. My heart free falls with the silent babies. "What are you doing?"

"This carriage is late as it is. I have to get home. We can chat while I work. Tell me everything you've been up to."

"You killed them." I put myself between her and the carriage.

"What? They're fine. The baskets are imbued with protection. I'll hike down after and bring them to the shelter like I always do." She tries to shove past me, but I block her.

I can't wrap my head around it. She dropped them right off the edge. I force myself to believe her, so I can breathe again. "How could you take part in this? These babies' mothers are crying for them. Sonnet is their home."

"Don't make this difficult, Everielle. You know how much I care for you, but this isn't about you."

"I know what the Centress is doing."

She softens, folding her arms over her chest and letting her eyes find mine. "I've known her a long time. Longer than I've known you."

Maybe I don't want to hear the answer, but my words spill out anyway, unsure if they're asking or telling. "Then you know who she is."

Cam taps her fingers against her arms, frowning. "You know."

I lose it. "You knew I had family all those years and never told me? You let me go from home to home my entire childhood."

"There was no other way."

"You could have returned me to her," I yell.

"Oh, hun, don't you see? She didn't want you. I was sixteen when she handed you over in a basket and told me to find you a home."

It's no different from hurling me into a solid wall. The pain breaks me just the same. I can't escape it. It's too strong, too deep. Too real.

All this time, my mother knew where I was, how to find me. She didn't want to make the time to keep me—not even for that one year before sending me to live at school. She didn't want to know me. I truly was a waste of space in her eyes, a burden she didn't care to take on. She sent me away like every foster parent did.

"She's doing what she has to do," Cam offers, as if that makes it alright.

"How long has she been doing this?" Tears well in my eyes. How many babies grew up without mothers because of her? Grew up like me?

I break into pieces—one for every home that took me in, one for every time I believed it would be the last time and one for every time I was wrong. I'm too broken to let the tears loose. The years of searching, the library trips, the records office, the wondering. Ugh, and the *hoping*. That's the worst part... the years of hoping. I wouldn't wish that on anyone. My blood snakes through me, thick with grief.

"That's enough questions." Her chin lowers, and she glances toward the carriage behind me.

"No, I have more. I need answers. I have to find my friend, and I'm going to fix this fucked-up situation. I won't let her break more families."

"Watch your tongue."

"I'm not a damn child anymore." I take a step to the side, anticipating her next move. "And I'm not going to let her control Calderans with that elixir either."

"Actually, it's time for you to take a concentrated dose of the elixir and ride this carriage back into Sonnet. Your mother will be looking for you." Cam dives, tackling me to the ground—not the move I was expecting. A rock bites into my side, and the crack of bone rivets through me. I cry out, breathless and sharp.

"Cam?" I mutter, unable to accept this reality. She was my person growing up. My only one.

She sits on top of me, black hair wet with mist, sticking to her face, holding my arms flat at my sides against the grass. "This kills me. You don't know how much."

"You can let me go," I gasp out through the pain, trying to bury it somewhere deep, far from my awareness. "I won't tell the Centress I saw you."

"I'm still me. But I have needs too." Her quiet voice is too much like the one that guided me through those early years, the one I so often hear in my head.

"What do you get for turning me in? Magic?" I can't hide my disgust.

"The Centress will take care of you. She'll give you all the escape you need. No more pain or visions. You'll be happy."

I scoff. "Does that make it easier for you?" I never dreamed of happiness. I'm not delusional—just unstable. "She's lying. What do you get?"

"This isn't easy for me." Her grip slackens ever so slightly, softening with her voice.

"What's she going to give you that's worth my life?"

She's quiet. Too quiet.

Then she laughs softly, a vibration against my thighs where she sits on me. "If anyone else in Sonnet found you, they'd hand you straight over. But I'm the one who cares enough *not* to turn you in. I'm the one she was worried about finding you." She laughs again, harder this time. "So what does she do? She offers me something I can't pass up. An out. If she has you, I don't need to be responsible for ripping babies from their mothers anymore. She won't need their magic. I get to walk away— all I have to do is give you back to your mother." Her maniacal laugh travels down my neck.

I can't appreciate the irony of it amid the pain. "Please, I'll make sure you don't have to do this anymore. Let me try." I twist under her weight, a broken rib stabbing at my insides.

Cam's tears splash onto my chest. "Know I love you, Everielle."

She lets go with one hand to reach for her pocket, and I try to push her off me. She's too fast. Something glints in her hand as she grabs my arm again and slams her weight down on me. My body convulses, rib breaking all over again. Pain anchors me to the ground. She slides her knees on top of each of my hands, pinning them at my sides. My knuckles crack under her grinding force despite the cushion of the grass.

Cam squishes my cheeks, forcing open my mouth, and holds a glass vial to my lips. With a sad grimace, she pours the liquid in. It splashes against my teeth in cold drops, coats my tongue with bitterness and puddles in the sides of my cheeks. I close my throat, refusing to swallow down the falseness. I don't want to lose myself to the elixir—even if it comes with an escape. She pinches my nose, her long, square nails gouging into my face.

Her eyes go misty. *I'm so sorry*, she mouths, then rams her palm under my chin.

My teeth smash together, my tongue caught between. Blood fills my mouth—real blood—mixing with the elixir. The need to swallow climbs my spine, the need to breathe.

Right beneath her bony knees that hold me down, I rake my fingers against the dirt, forming squashed fists. Green spikes of grass poke between my knuckles. Breathless, racked with pain and a mouthful of swirling life and lies, the white energy returns with a vengeance. There's no quiver, no gentle prodding or guiding. It explodes beneath the ground, magic traveling through a million tiny grass roots, jumping easily from one to the next.

The ground lurches. My lower half flies up into the air, ripping Cam's fingers from my nose and throwing her away from me. Her legs slam beneath the edge of the carriage.

I sit up and spit the mix of elixir and blood into the grass.

"Everielle," she cries. My fists contract.

Another explosion of energy—beautiful, raving, undeniable magic. I grip the grass blades tighter. The ground jerks and rolls again at the surge from below, and Cam slides further under the carriage.

And right over the waterfall's edge.

"Cam!"

She answers with an ever-quieting scream.

My whole body trembles, and the earth below me jolts again.

The carriage rolls after her. I push past the agony in my rib and scurry to the edge. Taking hold of the carriage, wrapping my murderous hands around that old, splintery wood, I pull with everything in me. A strength that can only be gained from surviving ten thousand deaths.

But even that strength—conjured from years of visions and drawn from the deepest pockets of pain—has no effect, no special power. I'm no one special. The weight of the carriage wins. The heavy sacks of freewill-killing elixir, the five remaining babies, my self-worth—they tip over the edge into the mist.

Gone forever.

CHAPTER 42

L oneliness hurts more than death.

Staying behind, living—that's what kills me.

Being so alone that my own breath is a slap in the face, a constant reminder of my own existence—it's enough to rip the life right out of me and set things right.

I don't know how long I lay there, the warm sunshine mocking me, the mist wetting me in wispy layers, staring up at that arch of colored scribbles in the sky. Every cursed color there is. *Take my breath away.* I begged for it.

And I prayed. I prayed to the gods, not because I suddenly believed in them, but because that's how lonely I got. Not the kind of loneliness like when I hid alone in my room for days on end, or like rotting in a cell for weeks or missing Kelter. No, I talked to the keepers of the Immortal Realm because guilt hollowed me out, leaving me so deep and hidden inside myself that I couldn't feel.

I lost myself in that patch of grass, and without even myself to keep me company, the real loneliness set in, and I sought out shadows and gods for company.

That's when I knew loneliness was lethal.

I'd still be there now if the dark shell I left behind weren't so stubborn. Only a fool walks back into a realm of enemies and traitors and memory-stealing magic. So what? I'm a fool now—whatever is left of me. A fool who won't let another child grow up with pain like mine. A fool who wants free will for a realm of people that laugh and judge. A fool who won't leave a friend behind, who keeps deals with darkness.

After passing through the strange, flattening sensation of the border, I follow my mental map back toward the heart of Sonnet, no trace of the carriage tracks. Each step takes me farther from the haunting faces of the babies in their elixir-induced sleep, and closer to my foolishness.

For once, the sky is dry—as if it shriveled up along with my sanity—but it leaves me without liquid. It would have been a good idea to quench my thirst at the falls before I set on my way, but I couldn't drink from the water that holds Cam's body. So I have no plan, no food and no water, and in this state, at least a few days' walk ahead of me. Maybe I'll reach the river before I pass out.

Evening arrives. It's as unwelcome as the jab of pain in my side with every guilty breath. I try to keep watch. I don't need sleep. Sleep is for the living, and I don't know how to live anymore.

I hug myself through the bluster of thoughts and the visions of death that stir to life when I close my eyes. I wake up from a half-sleep again and again, sitting against a tree trunk, shivering from a sticky, cold sweat—the only trace of the nightmares that stalk my unconsciousness with boldness, as though they own the place.

The light of day isn't much better. I walk for hours, a simple agreement between my feet and the ground to keep me going. The earth pushes me along through the endless trees when I can't take another step. I no longer know which way I'm going or where I've come from. Nothing looks familiar. After spending years mapping every inch of ground I covered, I'm lost, and the nature I once trusted is as unpredictable as everything else.

I wander, scanning the bushes in the undergrowth of the trees for berries, anything edible, but nothing grows here—nothing but desperation. The hunger pangs mingle with the skewering pain from my rib, and I welcome them. I stomp as I go. If I can keep feeling that sweet pain, then I'm awake and far from the nightmares.

Tonight is worse than the first night. I dream of screaming. Cam's scream, my scream, it's all the same. It never fades or ends. It severs my mind from my body and lives on in both, somewhere under that morbid rainbow that follows me from one nightmare to the next, until rough hands cover my face, trapping the scream inside me and sealing my mouth shut with the scraggly violet tendrils of the rainbow's end.

The nightmares don't even earn their name compared to the onslaught of my waking visions—the waterlogged deaths that drop me to my knees and leave me scratching my eyelids, sharp nails tearing at my skin.

Water is all I can think of when the cloud-blocked sun marks another gray midday. My throat is so parched that even my soul begs for a drop of liquid, fearing it might dry up with my body, now as light as the breeze that shoves me along. My brain is sharper than ever with the lack of food, and my body finds renewed energy that has me putting one foot in front of the other, hour after hour. What did I ever need food for?

And sleep? Crutches for the weak. I don't need them.

The birds come for me before the sun sets. They fill the sky. Their magical wings match the slow beat of my heart. It's peaceful when they sing, a chorus in the wind. I find a spot to curl up, grateful to finally be so far from the death that haunts me, even as my own edges near. Warm wings wrap around me, and the rumbly purr of a free blitzer lulls me into nothingness.

"Get off her, get off!" A man's voice, then wingbeats. So familiar.

Cold hands roll me over. "Never."

I'm not here, I tell him, but nothing comes out.

Smooth, icy metal prods at my lips, and a silky liquid trickles over and through them in tiny, lifesaving kisses, stinging the tooth punctures on my tongue.

"Never." Eli traces my brow with his thumb, sharing scents of earth and trees and the faint prick of cloves. A breeze wisps over me, warming me from the inside out. His lightness tugs at my soul. "Come back to me."

I open my eyes—a battle of wills at this point. It's early morning. Black ringlets hang like a mobile above me. My head is nestled in Eli's lap. It takes me a while to locate the rest of my body. I'm still lying on the ground, a bed of decaying leaves beneath me, surrounded by the solid, unfailing comfort of trees.

"Never," I rasp, my voice dry. *Because I'm gone. I can't come back. I was washed over the falls.*

"You have to come back. I need you." A small smile curves his lips. His fingers pinch my ear and tug, as if he missed it. "Drink. You look terrible."

"Elivander." As it comes out, I remember—how I called him *Eli* as his fingers tore me apart so perfectly, the sight of his back, cuffing him. I want to jump up and put all the distance in the world between us, but I'm too weak.

"You were at the falls," he asks and states at once.

I look away in response. Whatever part of me was at the falls is still there now—rotting.

"You could have gone home, but you came back." He runs his finger over my lips, sliced and split, the contact unnervingly gentle.

I jerk my head back the other way, trying to escape his caress, but his touch follows. "I can't leave Kelter here."

"You came back for *him*." His finger falls away, and his legs go rigid under my head. I can almost feel the surge of angry blood coursing through him.

"And to stop the Centress," I add.

"I thought you'd go back to Caldera after seeing…"

"The towers?" My heartstrings twine and tangle, the image of the tattoo all caught up in them, reminding me that he's the one who got Kelter and me into all this. He let his people hurt me. I shouldn't care. Not when I've done much worse, when I've taken a life, maybe more, sent them over the falls with whatever wretched magic seeks out my hands.

But I do care. "Hating you won't keep me from Kelter."

I try to roll off his lap, but he crushes my head against his stomach, his fingers buried in my hair and ammo-filled suspenders mashed into my cheek—a hug. I close my burning eyes, too dried up for tears, wishing I could go back to the escape I found in him. But no. He can lock me behind bars, push my body and mind, test my boundaries. But pushing my heart past its limits? Looking so deep that he managed to trick me into the slightest flicker of trust—just to demolish it? That's brutal.

"Let me go."

He looks down at my face smushed up against him, his expression unreadable, every emotion packed away tight behind the black and brown and white of his eternal eyes. I take in the contours of his face—the cut of his jaw and the scar that slices through it, the high domes of his cheeks, the angled fret of his brows—then try to loathe them as fiercely as his betrayal blisters my heart.

He fastens an arm around my shoulders, pulling me so close that I fold, pain drilling into my side from the broken rib he doesn't know about. One finger strokes my nose, bridge to tip. "How many times do I have to tell you that I'm never letting you go?"

A wave of nausea pushes me under, shrouding the pain in black bliss.

He hasn't moved.

My head is still in his lap, his hand resting on my face. His dark aura swirls around me, the scent of earthy depths. It's been hours, based on the daylight struggling to push through the heavy layer of clouds. Freshness thrums through me—like I've been brought back from the dead or just had a vision. I sit up and scoot away, the pain in my rib somehow only a dull throb.

Trees surround us, the scent of pine overwhelming me. The green of the foliage is saturated, the brown of the bark too rich. I stare at Eli, every line and angle of his face jumping out at me, his eyes dancing with life, every golden speck glaringly obvious. He has a pack at his side, similar to the canvas backpacks in Caldera, but seamless and made from a thick brown fabric that looks like dried leaves. A drawstring cinches the pack shut, its ties like roots.

"How did you find me?" I throw the question out between us, accusing, not inquiring. My matted hair springs back up when I smooth it. My clothes are crunchy and crusted, my arms coated in dirt and dried blood from the scratch of branches. The last few days still hang over me, but my feelings are a mirage, out of reach and impossible to chase. Even my anger with Eli is muted compared to the thoughts of him roiling in my mind.

Eli pockets his lucky stone, pulls his knees up in front of him and wraps his arms around them. "You went the wrong way. We're in the far north now. You must have walked in the wrong direction for days. I could feel—" He pauses, his laced fingers writhing as he devises an obvious lie. "Luck. I left as soon as Milo uncuffed me, but I had to pack supplies first." One brow shoots up. "We still need to have a little chat about that."

"About what?" I pick at a fresh scab on my arm, the brown-red color vibrant.

"You running away. Again."

I look up—straight into those striking eyes. "You mean when I realized you've been lying to me about my abduction this whole time, then pretended I wanted your cock in my mouth so I could cuff you and leave you in the woods?"

Utterly unperturbed, not a muscle twitching, he says, "I lie about everything."

"*That's* your defense?"

"I don't need one." He pulls a bar from his pack. "Eat before the elixir wears off and you're too miserable to chew."

"You gave me the elixir?" *A Hollow dosage won't work...*

"Not the Hollow elixir. That's already in the water. It's Milo's invention, his morning-after elixir."

"What kind of activities need a morning-after elixir?"

"Eat." He wags the bar at me. "It only lasts so long, and you've slept through most of it."

So that's why I feel so... fresh, as though I've downed ten cups of coffee and managed to escape without jitters. I snatch up the bar.

"Just a couple bites, or it'll hurt. You haven't eaten in days."

"And you care about that?" *About me?*

I stop stuffing my face, already in pain from my wounded tongue, and pocket the rest of the bar, hating that he's right. I swear he's about to have a fucking seizure with the way he blinks at me, a hand pulling at his curls.

"Either you care or you don't," I add, staring at his arrested features, waiting, but neither response would set me at ease. And I can't take it anymore. I swipe a canteen from beside his pack and run.

I dart between trees, dodging branches and leaping over roots, powered by Milo's elixir. It's my only chance of escaping Eli before my rib pain returns and my energy wanes. I'll find Kelter on my own. If he's still alive. I ignore the doubt weighing down my steps and look over my shoulder to see how far behind me Eli is, but he's nowhere. Goosebumps creep over me. What made me think I could outrun him? I spin around, frantic, pick a new direction and run.

Every sharpened sense has me snapping my head left and right. The thud of boots. The stretch of a shadow. The crack of twigs. The whiff of cloves. Where the fuck is he?

Maybe it's all in my head, and I managed to lose him. Passing trunk after trunk, I convince myself each one hides Eli, pressed flat to the other side, waiting for me with cuffs. I can see him—dangling the metal before my eyes. I can hear the click, the steel locking into place, and feel the pressure on my wrist bones. No no no, he likes it too much to let him win.

Anger is my only option. I can't linger on the memories, can't let him pull me in. I search for him again, nearly smacking straight into a tree as I look behind me. I push off the trunk and run on, my calves burning, cold air stinging my flushed cheeks. I shove my hair from my eyes. *Find Kelter. Stop the Centress. Go home.*

I aim for dense patches, the darker the better, running freely, my heartbeat wild. I don't need him. Or his ear tugging. Or smirks. Or protection. Or—

I scream. The canteen flies, and I'm thrown to the ground, arms bent behind my back, cheek pressed to the dirt. Sticks stab me, and a body sits on my ass, smashing my hips into pebbles and bark.

"Got you," Eli says.

His deep, haunting voice does obscene things to me. Heat swells between my legs, and my smashed nipples harden beneath me, my breasts aching. "Get the fuck off me."

"Want to play again?" he asks, lifting the hair from my face piece by piece as I struggle beneath him.

I resist relaxing at his touch. "It's not a fucking game. I need to find Kelt."

"It is. You run. I chase—and catch." He pulls on my restrained arms then folds himself over me, hot breath on my face. "And you're my prize, little Never. I get to take you home."

Fuck. I want to run only to be caught in his arms again. "I don't have a home here."

"You do," he says, stroking the shell of my ear. "With me."

I almost roll over and angry-kiss his damn face, but I'm trapped, and I must have some remaining self-control because I don't even try. I turn my head away from his touch, nose in dirt, and remind myself why this man deserved to be cuffed and left in the woods. "All the more reason to run."

He rotates my head back to the side and lets his full weight fall along the length of me, squashing my twisted arms into my back. My lungs flatten, my body immobile.

His lips find the pulse on my neck, and he whispers into my skin, "Just because you're not behind bars doesn't mean you're not mine." He bites my neck, a sharp pinch, and flicks his tongue over the captured skin. I release an airy squeal as his teeth free me. "I don't need cuffs and chains to keep you. You *want* to be caught. Your noisy little heart says it all. It talks to mine."

I know I should hate him, but the way he has all the control, the way he thinks our hearts talk, the way he craves me... and declares me *his*—it will end me. Because how can I run from someone who feeds the dark spots on my soul and lures out the fight in me that I let lie dormant? Someone who reconstructs my heart and makes all the wrong feel right?

"You're fucking heavy," I force out through broken breaths.

He shifts his hips to nestle his cock snugly between my ass cheeks, as if it belonged there. "What happened to the carriage?" he asks.

Desire drains from me. "Why would I tell you?" My brain may still be numb from Milo's elixir, but it's not stupid. I don't want to relive that. If I did, I'd have to admit Cam was at the falls, and if I do that, then I have to admit to myself that she's not there anymore. That she's not anywhere at all.

Because I killed her.

CHAPTER 43

Milo's elixir wears off, and the weakness and pain creep back in as we trek through the endless expanse of dark browns and greens of the ancient woods. I don't bother trying to run again. He has the water, and I can't seem to leave his side. By the time the cloud-blocked sun sets, I can hardly feel my legs, and my head hurts from the thoughts I've flung around all day. Even this far out, it's too risky to have a fire and lead someone straight to us, so we let the darkness fall.

I sit against a tree, rough bark scratching my back and Eli a foot away. The cold night air invades my body, a distraction from my rib—but nothing pulls me away from the deeper pain, the guilt gnawing at me, breaking off frostbitten parts of my soul and shattering them.

Hours pass before Eli's lightness edges in with an encompassing warmth. Even with all the anger I've packed inside me and stoked so consistently while brooding all day, I'm tempted to crawl into his arms—maybe another attempt to escape myself. But they're cold, and whoever it was he kissed and touched so thoroughly, she's lying in the grass at the falls. Dead.

His feet tap the hardened ground, the beat to the song of the swaying branches and the gossiping leaves playing over and over until sleep takes me.

I wake up to find Eli's eyes on me, watching me sleep, my back to a tree. He sits in his usual position next to me, pack at his side. Dew finds every surface of the gray morning, occasional cold drops making their way down from the leaves to my head and shoulders where immaterial fingers brush down my chilled back. His darkness is out this morning.

Perfect.

"You didn't tell me what happened," he says.

"You didn't tell me you put a sack over my head, hauled me through the forest into another realm and dumped me in a dark room." I turn on my bottom, pushing myself with the heels of my boots, giving him my back. "How come you were in Caldera?"

"It's—I can't say." His words come out thick and sluggish.

I flip back around so fast that I swear my rib stabs straight through a nerve. "Not even to someone you were going to fuck?" I heave from the pain. Emotional, physical—I can't tell which. Both are debilitating.

The man smiles at me. "I am so close to dragging you the rest of the way back."

I purse my lips and crank my brows up. "Did you bring a sack?"

"I wouldn't want to keep you from kicking and biting. Or muffle those screams of yours now that they only make me think of—"

"Do not finish that sentence," I warn.

"—my fingers in you."

Dammit. He has me wet just like that, remembering the delicious pain of a four-finger fuck.

"This is all your fault."

"You're the one who likes it rough. I simply give you what you want," he says, wiggling four fingers.

"I've had better. And rougher." *In my head... thinking of you.* "But no, it's your fault that I'm in this situation and Kelt is locked up, and that I wandered lost in the woods until I passed out. It's all your fucking fault."

He's quiet, slow breaths coming and going as he looks at me. "I wasn't the one who ran away."

I punch the ground, my fists landing as solid as a damn tree, but rootless, unanchored, searching for something to take hold of. Why can't I understand this man? And why do I want to?

My arms wobble. "Of course I ran away. And I don't know why you insist on keeping me around. You have no idea what you're doing or what you want, with me or anything else."

His head ticks to the side, dark eyes angled at me. "I know exactly what I want from you."

"I'm not talking about fucking me."

"Me either." He shrugs, that rogue brow lifting. "But if we were, I'd rather *show* you exactly how I'd hold you down and shove my—"

"Shit, Eli. Stop." *Don't make me want you.* "And if I don't give it to you? The other thing you want, I mean."

"You will."

"What kind of self-serving—"

"You have no idea what it's like!" He loses his mix of smirks and cold restraint, threads of desperation unraveling around him.

"Then *tell* me."

"You don't know how much I need you." His hands clench around his bent knees, every muscle and vein as strained as the air between us, yet vulnerable, brittle, as though I could shatter him with one word. "You'll do what I fucking say. There is no other option. *I* don't have another option."

Maybe I would if I could, if I had any control over this magic. If you would explain.

But he won't, and I'm not whole. I don't know what's inside of me. And I tell him as little as he tells me... because I can't trust him again. He could do anything. Worst of all, he could leave me—like everyone else—so I have to run, before he does.

But as much as I came back for Kelter and to stop the Centress, I came back for him, too, if I look past my own lies. Maybe just to understand what lurks behind those tempting brown eyes. Or to punch him. Or kiss him. I don't know. But I build up my walls. I cement them in place. I hide behind them—and I push him away with words and spite.

"You don't need me. Nature is all around us, and you aren't even trying to get me to take the magic again." Magic that I shouldn't be able to take, magic that Hollows were never capable of stealing to begin with, that not even Vaile can pull from the plants. So why can I? What am I?

He grabs hold of my shoulders, his voice as lethal as my grass-fisting hands. It's at total odds with the smirk lifting into place on his cheek. "I'm not trying to get you to take magic right now, because apparently, it takes two guards beating the shit out of me for you to figure it out."

The glowing plants at the lake... "That wasn't because of you. I was scared."

He dips closer, his face in mine, and slides one hand so damn slowly up the back of my head, closes it around my hair and bends my neck back—like when he kissed it. My breath stutters, ragged at the images he stirs up—his mouth on mine, the desire I fight.

"Scared for me," he whispers.

I shake my head, stilling instantly at the tug on my scalp. "No."

He slides his lips down my neck with a steamy breath and pulls back. "I'm starting to think you lie more than me."

The rest of the day goes similarly, each interaction and the moments in between brimming with tension—the perfect distraction from being a killer, from babies. From my mother and Kelter too. The occasional showers give way to a downpour as we round the base of a mountain. It blocks some of the wind, but none of the droplets that rap the top of my head.

My black shirt and pants hang heavy, drenched. I drag my boots through the mud, cold and wet on the outside, fuming and crackling with heat and fury on the inside—fury that I try to keep alight. But it's harder to stay mad when Eli finds me a dry spot to sit and eat. When he stops every half hour, without fail, and hands me an open canteen. Or when he holds my elbow through the muddy areas, ensuring I don't slip. That fury falters.

It's late afternoon when I stop, panting, unable to take another step. I lean against a tree.

"Are you going to tell me now?" Eli steps in front of me.

"Tell you what?"

"What's hurting you." He scans my body.

"Nothing."

"My little liar. You don't have to be so strong all the time." He leans in and slides his hand over my side and onto my back, as if he knows. "What do you want me to do? Touch you all over until I find where it hurts?"

Yes. I mean—"No."

"Are you sure? You decide where these fingers start." He taps them against my back. "I decide where they end up."

"Is that all you can think about?"

"Mostly," he says, shameless. "I can't give you medicine if I don't know what's wrong."

"You have medicine?" I hate to sound so hopeful.

He pulls away and sticks his thumbs under the straps of his pack. "Milo gave me one of everything he had."

I give in. Pain occupies every thought. "It's my rib. Back here." I reach behind me. "I think it's broken."

Fists form around the pack straps. "Who the fuck hurt you?"

I startle, but can't look away from the trembling line of his jaw, the failed attempt to calm the explosive breaths escaping him.

"Because they're dead," he adds in a tight whisper when I don't answer.

Too late. I killed her.

"You *will* tell me." He lowers his pack to the ground and kneels before me, digging through the contents—glass plinking—then pulls out a vial with a cork in the top. "One sip. It's strong." He hands it up to me, his head down, other hand still searching through the pack. But I'm utterly distracted by the sight of him on his knees before me, so close… so perfectly positioned. It only worsens when he looks up at me—and smiles. "Wet yet?" he asks despite my sopping clothes, as if he could smell the arousal coiling in my core.

I take the vial. I have no idea what's in it, but I swallow the bitter blue liquid—all of it—and give it back. Maybe it will take away more than physical pain. I dreaded the idea of the elixir robbing me of my free will, but I'll swallow anything to feel numb, to forget, to pull me out of the frequent dark spiral that always lands me back on that patch of grass, the roar of the water blasting through me, the mist drowning me.

Eli stares at the empty vial in his hand and looks back up at me, straight-faced. "That's quite a load to swallow."

I close my eyes for an extra long second, suppressing the smile sneaking past my walls. "Your little comments aren't helping."

"I disagree—and so do your soaked panties." He stands and slings the pack over his shoulder. "You might pass out from drinking all that."

"I'm not sure passing out in your presence again is a good idea."

"It's not." He grins, diverting the raindrops gliding down his face. "You'd miss all the fun. Either way, it won't hurt anymore soon, and it'll heal faster. Let's go." He turns to walk away.

"Wait."

He halts, leaving his back to me.

"I'm cold."

"Then keep moving." He takes a step.

"I'm wet," I try, risking another suggestive response from him.

"It's raining."

Clueless man. "I'm *exhausted*."

He slowly spins around and stares at my dripping body and pleading eyes, his forehead wrinkling.

"I need to rest."

He takes my arm and starts walking, silent as he steers us toward the mountain's incline. Thoroughly soggy and shivering, I trek up the hillside without complaint or question, even as we reach solid rock and have to find our footing with each slippery step. He never lets my arm go, and as the last of the gray daylight hides itself beyond the horizon, he lifts me up and lays me flat on a muddy rock ledge before climbing up next to me. I nearly lose myself, staring at the hole carved into the rock wall of the mountain, as deep and dark as his eyes.

CHAPTER 44

"Come on. We'll sleep in the cave," Eli says.

That darkness has curled around him all day, but it doesn't stop me from questioning him anymore. It doesn't make my skin crawl. I feel it, like a shadow I can't see, a cool, pressing embrace all around him, in him… in me.

Not bothering to lift my cheek from the rock, I ask, "Is that safe? How did you know this was here?"

"It's a bit of a family spot." He looks at the dark entrance behind him. "No one outside my family has ever been here."

"Your family spot is a cave?" *And you're letting me see it?* "Why does that not surprise me?"

He slides his hands under my arms and pulls me to my feet. The mud thins as the rain trickles down my pant legs in brown rivulets.

"Would you rather rest out here?" He doesn't wait for an answer before taking my ear and moving toward the cave.

I stop short and jerk my head free. "I have a hand you could use."

At the mischievous glint in his widening eyes, I specify, "Not for *that*."

He pushes the dripping curls from his eyes. "I hurt you?"

"No… It's just not what people do."

He waits, staring, as if I'm holding back a better explanation. I'm not.

His hand goes to his own ear. "I'm not like other people."

No, you're not. And neither am I. I look up at him, blinking the rain from my eyes.

He reaches back out and slowly takes my ear again. His cold fingers slide over the wetness, and he doesn't let up on his deep stare as he tugs me one step, and another, walking backward, gently guiding me out of the rain.

"And I like your ears," he says.

I can't find a scrap of anger in me at this precise moment, and I'm rummaging through my feelings in a frenzy trying to find some.

I'm mesmerized the second we're inside. Our wet clothes drip onto the cave floor, each drop echoing. The curved walls are midnight blue, covered in names written in an elegant, swirly script. Thousands of names, crafted with shimmering white letters, much like, if not exactly like, the writing on the notes Eli left for me each day in the castle. The names twinkle on the blue background, everywhere the moonlight reaches, as though they've been written with stardust.

I extend my hands without thought, drawn to the textured walls and the calming color. My fingers dance over the names, rings rasping gently as I trace the connected letters, dotting the i's, swerving and looping. "Who are all these people?"

Eli rolls his head around the cave and back to me with a heavy, burdened look, unlike his usual unreadable one. "They're my ancestors. Every father of every son."

"Your family can be traced back that far?"

"All the way back to the beginning."

"No daughters?" I drag my hand along the wall, stepping deeper into the cave. Rain beats the mountain outside.

"My family line doesn't have daughters."

I pause. "At all?"

"Not one in all the millennia."

"That's not... natural."

He tugs on his earlobe, eyes flitting from wall to wall. "I know."

His admission has me searching for somewhere to look besides his face. "How did you know the Centress was keeping Milo and me at the Ring?"

"I'd followed her there before." He tosses his pack against the wall, and his hands settle on his suspenders, pulling the straps and snapping the ammo against his chest. "I found out she goes every night, but I didn't know why."

"To choose which babies stay and go, and to take their magic?" I ask.

"It seems so."

"Why were you following her?"

His jaw clicks back and forth as he hesitates. "I was looking for someone."

"Kelter?" The possibility flickers through me like tiny wings in my veins.

"Only to save me the trouble of finding him later." He drops his gaze to the floor, toeing figure eights into the thin layer of mud with his boot. He's different inside this cave... looser.

But he's responsible for us being in Sonnet. It's his fault Kelter is being held by the Centress, yet knowing that he was looking, that he's planning to keep his end of the deal—it makes it even harder to be mad.

"How did you make the pain stop?" I blurt out. "The Centress put her hands on me, and I thought it would never end, but then you were behind me, holding me... and it was gone."

His head pops up, daggers in his eyes. "She must have pulled back her magic."

"I don't—" The look in his eyes turns desperate, silencing me, but I have no doubt that the second his arms wrapped around me, the pain started to wane. I fold my wet arms over my middle. "It's freezing."

Eli leans back, one knee bent with his boot flat to the cave wall while he stares at me, and I'm reminded of Kelter back in the stone room—how he leaned against the wall and said everything he could to upset me solely to keep me warm, when all I really needed was his arms.

Minutes pass before he severs the silence. "Take off your clothes."

"What?"

"You heard me. You'd be a lot warmer without the wet fabric on you. Your body can't keep up." He cracks his face into a brazen smile. "And I wouldn't mind."

Right. True, but—"I'm not doing that."

"It'd help."

"What is it about you?" I hug my stomach tighter. *Hold on to the anger.* "You're a jerk to me in front of your friends, and they don't even notice or care. They stand by you no matter what. But the other guards think you're beyond awful. Then you're nice to me—you act like you care, and you kiss me like you mean it. Then you want to fuck me, yet you think it's okay to lock me up so I won't... what? Leave you? I don't know what I'm supposed to think."

"Nothing."

"I'm supposed to believe *this* is nothing?" I gesture between us. "Tell me I should think nothing of it."

He hides his face with another look at the floor, his voice low. "What if I said you were just convenient? Could I make you hate me forever?"

Convenient? "Is that really what you want? For me to hate you?" I grip the excess length of my wet shirt, shaking. "Because I wouldn't fucking believe you."

Or maybe I would. That's all I was to Reggie Junior and Maverick J.—a convenient fuck. Why would I be anything more to Eli?

He keeps his head down, his waterlogged ringlets the only thing visible. I pace along the wall, working myself up as I rant. "You lie to me. You lie to your friends. You told them you wanted to see how a Hollow takes magic, but you keep telling *me* that you need something from me, and of all the things you lie about, I don't think that's one of them." I stop and lock my limbs. "So what is it?"

Because I'm not a Hollow like you thought. I don't have whatever you need.

His hands grab at the cave wall, fingers curling like he wants to ball it up into his fists.

"What makes it worth getting yourself and all your friends in trouble? And almost killed?" My voice rises, trembling with cold and a bone-deep need for answers.

"Stop talking," he warns, lifting his head.

"What makes it worth walking through the woods for days to find me? Who would do that?"

"Never…"

"What's so important that you would put up with *me*?" I gasp, the weight of my entire past piling onto my chest. How could I be worth any of that? How could anyone *care* enough?

"You are," he yells and kicks off the wall, striding toward me with soggy stomps. Once his boots meet mine, he shoves my spine against the curly letters, an unsteady hand pressing my chest. "You want to know what I need, what I want from you?"

I stare at him. Now I'm the one grasping the wall, wishing I could hold on tight to keep myself from taking his troubled face into my hands. His brows cage his eyes, but nothing could contain the fear sparking in them, the despair leaking out.

"Do you?" he asks, his features breaking with emotion. He moves his hand to my throat, offering an air-stealing grasp before his touch softens along with his voice. "Do you?" His thumb traces down my neck and lands in the notch between my collarbones.

"I asked you." I'm quieter than him.

He levels our faces and touches his nose to mine. His voice is tight, strained, as his thumb jabs into the hollow of my throat. "I need you to fix me."

CHAPTER 45

My fist flies up at Eli in defense, clobbering his face. He grunts and throws his hand over his mouth, his eyes wider than ever before. I don't know if he's more shocked by his own harsh touch or mine.

I hold my throat. "Fix you? How?"

Eli backs deeper into the cave and drops to the floor with his back against the wall. "You made me bleed." His voice is muffled behind his hand.

"You fucking love blood."

"Only yours." He clutches his face harder, fingers depressing his cheeks. "No one makes me bleed."

It's the disbelief in his voice that has me crossing the cave and kneeling in front of him, the cold creeping back to me with the shift in my nerves. "Let me see." I reach for his wrist and tug it away from his face.

"No."

I scoot closer, my knees bumping his legs. Damp curls stick to his forehead. "Don't be so damn difficult." I pull again, but his hand is locked in place, squeezing with a bruising strength. "You're such a baby."

My own words crush me. The babies. The falls. Cam. *Killer.*

Maybe it's the destroyed look on my face, or the way the shivers take me so violently, or the soothing blue walls, or maybe it's something in him that I can't see behind the black and brown and gold-flecked pools of his eyes, but he lets his hand fall away. Blood dribbles from the side of his mouth and down his stubbled chin, almost black in the dark of the cave. His darkness peels away, leaving behind a lightness, a warmth that slips through me.

"It's only blood," I say, steadying my hand the best I can. It reminds me of the blood on Kelter's face the last time I saw him. One firm stroke of my thumb at a time, I wipe the blood from Eli's face, already thick and sticky, cooled by his skin. Then I shift to his hand, rubbing it into my palm until the blood rains down in dry flakes. He watches me, pain in his eyes that's all too familiar. The scent of the cave air strengthens around us, and I force myself to back away.

He grabs my wrists and pulls me back to him. "Kaleida told you about the gods?"

"Yes."

"About Ametrine and the three Vaile she shared her essence with and turned into gods?" He rubs his thumbs over my collarbones, the softest touch from his cold, rough hands. My heart swells, and I smother it in guilt and emptiness, sacks and chains, deadly rainbows and wretched green grass.

"The gods aren't even real, and—"

He leans forward, squeezes the sides of my face and plants a bloody kiss on my lips, and as he pulls away, he shushes me. "Shut that little mouth and listen for a minute."

The kiss lingers, salty and sticky. I seal the blood between my lips.

"One of those gods, Peridot, also used some of her essence from Ametrine to create her own being. The Vaile and Hollows each have a part in the cycle—magic moving through the beings, to the plants and back to the gods. It was already a perfect design. As long as magic keeps flowing and never leaves the cycle, the Vaile continue to receive gifts from the gods through the connection to their Immortal Realm. But Peridot wanted a safeguard in case the cycle was disrupted, causing magic to die. She made another immortal who was to be the source of new magic if ever needed, but"—he casts his eyes down and takes my hands in his, trembling fiercely and holding so tightly that I keep quiet—"she made a mistake."

He blinks far too slowly. "The new being couldn't do the one thing he was meant to do. He couldn't create magic. He could only block it. Peridot was fucking livid. She was given one opportunity to create, and she wasted it on a mistake. So she took the essence back from him— violently."

He hauls my hands to his chest. "But it couldn't be used to make a new being, and Ametrine couldn't give any more of her own essence.

Peridot ruined the only chance at creating new magic, and she didn't want Ametrine to find out. So the cruel bitch goddess lied and kept her mistake locked up in a cage for thousands of years, leaving him just a shell of a being without the essence used to create him. When Ametrine found out, she was furious that a being in her world had been locked up like that, so she freed him and punished Peridot. Ametrine sent the being to live with the Vaile, and eventually he fell in love with one of them."

Love. I didn't think he knew that word.

"And they had a son, who grew into a man—half-Vaile, half-mistake. And when the being died…" He pulls me closer. My knees bump my chin, and he wraps his arms around my back, trapping me in a ball against him, my hands still on his chest.

"Eli—"

He shushes me again. "When the being died—"

"I thought the being was immortal."

A sad smile finds his face. "He was. Is. But without his essence, his immortality was broken. His body died, but his mind and soul joined his son's—they merged into one, inside the son's body—and then his son had a son, and every time a father died, it happened again… and again, eventually merging thousands of souls into one."

He stares at me.

I stare back, unsure of what to say and still shivering.

So he continues. "And sometimes the son knows it's coming because the father tells him and prepares him for the combined future that awaits them after his death. And sometimes"—he hugs me tighter—"he doesn't find out until he comes home to his mother standing over his father's dying body, watching him bleed out on the carpet with a knife in her hand. And with the final beat of his father's heart, his body changes in an instant. Colder, thicker skin, stronger—so much so that he doesn't know his own strength—and other things too."

"What are you saying?" I grit out.

"I'm saying… I'm a mistake."

"How? I don't understand."

"Never—" he sighs a lifetime's worth of sighs and kisses the tip of my nose. "I've lived thousands of lives, and every time I die, my soul and all my memories and thoughts from all my previous lives join with my son's mind and soul and body, and we become one."

I'm not sure if I'm more terrified of the words he's saying or the fact that he's saying the words, opening up to me—with pure fucking nonsense.

"Your son? You're not making sense."

"So many sons," he says, eyes glossy.

He's serious… and not at all sane. I've found someone as unstable as myself.

I humor him. "So, you are your father?"

"And my grandfather and my great grandfather and—"

"All the way back to the beginning," I finish for him, my mind swirling.

"Yes, but I'm also me. Mostly me." He touches his forehead to mine. His curls graze my eyebrows, and the beat of a thousand hearts hammers into my hands. It's too gentle, too intimate, even with his tight hold. *Who is this man? These men?*

"But they're in you?"

"Yes." He nods against my forehead.

"They talk to you?"

"It's more like I sense their thoughts and feelings. And I have memories from all of them—who they loved, things they did and said, places they went. They're part of me now, as if I were the one who spent thousands of years in a cage and lived all the lives after. I remember every minute of every life like yesterday." Pain pours from his eyes.

"That's…" *Disturbing. Creepy. Torturous.* "Fucked up."

This man of endless fortitude simply smiles, accepting my broken form of comfort. "Such a way with words."

I snort a quiet laugh, taken from the moment. "You only like it when I say *fuck*."

"I do."

"Why?"

"Because you don't let anyone take that from you."

His conviction rattles me. He's wrong. My foster father took my voice. And Mallace with the serum. And the man in the woods. But with Eli, I'm not afraid to stand my ground. I look away, something much too close to affection stirring in his eyes, and I can't handle that. "So your mother that you won't talk about—she's your father's…"

"Lover," he whispers.

"But that means—"

"I know. But I'm not my father, not completely. He's just here. In me."

"And she killed him?" I ask.

His eyes confirm with heartbroken blinks.

Before I can embrace the compassion sneaking up on me, a wall slams into place, and it's gone. I try to pull away, now realizing why he locked me in. He knew I'd want to get away.

"Of all the realms, Elivander. Fuck. This is one messed up lie." *Or a truth I don't want to believe.*

He pushes me onto my back and lowers himself over me. Our wet clothes mesh into a thick, unwelcome layer between us, and he puts his face in mine. "It's not a lie." The warmth is gone, the caressing breeze, the fresh scent of dawn—replaced with the taste of blood and fingers on my neck and back.

"Why are you telling me this?" I try to roll out from under him. I want it to be a lie.

"Because I need you. Whatever's inside of you, I need it to fix the mistake."

I rake in musty cave air. "You need me to fix you? Why the fuck would I? I don't even know how to fix myself."

"Because…" His voice shakes. "You're my only godsdamn chance. I'm stuck like this without you."

"I don't have what you need." I reach a hand up to his cheek and slide it back through his hair, dropping my voice to a whisper. "I'm not even a Hollow."

"I know."

"What?" Shock zips through every nerve in my body, and my hand falls away.

His legs hug mine, trapping me in place. "From the day I saw you touch that seedling, the way it lit up, I knew. I was around before the Separation, back when Hollows and Vaile lived together. I know the Centress is lying to everyone—Hollows can't take magic from plants."

"And you let me believe I was a Hollow and put me through all those triggers for nothing?" I try to shove him off of me, but it's like trying to move a wall.

"I had to go along with it. And triggers are how we wake up magic.

It was the only way to get it out of you, Hollow or not. You *do* have what I need."

"And what is that exactly?"

"You. I need *you*. I don't know why you can take magic or what happened at the lake." His desperate eyes search mine, his bloody lip pinned by his teeth with no escape, so forceful, yet delicate. His stare hits my soul. "But help me, Never. Whatever is in you is not typical magic. It can fix me. Help me escape this damn nightmare in my head."

"Eli…" My heart melts. "I can't. I don't know how."

He pulls back, moonlight seeping into the brown of his round eyes, endless years in them. "Me either."

I swear the cave echoes his quiet confession, bouncing off every perfectly written name, every inch of my body beneath him. I wrap my arms around his neck. "But I'll try."

He almost collapses on top of me, relief taking over his face. Then he sits up, his muscled frame hovering over my hips. He's near breathless. "I'll do anything to keep you."

I'm speechless, seconds ticking by. Saliva collects in my mouth, warm and sweet on my wordless tongue as I attempt to decipher his words. Silence gnawing at my sanity, I force the question from my lips. "Until I fix you?" *Until you don't need me anymore?*

He smiles down at me and runs a thumb over my mouth, a full circle, and lets that delicious darkness of his fall around us in invisible drops. "No, my little Never Ever. I've been telling you from the start—" He leans down and kisses me just above my lips. Then below. Then right smack on them. "You're mine, and I'll *never* let you go."

CHAPTER 46

His tender kisses hurt. I retreat to the opposite side of the cave, leaving Eli alone. Hours pass as I let his words sink in. Between visions of death, my thoughts bounce from his story and plea to his claim on me—fuel for denial. I can't process this vulnerable side of him while sorting through my own muddled feelings. I pretend nothing has changed, but the quiet space between us seems to collapse like a disorienting dream.

I hold my necklace and shiver against the white letters of the cave wall, my teeth clacking together after another vision. The cold consumes every breath, every ticking part of my body, every pump of blood until the rattling reaches the crux of my existence, taking over any remaining shred of self-directed thought until I'm not thinking at all. And like the night I rolled across the floor to steal the stone from Eli's pocket, I roll my body across the muddy cave—my clothes still damp, my skin like ice, my heart like fire. I get closer and closer.

He's on his side, his back to the opposite wall, and when I almost reach him, I stop. Some seditious, logical part of me tries to prevent one more roll into his arms. It's too dark to tell if his eyes are open or closed.

I lie in utter quiet, except for the chatter of my teeth, one foot away, trembling head to toe. I wiggle my feet in an attempt to overcome the numbness, my boots scraping. Minutes pass. The longest minutes that feel like hours.

And when my heart is so slow it might give up, Eli sits. My eyes open to see his arms rise, his shirt following. He tosses it aside. Then his hands find my waist. He says not a word as he lifts my shirt, and somehow I'm sitting, my arms in the air as if this is exactly what I wanted.

He pulls the damp fabric over my head, wraps an arm around my middle and pulls me up against him as he lies back down.

My back melds to his bare chest. My hips find his, and I tuck my head under his chin. Coarse stubble pokes my scalp. *I'm dead.* Can't he tell? *I'm not here. I'm under the mocking rainbow in the green Calderan grass, a killer, rotting in the prison of my mind.* But I let him stay, touching the stranger I've become. Maybe because he's hurting inside, like me. Or his arms are a safe, dark cocoon. Or maybe because I see another side, an Eli that holds a dying child, that drums and sings and bleeds. Or maybe because I see both sides—and I don't want to run from either.

He's so cold against me that I'm sure I'm the one warming him, but still, my insides heat, churning with desire. He works his hand up my side and over my chest, his fingers creeping until they find the cup of my bra. They slip inside, missing my treasures. I jerk from the contact—cold fingers on my nipple, a rough hand holding my breast. Then I exhale, releasing all the gnarled, crooked feelings as arousal edges in, a slow climb from pulsing to throbbing. Eli's hips rock into me in a steady rhythm. His cock hardens, going from a gentle nudge on my bottom, to an insistent, solid bulge I can't ignore.

It's a struggle not to turn my body and face him, not to take him in my hands and push his length inside of me, to escape in ecstasy. I contract every muscle to resist, clenching my legs and holding my breath… because how can I let go with my body when my mind is a broken mess? How can he?

But escape is exactly what I need.

He holds me like that for so long, thumbing the bud of my breast and nibbling my ear, his hips rolling against my backside, that not a single other thought makes it past the pleasure.

The silence is palpable after the obscene amount of words he spewed in the woods while torturing me into rapture, but it disintegrates when he pinches my nipple so tight I scream. It echoes off the walls. Then he twists, and it burns in the best fucking way. I reach behind me for some part of him—any part I can make mine. My hand lands on the hair over his ear. I take ringlets and flesh into my fist and pull as his knuckles roll over me.

He doesn't even try to move my hand, so I yank harder. He growls and sucks my ear into his mouth. Two fingers clamp down on my nipple, twirling and tugging until I run out of curses. My moans roll through the cave. I free his ear and stir against him, pressure building in my core, pounding through me. My fingernails spear the hardening mud on the floor. He reeks of musk and man and blood, mixing with the damp earthiness of the cave, and I haul it into my lungs as I come undone, my breathing frantic and heavy.

I'm still shaking, wet and pulsing and panting when his chest slams into my back, his hips searching wildly for contact. His hand dips between us, releasing his cock from the restraint of his waistband and pushing it against my ass, still tragically covered with my pants. He rolls me onto my stomach, and his own body follows, his weight on my bottom and legs. He props himself up on one elbow, his other hand under me, still holding my breast. He's almost quiet, strangled moans stuck in his throat as he bucks into me.

"Don't hold back," I command, struck by the realization that his strength is part of who he is. "Give me the real you." He shouldn't be hidden by self-restraint. I *want* to feel his powerful body with no escape. I *want* to be trapped by the uncontrollable urges of a man who needs and desires me to the point of chasing me down and locking me up, whose mind and future depend on me.

And I want to fight him every damn step of the way.

"I'd break you to pieces," he says, his voice strained.

He'll slaughter anyone who even thinks of hurting me. He'll protect every last drop of my blood to have for himself. I'm his in a way I can't comprehend, and I'll embrace all his sharp edges. I don't care if they scratch and slice. I'll guard them like he guards me and never let a fucking soul near his heart.

"I'm already broken," I yell.

"No," he grinds out, yet triples his force. My hip bones crash into the muddy cave ground over and over. I slide forward with his thrusts, my clit rubbing against the floor and my hands out flat in front of me, nothing to hold onto. He doesn't remove the fabric over my ass that keeps him from filling me. He takes me like this, with the urgency and unrivaled carnality of a man unraveling... for me. And I don't want it to end, but his entire frame convulses in violent spasms. He clenches my breast. I swear he nearly tears it off in passion, and those teeth of his bite down on my ear, all control lost.

With the final jerks of his cock up against me subsiding, his breathing slows, his movements settling back to a slow rock. He rolls us back to our sides and pulls me closer to his now-clammy skin, his fingers skimming lazy circles over my hips.

"Sleep, little Never." He licks the drops of blood from my ear, following with tiny wet kisses over each tooth mark. His tongue soothes the sting as he pulls out his knife. I tense, but he only smashes my body tighter against his, draping a heavy leg over me. I fall asleep to him suckling my ear, his knife across my chest, protecting me. All night his cold skin against mine keeps me pumping with heat.

We leave the blue cave of names, slog down the muddy mountain and cross the river that the baby and elixir-filled carriage bumbled over days earlier much farther south. The water is clear, making it easy to step from one slippery rock to the next in the shallow current. Rain pelts our shoulders and drips down our bodies, rinsing the white stain from the back of my pants—a reminder of his arms, the safety… and the sweet, unchecked savagery.

It was more than an escape.

He refills the canteens and sits down to go through his soaked pack. A change of clothes is stuffed into the bottom, as saturated as everything else, including the mushy bars we force down.

"They'll be looking for us. And for Milo and the others too." He tightens the drawstrings of his pack and stands, hooking his thumbs on his suspenders, tone confident. "Now that we've crossed the river, they could be anywhere. It'll take longer, but we'll travel along the northern edge of Sonnet to avoid the village and any other common areas. We hide if we hear anything. I fight if I have to."

We walk for hours. My tongue is mostly healed, and the medicine took away my rib pain. I don't mind the light throbbing of my ear, reminding me of Eli's feral lack of control. The rain finally slows in the evening, and we share a tree to sleep against when night falls, only inches of bark between our heads.

Gripping my raised knees under the gray night sky, so few stars visible behind the thick clouds, I imagine seeing Kelt again, his warm smile and his ears that stick out. I'm so close to getting him back. I try to push myself off the cliff of consciousness and into sleep with those thoughts coiled around me and Eli close by, but sleep doesn't come, leaving nothing left to do but ask questions I don't want answers to.

I speak into the darkness between us. "So you've lived thousands of lives?"

"Yes," he responds with a tone of caution.

"And have had thousands of sons?"

Silence.

Then—"Yes."

"Do—" I brace myself for his answer. "Do you know my father?" I wait.

"I know nothing about your family."

Dammit. "Me either," I whisper. My rings burn as I turn them faster and faster. "And you've died thousands of times?"

More silence.

"Yes."

Everything seizes inside me. I'm broken and rotting because I die imaginary deaths every day when this man—this ancient, afflicted man—has actually died over and over, if I dare believe? Could he understand the visions that haunt me every day? Could the endless life he conceals within rival the death in me?

"What happened at the falls?" His voice is quiet, heavy with idle hope.

Nothing and no one I want to talk about. That's one death he can't understand. I scoot away, my muscles wrapping into bands of guilt.

Chapter 47

W e're up at the first sign of dim daylight. We stop and huddle behind trunks and boulders every time Eli insists he hears voices and boots in the distance—noises I don't hear. He claims his hearing is better, his other senses too, which I doubt, purely because the thought of him smelling my desire every time I gushed in my underwear is disturbing—and arousing. I tuck myself in at his side and hold my breath while we hide.

He crouches, knife in hand and suspenders loaded with slingshot ammo, and holds an arm extended across my chest, keeping me in place. When he deems it safe again, he pulls me to my feet, and we walk on.

Gray clouds shutter the late morning sky. Eli's demeanor changes, his steps faster. He takes my arm and pulls me along, the warmth of his lightness and a light breeze hitting my skin.

"Isn't the castle that way?" I ask, recognizing portions of my mental map from the few times I was taken around Sonnet.

"We're not going to the castle."

"Are we going straight to the Ring to search for Kelter? What if someone finds us?"

"They won't," he snaps. "Not where we're going."

"That's what you said about the lake."

He grips me tight. "This is different."

I take long strides to keep pace, and after over an hour of winding through trees, he lets go of my arm. I follow his figure through the dark shades of the woods, all in black with the brown pack on his back.

"Where are we going?" I ask for the tenth time and finally get a response, as vague as it is.

"I have something to show you."

He gives me no clues despite my torrent of questions. We hike farther east under the menacing clouds, and the edges of my map expand and push the boundaries of my mind.

"If the Centress is so confident that magic is diminishing and causing weather disasters, why doesn't she stop the magic from dying instead of taking it from babies, especially if she is only moving magic from one part of the cycle to another and not replenishing anything?" I ask instead of offering another guess at where he's taking us. "And if the cycle was designed to reuse magic and not let it die, why is it running low after all these years? You didn't answer when Sypher asked, but you must know."

"Besides the fact that I'm a mistake and can't create new magic to fix the very problem I was made to prevent from happening?" he asks, clearly a tad sensitive. "It's cruel. I'm stuck waiting almost twenty-four years of every lifetime to be gifted a shred of magic. I should be its source, but all I can do is block it."

Made, not born—yet both are true if his story is. I wait for him to keep talking as we push past low branches.

He snaps a twig off a tree on his way by and proceeds to break it in half over and over as he speaks. "It's the Separation. The loss of magic was almost nonexistent until the border around Sonnet was put in place. Hollows and Vaile aren't meant to be apart, and magic isn't meant to be contained and concentrated like it is now in Sonnet. Hollows haven't been allowed to take part in their role in the magic cycle since the Separation. It's breaking the natural flow and destroying magic faster than ever before. The disasters come every few months now, but it's not only the weather that's a problem if magic gets too low—the connection to the Immortal Realm will be severed, and Vaile won't receive gifts anymore. It's an unintended consequence of the Separation, but the Centress isn't willing to take on the risk of undoing it and bringing Hollows and Vaile together again."

"But if Hollows don't actually take magic, what's the risk?"

He tosses the last bit of broken twig aside and holds a low-hanging branch away from my head as I walk between two trees. "The risk is eliminating all Vaile. Before the Separation, Vaile started mating with Hollows even though they were linked with another Vaile, but the children born to the mixed parents were always Hollows—without the gift of magic. After a few generations, hardly any Vaile were left."

"So either the magic dies due to the broken cycle and extreme weather destroys the land—or all Vaile and their magic die out?"

"Basically."

"And which side are you on?"

"Both. I don't know." His steps slow. "I only know that I can't let the connection to the gods in the Immortal Realm be cut off, or you'll never be able to help me."

"Oh right, *the gods*."

He stops and sneaks a finger under my chin, latching his eyes onto mine. "You can't believe in magic—and what I am—and not believe in the gods."

I can. Denial is much easier than blindly believing.

But I give him this one thing, this one truth. "I believe in you, who you are. Not because of the gods and the Immortal Realm that don't exist, but because—" I struggle with the words, the emotions I lay bare with them, my throat closing. "Your eyes." I rake in a shaky breath. "When they're looking into mine—it's as though thousands of eyes are looking back at me, thousands of hearts and souls captive inside you."

Pain sinks into his features at the truth in my words, and something else… vulnerability, like the way I feel when he stares so deep, when I'm *seen*.

His past is much longer, and far more painful than mine, his mother more despicable. And those names on the cave walls—they belong to him, each one a lifetime, a death. Each one a person he once was, and still is.

He swallows whatever words he can't spit out and releases my chin, then takes my ear, and we walk.

The sound of rushing water grows louder, and I stiffen, pushing through each step as though wading through thoughts. *It's fine. I'm fine. We're not at the falls. It's a river.* A light rain trickles from the clouds and makes its way through the maze of branches above me.

We reach a narrow bridge hanging between two skinny logs for handrails. Eli crosses first, the path of wooden planks swinging and bouncing under his feet, the rain splattering freely on his finally dry clothes. I rally the muscles of my legs into obedience and step onto the bridge.

Near halfway across, the slightest glance down makes the white rapids far below bubble into view. The mist rises like at the falls. I can't move one more step. Cam's scream plunders through me, taking every bit of strength I have left. I fall to my knees, hands on my ears. *Crack*. I can't tell where the sound came from. The rain rushes to drench me as though it might wash away the filth staining my conscience. *Too late*.

How quickly I spiral. I bury myself in the torment. I try to block out the screaming, try to erase those babies' faces like I erased their chance at a family. I try to hide behind walls of guilt, letting only the musty, wet stink of this bridge reach me. But I can't hide who I am, the choices I've made. I can't blame an elixir that doesn't affect me. Every thought is truly, painfully mine. Every choice is born from a free mind, and I own my existence, from my soaked skin to my unbelieving soul. I own it.

And it's too fucking much.

My name falls with the raindrops around me. I toss up another shield, another wall, trying to shut everything out. But it doesn't stop— my name, dripping and dropping around me.

"Never!" Invisible darkness tears down my walls. "Look at me!"

Let me hide.

"Never!"

Go away go away go away.

"Never!" His voice strums the invisible threads above me in urgent chords, and my head rises to his call like a soggy marionette. I can't fight it.

He kneels at the other end of the bridge, sopping curls and rain-soaked face. "Hold the rails."

I drop my hands from my ears and wrap my arms around me. The pelting rain hammers to the center of my brain, almost drowning out the roar of the river. "I can't fix it all. I can't save them."

"Hold on to the sides."

"I can't beat her." My temperature rises with every word. Diluted tears stream over my lips. How am I supposed to stop my mother from taking babies? From drugging Calderans? From killing Kelt?

Eli pulls at his wet hair. "You only have to beat the thoughts that hold you back," he yells over the rain. "Let me help you."

"Help me? You don't know—" *How broken I am. The death I see.* Hotter and hotter.

He looks up at the rain and back at me. "If you would—"

"How? How can you help me?" *Please help me.* I'm burning now, but it's not me at all. It's the rain. It falls in steaming sheets, carrying every earthy scent of the woods with it.

"For starters," he shouts, whipping the hair from his face, "I could stop you from falling into a freezing river."

My head drops. Hot raindrops massage my neck and slide down my back. The two planks at my knees are cracked down the middle, dangling down from a split center beam. The river eddies and lashes below, vapors rising as the rain batters the surface. I trace the fracture of the beam all the way to the other side of the bridge, visible in gaps between the planks. The bridge could collapse at any moment. It's as fragile as my sanity.

The vision comes like a crashing wave.

Falling to the rapids below. The rocks waiting to break bones, tear flesh. The breath-stealing cold. The blood mixing with the froth. The end.

My senses surge with life. I roll my head and grab the rails, pushing the vision away, down into the rapids. One movement forward would have landed me on the jagged rocks jutting through the water.

"Keep holding the rails. They'll be there even if the bottom drops out." He stands, arms out, beckoning me.

"That's really fucking encouraging. Don't you have a rope or something?"

"You have to cross."

"What if I slip?" *What if I fall like Cam, like I deserve?*

"Come to me."

I'm frozen under the hot shower, unable to pick up the pieces of myself. "I can't."

Eli reaches out over the rails, looking at me in the most devastating way. His hands dance and drum against the wood, fingers rapping out a familiar, jumpy beat, backed with the pit-pat of rain, now unbearably hot. His whole body absorbs the rhythm and moves with him.

"What are you doing?"

"I'm going to summon you." His eyes narrow and darken like coal, and the side of his mouth quirks up.

"Summon me?" I tighten my grip on the rails. He's lost it.

"Right into my arms." The beat quickens.

"You can't do that."

"Oh, no? Didn't I say I control you?"

Then this man, this gorgeous, wet, drumming man sings. His song ricochets off the raindrops, straight into me.

There's not a step worth taking
A breath worth holding
A neck worth breaking
If no one's waiting

So why should you hold on?

I recognize the lyrics. They push me to my feet and over the missing planks. They nudge me forward one tiny step at a time, grazing my calves and prodding my shoulders. They stick my hands to the rails and silence the creak of the beam and the thundering river. They extinguish the scalding rain—and carry me to him.

Summoned, I collapse into his waiting arms, hot and steamy from the rain. He holds me, and I know—I *know* that if he lets go too soon, I'll fall apart.

But he doesn't, and once I can breathe without shuddering, without visions flashing and death crashing through my mind, we walk. It's not far before he steps in front of me and grabs my shoulders.

"Ready?" His dark brown eyes flicker with excitement.

"For what?"

He pulls me past dense trees, so close that their bark scrapes the bare skin of our arms. My boots sink into the layer of moss blanketing the ground. The trees tower above in a tight circle around us, forming a canopy that blocks the gray sky. Inside the ring, smaller trees with waxy leaves and bunches of bright red fruit crowd the space. The air is thick and balmy and smells of jasmine.

Mouth clamped shut, fingers fidgeting with his ear, Eli watches me take in the scene, my eyes traveling from the canopy, to the drapes of fruit, to him.

CHAPTER 48

W ell?" Eli asks, leading me to an open circle of moss in the center of the space.

I take another look at the trees around me, laden with bunches of fruit that look like ripe cherries. "Are these... coffee plants?"

"Yes. I had Milo show me where they are. He planted them years ago." He slides a hand into his rain-drenched curls, removing his pack and tossing it aside as he sits on the moss.

"Coffee," I stammer.

"You hadn't had anything to eat or drink in two days, and you asked for coffee. I thought you wanted it as medicine, then I remembered seeing Hollows and Vaile drink coffee before the Separation. We only use it for headaches now, and even then, it's rare."

I touch the nearest leaf, but my eyes stay on him. "This isn't what I expected."

His face falls. "Oh. It seemed important." He reaches for his ear again, then snaps his hand away when he catches my eyes following the movement.

"I mean, I didn't expect this from you." I sit down and fold my legs, a soft breeze playing over my cheeks. "It's perfect." Those words do nothing to capture my thoughts, but it's all I can manage with him across from me. Looking like he does. All dark and hopeful.

"Not hideous?"

I bite back a smile, thinking back to my response at the lake, the feel of his fingers dipping past my waistband. The heat in his eyes flares, luring out the golden specks. But just as I let a sliver of joy show on my face, all the doubts and feelings I thought had fallen into the river rush back, and my smile fades. Maybe I forgive him for dragging me into Sonnet, but what am I doing here, with him, pretending I'm not a killer? That I'm not as broken as he is, that everything isn't a mess?

I lean in. "I need to know, Elivander. I need to know how you do it."

He looks up from his hands in his lap, flinching at his full name. "Do what?"

"How you embrace the darkness. How you carry it with you, but it doesn't eat you alive. You still function. I want to be like you, so it won't hurt so fucking bad." I scoot closer to him, our bent knees kissing. "Show me how."

He stares at me for a long time, his eyes locked but walled off behind the brown. "Why would you need me to show you that?"

He won't help me if I don't tell him, and I'm dying here, shriveling up inside myself. I swear I hear my walls come crashing down with every word.

"There's something wrong with me," I whisper, my resolve strengthening. "It's always been there, and it's getting worse. I feel it in you—the darkness mixed in with the light. I'm drawn to you, but you have these walls up." My hands creep forward in my lap. "And I see myself behind them."

Fingers down my back, blood in my mouth, the tempting scent of the darkest cave—they all bombard me at once. His face twists into a crooked smile. He crawls forward, and the darkness leans in. "You think there's something wrong with you?" He breathes into my ear.

My heart breaks records in my chest. "I know there is."

He shoves me onto my back and leans in again. "You think you're dark?"

"Black-hearted."

He scoffs. "Want to know what I think?"

"What?" I gulp back a trace of regret and glance at the canopy far above, the tiny pockets of gray sky that push through.

He lowers himself to my ear again. "There's not a speck of wrongness in you, not a shade of darkness."

"You're wrong," I tell him. Because I feel it. I feel it lurking in my mind, infecting my blood.

He sits up and raises his chin. "Then show me your darkness. Show me where it comes from."

"I don't have a—"

"You do if you're truly dark." He reaches into a pocket. "I'll find it. I'll cut it off at the fucking source." The silver shimmer of his knife looms over me.

I silently call his bluff, not even flinching. But the blade grazes my stomach. A slow, precise touch. He slices my shirt straight up the middle. I hold my breath, savoring the wisp of his fingers on my skin. He reaches the collar of my shirt, the knife at my throat. With one more gentle tug, it's free. My shirt falls open at my sides.

Eli sucks in a breath. His eyes prance and flit over his prize, at the nervous flexing of my abdomen and the embroidered scene on the cups of my bra. He scrapes a circle around my navel with the blade, then folds his body, landing his lips on my belly button. I suck in, pulling the sensitive spot away from him, and he follows it down, flicking his tongue inside before pushing himself back up.

I gasp, clamping my hand over my stomach.

"Stop that."

"No darkness here," he says, flipping me over, my cheek pressing into the mossy ground.

The tip of his knife glides across my back, pushing my damp hair up and over my shoulder. The slice of my shirt and the neck loop of my bra send a trail of whispers up my spine. He brushes the pieces away with the knife's edge, sliding the sleeves down my arms and past my hands, then flattens himself over my body. Breathless and trapped, desire pounds through me.

"No darkness back here."

I spit the hair from my face. "It's on the inside."

"Oh, don't worry, I'll check there." He rolls me onto my back again.

Looking down at me, hunger and lust leak from his features. His tongue spills over his lower lip, his cheeks kissed pink.

"Eli..." It slips out of me, a breathy plea.

"Busy," he drums back, slicing up one leg of my pants, then the other, the swipe of his knuckles tickling my shins and thighs.

I'm deathly still, need flooding my senses. Gentle knife swishes peel the pants away from the sides of my legs, and cool metal frees the fabric from between my thighs.

"Nothing dark here."

He puts me on my stomach again with an effortless roll, rips away the scrap of pants stuck to me and I'm all his. Nothing but the string tie of my bra and the thin fabric of my underwear block his search. I'm exposed—like when he looks so deep into my eyes.

"Not a fucking thing here." He slaps my ass with the flat of his knife. I look over my shoulder at the stinging line of fresh blood seeping into my underwear and flip onto my back to properly glare at him.

"I told you. It's—"

"I'm not done yet." He climbs on top of me.

My hands grip his thighs, riding up the hard muscles that hold back his full-weight from crushing me. Knife now at his side, he bunches up the sheared fabric scattered about and pulls out a fire stone from his pack, as if he were about to light up a teva roll. The stone flares red, and he holds it up to the ball of sliced clothes. Though still wet from the rain, they go up in flames and blast my face with heat. Ash flurries down, covering the mountain and waterfall on my bra in gossamer layers of darkness.

"Show off," I say.

He reclaims his knife and holds the point to the bottom of my throat. "You say you're drawn to me." I nod, not trusting myself to open my mouth. "What is it? Is it the darkness you like? The doubt that crawls under your skin?"

I look up at him. His brown eyes search mine, flicking back and forth beneath angled brows.

"Tell me," he says.

"Maybe. How the fuck would I know? I can't figure you out."

He sits back a bit, my thighs under his. "That's too bad."

"What?"

Keeping the knife in place, he scoots down my body and lowers himself over my chest, my legs hugging his sides. His chin rests in the hollow spot between my ribs, right over my birthmark, roughly the shape of an eye. "It's a curse."

"Curses aren't—"

"They're as real as your naked body under me, Never. Do you want to deny that too?" He shimmies his hips back and forth, desire igniting at every point of contact.

Somehow his words make the reality of our closeness palpable. I bury the denial, for him. "Your many lives are a curse?"

"No, what I am is the mistake. The curse is different."

"So... you're doubly fucked up?" I pull on a curl resting on his temple.

"You could say that." His chin presses into me as he talks, his stubble scratchy. "I was cursed as a baby. My mother's other lover did it out of jealousy of my father."

The blade quakes against me in his grasp. "It forces people to see me a certain way. Either they look at me and see exactly what they want—someone they trust, someone they follow, even if they question it. Or they see the opposite. They fear and despise me, avoid me, and never trust. My whole fucking life. It doesn't matter what I do or say. My actions are pointless. The curse sways them one way or the other."

He lifts his head, pain-stricken eyes peering at me past the tips of his ringlets. "Do you know what that makes me?" Cool air blows from his lips over my chest, and the ashes float up, dusting my face in soot and catching on my lashes.

"No." A fist takes my heart in its unforgiving grasp.

He swipes the knife down from my throat through the braided center string of my bra, marking me with the faintest red line as the blade drags between my breasts, then scrapes away the fabric. The blue stone and ring slide down my right side, and the key and jade button tumble over my left breast and onto the moss beside me. My face heats, my chest moving with sporadic breaths.

Knife tossed aside, he sits up straight and darts his eyes over the treasures he uncovered, breasts and blood and trinkets alike. And as though he has all the time in the world—which apparently he does—he tucks my mess of hair behind my ear then runs his tongue up the center of my chest before sharing the metallic taste with a rough kiss to my lips. Picking up the key, he positions it over my heart, then sticks the button in my navel and gives it a tap with a satisfied curl of his mouth.

I watch his every move, entranced, waiting for him to answer his own question. He bends until his body is flush with mine and plants a kiss on the stone of my necklace, setting off a sizzling heat, then another on my birthmark. The key tumbles to the moss, and his eyes find mine.

"Invisible. It makes the real me fucking invisible." He blows again, a tiny hurricane against my breasts. My nipples harden, and I curl my fingers around the suspenders on his back.

"I see you," I whisper, barely able to breathe.

"And you know what the worst part is?" His eyes are raw, buried in hurt. "I'll never know if the people who claim to care about me truly care, or if it's the curse that has them following blindly. If I can't tell what's real, then what's the point?"

I simply look at him. This tragic man.

"I used to try. Growing up, I didn't understand why some people hated me even though I was as nice as anyone else. Then my father died, and I got his memories of the fight with my mother. I learned about the curse that they never bothered to explain to me. It all made sense, but these people in my head..." His eyes close for a lengthy moment, long black lashes skimming his cheeks. "All the things I learned about the past. All the voices and memories. It's too much. I stopped trying to make people see past a curse. I give them what they'll see anyway—a reason to run."

He snakes his tongue over my nipple in tiny circles of wrath. I slam into him, arching my back and moaning through the entire assault.

He continues as though I hadn't moved a muscle. "So, it's either one or the other. But *you*—" I writhe and gasp under the pinch of his fingers on both my nipples, rolling so casually as he talks. "You see both sides of the curse. I don't know why." He twists so hard that I cry out, then frees my nipples from his vise. "But will you ever really see me? The man behind the curse?"

Tears trickle down my ashen cheeks, but not from pain. It's the torment in his question, the way his voice cracks. My hands cup his cheeks, coarse hairs pricking my skin, and I'm reminded of how Kelter holds my cheeks and looks at me so tragically after my visions. I don't want to be like that with Eli. I don't want to hurt him—not his heart—but I do need to know...

"Why do you care what I see in you?"

He covers both my breasts with his hands, his thumbs stroking up along my nipples. His face changes, a look so sincere and vulnerable with the smoothed lines of his jaw and his softening eyes that I want to look away.

"Why wouldn't I want you to see me when I see you?" he asks.

What's there to see? I'm no one. "You locked me up."

He bites one nipple, then the other, and follows with kisses, his lips a soft tease. Taking his time, he looks into my eyes. "I've lived enough lifetimes to know you're worth keeping."

His words cripple me, much more than those lips of his. But I don't let up. "You chained me to a fucking tree."

His brows bounce up, a smile breaking. "Foreplay."

"You made me bathe in a bucket."

He rests his head over the stripe of red on my chest, wet black curls spilling over my skin, and in a voice so low that I doubt he wants the words to come out, he says, "Maybe because all I have at the castle is a shower, and giving you a bucket instead meant I didn't have to see the terror on your face like that day in the shower room… even if it meant not seeing everything else."

A smile works its way onto my face. I lift his head up and turn it to face me. "What makes you think you'd be watching?"

"I wouldn't miss it." He sucks my breast into his mouth, taking in all that will fit. I wrap my hands around his head and pull him closer, cradling him in my arms. I stroke those unruly curls and pull them into my fists. His tongue rolls and kneads into me, his head moving with the deep gulps. I watch him suck me so thoroughly, his brown eyes wide and locked on mine, unblinking. Fuck. He'll take me apart like this. Piece by piece.

"I see you, I do," I choke.

"Maybe, but if all you want is darkness…" He switches to my other breast, and I smash his face against me until he pushes up for air.

"No, that's not it." I grab his ears and pull his gaze back to mine, only smoky, jasmine air between us. And all those clothes he still has on. I tug on his suspenders, but he slips away, down.

He speaks into my skin. "But you think you're dark. And I don't. So unless you're cursed like me, I need to know how I could be so wrong."

Wet kisses leave cool patches across my chest and down past my belly button.

"No." I can't let him see.

He sucks my hip bone and marches his lips across to the other with small smacks. My hips fly up beyond my control, wild for his touch between my legs. With his cheek resting low on my belly, he presses me back down.

"Tell me, and you won't regret it." He bites the round top of my mound, right over my underwear, then moves lower. "Why are you dark?" His rough chin spreads my thighs apart. Hot air teases my slit. I whimper through heavy breaths. My leg muscles tremble, and I squeeze his head tight.

"Open up." He turns his head and bites down hard on my inner thigh. I cry out at the sweet pain and spread my legs wide for him. "Keep fighting, but every bit of you is mine, and I told you I take care of my things. So you're going to let me fuck your precious little pussy with my tongue until I decide we're done. Now tell me," he says into my lips, brushing against my underwear with a low moan.

I try to push up into him, his lips, his tongue, his teeth—any part of him—but he digs his arms into my thighs and holds me down, depriving me of everything I need.

"Okay, okay!" I yell. "Just do it already."

"Good girl," he coos, then licks my core and nuzzles his face into the fabric.

I groan. Desire overtakes my mind and body, wrapping me up tight in burning ribbons of pleasure. "I see death!"

CHAPTER 49

I t all comes gushing out. "Visions of death. Like my soul can't live without it. My death, Kelter's, yours—anyone's. Every damn day, over and over."

I sink into the moss. It's so trivial compared to his real deaths.

But he doesn't judge me. No. He takes my underwear in his pearly teeth and pulls it to the side like the opening curtain of a grand show.

"The blood, the bones, the terror, the loss. All of it," I cry, winding up tighter.

He pushes my thighs, rolling me until my back is off the mossy ground and my neck is bent, my hips and ass rising to his waiting mouth. My legs hang over my head, my wet boots in the air. He gets up on his knees, slides them under my raised body and palms my ass cheeks in his hands before sending a chilled breeze over my scorched opening, torturing me with the lack of contact.

"And it's my fault the babies went over the falls, and that all of Caldera will be under the Centress' control. And I killed Cam. I sent her right over the waterfall." He tightens his grip, a sharp breath over my entrance. "And I burned down a house. With a family inside. On purpose. And I fucking liked it. And I steal things when I want them, just for the rush."

My whole body moves with my panting breaths. Eli doesn't say a word. He clamps his hot mouth over me and sucks away the pain, making good on his word—I don't regret it at all. I reach up and hold his head against me, forcing him to lap up all the darkness. My fingers lace through his hair as it brushes my thighs. Over and over, he lets go, nips at my folds and captures me again while I confess every atrocity, down to the smallest, most forgettable thing. Except I can't forget.

And once he has sucked me into silence, his mouth covering me so fully—the pressure and the pull and the scrape of his teeth drowning me in pleasure—his head rises between my dangling legs.

"Anything else?" he asks, reaching for his knife while the other hand holds my hips high in the air.

"Not right now," I whisper.

"Good." He glides the handle down my slit and presses the end against my entrance, spinning it. Silver flickers between his fingers.

"Fuck, that's cold." The beat in my chest goes berserk, my mind even more maniacal, the thought of him slipping the smooth metal inside much too enticing.

He laughs. "Next time, my little blood luster. I have first dibs on fucking you." He sucks my juices from the handle and flips it around. "And the only thing I want to hear now is you begging me to stop." He cuts through my underwear, across my center and up the front, then flings the scrap of fabric into the nearest tree.

"Not begging for more?" I ask edgily, unsure I still want to be trapped in his grasp and fully naked.

"I doubt it." Then his hands squeeze my cheeks and his tongue is on me again, sliding down and down, from the top of my slit, past every hole and back up again. He rocks my hips to the rhythm he sets with his tongue.

"Eli," I warn.

My hands grasp the moss at my sides. Every lick is eager and relentless. His grip tightens on my ass, and he moans into me, taking his time. Burrowing deeper. Enjoying himself. The sensation pulses through me, my entire body drunk on the touch of his tongue. His licks become ravenous kisses—sloppy, sliding kisses and hungry bites—more and more frantic and insistent, reaching my thighs, my cheeks, my fucking everywhere.

Adjusting his hold on me up in the air, his cold fingers walk inward until they reach my entrance. They force it wide open, my skin stinging at the stretch, and he thrusts his tongue inside me. I'm lost in bliss, lost in every deep thrust, lost in the slippery assault, his groans vibrating into my core, lost in *him*—everything about him.

It's too much. It's too perfect. Too perfected... experienced. It dawns on me.

"You've fucked thousands of women."

His tongue stops, and he reclaims it with a long, lingering lick. His lips and hot breath flirting with my slit, he says, "Hundreds and hundreds of thousands of times."

My heart flattens. I'm just another fuck on the eternal timeline.

As if he feels my soul deflating and my heart withering in its dark chamber, he pops a kiss onto my clit, spreads my legs and rests his chin on my mound where I can see his face between my thighs. "But not in this body." My lips part, my breath catching. "Not once. I'm brand fucking new... for you."

I lock onto his warm brown eyes, a sweetness in them I've never seen. Then it's gone, leaving piercing, angled slits.

"And soon I'll be inside of you, feeling it—not remembering it."

I moan at the sheer thought.

He rolls me back down flat and slides his arms under my shoulders, lying on top of me. He's heavy, inescapable. I shiver under his damp clothes and cold body. His face hovers an inch from mine, my scent on his breath. He takes hold of my hair, a hand on either side of my head pulling tight.

"I want to memorize your face screaming for me to stop and the warmth of your tight pussy squeezing my cock, so deep and hard inside you that you mold to my shape forever." A whine rises from my throat. "Never, I promise fucking you will wipe my mind clean of the thousands of times before. You'll be the only one, since the beginning of time."

"You lie."

He groans and rolls his hips, jabbing me with his length. "Take it or leave it."

He kisses my lips, my chin, my chest, all the way back down to my other waiting lips. Then his tongue is everywhere, his lips sliding over the wetness, and I don't care how many times or how many women. I don't even care if all the thousands of them—all the lovers—want to stand around us and watch. As long as he doesn't stop.

He pushes my legs apart, flattening them to either side of my hips and securing them with his elbows on my inner thighs. I smack his head and try to wiggle my legs free from the burning stretch and poke of bone, but he lifts his mouth just long enough to growl a single word. "Behave."

I squeal and try to roll away, but he's back, his lips fixed on my clit, his cheeks hollowed and a finger toying at my opening while he holds me in place. Whimpering, I arch my back, trying to escape the slow slide of his finger, but my hips are pinned.

"Damn you!" I struggle and squirm, pulsing with pleasure.

His deep laugh vibrates against me, burying his nose in my heat, his stubble scraping over my delicate skin. "That's not begging."

Before I can complain, he fills me, uncountable fingers all inside me at once. The elation—I scream. And he twists. I shriek. And he licks, his tongue furious, rolling over my clit in forceful waves. And the sight of him between my legs, devouring me, the curling of his fingers, the unbearable fullness—

"Stop!"

Instead of his fingers slowing, his tongue abandoning me, he chuckles into my folds. "Better…"

And with renewed strength he pushes my legs flat with those damn elbows, spreading me wider as he heals me with torture, inside and out. Too many fingers, too much tongue. Too intense. My toes curl. I cry for him to stop. But when he does, even for a breath, I push his head back down and demand more. I'm as rapt with the control he has over me as I am with the perfect amount of pain, but I give the man the fight we both want. And he fucking loves it. His hands and mouth attack with feverish passion. I pull his hair, his ears. I beg. I scratch. I curse. I hit. He comes up gasping for air, laughs and goes back for more.

My body shakes, contracting from the inside out. I reach for the moss at my sides, grasping at the mat of fine leaves—something to anchor me, to keep me from succumbing to the torment. All around us, the bed of green lights up. The surrounding trees whoosh back, hit by a tidal wave of air. The ground jolts beneath us. Magic shoots up my arms and spreads, winding and searching, vibrating energy steering through me and settling within.

Eli pops his head up, smirking hungrily. "I would have started with this if I'd known."

I shove his head down, and he goes back to pumping those fingers and nibbling my lips as the white glow falls away into the ground and disappears. His elbows slip off me as he pushes my thighs farther back, his ravishment near frantic, and in a second I have them up and over his shoulders, trapping his head between them. Each savage stroke of his tongue undoes me, but I need more of him. I pull on his suspenders, stretching the black twists until he finally looks up at my pleading face.

"Get the fuck inside of me, now."

He pulls away, fingers sliding out of me as he lowers my hips to the ground and kneels between my legs. The emptiness, the lack of his touch, rearranges my soul.

A smile breaks across his face. He licks his fingers one by one, then wipes my juices from his mouth with the back of his wrist. "Nothing there either. No darkness inside or out. You were wrong." He slips the suspenders off his shoulders and pulls his shirt over his head.

My world spins, faster and faster, forcing me to the edges of space and time and right into Eli. I thought I was drawn to him before, but this? It's unreal. The curves of his muscles. The soft brown skin. The scars. I want it all. I sit up to take it, but the knife is poised in his deft hand again. I freeze.

"You're spotless, but that's not the case for me." He slashes the blade across his chest, drawing blood in a furious flash of silver. Black blood—thick, black, oozing blood.

"Do you still want me?" He holds out his arms, letting me take it all in.

My heart screeches to a halt—then beats again, for him. I scramble onto my knees and tear down his boxers and pants with a violent shove, leaving the waistbands around the thick muscles of his thighs. His icy exterior is nowhere to be found when I wrap my hands around his cock and indulge in deep strokes. And the noise he makes—it's the most beautiful groan straight from his chest.

He wraps his arms around me, holding me tight, my cheek mashed against his bloody chest. I suckle at his skin, working my way down, thinking if I didn't already know better, I'd expect him to come in spurts of sticky blackness. My lips slip along, finding the perfect spot over a rib. And I bite him. My teeth break his skin, and a drop of blood finds my tongue, cold and... *spicy*.

He shoves my head away, chuckling.

"A taste for a taste." I grin and collapse before him, opening my mouth. I want to make *him* beg me to stop. He won't even know I've never done this.

"No, not after your stunt—this one or with the cuffs," he scolds. "When I let you suck me, it'll end in me fucking that hot little mouth and coming all over your pretty face. Then I'll spread it around and let you lick my fingers clean."

I look up into his eyes as he takes his cock from my hands and slides the dripping head in hot lines back and forth across my parted lips, mixing the black and white.

I kiss it.

"Fuck." His hips pull away, and both hands move to fist my hair. "But right now, the only place I want to come is inside that sweet pussy, and I'm not sure I could hold back if my cock were down your throat."

I swallow. It's all I can do.

He pulls me up by my hair, then crushes the sides of my face in a cold embrace. "You're fucking mine, Never." He smashes a kiss onto my wet lips. "And so we're clear, the only one who's going to be in cuffs again is you."

"Very funny."

He grins and throws me on my back, my feet over his shoulders. "Not a joke."

One hand lines up the scorching head of his cock at my entrance, and our eyes meet as he makes a slippery circle around it, then pops the tip inside and back out, leaving me crying out and punching any bit of him I can reach. "Hurry the fuck up."

He does.

His full length rams into me, filling all the emptiness in every way. So deliciously complete. Nothing slow or careful or tender about it. Groaning, my breasts held tight in his harsh grasp, he gives himself to me—for the thousandth time, and for the very first time. All mine. No gentle roaming or kisses, just a primal beast tearing me apart. I ache with every slamming thrust, his touch filling my mind and body beyond my depths and stretching me into a new existence.

My thoughts fracture with the way he crashes into me. He pounds me back to life, luring my body to him from the green blades of grass. *Live. Live. Live. Live.*

I watch him—his movements, his features tightening, distorting, fierce and uncontrolled. He's brutal. And gorgeous.

"You have to promise," he says between strikes.

"Anything." I'd sell my soul to stay in this moment.

"Never fall in love with me." His voice crackles with pleasure.

"What? Why the fuck would I?"

"You have to promise—"

Strike.

"To never—"

Strike.

"Fall in love with me."

I drop my legs from his shoulders, and he falls against me, chest to chest, a solid weight to keep me from floating away.

"Promise!" He stops, waiting and pulsing inside me.

I claw at his back, forcing him deeper, desperate for more, scratching until my hands slide freely over the fresh cuts I made, marking him with love he'll never have from me.

"I promise. I fucking promise." My cries bind my heart.

"All of it!" He pulls out, dripping with satisfaction, leaving me empty, so dark and empty.

"I promise I'll never fall in love with you!"

And he fills me again.

He gives and takes with slippery jabs, faster and harder. His black blood smears between us, over my heart, seeping into me, sealing my promise with the bloody kiss of our chests a hundred times over. His hips knock into mine with each consuming entrance into me, our sticky skin smacking together. I close my eyes, feeling him so thoroughly and savoring the in, the out, the fullness, the ferocity.

He shifts his weight back, then his hand is snug on my throat. The other grabs a fistful of my hair. "Open your eyes and watch me fuck you, little Never." My eyes fling open, catching his merciless gaze. "And when you come for me, I want every curse word you know rolling off that tongue, louder than all your screams combined."

That's it. I'm not going to make it much longer. Not when he talks like that. I dig my fingers into his back while rocking my hips. I'm tugged and bound and strangled from the inside out, my back a shadowy rainbow arching toward release, my hips the rolling rapids of a river, speeding toward the waterfall's edge, teetering on the brink—all those terrible moments about to fall away for good as he fucks me into forgetting. My thighs convulse.

Him on top of me, his bare chest, every burying thrust—he's a drug, the best escape. I want him over and over. In and out. Slick and hard. The angle spot-on. His nose scrunches up, his lip held captive by his teeth while looking down at my bouncing breasts. And for a second, he glows, a product of my mind lost in euphoria. My fingernails gouge crescent shapes into his back, his hand still flexing on my throat. I cry out and grind up into him.

"Never… you're killing me," he pants.

"How long until you come back to life?"

His face screws up. An animal groan builds within him, low and threatening. He drives into me with a wicked fury, rubbing me just right with every blurry stroke, sending me plunging over the misty falls, beyond return, thrashing against his cursed hips. Heaving, moaning breaths rack my whole body, and I writhe beneath him, dizzy, my body jerking with torrents of tension.

And just as relief finds me, he releases that groan. That visceral sound of an ancient being—*his* sound—intensifies every sensation. Waves roll over my nerves, and I want him closer, deeper. I don't want it to ever stop. I could stay here. I could spend an eternity like this—my mind free, my body raptured, death so, so, so far away.

He watches me, an intensity in his stare as though he could feel my raging pleasure. And I have no shame. No awkwardness. He's seen my worst. My tears, my fury, my violence, my turbulent mind.

I don't need to love him. No. I'll hate him. I'll hate him with every piece of my heart so it's never without him.

"Don't you close those eyes," he demands, his fist pulling my hair tighter.

My walls clench and release around his cock, and he surrenders his final shred of restraint, unleashing himself on me, his hips bucking. He slams into me with unnatural force, as fast and urgent as his ragged breaths tear from him. The strength and savagery of a being forced to live on, death after death, sharing his mind with the many thousands who came before.

"Eli…" My eyes roll, threatening to close.

"Eyes on your guard," he orders, his voice dangerous, deepening with the grip on my throat. I blink up at him, and he loosens his hold. His whole body is strung tight as he lifts my head by my hair and presses the softest kiss to my lips between thrusts. "My forever prisoner."

I move my hands to his curls, threading them through my fingers. I look straight into those boundless eyes. "The only mistake you are is mine."

He throws back his head, his neck corded and red, dripping with jewels of sweat. With a gasping breath he pleads, "Don't break your promise."

A grimace of agonizing pleasure takes over his face—eyes pinched shut and mouth open with a silent roar. He bends, his muscled body crumpling as he comes, emptying himself deep inside me with one exquisite spasm after another, an utter loss of control. And in this moment, he's as far from invisible as he can be. I see him—even as the darkness devours us.

CHAPTER 50

W e're on our backs, streaked with black, admiring the leafy canopy in our sweaty paradise. I don't know how long it's been since we untangled ourselves. Unanswered questions hang in the muggy jasmine air and mingle with the dripping, swollen afterbuzz of carnal satiation. Only some are approachable.

I promised away love I know nothing about, and he pleasured me into submission and drank up my innermost secrets. I tore open his back, and he tore down my walls. He bared the curse that haunts him, and I bared my ass.

We're even.

I roll to my side and trace my finger over the fresh knife cut on his chest and the dry black blood. Another wound marks his abdomen, the one I glimpsed in the woods while running my lips down his front.

"What's this from?" I tap the fresh scar.

"Jace stabbed me at the lake." He doesn't offer any emotion with the information.

"That's why she thought she left you for dead?"

He confirms with a deep sigh.

"But you were fighting the next day." *And kissing me.*

"Perks of being a mistake," he says, but even his bitter tone doesn't detract from the aura of lightness that hangs in the air around him, its wind riding over my exposed skin.

I drag my hand back up to his chest and rest it on his heart, formulating my question. A being all his own. And a curse. The unluckiest man of all time. "Milo and Sypher and everyone, they know about your many lives?"

"No. Only you."

Oh. "And they really can't see your dark side?"

He stares up at the trees, and I watch the subtle movements of his jaw as he speaks, the stretch of his scar. "They all see my light side. I could break Sypher's neck, and they'd still follow me anywhere, do anything I ask. That's why they gave up their loyalty to the Centress. It wasn't actually their choice."

"But Sola threatened you."

A look of affection crosses his face, softening the hard lines left by my previous questions. "I let her believe she's in charge. It keeps her happy. And Milo, he likes to think he can rein me in."

"Do they know about your other side?"

"Just Milo."

"So they think you're completely wonderful?"

"Aren't I?" He grins and tugs on his ear, and I wonder if that little habit is truly his, or one from a previous life.

"I wouldn't really know, would I?" I ask, realizing how much of myself I've given to a stranger. I *see* him, but am I seeing clearly?

"Everything I say and do is real, but you see it the way the curse wants you to see it. It takes my words and actions and tells you how to think and feel."

"Then how do I know what's behind the light and dark sides of the curse? Who you are. Is it real—what I think of when I look at you?" Recollection ripples through me. "How I feel when you touch me?"

Eli turns to me, resting his head in his palm. His hair is a mess, curls sticking up all over from all the pulling I did. He strolls two fingers over my eyelids, shuttering me in darkness. "Don't you ever believe in things you can't see?" His hand frosts down my middle, and lower. At least, I *believe* it's his.

"Why would I?"

"Would you be okay with a world that stops breathing beyond your sight? That turns to nothingness behind your back?"

"No, but—"

"Then believe." His hand latches on to my belly. "Believe that every time you blink, it's me you're not seeing in that fraction of a second, but I'm there. Me, not a curse."

I hold my eyes shut and move my hand to his, feeling his strength. "What is it that I'm not seeing?"

He loosens his hold on me and sighs under the burden of invisibility. "I guess it's that fine line between trust and distrust, the feeling between wanting to run at me and run away from me, the gray between the light and dark. I'm somewhere in there." His hand tightens again.

"But who are you?"

"Elivander Merinson Hux the Second. My father thought it'd be easiest to have the same name. You know, for when we merged together." Sad pride perforates his words. "Beyond that, I don't really know anymore."

I crack open an eye. "Merinson?"

"My grandfather."

I roll my naked body on top of his and kiss his stubbled chin. "It's a very sexy name—for a grandfather... which you are. And I fucked you anyway." I sit up, straddling him, and trace the rising edge of his ribs, the bite mark I left. "Do you wish I were a Hollow?"

"No."

"Why are you obsessed with them?"

"I'm not."

"But Milo said—"

"He was wrong. My obsession is far more specific, Never." He lifts his head to watch my moving fingers. I shut out his words, the implication, and continue my exploration of his chest. He lets loose a breath. "My skin is thinner with your touch."

"How so?"

His brows knit together, as if he were debating revealing more. "It normally takes a blade to make me bleed, but you cut me open with only your nails and teeth. Even your fist against my tooth split my lip inside. And I'm not as strong around you. It's getting worse. I could barely fight off Jace and Poett at the lake while you were close."

"Oh."

"It makes me wonder... What else are you capable of doing to me?" He eyes me with suspicion.

"We could find out." I reach behind me, taking his semi-hard cock into my hand. But I don't tell him I might be starting to resist his curse, the push and pull, that I might be seeing the gray.

His body jerks beneath me. "We *will* find out." He takes my other hand in his and fiddles with my rings. "You know…that ring is Milo's. You have to give it back, little thief."

"I just—"

"Shh." He plucks the red ring from the moss and adds it to my collection, wrapping the fabric strip around my finger and tucking the end under the band. "Hold on to it for now."

"It will be safe right here with my other rings." I inspect my fingers, recalling the homes I was sent away from… and Cam.

"What other rings?" His thumb brushes over the new addition.

What? But before I can ask what he means, he picks up the key. "Where did you get this? I didn't think of it earlier, but it looks like something from before the Separation, which can only be found in Caldera and…" Long lashes frame his widening eyes. "You didn't."

"I took it from your house."

He pushes me off him. "Shit. That was forever ago."

"What's wrong?"

"Everything within those walls is bound to the house. Removing even one thing breaks the protections. They start weakening until they fall. Anyone could find the house now. We have to go."

"You don't happen to have my old underwear in your pocket, do you?" I ask, glancing at the sliced up fabric hanging from a branch.

"It got crunchy. I left it behind," Eli says and collects my underwear scrap from the tree. He brings it to his face, inhaling my scent, then stuffs it in a pocket. The pieces of my bra follow.

"*Crunchy?* You're disgusting."

He gives me a cocky smile along with a spare shirt and pants from his pack. They reek of stale dampness. Then it's a rush of yanking wet clothes over my sticky body. I stuff my treasures in a pocket before we take off toward the castle.

Reaching the river again, we stand at the edge of an alternate bridge, my heart already trying to flee its cage. Eli doesn't ask, doesn't speak or hesitate. He simply lifts me into his arms and carries me across. I rest my head on his chest and tuck my fingers into the neck of his shirt, holding tight until he plops me down on the other side, safely past the mist and rapids, and we continue on.

Even so soon after our escape amid the coffee trees, after being dismantled and put back together by him, my mind starts stirring. I don't know what just happened with him—what I think of it, what I want. I can't attach a meaning to it, only a sense of belonging that I've never felt before.

A lost piece of me wants to feel more, to feel the very things I try to protect myself from, but the miniature fortress erected around my heart holds me back. With all the walls that he's knocked down, *those* seem indestructible, as if an external force reaches inside my chest and holds them in place. I can't let him in all the way... even if I want to.

He healed something in me, though. Brought back the part of me I lost at the falls—the last buried remnant of my hope and trust, so suffocatingly deep it had shriveled to merely a shadow of a concept. I have it back, but I don't know where to put it. What desire is worth the risk of hope? And how can I trust him again when I don't trust myself?

I can't.

But he's the only one who knows about my visions, and he's not running away.

I see his two sides—his lightness and darkness and everything beneath and behind and in between—and I accept it all.

I jog to keep up with his panicked pace, my mind shifting to the castle. Faster and faster we go, only stopping when a vision hits, when I die, crushed by the heavy trunks of fallen trees. Eli takes me in with those consuming eyes of his and presses on when I return—no pity, no judgment.

I slam one foot down after the other on the mushy undergrowth of the woods, my boots sticking to the mud and peeling away with loud *smacks*. I force my stride to lengthen, my thighs burning, until I match Eli's rhythm at his side. He reaches down between us, not slowing, not looking my way, and takes my hand in his. Hesitant fingers lace through mine in an awkward tangle. I almost reach for his ear in return.

And we run, the towering trees zooming by. I'm aware of everything I see—and don't see. Every blink, once unnoticeable, now has me searching the shadows, reaching through darkness, *believing*.

CHAPTER 51

W here we expect the pointed roof of the house to jut into the sky, dust lingers in its place. Carved wood dominates the pile of rubble—shelves upon shelves, slices of walls, beams and floorboards tossed together and topped with mangled silver pipes, cracked stone basins and ripped sofa cushions. A golden spiral staircase gleams through the dust—twisted, cracked, buried in chunks of wall and the occasional chair leg.

Trinkets and gadgets and everyday things litter the ground, Calderan items from before the Separation—candle holders and cast-iron pans, ceramic jugs and metal teapots. And rising from the remnants of the house is a soft whimper of defeat.

His home. His home for thousands of lifetimes, held together by the oldest magic. Destroyed.

I did this.

Eyes like dark crystals, he looks over the heaping pile, his memories, his pasts, then snaps back to no emotion. "Where is everyone?"

We run to the hatchway doors, finding them splayed open. Debris blankets the stairs. My heart is raw as I take the steps two at a time. Earth spills through the broken slabs of stone of the caved-in walls and pipe-covered ceiling, hanging low, angled, bearing the weight of the fallen house. Cracked doors lay flat on the floor, torn down by the collapse of their frames.

Eli surveys the wreckage, his shoulders stiff, jaw tight. Only his feet move, shuffling in a circle beyond the bottom of the staircase until he stops with his back to me, staring across the room at the desolated cell I

I slept in for weeks. The bars bend and twist like the blitzer's cage after I'd had my way with it. I step forward until I reach him, my fingers working up his shoulder, then higher. And I tug on his ear. His muscles tense at my touch, but minutes pass before he turns, looking down at my teary face.

I'm sorry. I'm so sorry.

He lowers his head, nearing me with scouring eyes and a hard-angled jaw, his dark aura closing in, his scent stronger, imaginary blood pooling in my mouth. Then he kisses my forehead, so softly it hurts, and turns his back to me once more. I peek around him, following his gaze to the one thing left intact: that hideous brown couch. A leaf-shaped note waits on the lumpy cushion. Eli wades through the destruction, plucks the note from the couch and reads it aloud.

Dearest Everielle,
It looks like I've missed you. I'll be waiting for you at the Ring.
Fortunately, I have plenty of company, including your delightful Kelter.
Mother

Eli's eyes go straight from the note to me. "Everielle?"

"Don't ask." His brows rise, but there's nothing more to say. I was given a name too soft, too elegant to live up to—at least on the outside. "She has Kelter. And your friends." I choke on the surge of dread rising in me.

Eli folds the note, zipping his fingers along the creases. "You're staying here."

Fear flips to fury. "No. I'm going to get Kelter."

"She's using Kelter as bait to get to you."

"I don't give a fuck. Let her. Kelt needs me."

He crushes the note in his fist. "He doesn't deserve you."

I don't quite know what to make of Eli's words as I step over pieces of broken cabinet, making my way closer to him. "If you leave me here, I'll follow you. There's nowhere to lock me up." I gesture to what's left of the cell and the broken doors.

He looks away and jingles the cuffs in his pocket, a wordless threat.

"Cuffing me only offers easy prey to the guards when they show up to check the place out." I take another step and poke a finger into his chest. "You said you'd never let me go. So don't fucking leave me."

He tightens his mouth and settles his pained look on me. "Give me two minutes." He disappears on hands and knees through the collapsed hallway, returning with a dry pack and a handful of notes from his nightstand.

How… *sentimental.*

He slaps them into my hand. "You'd better behave, my little Never, or you'll find yourself half-naked and cuffed in the woods like you left me."

We leave the crumpled walls sighing and whining behind us as rain falls from the gray expanse of clouds above. I keep a steady pace next to Eli, navigating through the maze of trees. My mind teases me again, showing me the little boy's face in the distance. I look away. I'm tired of seeing things that aren't there.

Eli pulls a teva roll from his pack and lights it with the flick of a fire stone, not even a struggle with the wind and rain. In goes the air, inflating him, and out puffs the purple smoke. He hands it to me, knowing I need it.

I inhale, the crest of a red circle burning toward me and a metallic kiss of spice on my tongue. I exhale the fear and the hurt.

The nearby river merely whispers at my nerves thanks to the teva softening the memories of the rushing sound of Caldera Falls. Eli's posture morphs once we're near the circular building of the Ring. His steps become focused and harsh, body poised for battle.

"I can't use the roof again." Eli points with his knife. "They'll be expecting that, and every entrance will be guarded. I'll sneak in the back and look for where she's keeping them."

"How are we supposed to get in the back if it's guarded?"

"*We* are not doing anything. I need my strength… and you distract me."

"I'm not waiting out here."

"You are." He pushes me against a thick trunk.

"You're going to chain me to a tree again?" I tease.

"No, I'll save that for when we have time to enjoy it." His unflinching face nears mine. "You're going to stay hidden here and wait for me to come back because you want to be alive to see your little Kelter again."

Fine. I let my weight fall against the tree.

He pulls back, satisfied. "That note could have been from days ago, and we've been gone for a full week. Hopefully I'll catch them off guard."

"That's your plan? Hope?" I believe in that even less than the gods. I stare at my feet. He's going to get himself killed in there, but the way he hangs on to hope despite all he goes through reveals a strength far deeper than his layers of muscle.

"Yeah." He positions the tip of his knife under my chin, raising it until I meet his gaze. "You might want to try it some time."

I crack a little inside, too many emotions trying to escape.

He lowers the blade. "Don't do anything stupid if you see Kelter."

I shove him. "Go."

He presses his full body into me, my back to the tree and his knife at my neck. Darkness trails down my spine, and his hips rock forward with the untamed growl he lets loose. "Fuck, Never." He shoves his cold hand up my shirt and clutches my breast. With a pinch of my nipple and a bite on my cheek, he slides his hand over my heart. It covers my chest. Every touch has my head spinning in reckless, giddy circles, even the metal shifting at my throat.

"Feel that?" he whispers into my lips. "I hear every bloody beat from miles away. It sets the rhythm. Your heart skips a beat, mine does too. Your heart pounds—like now—so does mine." He pushes harder on my chest. "So slow it the fuck down, or I won't be able to walk away without leaving you sore and dripping."

He can't be serious about our hearts, but that untethered desire for me already has wetness trickling freely down my thighs.

"With come or blood?" I ask.

"Both."

"Yours or mine?"

"Both. We'll make a fucking mess." He taps the blade on my neck to the rapid beat of my heart and pulls his hand from my shirt to squeeze my cheeks. His tongue forces past my smushed lips in a rough kiss, so urgent and consuming it's as though he needed it in order to keep breathing. "You will behave so we can get out of here alive. I have so much more I'm going to do to you. And fuck you against a tree just got added to the list."

I grab his suspenders. *One more kiss.*

But he pulls away.

My knees weaken, and I flatten my back to the tree and watch him approach the vine-covered outer wall of the Ring. He sidesteps along the curved exterior to where the carriage was loaded with babies and the elixir the night I followed it. Another carriage waits in its place, full of sacks—a reminder of my failure. I grip the tree, clenching my eyes shut. The babies. The mothers. Caldera. The thoughts become threads of energy from the bark at my fingertips, passing through my hands and climbing my arms. Magic streaks through me, into me, beyond my control. I pry my hands from the bark and open my eyes. The glow fades from the trunk at my back.

Eli peeks around the outer wall into the back room then disappears through the doorway, leaving me alone with the dwindling gray light and soft sprinkle of rain.

I watch for him to return, to exit the Ring with Kelter behind him, and Milo and Kaleida and everyone else, but a scrawny Life Cycle worker appears instead. He lifts a basket into the carriage, talking over the shoulder of his gray jumpsuit.

"Did you see the Hollow was moved?"

Ash follows him out on her twiggy legs, a basket against her chest. "Yeah, to the underground storage with the traitors. I don't see why he's still alive."

My breath hitches. Kelter. I have to tell Eli where to find him.

"I'm glad the suites are finally back to being used for birthing, not prisoners," the man says, taking the basket from Ash.

I practice the obscene act of waiting as baskets of drugged babies are packed into the carriage. When the workers retreat, disappearing back within the walls of the Ring, and the carriage door swings shut, I'm ready. The ancient wooden wheels spin, and it takes off, more babies stolen from their mothers. I don't let myself follow, not this time.

I drop to my hands and knees and crawl over slippery leaves and sharp twigs. Five feet, then I stop, listening. Then another five. And two and three and four more until I'm outside the door, peering into the back room. Baskets and tea carts and blankets. My stomach churns. Waterfalls and rainbows and death.

I stay close to the wall, listening for the heavy breathing and painful cries of labor from the other rooms, but it's eerily quiet—save for the patter of rain. And dark. My knees go numb on the hard marble floor, my wet hands slipping and squeaking. I shove used syringes out of my path, avoiding the prick of the needles as I make my way along the wall.

A whistled tune sounds—not a song; that wouldn't be allowed. No, it's a menacing taunt, like a hunter laughing at his prey as he lures it to its demise. I tuck myself behind a large wooden barrel against the wall and search for the source. And there, beyond the entrance to the moonlit atrium, a guard in a black jumpsuit stands in the rain, club in hand, death tune on tongue.

Dammit. I can't find Eli if I can't get past the guard. I debate going back, returning to the safety of the tree and letting him rescue them on his own, but he might not know there's an underground room. So I stay. I'll find Kelter myself.

I scoot closer to the barrel. The cold pinches my skin, and every puff of foggy breath might give me away, but my frozen fingers come across a hinge. I slide my hand along a gap in the marble and hit the rounded top of another hinge. My fingers follow the crevice in the shape of a square—then in… to a handle.

A trapdoor. It must lead underground. To Kelter. To warmth and hugs and home. I grab the handle, cold metal biting into my palm. And I pull. The hinges creak. The marble squeals. And the door lifts an inch. I hold my breath, but the guard doesn't come running. He whistles that awful tune and swings his club at his side.

I raise the door another inch, and another, each motion producing the slightest whine from the hinges. Pitch black peers up at me. I keep going, bit by bit, lifting the heavy marble door higher, and when it's halfway open, and I'm that much closer to seeing Kelt, the whistling stops.

And boots stomp.

I freeze, still on my knees, one hand holding the trapdoor open, one gripping the edge of the floor, fingers dipping into darkness.

The guard approaches and halts on the other side of the barrel, sliding a hand through his golden-brown hair.

I'm as still as death. I beg my heart to stop banging around long enough for him to move on.

I'm not here. I'm the dark of night. Walk away.

But he doesn't. He shoves the barrel over, sending it slamming down on top of the trapdoor and closing my fingers inside. Sharp, clinking objects tumble over my back, piercing my skin. I scream, and a vision steals me from the pain and panic.

Fat needles stab into my veins, hundreds of them, draining my blood through tiny tubes. I rip them out one after another, but I'm weaker every second. Sweat coats my skin, my sight a cloud of black. A final needle jabs into my heart, siphoning my last drops of life.

"Never!"

Eli. I'm pulled from the vision, life hammering back into me with the throbbing of my squashed fingers. I try to crawl backward to escape the pile of porcelain I'm buried beneath, but my skin slices in a dozen spots.

"Never what?" a man says.

He's talking to me, jerk.

The guard digs through the broken teacups from the barrel to get to me, clearing enough porcelain to find my head and shoulders. He yanks me out of the mess and wraps a bloody arm around my neck. Eli is splayed on the ground beyond the doorway to the atrium, his pack and knife tossed aside and the guard who took Milo and me from the lake perched on his back.

"Godsdamn Eye of Malachite, Rayde," Eli yells as his head is whacked into the white stone.

The guard he called Rayde rolls up the sleeves of his black jumpsuit, grips Eli's curls and smashes his head down again. Bone on stone.

My mouth fills with saliva. "Get the fuck off him!"

Eli's back is to me as Rayde drags him away, arms kinked, but his words still find their way to me. "You will *never* be their prisoner."

My heart trips. *Only yours.*

Footsteps thud across the atrium, the accompanying voice too familiar. "Lock them up," my mother says. "And Jace—you fail me again, you're dead."

CHAPTER 52

J ace comes for me, her face pinched with wrath and still bearing Sola's blue-gray handprints on either cheek—now wrinkled and peeling. Her rapid steps are unhindered, even in the fitted jumpsuit. "Give her to me."

The guard hands me over with a grunt and a shove, a deep scowl on his face as he watches Jace haul me backward across the atrium. We pass the Centress, rolling her neck and tapping her foot as if the art of abduction bored her.

Jace pushes me through the door of a birthing room and slams me into the wall, knocking my head against the white marble. The room is like the one Milo and I were locked in—windowless walls and a narrow bed in the center with stained sheets, guardrails and chains. She holds me against the cold material with a hand to my throat, her eyes twitching, pressing until my airway closes. I fight the tears building up from the pain and try to pull her fingers away, cursing my weakness. She lifts a knee, and with a hateful grin, smashes it into my hip, pinning me in place.

"There's no one left to save you, Hollow. I hope I get to be the one to finish you off when the Centress is done with you." Drops of spit hit my face as she speaks.

She still thinks I'm a Hollow.

Knowing she'll let me live doesn't stop the panic of not being able to breathe, the urgency. Tears fall in warm streaks down my cheeks. Black spots dot my vision. Pressure builds. I can't find the fight in me that surfaces when I'm with Eli.

The door opens.

"That'll do, Jace," the Centress says, tossing her hair behind her shoulder.

Jace releases my throat, then cradles my head and conks it into the wall again. My brain rattles. Lights twinkle behind my eyelids as I gasp for air. She tugs my head forward, and I brace myself for another blow, but she gathers two fistfuls of my hair and pulls, distorting the handprints on her cheeks with the glowering look she gives me. With a final breath of hot rage in my face, she drops her knee from my hip and frees my hair.

The Centress steps to the side, letting Jace leave, then closes the door. I wince at each heavy lungful of breath, my back flat to the wall, and let my gaze roll to her midnight eyes and fair face.

"You've caused quite a stir in Sonnet, Everielle." She tilts her head to the side, inspecting my baggy black clothes. She wears black as well, a sweeping dress with long sleeves and a high-cut collar.

I refuse to give her the satisfaction of a response. If only she couldn't see the tears still dripping from my jaw, hear the rasp in my throat. I want to ask about Kelter and the others, but I hold back and focus on sharpening the daggers in my wet eyes.

"Calm yourself, love. I have to thank you."

"For what?" I bite my tongue at my lack of control.

"For returning my rogue guard, of course. All Eli had to do was wake things up in you and bring you back to me." She purses her pale lips, and her words wrap around my throat, taking my breath. "It was a simple command—take you from the cell, hide you away who-knows-where and finish the job for me without the eyes of every Vaile on you. I couldn't let anyone else see what you possess. As disturbing as Eli is, he was the convenient choice with a history of loyalty and already your guard, but oh—" She clicks her tongue. "What a mistake."

No. He wouldn't do anything for her beyond his regular job. He may have been selfish, taking me from the black room and locking me up for his own reasons, but to help *her*? He couldn't. My arms and legs tingle, all the blood rushing to my face.

"No."

"Oh yes, dear," she says, much too sweetly. "I knew you didn't steal any magic, but I had to see what was inside you. When I saw it, saw you lighting the room as you shook in pain beneath those rocks, I knew I had to get rid of Mallace. I broke his neck—and four of my nails while disposing of his body." She looks at her fingernails, flicking them. "That was more satisfying than just taking his memory. But I couldn't let anyone else find out, and the only reasonable way to explain stopping the sessions was to have you go missing. So I asked Eli to take you away."

Stop talking. Stop stop stop.

"But I should have listened to my instincts not to trust him. He didn't bring you back to me when he was supposed to. Nobody could know what I'd asked of him, of course, so you can imagine how unhappy I was to see him showing up for his shift each day, that smug look on his gorgeous face, and not be able to do a thing about it. I had to send every Vaile in Sonnet out in search of you."

My jaw clamps shut at the thought of her enjoying his face. I can't feel my legs. Only my locked knees keep me upright.

He would never hand me over to her.

She nears me, her tall body making me tremble, and runs a gentle hand over my knotted hair. "But you're here with me now. I won't let him hurt you anymore."

My mouth opens. And closes. And opens, searching for a response that could possibly begin to express my ire. "What? You—"

"Hush now." She places her hand on my cheek, tightening her grip when I try to escape. "Nothing but lies come out of that man's mouth."

And truths and secrets and pains.

"He should have obeyed me." She slips her fingers under my chin, tilting my head far back to look at her. "I even offered him the most coveted reward in Sonnet for a job well done—let him kill a Hollow. He was plenty motivated to get his hands on him."

Kelter.

That can't be true. Eli was looking for where she was keeping Kelter so he could rescue him, not kill him… but he's hated Kelter all along. Would he hurt him to keep him away from me? I don't want to believe that.

"Don't worry. He'll be punished." She pushes up on my slack jaw and steps back, allowing me to see her face better. "And I'm going to get what I want from you. If pain is what it takes, that's what you'll get. We'll see if you're ready to cooperate tomorrow after a visit from my guards."

"What do you want from me?"

The tiniest hint of a smile pushes at the Centress' lifeless lips. "Your essence, love."

"What essence?" The same kind the fake gods have? She's crazy.

"That's what's inside you, a special kind of magic. You hold it in your memories—what makes you who you are. It had to be woken up before I could access it. I heard what you did at the lake. Thanks to Eli, your essence is ready for me, but you resisted my gift when I tried to take your memories. That mind of yours is too resilient."

An essence? That can't be right. It's not even real.

"Now I have to weaken you, make it impossible for you to resist me." She wipes away my fresh tears. "You brought this on yourself, Everielle."

I slide down the wall as she exits, her black dress dragging behind her, hair swishing. Moonlight slips through the grate at the bottom of the door, the only light to keep me company through the cold night. The lock clicks, and I fold my arms around my knees and tuck my head.

The visions come throughout the sleepless night—*of Jace holding my throat until I watch myself slump down, dead and alone. Of guards ripping away my limbs, a slow stretch popping the joints and tearing the skin. Visions of Kelter beaten to a lifeless pile of blood-soaked skin and broken bones.*

Each time, the surge of life returns sharper, more intense. My senses heightened. The silvery shine of metal chains, the rusty smell of old blood, the dampness of my boots. The cries of women and babies ring out, crisp and piercing, as if they were coming from me.

My eyelids are drooping when the gray morning light sends the night shadows into hiding. A canteen is shoved through the grate, falling to the marble floor as dark fingers pull away. More elixir-tainted water. It may not dull *my* free will and force me to do what they want, but that's exactly what it's doing to Kelt... and all of Caldera. I crawl to the door as the footsteps fade, then unscrew the cap and glug down the liquid.

With a full belly of water, I sit against the wall and pull the notes from my pocket, all the ones Eli left for me during the week I spent locked in his room.

Never,
My whole room smells like you.
Eli

I press it to my chest.

Never,
Did you know you snore?
Eli

I do not.

Never,
Miss me yet?
Eli

Tears splash over the beautiful script, written with those damn talented fingers. He *did not* put me through trigger after trigger to help the Centress wake up this stupid thing in me. I curl into a ball on the floor and stay like that for hours, listening to the sounds of labor. I pull my body tighter when the door opens and shuts.

"Hello, little Hollow." A man's voice slithers down my spine. "You're not as wet as when I last saw you."

I can't hold back my whimper as I place his voice. I don't dare turn my head to the black eyes I know I'll see, the gaunt cheeks and the long hair Eli once pulled to heave him over my head and into the lake.

"And you don't smell as much like vomit," I say into my knees, not revealing I saw him after that, getting walloped by Sypher.

Poett's hands clamp onto my sides, lifting me effortlessly from my safe ball on the floor. He shakes me, trying to get my arms and legs loose, but I stay tucked tight.

Go away.

He groans and tosses me onto the bed. My back hits the stiff mattress, and he leans over my bent legs. I keep them pulled against my chest.

"Let's see what was so special that Eli would give his life to fuck you." His pale, swollen face looms over me, at least four teeth missing, his nose narrowing as he scents me. His hair falls over his shoulders in greasy clumps.

"Get away!" I kick my feet into the black jumpsuit over his stomach without thinking, the small act of violence coming so easily.

He stumbles back then dives forward with renewed rage, grabbing my legs and chaining me to the rails with the dangling cuffs. I sit up and try to fight him off, but he shoves me to my back with one palm, pulls my arms up over my head and chains them too.

"That's better. Now I can see what I have to work with."

I pull on the chains, twisting and writhing while he laughs. "Are these hard for me?" He flicks my cold nipples through my shirt, and I silently curse Eli for slicing up my bra.

"Fuck off, asshole!" Finally—a voice when I need it. I try to turn away from his touch, but he runs a hand down my chest to my belly, then tugs at the front of my pants.

"No underwear either. He likes it easy, puts you in his clothes for quick access." He snaps the waistband against my skin. "And nothing in the way." His fingers trail from one hip bone to the other. "I prefer a challenge, maybe a chase, but thanks to you, I've been forced to work double shifts. I haven't had a spare minute for release."

"Don't. Touch. Me." Tears threaten me again.

"Don't get too excited, Hollow." He pats my mound, bending his hand to my shape. "I'm not here to give you pleasure—only pain." Then he plunges his elbow into my stomach. Lips to my ear, he whispers, "But sometimes it's hard to tell which is which."

I groan, my body trying to curl up but stopped by the chains. Gasping, every muscle across my middle cramping and burning, I let the tears fall.

Even through the watery blur, I see Poett's face light up with delight, the slow lick of his lips. "Is that the sound you make for the traitor when he takes you?"

"Please." *Don't hurt me again.*

His eyes narrow, a sick hunger in them. "I bet he likes your face full of tears, gets off on your pain while you beg for more."

A pounding sound comes from beyond the door, sudden and desperate, as if someone wanted the pain to go away as much as I do.

He rests a hand on my lower abdomen, his thumb toying with my waistband, fingers caressing. I scream. I curse. I cry. His touch is sickening. He keeps his hand in place, waiting to speak until fatigue quiets me.

"You're lucky the Centress didn't send someone that already has their gift. They could burn your hair off, freeze your fingers before shattering them... or worse."

"Lucky? Fuck you."

His elbow lands on my thigh this time, and I can't stop the gurgling sound of agony that escapes, the groan and whimper that follow.

The pounding strengthens from somewhere across the atrium.

Poett stands next to the bed, glaring down at me. "I've spent my whole life being warned about Hollows from Caldera, how your people could ruin us, how all you care about is taking magic from our land. The only thing that let me sleep at night was knowing the elixir kept Hollows away. Then you showed up." He punches my chest, forcing the air out of me. "We are nothing without magic."

The distant pounding continues, and I close my eyes, letting it become a beat in my mind, a comfort as I wait for my breath to return.

CHAPTER 53

The Centress slid into the room after Poett left me bruised and quaking. I retreated to a corner, trying to hide in the darkness of the falling night, but she picked me up off the ground.

Are you ready to stop resisting, Everielle?

That was all she said before her hands slid onto my face and unleashed her gift. Pain cracked through me, then I felt the pull on my mind. I fought to keep my memories, putting every remaining scrap of strength into holding on to the little moments I thought I didn't care about. She slapped me across the face when I didn't let go of a single one. I was too numb to feel it.

Poett and Jace returned over the next two days, pushing me to my limits, weakening me for the Centress' visit each night. Every breath is tight with pain. Every movement spurs regret. My legs and arms and stomach sting where Poett cut open the top layer of my skin in slow, torturous slices, right through my clothes. I tried not to cry out with every entrance into my flesh, but I couldn't even muster the thought of silence when he wiped the bloody knife over the scar on my neck—too painful a reminder of where it all started.

The pounding sound always comes with the physical pain, then returns when I'm left alone, falling apart inside.

My visions of death are the only escape. How ironic that the gory end of life and crushing loss feel like a comfort compared to real pain. But the relief dissolves when my senses come to life after my visions, spiking my pain to cruel levels. I'm weak without food for three days, unable to chase that invincible high I felt in the woods before Eli found me. But I won't let my mother ruin me. I won't.

"I gave you a chance to cooperate, and you didn't take it," the Centress says, pulling my sore limbs upward and forcing me to stand. She unruffles the long skirt of her crimson dress. "I expect better from my daughter." Her words slice past my thickened skin to the vulnerable layers beneath, and my toxic mind scolds me for letting down my mother.

"I don't have what you want. Please let me and my friend go home. I won't come back to Sonnet. I won't say a word to anyone in Caldera." I don't care about saving anyone else right now, about elixirs and babies and doing the right thing. I can barely think. I want it to be over. I should never have left that stone room. I should have listened to Kelter.

She blinks her beady black eyes, her hardened face unreadable. "Your home is here with me."

Her simple statement turns my despair into outrage. "You're nothing to me. You got rid of me. You wreck lives. You separate mothers and babies. You drug Calderans, and Cam's death is your fault too." She stiffens at my words, and I throw more at her. "If you weren't forcing her to take the babies into Caldera, she'd still be alive." *And I wouldn't be a killer.*

Rain smacks down on the stepping stones of the atrium, thunder rolling.

"Cam?" Her face ices over. She clamps her hand over my mouth, shoving me back against the wall. "I don't know who or what you're talking about," she says. "You're delusional. The imbued carriages take care of everything. And I told you that I don't need to take the babies' magic to put back into the cycle now that I have you. They won't have to be separated if you cooperate." Her hand peels away, letting my shallow breaths free.

"You're lying." *Everything's a lie.*

"Come to me, love. I'm not going to hurt you." She pulls me against her, my head landing on her ribs.

"You already did." I shove her away, and she lets me, taking a step back. "You used rocks to rip me open." My chest caves in at the memory, the pain. "You put your hands on me."

"I needed to see what you were given. I was simply gathering information. Any mother would." She holds out an arm to me, long and elegant, beckoning, as if I would willingly go to her.

"You sent guards to beat me." I gesture weakly to my bruised body.

"Which could have been avoided if you weren't so stubborn."

I let out a defeated sigh and unstick the fabric from the scab-crusted cuts on my belly, grazing my fingers over the dry blood. "What's happening to me? Who... what am I?"

"I'll tell you. I'll explain who your father is. I'll tell you everything I know about the magic he gave you and the birthmark on your chest that comes from him."

My head spins. My father? I press a hand between my ribs, clutching my birthmark. Another *boom* of thunder rumbles the building.

She reaches for my hands. I'm too slow as I pull them away. The warmth of her skin travels up my arm, spreading through my core and out to my limbs like the magic that finds its way into me. It's what I've always wanted. All the answers. All the possibilities. A mother. I'm caught, feelings smeared all over my face. How could *she* have this effect on me?

"You're my daughter—of course I want you to know who you are." She steps closer, her dress sweeping over the toes of my boots, and I take in her scent of wildflowers, the ones that spring up in the rare patches of sun that make it to the Calderan forest floor. The ones that I stomp flat as I make my own path. Her tall frame soars above me, and I feel like a child again, so small and helpless.

I bury the absurd ideas strutting through my mind—a mother's shoulder to cry on, someone to confide in, someone who can't turn their back on me. She's not that person I invented. She's not the mother I imagined in my head year after year, the one I fell asleep to as a child, when I still believed in hope.

She's a fucking nightmare.

"I need to take away your memories first. We'll start over," she says.

I pant, blood surging through me with no direction as I look up at the Centress—my mother. Her tight mouth and emotionless expression look back at me. She's the definition of composure, of control.

She's everything I'm not.

"Don't touch me." I rip my hand from hers and fall into a vision. *Instead of my mother's vacant black eyes looking down at Kelter fighting and thrashing in her lap, they're warm and fierce, tormented and questioning—my own indigo eyes. Full of tears. She slips her hands around his neck… and snaps it. Then he's still. So sickeningly still. Until his neck cracks back into place, and his hazel eyes flash at me, green and gold and honey, throwing me out of the vision.*

I gasp, my head pounding like the rain outside, the plain room now vibrant and overwhelming with detail, with life—so much life after death.

I'm not like her. I'm not… but I'm a killer. And so is she.

Her jaw muscles spasm under her cloak of self-control. "Can't you pay attention?" she scolds, like so many before her.

I cover my face with my arms, trying to escape my overactive senses—and reality.

"You may not be pleased about it yet, but there are perks to being my daughter." She lowers my arms and tips my chin up to her. "I'm going to let one of your lovers live." Panic cracks through me as her dark eyes dance with delight. "And you get to pick which one."

CHAPTER 54

My mother tows me across the birthing room and out into the atrium, under the gray sky, into the rain. We stop just feet away from Kelter and Eli, each held by a guard. I'm not sure I really see them. My mind is fogged, my body weak, my heart in pieces.

Only denial slips out of my mouth, unfeeling words. "They're not my lovers."

"Call them what you wish," she says.

Kelter. It's actually him. Alive.

Brown hair slicked back in a low tail, lips folded in determination and a club in hand, Poett holds Kelter's arms behind his back. The patter of rain gushes through my ears, consuming all my thoughts until a woman wails in pain from behind a closed door. Another baby on the way to be stolen from its mother.

"Give that woman tea," the Centress yells. "Give them all tea. I don't need any distractions." Two workers enter the atrium from one of the rooms, bow their heads and run off, one toward the room with the tea carts and another toward the woman's suite. "And take this one, Jace."

Jace runs up, yanks me from the Centress and bends my wet arms behind me.

"Ever, what are you doing here?" Kelter asks, snapping out of his shock and sweeping his gaze over my fist-sized welts and the sliced skin showing through my ripped clothes. His honey-tinged hair is longer now, his body thinner, cheeks sunken. Freckles hide beneath layers of rain-streaked dirt and an inch long beard.

"I came for *you*," I say, still taking in Kelter as though I haven't seen him in years. He's wearing black pants like mine and a white shirt that's torn and stained brown and gray, as if he'd been wearing it for weeks. His gauntness makes his protruding ears even more obvious despite the hair that hides the tops of them, and more than ever before, I want to reach out and grab them to know he's real. "Are you okay?"

My mother speaks before Kelter can answer. "Which one gets to live?"

She's violent and twisted and heartless. I want to believe she wouldn't kill one of them, but I can't—because she would.

I pry my eyes from Kelter to inspect Eli. I don't want to look at him, to be pulled in by his dark eyes and perfect amount of stubble, not when my heart fractures at the sight of him like this. Rayde holds him in his crushing arms. The bits of his forehead visible through his wet curls are bruised, and his knuckles are purple and swollen, as if he'd been punching a wall... or pounding on one. Over and over. Trying to get to me.

"Never—" Eli says, endless regret lining his forehead. "Fight."

"Shut up, traitor." Rayde jabs the end of his club into Eli's cheek, silencing him.

I flinch. I want it all to be a vision. I want to open my eyes and everything to be better again. I look at my mother. "You can't do this."

"I'm the Centress." She rests a hand on her hip.

I fight the acid rising in my throat. "I'm not choosing."

"Alright then, they both die." She runs her fingers over her sheet of dark brown hair and bends the wet tips to inspect them, not bothering to glance at the two guards standing behind Kelter and Eli, positioning clubs under their chins. Terror streaks across Kelter's face, his hazel eyes round, his mouth gaping. Eli simply lifts his chin, nostrils flaring.

"No!" I try to leap out of Jace's grasp. "Don't hurt them."

"I really thought this would be an easy decision for you." The Centress pivots and swoops in front of Kelter, caressing his jaw with a single long-nailed finger on her way by. "What reason do you have to let a Vaile live, especially this one?" She passes Eli, running that same finger over his cheek and down his chest.

Every reason. "Let them go. You can have me."

"I already have you." She huffs a sigh and flops a lazy hand at the guards. "Carry on."

Rayde and Poett pull back on the clubs, holding them tight against Eli and Kelter's throats. Kelter shoves his head back and pulls down on the club, frantic, his hands slipping on the wetness.

"Why are you doing this?" I cry, still struggling against Jace.

Eli bashes a heel into Rayde's shin behind him and twists, jabbing him with his elbow. No fear on his face, just fury.

"Because, Everielle, even days without food and endless hours of pain weren't enough to get you to lower your walls. You keep fighting."

She doesn't realize how close I am to breaking, but not from crippling pain and hunger pangs. I'm on the verge of collapse from knowing that every bruise and cut, every minute of agony, every lonely breath is the product of my mother's rejection. A reminder that I'm not wanted, not loved. But maybe if I didn't spend every day dying, losing myself, losing others, impaled and crushed and breathless and burning and bleeding and pleading for it to end—maybe then it would have been enough.

"Now I see that only the strongest emotions will let me in deep enough," she continues. "I have to break you to get what I want. Plus"—she rolls her head toward Kelter and Eli, watching them battle against the clubs at their necks—"someone has to be punished for making me wait."

Kelter clenches his teeth, panic marring his face as peaceful raindrops gather on his beard.

I need to buy time. "Okay, stop. I'll choose!"

"Go on." She mocks me with her calmness.

"Tell them to stop. Let me think."

"Oh, that's not happening, dear. Think quickly, or they'll both be gone."

She's serious. She's letting the guards kill them. A blue hue clouds around Kelter's mouth. His grasp weakens on the club, his knees bending beneath him. Eli continues his fight, but the club stays firm at his throat, a shade of gray crawling up his face.

Damn her. She can't do this. My breaths come faster, the helplessness crushing my chest. My insides are torn out, tied in knots and shoved back in, my head and heart at odds with each other.

"Stop, please stop," I beg as my mind runs in circles. My Kelter, my friend. I can't lose him. And Eli—he needs me. He sees me. I see him. But Kelter would never lie, never betray me.

The clubs press harder. Kelter's eyes find mine, the greener one gleaming. I can't look. My whole body is shrieking. I'm going to lose them both.

Too long.

Too much time.

Too little air.

The ticking seconds rap through my blood.

"Kelter! I choose Kelter!"

Golden specks flare in Eli's eyes as they lock onto mine.

"Release them." My mother extends her hand out flat. "The knife." Kelter and Eli gasp for air, color rushing back to their faces.

Poett pulls a knife from his pocket, unsheathes it and shuffles forward with Kelter. With a quick scan of the silver blade, he lays the handle in the Centress' palm.

Eli's knife. I'd know it anywhere.

Kelter coughs and grabs his throat, tears falling from his bloodshot eyes. I don't see the rush of relief I expect. His face is ruined with pain. He turns to Eli and grabs him, so tight his knuckles go white and blue veins bulge. Eli rolls him off his shoulder, whipping him away without a glance. Kelter's hand falls to his side.

Why would he care what happens to Eli?

The Centress cocks her head stiffly to the side as she watches their interaction. She prowls toward Kelter and wipes away an escaped tear, lost among the raindrops. "You have a second chance at life, young man. All you have to do to save yours is take his." She rolls her head to Eli.

"No!" This wasn't the plan… I had no plan. I wanted to delay. I needed their throats released.

"I-I can't." Kelter blinks rapidly, wet lashes fluttering up and down.

"I'll make it easy for you. The guard will hold him, and all you have to do is take his life." She gently takes Kelter's hand in hers and turns it palm up. "I know you well now. You're stronger than you think." She traces a crease to his wrist and sets the knife in his hand. "Be smart with this and do what I asked. You wouldn't want anything to happen to Everielle, would you?"

CHAPTER 55

Kelter closes his trembling hand around the wet handle. Those green-and-gold eyes flick up to me.

"You can't ask him to do that, you twisted bitch." I can barely find the breath to speak. He didn't grow up like the children here. He's not like *them*.

"Oh…" Sugar coats the Centress' tongue. "So sorry, love. Did you want to do it?"

I try to tear myself from Jace's grasp again, pointlessly charging toward them, but I'm locked in place. "No, *please*. Don't make him do this. I'll do anything. Don't hurt them."

She smiles. She actually smiles at me, breaking her porcelain face in the process. "That's right. You will. I'll have your essence by taking all your memories, and after, you'll love me as your mother. You'll have the family you always wanted."

Each person in the courtyard tenses, disbelief all around, but Kelter's frantic eyes, fixed on me, must be the widest of them all.

"But first," the Centress continues, "I'll make it clear that I don't allow anyone to disobey me—and live."

Rayde shoves Eli a step closer to Kelter, wrenching his arms behind his back. Kelter looks my way, desperation carved into his drenched face, his body weak and overcome with shallow breaths.

"Don't do it, Kelter," I say.

"Go ahead. You know you failed to protect her. Now is your chance." She can hardly contain herself, her soft words settling over Kelter as she massages the rain into her anxious hands.

Kelter's eyes drift shut. He bites his lower lip. His shoulders rise and fall, the white shirt now stuck to his body, every rib showing, every breath forcing him to face reality.

Talk to me, Kelter. Tell me you're in there.

He opens his eyes and looks at me again, as if he heard me. I swear he begs me to go back in time and fix all of this. I know salty tears must be finding their way out those hazel eyes and down his cheeks with the rain, even if I can't see them anymore. The wind hits my face as hard as the panic and pain.

"Don't let her make you like one of them," I say. *You're different. You're gentle.* I don't know what I expect him to do, how to get out of it, but he can't do this. He won't.

Eli blinks at Kelter, his face hard but almost relaxed. If he's scared, if he's silently begging him to throw the knife aside like I am, it doesn't show.

Kelter swallows, slow and forced, as though the blade were lodged in his own throat. The look on his face says the same. "I don't have a choice, Ever. She'll hurt you if I don't do it, then she'll take me from you—and you need me." Arm shaking, he raises the knife.

I need both of you.

Another vision takes me, my exhausted mind barely holding on, falling further into itself.

The Centress has Eli frozen on his back as she licks down his neck with the long, slender tongue of a reptile, making figure eights across his chest and pausing at his nipple. Her tongue becomes a dagger, and she drives it into his heart. It fades to soft pink again, and she slurps and laps the oozing black blood from his chest until he's clean.

Dizzy, my head imploding and my senses on fire, I'm unable to push the bloody scene from my mind even after it ends.

Eli's jaw shifts back and forth. I feel him looking at me, but I don't let my gaze meet the dark caves of his eyes—I might fall in. I lock my stare onto Kelter, but from the edges of my vision I see Eli tilt his head back, exposing his neck in defiant acceptance of his fate.

No. This can't be happening.

"Please Kelt, no, no..."

But Kelter takes the silver blade of Eli's knife—the one that I held to his heart, the one that cut my clothes and spilled blood from his chest—and with a firm grip on the handle and a quick step forward, he slashes Eli's throat. Straight across, deep into his amber-brown skin.

Lightning sears the sky, the angry roar of thunder following.

Thick black blood flows down Eli's front. His eyes bulge with shock, and for a moment, the wind dies too, perfectly still and silent, not believing.

"It's… it's black," Poett mutters.

"What the fuck?" Rayde releases Eli's arms and jumps back, leaving him gurgling and choking on the blood as he collapses on the wet stone.

I'm struck from every direction. A hole drills through my heart. I turn away, twisting in Jace's grasp. Gusts of wind lash against my wet skin. Nausea coils in my gut, and I retch, dry heaving from my empty stomach.

"You're both gross." Jace holds me at a distance.

Kelter is frozen, bloody knife in hand, black liquid washing down his arm with the rain.

I don't know if I'm breathing, if my heart is beating. Eli is in a heap on the ground, lifeless. The man who left me notes and drummed his way into my heart, the man who knows death better than me, the man who cares to *see* me—dead. Gone.

The pain and loss of every vision of death stacked up can't compare to this, to the way my chest aches as though my heart were pushing right through the walls, tearing me open and falling to the ground. I harden inside. My veins turn to glass, my nerves to stone, but I still feel every agonizing moment.

"Come, dear." My murderous mother takes my arm, pulling me away from Jace, her eyes locked on the black mess spilling from Eli. "Take that knife and restrain him," she says to Poett, pointing at Kelter. She hisses in my ear, "Ready to say goodbye to your memories, love?"

But Eli's gone. Memories are all I have left. And now I'll lose them, and it'll kill me. Without my memories, I'll cease to exist. Cam will be gone, my forest, every sunrise with Kelter, every dark look from Eli… every touch. Every blink. Gone forever.

The world is suspended around me. Time quits.

I weep. Tears of tiny moments that will be washed away. Tears of love and loss, of life and death. Of me before, wanting to forget it all, and me now, wanting to hold on to every moment. I cry for Eli and Cam and the Kelter I lost when that knife took a life—and for myself.

"Why do you have to take them?"

She lifts my chin, her voice sweeter than vengeance. "Why does it matter if you won't remember the reason?" Her hand smoothes my wind-swept hair, reminding me of the mother I never had.

"How can you say you're my mother and still do this to me?"

"When you're a mother, you'll know there are no limits when it comes to your child. You defy gods. You cross realms. You kill, you lie and you bleed for them." She holds my cheek. "And you expect them to do the same for you."

"None of what you do is for me."

"I've done all of that for you and more… if you only knew. I've risked everything to save the land from total destruction and give us the future we deserve. You think it hasn't cost me? Why isn't everyone lining up to thank me? You of all people should be grateful."

I can almost see past her glassy black eyes and stone face. To the broken mind inside. "What are you going to do with my essence?"

The Centress turns me around, pressing my back to her chest, and wraps her arms around me. She speaks over the fierce wind that pierces my skin. "I need it to see your father again. The only way to get it out without killing you is by taking your memories. I'm saving your life, Everielle. And after, we won't have to worry about the loss of magic or the worsening weather anymore because we'll be safe with your father."

My father.

Maybe I'll get to meet him after I'm erased.

The wind whips at my baggy shirt and pants, flapping and snapping them around my exhausted limbs, and my mind shifts, building a shield around itself and blocking the fear that coils and tightens and strangles.

Erased.

I won't have to hurt inside anymore, won't have to miss anyone. I'll be beyond numb, beyond forgetting, beyond the risk of remembering. No more memories of rejection and cruelty, of thousands of deaths, no more trying to escape. No more hurting over Eli or blood spilling down his neck and chest. An empty mind in a purple haze. Oblivion.

"No! You can't hurt her!" Kelter charges forward, but Poett rips his arms back.

You're too late, Kelter.

"Ugh." The Centress huffs at the three guards. "Kill that one too and get out of here."

CHAPTER 56
KELTER

I didn't feel the knife go into my chest as I fought to get away, or feel it come out. It was Ever's face that told me something was wrong, the way it twisted in agony, too much pain for her scream to materialize. I thought the Centress' hands were already on her... until the warm liquid ran down my center.

I feel it now, though. Blood squirts out with every struggling breath. My body tingles, and my legs give out. I thought I'd make it out alive. I thought the Centress would spare me after what she did for me these past weeks. I drop to the puddle of Eli's weird black blood on the ground, quickly mixing and swirling with my own red blood and soaking into the moss-filled crevices. My knees crack into the stone, and I fall to his side.

I can't believe it was my hand that took a life, especially his. When it comes to survival—when it comes to Ever—I'd do anything, but I didn't save her *or* me. It wasn't meant to end like this. It's ironic, really. If only she knew... but I'm not supposed to care. Not about her.

I choke through every breath, each shorter than the last, each crackling with pain until all the miserable, excruciating work of taking in a breath is useless. I manage a look at the now familiar vine-covered walls of the atrium, and at her, hair thrashing in the wind, her tortured body backed up against the Centress. The affliction is gone, replaced with a slack expression and wide indigo eyes.

"This will hurt, darling," the Centress says.

How could that be her mother? How could she have magic? How the fuck did everything turn out so wrong?

"I know," Ever says so quietly that I miss her loudness. She makes that face, that brave face so full of terror, the one she makes a half-dozen times a day, when she seems to slip out of this world and into the only place I can't follow. A place so terrible she won't even tell me about it.

The Centress pulls her closer and stiffens, and Ever's brave face gives in to the pain. She needs me, and I'm dying.

The shitty luck.

I can't look at her a second longer, at her body shaking from the pain, at all the ways I've failed, how I've failed *her*.

Thunder claps, and my hearing starts to go, muffled and distant as though I'm underwater. The last of my strength gives out, and my head splashes into the warm blood and rain.

Then Eli hovers over me.

Damn.

I'm already dead—because I know *he* is. Blood still flows from his slit neck, black dripping on my face. I knew there was something off about him. Every time he was near, I wanted to get as far away as fucking possible.

"You will not die, asshole," he says in a harsh whisper.

Too late, I say, but only gurgles and spurts of blood come out.

"You need to live so I can kill your scrawny ass myself," he says.

You're dead. More gurgles. Too bad I didn't get a chance to tell him the truth before we died. Maybe he would have been less of a dick.

"I can't understand a word you're saying," Eli hisses and leans closer, his stupid curly hair hanging in my face, an oozing stream of blood hitting my mouth. I try to spit it back at him, but all my working lung can manage is a painful splutter. "You can't slit my godsdamn throat and get away with it."

You're insane, even when you're dead. I can only think the words I want to say. My body weakens with the blood loss. My ears ring, and the tingles fade, leaving my arms and legs without feeling.

"I said you will not die. Stop your bleeding. You need to get out of here before someone finishes you off, and I need to go help her." His eyes are frantic, his pupils exploding.

Right. Let me stitch my chest closed real quick and come back from the dead. My lips don't even move this time. My vision goes blurry, blackness shrinking my sight.

"Fucking Malachite. She'll never talk to me again if you die."

Who? Ever? Why do you care? I blink at him; it's all I can do.

Eli grimaces, grabs his ear—that ridiculous nervous tic of his—and smashes his hands down onto the opening in my chest. And the pain—pain like the world collapsing into me, pain like I'm torn and scattered amongst the stars—it ruptures my very being. It pulls me from my bones. It bores into me. Breath and death and life and loss. My head detonates, then he's gone. And so am I.

CHAPTER 57

ELIVANDER

I will not be erased. I will not be erased. I will not be erased from the one person who's ever looked beyond the curse. I repeat it as I drag my feet toward her, her pain plowing through me.

I don't know what the fuck just happened with Kelter, but I'll deal with it later, whatever we did. The bastard actually killed me. Or would have... if I could die. This world is stuck with me until I have a son to take on the mistake. It's worse, though—to feel all the pain and not be saved by death.

But now—I'll save her. She was mine from the start. I thought I'd do anything to get what I need from her. I was prepared to destroy her, to go to any length to escape this torture and never pass it on. But not anymore. Not since she worked herself so deep into my head, a better escape than drumming, a presence that distracts from all the rest. Not since I felt the fear of losing her. So early on, I saw the familiar torment in her eyes—and couldn't look away.

I can't lose her.

She's my Never Ever, my fucking addiction until the end of time. I need her breath, her body, her blood. Her little hands, that mouth, those eyes. I need all of her. I may not be able to die, but I swear if anything happens to her, it will take my life.

And that's where it has to end—with me. I've already let her get too attached. I can't tell her about the other part of this damn curse and how I fucked up and fell for her, how everything's at risk—if she falls for me too. I can't let that happen, and she can never know what I've done to stop it. It's ironic though... If she knew, she'd never love me.

I don't know how many memories the Centress has taken from her—if the earliest ones go first or the most recent ones, if I'm already gone from her head... if our last day together is gone.

I take one last look at Kelter collapsed on the ground behind me then scan the atrium. The guards haven't returned, but knowing they're probably getting their fix of violence with Milo and the others underground has me planning every detail of their deaths.

The Centress holds Never's back to her chest, her eyes shut tight as she pours pain into every cell of her body. I'll kill her for what she's doing. Nobody fucking touches her but me. No crazy bitch Centress erases me from her mind.

It's bad enough I failed to protect her over and over. What's the point of being what I am if I can't keep her safe, if all I managed to do when I felt her pain was pound the walls until my hands were black-and-blue? They drew her fucking blood, *my* blood. I wanted her to know she wasn't alone—but she was.

Never again.

She's drenched in rainwater, light and dark at once, sharp-edged and smoldering, like a star that fell too far, too damn stubborn to stop burning. Her body contracts all over under the pain, and even as I hobble forward to save her, the fierce wind trying to take down my weakened body, I can't get those moments together out of my mind—a constant problem since it's full of the thoughts and desires of the thousands of men that make me up.

I feel her again as if she's still under me. That's what she does to me. I can't help but notice her face is screwed up like when I twisted her nipples until she couldn't take it anymore, and her cries are the same as when she came, pulsing around me while I fucked us both into oblivion.

Oblivion. That's where she's headed if I don't stop this.

The pain intensifies the closer I get, and it's not the would-be fatal gash in my throat—which is also wrecking me. She must be in pure misery if I feel like this. The storm is relentless now, a near constant barrage of thunder and lightning, though she doesn't seem to notice. I can't feel a trace of terror from her anymore, only a current of turbulent emotions I can't hold onto, like how it felt before my little prisoner cuffed me... my little rebel.

Her eyes are open, though might as well be closed for the lack of light in them. But that color, damn. It brings out the blue-purple tint creeping over her skin right now. And as fucking beautiful as it is, all I want to do is hold her in my arms and take away the cold and pain.

I'm too weak for a fight, so I slide up against Never and wrap my arms around her lower back, squishing them between her and the Centress... her mother. She's as unlucky as me. Her forehead falls against my chest, and the blood from my neck drips onto the top of her head. Even with the gutting pain she shovels into me, I don't ever want to let her go.

And I won't. I'll keep her. She'll never get away—and never want to. Just because I can't have her heart doesn't mean she won't have mine. I'll be there for every tear and nightmare, every smile and swear word. I'll be the face she sees after every vision. I'll be the arms that rock her to sleep and sing the song that plays in her head. I'll bring out the fight in her, the violence, and destroy anyone who gets in my way.

And through it all, I'll never ever let her love me.

The Centress' eyes are now open and glowering. She tries to throw me off, but she isn't willing to let go of Never to actually succeed. Neither am I, so I stay, holding her tight. She's *mine*.

I reach for my blocking, as ancient and instinctual as my heartbeat, and pour it into her, a wall of armor against the Centress' magic. *The pain will be over soon*, I promise her with a squeeze, and I speak into her ear, offering the only words that come to me—one last memory of me if no others are left.

But the pain doesn't go away. Hers or mine. It rivets through my bones, promising to leave them in shards. It's as though *she's* blocking *me*...

I can't take away her pain.

But I will not be erased.

I will not be invisible, not to her. I have to stop this, but I'm barely hanging on. I've lost so much blood, and whatever happened with Kelter made me even weaker.

Never's wet boot jabs me in the shin. Then again and again, kicking and kicking. Her trapped arms push on my stomach. I hold her tighter through the pain and focus on blocking. If I can get it to work, if I can stop it for long enough—

Her knee clobbers me in the balls. Again. What is her obsession with destroying them? I fall away from her, my hands slipping past her waist, and curl up in a ball on the wet stones of the atrium. Hot daggers stab through my core, sharpened and amplified by her waves of tortured agony. They shatter like glass inside me. I retch until my body shudders and my intestines tie in knots.

And I'm too weak to get back up.

I failed.

She's on her own.

One look up. That's all it takes to see the fight in her. If she's still fighting, there's still a memory worth fighting for.

Keep your damn promise.

CHAPTER 58
EVER

The memories flash through my mind like the lightning overhead. They're pulverized, one after another, the loss much more excruciating than her hands on me. I relive the torture and ridicule, the rejection and abandonment, the avoidance and loneliness—the chords of my past. She extracts them, wringing me for every drop. I've lost command of my body, and my thoughts can hardly make it through the torment shredding my existence. The wind and rain pound down on me, and they're the only things that keep me in the present.

I search through the pain for good memories to cover up the nightmares of my past. Kelter. Those ears. His laugh. But it hurts too much when every heart-filling moment is paired with the sight of a knife in his chest. And even though I try to hold on to those moments, my mind keeps finding Eli. The folded notes. The castle. Song. Feet. Lake. Kiss. Cave. Lips on my hips. Him inside of me—and Kelter, taking his life. The cut across his throat.

I can't take it. I'd rather forget. Not feel. Memories have always been painful, something I wanted to forget, and now I *can* escape. I'm forced to let it all go.

A high-pitched ring disintegrates my brain. The pain continues in waves, taking me further out into the deep blue, too far to swim back. It's not worth fighting anymore. Pain, no pain, it's all the same. Soon to be gone.

The years pass. The memories march on and away. Goodbye Reggie and your wretched friends. Goodbye burning house. Goodbye Cam and your words of wisdom. Goodbye Maverick J. and your orange vest and belly hairs.

They keep coming… and going. Meeting Kelt. Sunrises and stars. Coffee and curses. Maps and adventures. I didn't think I'd ever let him go, let every moment disappear.

Milo's boyish grin. Kaleida's stories. More slip through the cracks, and they're gone.

Each memory, each little piece of me that makes me who I am, even the visions, they're torn away, nothing but an ocean of emptiness up to today.

More arms wrap around me, squeezing me—Eli. I know those arms. But it can't be him. I must be too far gone. My mind must have conjured him as one last reminder of what I'm about to lose forever. But he holds me close, my only rock in the stream of time.

Those few precious hours together, his demand—*never fall in love with me*. It floats away. The dust cloud over the fallen house. *Gone.* The ugly couch. *Gone.* My mother. *Gone.* Kelter slicing Eli's neck. *Gone.* A bloody knife through Kelter's chest. *Gone.*

A voice drifts into my ear, deep and sensual, urgent and strained. It belongs to the arms squeezing me tight. No voice I can recognize. I know no one. Not even myself.

"I lied earlier, my Never, but know this—I see your delicious darkness, and it's so damn beautiful. You can choose to have me killed over and over, but remember—you're mine. You breathe for me. You scream for me. You come for me, and only me."

I go weak in the knees. My eyes close. I don't know who that was leaning over me, but his voice drove straight into my core. Wind slaps my face, and rain batters my head.

My final memories pass by.

Hands—merciless, painful hands on me—holding me from behind, taking me away from myself.

Gone.

The words in my ear.

Gone.

From somewhere inside me comes a warning, a call to protect. I kick and kick and knee the man's body in front of me until the two squeezing arms fall away.

Those saving, shielding arms that held me so close, they're all I know in the world, suddenly my everything, my only, my old and new.

Gone.

A blank canvas. No memories. Nothing left. No wind. No rain. Only pain.

I let go, sinking into the dark depths of torment, nothingness holding me in its tender embrace, a black bliss all to myself. Around me, above me, below me. Part of me.

I could stay here, in the emptiness, nothing to hurt me but pain itself. But a little piece of that darkness within—it makes me want to fight. Fight for moments worth escaping, for pain worth feeling, for me. Whoever I am.

I'm worth the damn fight.

A tendril of energy works its way through me. It's strangely familiar. I latch onto it, nurturing it, encouraging it, letting it belong exactly as it is. It grows and flows with a flourishing force, and the pain lessens.

The energy escalates. Faster, more vibrant. I force my eyes open. The source of the pain has me in its grasp, a woman's pale arms crossing over me. I look down at the two bloody, broken men on the ground. I don't know who they are, who I am. I reach for the energy, accepting it without knowing or caring, and let it become me.

The painful arms wrapped around me take on a white glow. I pull harder on that swelling energy, wrapping myself up in the flowing strands, and the pain goes away completely. My mind and body are mine again. Feeling returns. Cold air rushes against my wet clothes.

I slip from the arms and turn around. The woman falls back onto the ground, weak and trembling. Who is she? Crouching at her side, only terror occupies her black eyes.

Then, driven by something too deep within me to comprehend, I plant my hands on her creamy cheeks. Her entire body glows now, even her endless locks of hair. Her mouth is parted, her face lax, and I pull with the strength and steadiness of a deeply rooted tree from the beginning of time. I know I'm pulling something out of her and into me, but what or why—I don't know. Just that I must.

Then my memories rain over me, flooding and filling my head—the pain, the death, the laughs. It's all there.

I pull more and more from the woman on the ground, the rush building inside me, swirling madly, no hesitation or judgment. Then, I know her—my mother.

"Everielle," she whispers weakly, a last attempt to tug at my broken heart, but it's locked up tight and far beyond her reach.

I hold her unforgiving gaze, matching it and accepting every consequence that will come—the permanence of my actions, the end of my search for my mother—and I keep pulling. Like the plants, I pull the magic right out of her undeserving body, feeling as alive as I do after returning from a vision of death. She killed Eli and Kelter. Not with her hands, but *she's* responsible.

She goes limp, a defeated mess of tangled hair and limbs. I keep the magic flowing from her into me until it runs dry and her glow fades. Then I rip the necklace from her neck and collapse. I refuse to let her steal magic from another baby ever again. The wind dies down, and the rain slows.

An anxious presence twines around me, and I open my eyes. Eli is sitting at my side, looking down at me, enough worry in those deep brown wells to last him a lifetime, or a few thousand. *Wait.* His neck. How is he here? I only imagined him holding me. Him and Kelt, they're both gone.

But dead or alive, hallucination or miracle, Eli works his arms under my knees and around my shoulders, lifting me up and resting my spent body in his lap. I can barely move or think or feel. I can't even hug him and cry over Kelter.

"Do you know who I am?" He swallows hard, a silent prayer on his lips, to the gods I don't believe in.

"My favorite fucking mistake," I whisper.

A smile takes over his face, a hand at his ear. "That mouth." He holds me tighter with weak arms. "I won't forget you chose that twerp over me."

That twerp *is my dead friend.*

"I knew you wouldn't die," I lie, eyeing the blood everywhere, the red-and-black knife on the ground. How does broken immortality work?

"I don't believe you."

I shrug one shoulder against him. *Please don't ever let go.*

"You were devastated," he adds. His fingers poke through my sliced clothes and trace over the new cuts. "Which of them hurt you, Never?"

I snuggle into his chest. "Just hold me. Kill later." *Don't make me relive it.*

Every avoidant thought is ripped from my mind as Kelter crawls over to us and sits, one hand on his chest, another on his head. "What did you do to me, Eli?"

"Kelter—you're alive." As spent as I am, I try to get to him, but Eli doesn't let go of me. He pulls me closer. My final sliver of strength fades as Kelter's arms reach for me. His voice echoes as I fall unconscious.

"Hand her over, Eli. I'm here now."

CHAPTER 59

I'm sinking. The bed is too soft, the pillows too fluffy. But no nightmares followed me into sleep. The terrors and visions of the last few days must have been enough to satisfy the dark corners of my unconscious mind.

Gray light pours in through the sheer curtains hanging over two walls of floor-to-ceiling windows in Milo's spare bedroom. Color skips through the rest of the room—sky blue walls, coral teardrop flowers in the corners, a saffron carpet, green ivy flirting with the walls and windows and a rainbow of glass vials covering every possible surface. I actually miss the gray stone walls of the castle.

Yesterday evening fades into a blurry memory shortly after draining the Centress of her magic. Eli pulled his bloody shirt over his head and knotted it around the exposed flesh on his neck, possibly to avoid the questions as he freed his friends… or stop the black ooze. He sat me as far from him as possible while he and Kelter—both weak and barely functional—managed to take down the guards. I could only hear the sluggish brawl underground… and smell the fresh blood wafting my way. Sola and Coen appeared first, then Kaleida. She hugged me until I was close to passing out again.

Why did it take five days for you to show up? Sypher complained when he entered the atrium. Milo elbowed him in the ribs and threw an arm around Eli, but his blue eyes avoided mine. Perhaps he wasn't particularly pleased to find his friend cuffed in the woods. Only fuzzy images follow—Coen tackling Eli when he tried to kill the Centress without getting answers from her. Sola cuffing her and forcing her to her feet. A view of the muddy ground after Coen slung me over his shoulder for the walk back to the castle.

Whatever stroke of luck allowed Kelter to survive is beyond my understanding, but what's even harder to grasp is how he took that knife and sliced straight across Eli's neck, unaware he would survive the fatal wound. He killed him. My Kelter, my conflict-avoiding, unseen, soft-spoken friend killed him. He did it to save his own life, but what did the Centress do to him all that time she had him locked up? Did she change him, create a killer... like me?

I woke up this morning to a barrage of thoughts and questions without end or answers, those moments with all my memories gone still fresh in my mind. That's what it took for me to choose to fight for myself. I had to become no one to see I'm someone, to care enough to want to exist and feel again. I have no explanation for my visions, but the pain they cause—the rejection, the death, the memories—makes me who I am. Whoever that is... Hollows and Vaile can't take magic from plants, but I can, and I took it from my mother too—but how?

Ugh. *My mother.* Mentally, I'm going back to not having a mother at all—the only way I know to keep the little pieces of my heart from breaking off and falling to its chamber floor. The Centress can't take magic from the babies with her necklace or send them away anymore, but Calderans are still under the elixir's control. All Vaile believe drugging them is necessary to protect Sonnet when the real concern is the border—separating Hollows and Vaile, disrupting the cycle and causing magic to die. Hot rain and violent winds are a gentle ride compared to the disasters to come. Either we find a way to stop it or undo the Separation, because what Eli was made to do—create new magic—he can't. And if this essence in me is what he needs, I'm at a loss for how to give it to him, how to help.

I don't know why he made me promise not to fall in love with him. I only know that every breath I take is laced with *him*. I'm not alone. I'm not held back. He pushes me. He sees me. He gives me a voice that's heard and a rhythm to follow. I'm more myself with Eli than I knew I could be. And maybe my heart isn't capable of giving in to him, promise or no promise, matching beat or not, but I can secretly treasure whatever this is, giving my blood and body and fighting and fucking to feel alive. I can do that... with him.

Though I'm still streaked with mud and blood, someone changed me into snug gray pants and a white shirt while I slept—a foreign skin after wearing Eli's clothes since arriving at the castle. Sitting on the bed and still sore all over, I slip the Centress' necklace from the nightstand into my pocket and tug down on the shirt that hovers at my waist, attempting to cover the cuts and bruises.

I look up to see Kelter in the doorway, showered and wearing black pants and a navy blue shirt with bulky dressing wrapped around his chest beneath it. His unkempt prisoner's beard is now shaved, revealing that face I know so well. Despite the bags he sports under his eyes and his protruding bones, he has a new air about him, wiser and older, the green and gold pools of his eyes deeper and darker. He smiles, his light freckles giving him that innocent look—but he's not. He took a knife to Eli's neck.

He closes the door and comes in for a hug, pulling me off the edge of the bed and into his arms. He wraps his hands behind my neck, his thumbs resting on my cheeks as he shakes his head in disbelief. "Finally."

I shift my stance at his touch. His skin is too hot. He's too close. Words don't surface for the million things I want to say and ask. I rest a hand on his chest. "Does it still hurt?"

"I'm fine. I needed to see you." He moves his thumbs to my eyebrows, smoothing them gently, then settles them on my temples. His eyes don't leave mine, as though he can't bear to look away for a second. "Don't worry, I'll keep Eli away from you."

"You don't have to. He won't hurt me."

"He keeps your fucking underwear in his pocket."

Does he not see the appeal? It takes everything in me not to laugh despite his sudden change in tone. "I don't want to know how you know that."

"He sees you as his prisoner."

"No, he…" How do I explain?

But Kelter looks at me as if he knows exactly what I can't find the words to express, and he's not happy. "You do realize that he won't let you leave, right?"

"He will…" I look at the hideous saffron carpet, unable to hold his gaze. Or admit he could be right. "But I don't want to go home anymore. Everyone is drugged. Magic is *dying*, Kelt. And I have a father here somewhere." *And Eli.*

"Did you ever stop to think *how* he plans to get what he wants from you? You heard the Centress. The only way to get to your essence is to take your memories—or your life."

He wouldn't.

Kelt lifts my head back up, hands still on my face. "And trust me, Eli wouldn't take your memories even if he could... He's fond of them."

How would he even know what Eli wants? I push him back softly. "I have so much to tell you." *But not everything.*

"I know." He hugs me close, and I'm careful not to touch where the knife went in. My cheek rests on his chest, his body injecting heat into me. So warm, so safe, so... not what I need. He strokes my hair, plastering it against my skull, massaging the thoughts and doubts inside into an unreadable mush. "But first you need to eat... and shower. At least I got you out of his clothes."

"You *what?*"

He ceases the mind-melting strokes of his hand and tugs at the dried blood in my hair, his other arm low on my back, keeping me near as I try to get away.

The door bursts open, rattling the glass vials.

"I know what you're thinking, Kelter. Back the fuck away from her," Eli says from the doorway.

He's also clean, wearing his normal fitted black shirt, pocket-covered pants and those laughable suspenders. And he's pissed—squinty eyes below the bruises, twitchy mouth, rolling shoulders—but something's different about him, something I can't quite pull into consciousness.

Kelter's face lands somewhere between rage and torture. "Of course you do."

Chapter 60

"Don't fucking do it." Eli steps into the room, heavy boots thudding on the carpet. I taste blood, and those cursed fingers slide down my back. "It's bad enough that you slit my throat."

My eyes go to the light green patch stretched across his neck, a bandage of sorts, made from plants.

"Deal's off, man. You broke it." Kelter glances at me, hurt flashing across his pleated brow, his upper lip rising in disgust.

"What deal?" I shove Kelter away as Eli meets us in the center of the room. "What are you talking about?"

"I mean it," Eli says, tilting his head in warning.

Kelter balls up his hands and presses his knuckles together. "Yeah, I feel that. And I don't give a shit." He turns to me, his face crimson and seething. "You want to know? For starters, your precious Elivander doesn't want you to know that you're his personal guest in Sonnet."

Precious? I set a soothing hand on Kelt's arm, imagining all he must have been through in the last two months. "I know he was the one who brought us to the stone room. He probably wishes it was a different guard that saw us that day, especially after yesterday." I'm sure getting his throat cut open wasn't an expected outcome of doing his job.

Kelter snorts, letting out a dry laugh. "No, I mean he planned the whole thing."

Eli's body ripples, hardening from head to toe. I hate that I notice every muscle under his shirt, every ridge down his arms, even as that familiar crushing weight on my chest builds.

"What whole thing?" I ask.

"And you brought her straight to me," Eli lashes back.

"What?" I might as well be invisible. These two are made from the same material, both ignoring me, caught up in their hot tempers.

"Because you asked me to! You offered me a deal I couldn't turn down," Kelter spits.

Eli stomps nearer, pointing a finger at him. "And you forced me to agree to keep my hands off of her."

I look at Kelter. "You what? When?" I can't keep up.

"Which you failed miserably at," Kelter accuses. "Just because you can't keep your dick in your fucking pants doesn't mean you can go back on your word."

"Stop and tell me what the fuck is going on!" I yell.

Kelter cocks his head at me. "Lover boy showed up in Caldera asking me to find you then meet him at the border in exactly one year. I knew nothing about the crazy plan with the sack, and we were never supposed to be seen by anyone else. After you passed out in the courtyard, he came to my cell and begged me not to tell you, so I took the obvious opportunity to protect you from a total asshole and made him agree not to touch you." His shoulders rise and fall with his livid breaths.

"I didn't beg. I threatened to cut off your dick and shove it down your throat. We couldn't risk her telling someone." Eli pushes Kelter in the chest, right where he was stabbed. "I gave you a year to find her because I thought you'd need it, not so you could make a fucking friend. I couldn't take you straight to the castle because of the night guards. You guys were supposed to wait for me in the stone room so I could sneak you out during the morning briefing. I looked through the ceiling grate and you were gone. You never would have been in the Centress' hands if you had just waited."

"I tried to get her to wait!" Kelter yells back, somehow not doubling over in pain. "You know how stubborn she is."

"You could have had some fucking balls and stopped her."

I search Kelter's face. "That's why we're friends? That's why you didn't push me away like everyone else? Because Eli asked you to find me? Did you even—" I bury the pain with all the rest and try to stop the tears—the ones I cried every time Cam walked me away from another home. "Why you? Out of everyone in Caldera? Why would he ask you?"

Eli answers for him, his glare slicing. "He was the only one I knew. We grew up together."

I swear the walls crash down around me, clouds of dust billowing as I swallow down the feelings I can't handle. "You grew up in Caldera?"

"No." Eli looks at me warily, as though maybe he doesn't truly want to deconstruct reality as brutally as my own mind does. "Kelter grew up in Sonnet."

"Only until I was eight," Kelter says. "That's why I agreed to the deal with Eli. He offered to get me back across the border and hide me."

I gasp for air, forcing it through the narrowed tunnel in my throat. "You were here... in Sonnet." This is why he didn't want to go back to Caldera. It wasn't really his home. "You're a Vaile? Everyone knows you? That's why Kaleida was so nice?"

"No one recognized me." He bites his lip, letting it slowly slip from between his teeth. "And Kelter's not my real name."

His words strike like venom, spreading and destroying me, choking the life from that ignorant, blind part of me that let deception in with open arms. Endless questions spin through my mind, but there's one I can't let go.

I turn back to Eli. "Why would you ask Kelter to find *me*?"

He takes a deep breath and lets it go, relief spilling out with his words. "A little boy came to me. Messy golden hair. Freckles. Dirty and a little wild. He knew about me, somehow. He said if I brought you here, you could fix me."

The little boy came to him over a year ago? How could that—

"But all that's not even the worst of it," Kelter says, rolling his head to Eli.

Eli sets his jaw askew in smug defiance.

"You *do* know." Kelter puts himself between Eli and me.

"Know what?" I ask, though not sure I want to hear anything else. I move out from behind Kelter. The light blue walls close in. The vines creep toward the corners.

They stare at each other, face-to-face. Kelter stands inches above Eli, but his wasted muscles take away any menacing look he might have been able to achieve.

"Then I'm right, it goes both ways?" Kelter asks.

"Not all of it."

Kelter shoves him. "You thought you could pretend that I don't know what you are now, that I don't feel what you feel?"

"You *know* I don't think that."

"I'm not going to sit on my hands while you take her in yours. I've seen what you do. I've got all these memories in my head. What am I supposed to do with them? What am I supposed to think? I don't even know who I am anymore. I only know that I can't forget about every long look into her eyes, the hours you spent watching her sleep, the thought you put into those notes—"

"Shut your fucking mouth." A bruised fist forms at Eli's side. "Those aren't your thoughts to share."

"But they *are* mine now. Kissing her, the knife against her skin as you cut away her clothes, the smell of jasmine while I—you stuck your tongue inside her? I didn't expect she'd like it so rough."

"Kelter!" I whirl back to Eli. "Why would you tell him that?"

Kelter only continues. "It's all in my head, as crisp and real as if it had been me. And you think I can experience all that—after being the one who spent a year building an actual friendship—and ignore it?"

Kelter hooks my waist, pinning me to his side. "I can't." Then with a hand behind my head, he smacks a kiss on my lips. As though he'd done it before.

The colors in the room swirl around me. I escape—from the kiss, the press of his lips, the suffocating warmth of his skin. Everything about it is wrong. I don't want him like *this*.

"Let the fuck go of me, Kelt." I try to slip away, but his arm stays looped around me.

Eli is still. Quiet. Watching my reaction.

I spin my rings in frenzied circles. Rage against these two men festers and blisters in every cell of my body. I can't make words from the thoughts that bump and clash and bruise my fragile mind. I need Eli to tell me. I can't ask. I can't hold on to the pieces long enough to make sense of them, not when they fracture and flip, not when they hurt.

How does he know about those things? Between us.

"Eli..."

Calm and lethal, he untangles me from Kelter, his firm hands pulling me away. But I don't want *his* hands on me either.

He speaks in the most controlled tone. "Those are my memories. Just because you have them doesn't mean they're yours. And neither is Never. She belongs to me, and I swear I'll finish what my knife started if you can't understand that."

"How?" I sputter, ignoring the death threat for a moment.

Eli's gaze embraces me, that insatiable darkness, his ancientness now muddled with the comfort of a friend who will curse at the stars and drink coffee through sunrise, and those turbulent brown eyes of his now flecked with green and gold, tender and carnal. This can't be real. I want to run. But his scent dominates me, traps me—dank, cold darkness, so strong I can taste him.

"The little shit was dying. All I did was try to stop the blood flow, and somehow that healed him. But something else happened."

"What happened?" I say slowly, my stomach filling with lead.

Eli tugs on my pockets, walking me into the slice of dangerous space between him and Kelter. "I accidentally, somehow, merged us into one... all the way back to the beginning."

THE END

ACKNOWLEDGMENTS

Thank you to my love, Enrique, for believing in me since day one and giving me the time and space to write, for late night talks and coffee and for every minute of every day—and it was *every* day—that you listened to me go on and on about this book, these characters, this world, the process, the doubt—and for never telling me not to try.

To my son, Josiah, for reading *select* bits in the earliest days and loving it enough for me to keep going, for listening to me tell you the plan for the whole series only for it to change the next week and for your smile and your hugs and the music you filled the house with.

To my daughter, Tauriel, for your huge heart and fierce glare and for sharing every dream you have in the greatest detail—you make me believe in anything and everything.

To my youngest, Kalú, for smelling the coffee beans with me every morning and smiling like nothing could ever go wrong.

Thank you, mom, for your unending support, for being one of the first two readers back when I had no idea what I was doing and for raising me to believe I can do anything.

Thank you, dad, for reading to me, for making books a part of my life and for showing me how to get things done and not care what people think.

Also thank you to all my friends and family for being there through the laughs and tears over the years. I love you all!

Jessica, I love you so freakishly much. Thank you for holding my hand through every up and down of this daunting process, for three-hour plot talks and for keeping me—and my characters—in check. Thank you for accepting my brain as it is and encouraging me to write a story I love.

I could not have done this without my book team! Thank you to my editors, Joyce and Alex, for digging deep, knowing your stuff and stopping me from scrapping the whole thing. Thank you to Sarah for your editorial assessment; you helped me believe in my creation and let go of what I didn't love. Thank you to my cover designer at Miblart, my formatter, Judi the talented artist with Centaur Maps, and to my proofreaders, Larissa of FictionAlly LLC and Adele! You all brought this book to life.

Dear Megan A. Rockwell, Ashley Dronek, Sofia Gavria, Maddison Jade, Adele, Molly E. Sandwell, Megan Robertson, Mom, Jessica Harris and my anonymous beta readers, thank you for your honest feedback and guidance. You saw what I couldn't, and I'm beyond grateful for how you helped shape this story.

And thank you to my readers, one page or all, love or hate. You are incredible exactly as you are. Sharing this story with you is like sharing a piece of myself. Thanks for giving it a chance.

ABOUT THE AUTHOR

Jaime L. Tlax writes dark fantasy with darker romance. Betrayals of the Broken is her debut novel and the culmination of sixteen months without sleep. Her books are a lyrical blend of blood, desire and secrets, featuring morally gray love interests and heroines who quite literally bite back. When she's not plotting chaos with a heavy dose of banter, she's probably in a closet—hiding, reading or passed out due to lack of coffee.